NIGHT SKY

SUZANNE BROCKMANN AND
MELANIE BROCKMANN

sourcebooks
fire

Copyright © 2014 by Suzanne Brockmann and Melanie Brockmann
Cover and internal design © 2014 by Sourcebooks, Inc.

Sourcebooks and the colophon are registered trademarks of Sourcebooks, Inc.

The characters and events portrayed in this book are fictitious or are used fictitiously. Any similarity to real persons, living or dead, is purely coincidental and not intended by the author.

Published by Sourcebooks Fire an imprint of Sourcebooks, Inc.
P.O. Box 4410, Naperville, Illinois 60567-4410
(630) 961-3900
Fax: (630) 961-2168
www.sourcebooks.com

Library of Congress Cataloging-in-Publication data is on file with the publisher.

Printed and bound in the United States of America.
WOZ 10 9 8 7 6 5 4 3 2 1

Suzanne

To my writing partner, my courageous daughter Melanie — the strongest person I've ever met. May you keep learning how best to harness your own amazing superpowers, and continue to use them for good.

Melanie

For my mother. Thank you for teaching me that everyone is a Greater-Than in some unique way, and for showing me that the greatest superpower anyone can ever have is the ability to love.

CHAPTER ONE

I had not been under the impression that trophy wives owned guns.

Of course, my impression of a lot of things had been changing lately, so the idea of a homicidal contortionist with a designer handbag and a vanity license plate that read DRSWIFEY was, surprisingly, not very surprising at all.

"What's up with Little Miss Sunshine?" Calvin mumbled to me, tapping my forearm with his hand as we made our way to the front doors of the Sav'A'Buck supermarket. He motioned with his head for me to look behind him, and I glanced over at the lady. Huge, fake-looking boobs and even larger sunglasses. I doubted she needed them at nine o'clock at night...the sunglasses, that is. It *was* September in Florida, but come on.

"Dunno," I answered, picking up my pace a little bit. I was eager to get inside the store. Even without the sun, the humidity made the air feel like it was about ninety thousand degrees. I had a bad case of swamp butt, and my jean shorts were sticking to my backside uncomfortably.

Calvin laughed as I fixed my wedgie with an apparently less-than-discreet swipe. "Could you fix mine too? It's really bad. Horrible," he said, lifting himself halfway off the seat of his electric wheelchair.

I socked him once in the bicep. "Punk."

The linoleum floors of the Sav'A'Buck were sticky, and the place smelled like pig grease and stale cigarettes. But that's what we got for venturing outside our pristine gated community and driving across the proverbial tracks into neighboring Harrisburg to the only place open after nine.

"Man, you really want to buy *food* from here?" Calvin grumbled, while two small kids whisked in front of us, barefoot, their faces coated with melted purple ice pop. The woman working register four turned around, her disastrous mullet matched only by the disapproving frown she offered Calvin and me as we strolled by.

Neither of us accepted it.

"We're making s'mores," I insisted, my resolve strong. It had been a hellish week, and I wanted something chocolate. We had driven all the way out here; we weren't turning back now.

Calvin rolled his eyes. "Come on," he said, steering himself sharply toward the right. "Cookies and crackers. Aisle seven."

I followed behind him, breaking into a trot to keep up with his chair.

But Calvin pressed his brake and we nearly collided. "There she is again," he hissed, tapping my hand furiously. "Doesn't she creep you out, even a little?"

Little Miss Sunshine, as Calvin had called her, was busy inspecting the nutrition information on the backs of two different bags of corn chips. Her long, blond hair was swept up in an elegant French chignon. She hadn't bothered to take off her sunglasses.

I scooped up a box of graham crackers and left the aisle. Calvin followed me this time.

Once the woman was out of earshot, I told him, "The only weird thing about her is that she looks like she's rolling in dough, unlike most Sav'A'Buck customers." I shrugged. "But we probably stick out here too." I found the aisle for candy and grabbed a humongous bag of chocolate. "So give her a break."

Calvin acknowledged his two-hundred-dollar polo shirt and shrugged. "Eh, you're right," he replied, and popped his collar.

"That's lame, by the way," I said, and found an empty basket to dump my purchases into.

"What?" Calvin replied, his expression one of mock offense. "Girl, you are just jealous because you can't pull off the look."

"Sooo jealous," I replied sarcastically. I was perfectly happy in my jean shorts and plain black tank top. Nobody needed to know my mom had spent a fortune for both articles of clothing. If it were up to me, I'd wear clothes from the local consignment shop, thank you very much. People were going hungry these days, and obviously many of them were right here in Harrisburg. That was way creepier, IMO, than Little Miss Sunshine jonesing for cheap, salty grease.

Calvin poked his nose into my basket. "Would you mind telling me exactly how white girls from the north make s'mores? Where I come from, we use marshmallows."

"Dammit!" I'd forgotten to grab a bag when we were in the candy aisle.

"Come on," Calvin replied, and reached for my basket. He set it atop his lap and followed me as I sprinted back toward aisle eight.

"Skylar, slow your ass down!" Calvin whined, but when I did, he zoomed past me, laughing.

"Oh, it's on," I said, pushing to keep up. "I could totally beat you in a race."

It was Calvin's turn to roll his eyes when we both had to slow for oncoming traffic. "Oh, yeah? How much you wanna bet?"

"I'll have to think about it," I answered, and that's when the screaming started.

Calvin grabbed for my arm. "What the..."

I turned to see a little old lady frozen in fear at the end of aisle eight. Then other voices joined the chorus, including a woman reciting the "Our Father" in Spanish.

"Don't," Calvin said, holding my elbow to keep me from walking toward them.

It was then that the screaming was replaced by a loud *cccccrrraaaaaaacccck.*

All I could smell was fish. Lots of fish. Enough fish so that I hoped and prayed I would never, ever have to eat sushi again for as long as I lived. My nose burned, and I swallowed hard a couple times to keep from heaving.

And then, Little Miss Sunshine rounded the corner.

"Oh, sheee-it!" Calvin exclaimed.

And I had to agree.

At first, I thought her body was facing me, but after a moment

I realized that, somehow, her head had pivoted almost completely around. Her chin rested awkwardly on her shoulder blade, and she was walking backward just to see where she was going. It was like that old *Exorcist* movie my mom watched every year at Halloween, but this lady was real, and she was heading in our direction.

She was also smiling.

"Okay, eff the s'mores, Sky. I'm out," Calvin said, his voice carefully even. But I wasn't moving, and neither was he.

Little Miss Sunshine, on the other hand…*she* was getting closer.

I didn't know where her sunglasses had gone, but I could see her eyes now. They were wild. And she had a terrible smile, like the Cheshire cat had up and lost it.

"Sky?" Calvin said, and I knew for a second what it must feel like to be him—absolutely paralyzed. I couldn't move my legs. I was stuck in that spot.

And she was smiling *at me*.

People began to peek out from aisle eight to see what was happening. I spotted the old lady and the woman who had been reciting prayers. Mullet woman at the register was quiet too. In fact, the entire store had become terribly silent. The only sound was the canned music clinking through cheap overhead speakers. It was some terrible electronic version of an old Frank Sinatra song, complete with computerized steel drums. I swallowed hard, the smell of fish absolutely overwhelming me.

"Look what I can do!" the woman said, and snapped her neck back around.

"Ohhh!" the Sav'A'Buck crowd gasped. Little Miss Sunshine giggled. Her perfectly manicured hands held her head in place. She spun around to face me.

I've got...youuuuuu...under my skin...

The lyrics echoed eerily through the grocery store, and I looked down at Calvin for a second. He had turned a pale shade of green, which clashed with his chocolate-brown skin.

"Look what I can do!" the woman repeated, her voice horribly clear, her tone singsong, as if she were reciting a nursery rhyme. She clapped her palm onto the side of her face, and I watched her jaw completely dislocate.

"Mommy?" one of the little kids in the register line squealed, while the Hispanic lady said something fast in Spanish and fainted.

"Look what I can do look what I can do look what I can do!" Little Miss Sunshine repeated, and this time it sounded more like "Ooook Uuut Aaah Aan Ooo" because she couldn't close her mouth. Her eyes were wide, with a disturbing amount of white showing on the top and bottom. I watched her grab the top of her mouth and pull.

I've got youuuuuu...deep in the heart of meeee....

Four of her teeth fell out and landed on the linoleum floor, close enough to my feet so that I could see the blood.

"Oh God oh God oh God," Calvin uttered, and his hand on my arm was clammy.

"On the ground!" The security guard who'd been dozing out front rushed through the sliding doors of the store. He'd drawn a Taser from his belt, and he sprinted toward the insane woman, pointing the weapon at her and blocking both Calvin and me in the process.

"Do it! Now!" he said. He was a stocky guy with a big salt-and-pepper mustache and squeaky black boots. I was close enough to smell him—cheap cologne, stale cigar smoke, and more of that terrible fish smell.

Instead of getting on the ground, the woman chuckled. A rivulet of red-tinged drool fell from her distended mouth and landed on the linoleum. The cop took a split second to look where it landed. And in that moment, Little Miss Sunshine high-kicked the officer in the bottom of his chin with her stiletto-heeled shoe. He fell backward, and from the way he hit the floor, I knew he wasn't getting back up.

The Taser bounced and skittered, and I swear that I don't know how it happened exactly, but somehow the weapon found its way over to my feet. And then it found its way into my hands.

"Really? I mean, *really?*" Calvin exclaimed, as I held the weapon with two extremely shaky hands. I felt like I'd chugged ten cups of espresso, I was jittering so bad.

But I lifted the weapon to point it at Little Miss Sunshine's chest—the biggest possible target.

Somehow I knew, despite her bloodied, disfigured mouth and saucer eyes, that she was still smiling at me. Mocking me.

And then she knocked her jaw back into place with a horrible crunch.

"I think you should have listened to the officer," I said. "Get *on* the ground."

I acknowledged the cop with only a slight nod, not daring to look away from the woman even for a moment. I could see from my peripheral vision that he was completely still, in a heap between Calvin's wheelchair and the crazy lady. I inanely wondered how long people typically remained unconscious after being kicked in the chin with a designer shoe.

"Just pull the trigger, dammit," Calvin urged from between clenched teeth.

Fingers shaking, I aimed the thing and squeezed.

Little Miss Sunshine looked down at her chest, at the hissing and sparking Taser that should have sent her to the floor. Then she plucked it from the front of her shirt, looked up at me, and smiled.

"Look what I can do look what I can do," the woman continued, and yanked a massive-looking gun out of her bag.

Everyone in the store hit the deck at the sight of the gun—everyone except Calvin and me.

She pointed the barrel at my face.

A nasty wave of déjà vu washed over me. It was mixed with a hefty dose of panic and combined with at least a small degree of consolation that Calvin, as always, had my back.

"Oh, *hell* no!" he barked. All the fear had vanished from his tone, and now he just sounded pissed. "You wanna mess with someone? You wanna put your gun in her face? You're gonna have to shoot me first!"

And then, things got *really* weird.

"Hey!" someone called from behind Little Miss Sunshine. It was a girl, older than me but probably only by a year or two. She'd appeared as if out of nowhere, but she must've come in through the front doors while my attention was on that gun. Dressed in full motorcycle garb—a red leather jacket and black steel-toed boots—she hollered again. "Hey, you!"

Little Miss Sunshine whirled around.

Motorcycle Girl charged forward and flicked the pistol out of crazy lady's hands as easily as if she were removing a piece of lint from a buddy's jacket.

The gun spun a couple times before landing on the floor. Motorcycle Girl kicked it back into the air with her foot and caught it with one hand. She tucked it deftly into the back waistband of her pants and then slammed the crazy woman down onto the ground using the palm of one hand. I could have sworn Little Miss Sunshine took a nosedive before Motorcycle Chick even touched her, but then again, I'd been seeing all kinds of crazy things this week.

"Whoa," Calvin said, while the crowd gasped again.

Little Miss Sunshine landed, hard, and made a gurgling sound. She looked up once at me and pointed, still smiling that awful smile, before her face dropped onto the ground.

The room once again was silent. Mostly.

Sooo deep in my heart, that you're really a paaart of meee...

Motorcycle Chick turned, running a hand gruffly through her platinum-blond pixie cut as she looked at me and frowned, her eyes the color of icicles.

Calvin could have caught flies, his mouth was open so wide.

"God *damn*, this music blows," the girl said as she glared from me to Cal and back again, as if the soundtrack was from our personal playlist.

Around us, the crowd began to move almost as one, with everyone— shoppers and clerks alike—rushing for the door.

I was about to turn too—getting out of there seemed like a brilliant idea—when Motorcycle Girl spoke again. Her words stopped me. "Way to protect Tiny Tim here, Sky. What were you waiting for? A sign from God?"

I looked at Cal—Cal looked at me. And I knew we were both thinking the same thing.

How the hell does this girl know my name?

CHAPTER TWO

I'm getting ahead of myself here.

The crappola had really started hitting the fan almost a week before the infamous Sav'A'Buck incident. Of course, I didn't know at the time that a string of unbelievable events were about to take place that would forever change my life. But then again, who can ever tell something like that?

My week had started out completely normal. It was the usual. School, Calvin, babysitting, dealing with Momzilla—a totally typical few days. If anything, it was an uber-awesome week because I got to babysit Sasha an extra night. Extra babysitting equaled extra money. And, anyway, I loved watching Sasha. She lived right down the street from me, and her whole family was exactly what I wished I had. Even though Sasha's mom and dad were struggling with money and both needed to work two jobs because of the whole Second Great Depression that everyone kept talking about, they still seemed so *happy* all the time. And relaxed.

Nothing like my uptight mom and her crazy rules. Momzilla

always told me that we should consider ourselves "lucky" because we hadn't been affected by the world economic crisis or whatever. But seriously? No matter how much money we had, I still had paranoid Mom on my case constantly. And *that* didn't make me feel lucky at all.

Anyway, that Sunday night was the last "normal" evening I would have in a really long time. Sasha sat at her dining-room table as I stood behind the kitchen counter and mixed chocolate syrup into her milk.

"A lot, please," Sasha said, crossing her fingers together as she swung her pajama-pant-clad legs underneath the table.

"Not *too* too much," I replied, pouring more syrup into the glass.

"But too too much is *good!*" she exclaimed. Her brown eyes were big and almond shaped and quite serious. "Daddy and Mommy let me have as much as I want!"

"Well. You've got it made, then," I said. "*My* mommy won't let me have milk *or* chocolate."

Or beef. Or any soda pop with artificial sweeteners. Actually, the list of things my mom wouldn't let me eat was longer than the list of things that I *could*. Ever since the accident and then our move to Coconut Key, the rules I had to follow would have given a kindergartner a rash. Compared to me, Sasha was pretty much living it up.

I had to do my homework before I watched TV.

I was not allowed to get into a car being driven by anyone who hadn't had their driver's license for a full decade.

I had to be home by ten thirty on the weekend and in bed, lights out, by eleven on a school night.

And blah, blah, blah…

Because life was so dang dangerous now, unlike the incredibly safe and bucolic good old days of the twenty-teens, or whatever ancient but perfect decade Mom had grown up in.

"*Skyylarr!*" Sasha brought me back to the present.

"Sorry," I said.

"What's wrong?" Sasha's eyebrows wrinkled up. Her expression of concern made her look way older than a nine-year-old. But she acted way older than a nine-year-old too. Sometimes Sasha was an old, wise person in a little girl's body. But unlike some kids who had older sisters and were nine going on sixteen, Sasha still embraced her inner five-year-old and liked being babied.

"Nothing," I said cheerfully as I handed her the glass.

She took a long, luxurious sip before grinning up at me. She had a serious milk mustache and she knew it. She pretended to twirl it with one tiny finger—exactly the way her dad did when he was joking around. "Yumbo!"

I giggled. Sometimes she acted like a wise, old person…and sometimes she was her extra-goofy father's daughter.

"Okay. Big sips and then bed."

"Big sips, *tooth brushing*, and then bed!" Sasha reminded me.

"I stand corrected."

She drained the glass and then carefully returned it to the sink, making sure that it was rinsed out and set perfectly in the dishwasher before padding deliberately down the hallway to the bathroom.

It was pretty crazy—I had never met a neat-freak nine-year-old before, but Sasha was borderline OCD about certain stuff. It just added to the overall cuteness, though. She was as tiny as an elf, seriously small for her age, with little stubby pigtails and eyelashes that went on for miles. But her elfin appearance hardly matched her little-professor attitude.

I wished I could adopt her.

Or, better yet, I wished Sasha's parents would adopt me.

"You'll tuck me in?" Sasha called after she'd brushed her teeth (carefully, of course, complete with milk-mustache removal) and climbed into her bed.

"Of course," I said, going into her room.

"Thanks a bundle," Sasha replied cheerfully, curling up underneath her pink bedspread. She held her favorite teddy bear close, placing the soft, downy fur underneath her chin before smiling up at me.

I lifted the covers around her, patting the sides with painstaking precision, just the way Sasha liked it. "I'll be in the living room doing my homework if you need me."

"Like if I have a nightmare or something."

"Like if you have a nightmare or something," I agreed as I looked around at the immaculately organized bookshelves, her neatly arranged toys—her massive doll collection the little room's centerpiece. She owned about a trillion old-school dolls, with big glassy eyes and frilly clothes. All of the beautiful brown-skinned dolls were front and center, with the blonds and the redheads at the bottom and in the back. They sat in perfect rows—typical Sasha organization. "But I bet you won't have any nightmares tonight."

Sasha looked over at the window, with its chiffon curtains, and

I went to double check that it was locked—something Mom had trained me to do long before I was Sasha's age. Outside, the night was dark and silent.

"Or if I just get scared or something?" Sasha asked as I checked to make sure her collection of night-lights was on.

"Or if you just get scared," I answered.

Sasha sat up. "Unless you want to stay and watch my dollies dance!"

I gently pushed her back down. This kid was a procrastinator when it came to bedtime, because she was so afraid of the dark. She'd make her dolls perform an entire Broadway show if it meant I'd stay in her room a little bit longer. "I'd love to see your dollies dance," I replied. "But it's time for bed now, so we'll have to play with them another day."

"No!" Sasha shook her head fast and sat up in bed again. "They don't dance during the day! Only at night!"

I pushed her down again, this time sitting beside her on the bed and pinning her down with the blankets. "Well, maybe you'll have a good dream tonight about your dollies dancing. That way, you won't have any time for nightmares."

Sasha belly-laughed. "But you don't *get* it!" she exclaimed through giggles. "They don't dance *in* my dreams. They dance before I fall asleep! Like this!" She wiggled out from beneath the covers and sat up once more, letting her head loll forward, her arms outstretched like a puppet on strings as she shifted her body back and forth.

I laughed, mostly because the idea of those dolls dancing like that would've made Calvin freak. "Wow. That's amazing. I wish I had dolls that danced around my room at night. But it's late."

"I'll show you next time," Sasha said, her eyes suddenly solemn.

"Okay," I said, "but right now, it's time for all little girls and dolls to stop dancing and start sleeping. Because tomorrow you have to be up early for school."

"Ew!" Sasha said, her nostrils flaring.

"I know. School is ewwy."

"No, no. *Eeeeew*. What's that *smell*?"

I sniffed the air and the stench hit me. Like something had died and then come back to life just so that it could die again and double the stink. I mean, it was *intense*.

"Oh my lord, Sasha, for *real*? Did you just *fart*?"

Sasha had her hands over her nose, looking like she didn't know whether to laugh or throw up. "Nuh-uh!" she exclaimed, her voice muffled through her fingers. She burrowed her face into her teddy bear and made a groaning sound, like breathing the air was physically painful.

It was. My eyes were literally *watering*. "Well, it wasn't me!" I exclaimed, gagging before I covered my own nose and mouth with my hands. "Good God! You are never getting too-too chocolate milk again, woman!"

She laughed.

The awfulness was fading, but I was still thinking about maybe hurling—or at least offering a dry heave or two to the Gods of Terrible Odors—when Sasha initiated a tickle war.

"Don't!" I warned her, trying to catch her hands, but the gasping breath I took was filled with fresh, clear, un-stankified air, and I immediately recovered.

Before long, the two of us were hysterical, a jumble of arms and legs on Sasha's bed, giggling and out-tickling each other until finally we lay there exhausted.

"It's gone," Sasha said. "The smell is."

I turned my head to look at her. "Thank goodness. You're nasty."

She giggled. "*You're* nasty!"

I stood up, fixed the girl's covers, and planted a big ol' kiss on her forehead. "Go to bed," I said.

"Good night, Sky," Sasha said.

"Good night, Sash."

I didn't realize it then, but I should have said good-bye.

———————

Things went south fast, starting late on Monday night.

I'd gone to bed at my usual time, but I'd fallen asleep quickly and immediately had one of my crazy, super-detailed dreams.

This one started out pleasantly enough.

I was on a highway. It was a long, two-lane deal…a place that looked familiar, but I wasn't sure why. And it was foggy. So much fog that I could barely see five feet in front of me as I drove.

Ooh. I was *driving*. Way cool.

I think that's when I suspected I was dreaming. In real life, I hadn't gotten my driver's license or even a permit. It was just one more thing I resented about my mother. Everyone else my age had gotten their licenses, but after everything that had gone down in Connecticut, Mom didn't think it would be "a good idea" if I got mine.

Anyway, in the dream, I was driving, and I was trying to keep my eyes focused because it was so hard to see a thing with all the fog. Trees whipped by in my peripheral vision, and a light drizzle smeared the windshield.

Suddenly, the car slowed down despite my insistent foot on the accelerator. A light was flashing on the dashboard, and I saw that it was the gas gauge. I was running on empty.

There wasn't a soul in sight.

The car puttered to a stop, and the rain started to come down faster and harder, tapping like angry ghost fingers on the glass.

I could hear myself breathing. And I realized I was scared.

Blip. Blip. Blip. Blip.

It was a noise outside the car, something in addition to the rain. My breathing quickened, and I pressed the lock button on the inside of the door.

The noise got louder, an insistent little chirp that reminded me of a hospital heart-rate monitor. It was just a beeping sound, but for some reason I couldn't stand it, especially with the dripping of the rain. I shuddered, and the goose bumps on my forearms tingled.

I pressed my hands against the cool rubber of the steering wheel and looked down at my lap.

Why was I wearing a *dress*? I *never* wore dresses. This one was white with little blue diamonds. It reminded me of those horrible hospital gowns doctors gave their patients to wear in the emergency room, like the gown I'd worn when…

I looked up again, and there was a face at the window.

I jumped and smacked my hip against the emergency brake.

Contorted through the rain-smeared glass, the face was pale, ghost-like. I could see dark hair, an open mouth, dark eyes…as dark as holes.

Panicked, I tried to start the car again. It sputtered and stalled.

The face leaned in, and I recognized it! *Her!*

Sasha? I called, and suddenly I was desperate to open the door to let the girl in.

Why was she standing in the pouring rain, on the highway in the middle of the night?

Sasha! I called out again, and finally pushed the door open.

But Sasha had already begun to walk away from the car. Somehow, she was moving so fast and had gotten so far away from me. I just wanted to get her inside where she would be warm and dry. I wanted to get her away from whatever she was walking toward.

And then, just as fast, I was out in the middle of a field, and the sun was shining. I was still in that stupid hospital gown, and Sasha was gone. It was just me and a flurry of monarch butterflies…and the woman.

The woman.

Who was she?

Across the field, I could see her. Silver hair and a hat that covered her face. I felt okay for a second. For just a second.

And then I was in a room, and there was screaming, and there was blood, so much *blood*, and I was covered in blood, and I could smell it—

BOOM BOOM BOOM!

I woke up, gasping, flailing for the lamp that sat by my bed. The sheets were saturated with my sweat.

I turned on the light and sat up, breathing hard. My heart beat wildly in my chest.

BOOM BOOM BOOM!

"Holy crap!" I shouted, because the sound hadn't come from my dream. Someone really was knocking on our front door.

Correction: someone was *pounding* on the front door.

BOOM BOOM BOOM!

And apparently they weren't going to stop until somebody answered.

I lunged out of my bed, tugging my oversized nightshirt down so that it covered more of my legs. I felt sick from waking up so quickly, my nerves beyond shot from the horrible nightmare.

"Sky?" My mom stumbled out of her room and met me in the hallway, her eyes a mixture of grogginess and concern. Her terrycloth bathrobe was snug against her body. She crossed her arms over her chest, as if fending off a chill. Her hands were tucked into the robe's oversized pockets.

"It's okay, Mom," I said, and hurried down the stairs.

I could see the silhouette of a petite figure through the door's stained-glass panel.

BOOM BOOM—

I flung the door open, even as Mom descended the stairs behind me.

It was raining in real life, and the woman standing in the doorway was absolutely drenched. It was Sasha's mother. And she was sobbing.

"Skylar!" she said. "Lord help me!"

"Carmen?" I said disbelievingly. "What's wrong?"

"Mrs. Rodriguez?" my mom asked, pushing me slightly to the side in the doorway. I felt a twinge of irritation. "What's going on?"

Carmen Rodriguez wrung her hands in the doorway, her long, dark hair sticking to the sides of her face in the rain. She wasn't wearing a jacket, and the storm had brought the normally balmy Florida temperature down quite a few degrees. I shivered, imagining how chilly she must have been.

"Have you seen her?" Carmen gasped, her voice shrill with panic. She shifted her focus to me. "Sky! Tell me you've seen Sasha! Tell me you've got my baby here, and she's safe!"

Now Mom was looking at me too, but I shook my head. I hadn't seen Sasha since I'd babysat last night. And I still didn't quite understand. "Sasha's *gone?*"

Carmen's face crumpled, and she raised her hands to the sky as if imploring God himself to bring the little girl back. I swallowed hard as images from my dream popped into my head. Sasha walking so quickly from the car...how I hadn't been able to catch up with her.

"I tucked her into be-e-ed tonight," Carmen hiccuped, "and when I woke up to get ready to go to work, she wasn't there!"

As Carmen collapsed into my mom's arms, sobbing hysterically, I looked over my shoulder at the huge grandfather clock that stood beside the staircase in our entryway. It was four o'clock in the morning.

In a typical, allergic-to-emotion move, Mom hugged Carmen awkwardly, with only the top half of her body touching the shorter woman.

I glanced over their heads, trying to figure out where Sasha might have gone. Many of our neighbors were standing in their doorways as well, craning their necks to get a better look at the scene. Some people were wandering around in pajamas and with umbrellas. Others carried flashlights. I could smell brewed coffee. Apparently our door wasn't the first that Carmen had pounded on.

I didn't see Edmund, Sasha's dad, but then again, I wouldn't. He worked the night shift as a security guard at the fish market. Sasha and I had always laughed at the idea of fish needing a guard. Of course Mom had killed the funny by telling me—out of Sasha's earshot—that these days, in the part of town over by the fish market, people were so hungry they'd rob the place at gunpoint if the guards like Edmund weren't there, actively on patrol.

"We're going to find her," my mom said, patting Carmen's rain-matted hair. "She can't have gone too far."

"Who knows how long she was missing before I woke up?" Carmen sobbed. "It could have been *hours! Oh my God!*"

I felt sick. Why had I dreamed about Sasha? I *never* had nightmares. True, I'd always dreamed vividly, but never like this. So why Sasha? And why tonight?

Vaguely, I remembered a night several years ago when my friend Nicole and I called the Psychic Hotline and talked to a lady with a phony Jamaican accent who made us giggle uncontrollably. I wasn't exactly a firm believer in fortune-telling or prescience or whatever you wanted to call it.

Still, it was an awfully strange coincidence.

And it was Sasha—who was squirrelly enough at bedtime to

require three night lights and a teddy bear. Why in the world would she wander out of her house in the middle of the night?

Instinctively, I knew that she hadn't wandered anywhere. She had to have been taken. But who would do such a terrible thing?

Hoping I was wrong, I dashed upstairs to throw on some sweatpants and to get a scrunchie for my unruly hair. I grabbed my phone while I was at it, intending to call Calvin so he could help with the search.

As I clattered back downstairs, the image from my dream—of Sasha walking down the highway—popped into my head. I cleared my throat and tried not to remember.

Carmen was gone, no doubt to continue searching for her daughter in the rain and the dark.

My mom had already put on her raincoat. "We're going to the Rodriguezes' house," she informed me.

I stopped short. "Shouldn't we be searching in other places?"

Mom shook her head. "It's possible that if Sasha did wander off, she'll come home eventually. Someone should be there, in case she does. Plus, who knows? There's always the possibility that she's hiding somewhere. In the...dryer...or..."

"The *dryer*?" I said incredulously. Mom was ridiculous. Yes, Sasha was tiny, but she was a nine-year-old girl, not a cat.

"It's called *holding down the fort*," Mom replied, jingling her car keys worriedly. "Let's go."

Just then, my phone rang and I saw that it was Calvin. "Neighborhood watch just called. Have you heard?" he asked. Neither one of us bothered to say hello.

"Yeah. We're heading over to Sasha's house now," I told him.

He was excited. "Did they find her?"

"They totally didn't," I said, "but according to my mother, Carmen might not have looked hard enough, and we just might find Sasha hiding in an empty appliance."

"I see," Calvin said, and I laughed despite my ever-growing anxiety.

"You know Mom. Just humor her."

"Meet you there," Cal told me.

———

The Rodriguez family lived down the street, about halfway between my house and Calvin's, in a little one-story ranch, painted red with dark green shutters. Even though it was by far the least fancy-schmancy house on the block, it was the one with the most character.

Sasha's dad, Edmund, was a freelance artist by day and a security guard by night, and most of his daytime projects had made their way onto the Rodriguezes' front lawn. Sculptures in the shapes of eggs, cars, and giant quirky animals stood outside on the grass. A few of the neighbors had made a fuss about it, as it didn't give the house traditional Coconut Key curb appeal. But Calvin and I had always thought it was pretty cool.

Tonight, in the predawn drizzle, the sculptures looked ominous. Neighbors I'd never seen before hovered across the street, staring at the house as if the small building would somehow offer answers.

"Man," Calvin said, still on the phone with me as I sat in the passenger seat of my mom's white SUV. We'd driven over instead of walking, "just in case" we needed the car, but really because Mom never walked anywhere.

"There's, like, a Ken and a Marge on every corner with flashlights, looking in the ditches and even up in the damn trees!" "A Ken" is Calvin's name for a really old guy. "A Marge" is the female equivalent.

He pulled his car into the narrow driveway, right behind us, and we both hung up.

"You and Calvin stay close, you hear?" Mom said, cutting the engine.

I willed myself to refrain from a smart-ass comment. With every Ken and Marge in the entire neighborhood keeping an eye on us, I seriously doubted I'd be raped, murdered, mugged, or kidnapped.

Still, I nodded and got out of the passenger side.

Calvin's wheelchair ramp made a low droning sound as he slid out of his car and onto the driveway. His fro-hawk was tousled into tight curls from sleep, and sheet wrinkles marked his face. I looked down at his outfit. He was wearing a white sneaker on his left foot, and a green and black one on his right.

"You look nice," I noted.

"You're a dick," Calvin replied sweetly.

"Let's not dillydally," Mom said urgently, and I socked Calvin in the arm, deliberately not making eye contact with him because if I did, I'd start laughing inappropriately. His smirk was challenging.

Calvin was always on me about my mom using words like "dilly-dally" and "knickers" and—Cal's favorite—"bosom." He claimed my mom had a gangsta rating of negative five thousand.

Mom shuttled by, oblivious to the fact that we were both pretty much making fun of her. "You guys go ahead to Sasha's room. I'm going to search the rest of the house to see if maybe she's hiding somewhere."

"Don't forget to check the microwave," Calvin called after her, and I punched him again.

As we walked through the front door, I smelled it.

Again.

That terrible, awful, fart-of-doom, backed-up-sewage odor. Was that Sasha again? Was she here?

But the house was empty.

"Ugh," I said and covered the bottom of my face with my pink sweatshirt sleeve.

"What's up?" Calvin said alongside me.

"You don't *smell* that?" I exclaimed.

"Smell *what*?"

I looked at Calvin. "Seriously, the fact that you can't smell it is kind of disturbing."

But he shrugged. "All I smell is my own sexiness," Calvin said.

"Well, I'm sorry to report that your sexiness smells like crap. Literally."

I could hear my mom bustling around in the kitchen, and Calvin tapped me on the arm, smirking. He mouthed the word "mic-ro-wave," and I rolled my eyes.

"Guys, Sasha's room is the second one on the right," Mom called.

"I know, Ma," I replied in a singsong voice, my impatience cutting through. I had only been in Sasha's house about a *billion* times before.

As we walked past Carmen and Edmund's bedroom door and down the hallway toward Sasha's room, the sewage stink became stronger. I kept my sweatshirt sleeve up to my mouth and nose, swallowing hard to keep from gagging.

Calvin looked at me quizzically. I turned the knob to Sasha's room. Instantly, the foul odor was stronger. I coughed violently into my sleeve, my eyes watering desperately.

"Are you okay?" Calvin asked. "Hey, where's her bedroom light? I can't see a thing."

I used the hand that wasn't covering my face and found the switch on the wall.

The room filled with light.

There was a flash of movement, and I quickly turned to the window, where I saw some kind of creature, barely more than a shadow. Long, gray, gnarled limbs, one leg hanging over the open windowsill... One grossly oversized arm clutching a teddy bear...

"Calvin, oh my God!" I squeaked, and covered my face instinctively, as if shielding my eyes would somehow keep me safe.

"What is it?" Calvin barked, visibly spooked. "Skylar, what the hell is wrong with you?"

"You didn't see that?" When I took my hands away from my face, the ghoulish figure was gone.

"See what?" Calvin's expression was ten percent concern—and ninety percent irritation. "Are you *trying* to scare the hell out of me?"

I shook my head, pointing an insistent finger at the open window. Sasha's lilac chiffon curtains fluttered dreamily in the wind.

Someone had *been* there!

"I saw some...thing," I said.

"Like Sasha?" Calvin asked, and anxiously moved himself forward to peer out over the sill.

I couldn't bring myself to get as close to that window as Calvin did. Something in my very core told me that whatever I had seen was dangerous. Evil.

It sounded dramatic, but there was no other word to describe it.

"Definitely *not* Sasha," I said, shuddering, and took a few steps closer to Calvin...and the window. "But it was holding her teddy bear, whatever it was."

"It?" Calvin shook his head. "There's no one out there, Sky. You sure you didn't just see a shadow and get freaked?"

I was sure. Wasn't I? But the screen was in place. I frowned. "Well, I'm definitely freaked, Cal. I know that much."

I could hear Mom in the other room, still moving things around in her search for Sasha.

Calvin nodded. "It's freaking me out too," he admitted, his tone grave. "All of this is."

I finally mustered enough confidence to walk toward the open window. Peering outside through the screen, I saw absolutely nothing out of the ordinary. Hibiscus bushes lined the outside of the house, the red flowers dripping with rain. An old rope swing that Edmund had hung for Sasha a year ago creaked languidly in the breeze. The backyard was otherwise empty except for a few older sculptures that Edmund had decided didn't make the cut for the front lawn.

I shrugged, suddenly exhausted. "I'm seeing things, I guess." But I didn't believe that. I'd seen...something.

"You're not covering your nose anymore," Calvin noticed. "Did it finally stop smelling like dooky in here?"

I sniffed. He was right. The terrible smell of sewage *was* gone… It didn't make sense.

Nothing about this made sense.

"You guys doing okay back there?" my mom called from down the hall.

"Just fine," I called back.

"So the *it* you thought you saw was holding a teddy bear?" Calvin continued, glancing around the bedroom.

I nodded. "Sasha's bear. The white one with the chewed-up nose."

Calvin looked skeptical. "You saw the state of the bear's nose, but you don't know if you saw a person or an *it*?"

"I don't know, Calvin," I said, giving in to my annoyance while trying to remember exactly what I'd seen. It had been just the flash of an image, like a low-res YouTube video, playing on an even worse Internet connection. "It was vaguely female. Kind of a she-ish, witchy it." I started sifting through Sasha's unmade bed, looking for the teddy bear in question. "What I *do* know is that Sasha doesn't let go of that bear for a second when it's dark outside." I looked under the bed. "It's not here."

Whoever had taken Sasha had snatched her up quick, stopping only to put the screen back in the window—if that was, in fact, the way they'd taken the little girl from the house. Not only was the bear missing, but her bed was a tangle of purple and pink sheets.

If it were up to Sasha, she wouldn't leave her bed unmade for more than thirty seconds upon awakening.

"And look at her dolls," I realized.

"Do I have to?" Calvin shuddered as he glanced at the shelves where

Sasha kept her collection. "I hate those things," he said. "I wouldn't sleep with them watching me. I'd spend the whole night making sure they weren't gonna do some evil while my eyes were closed."

"I'm not asking for your opinion about them," I said as patiently as I could. "I'm pointing out that everything's out of place. These dolls are all mixed up. Some are upside down…"

Calvin knew that in Sasha's world, this would be unacceptable. I'd told him that one of the things we'd done on Sunday was alphabetize the emergency contact list that her mom kept on the fridge. Whoo-hoo! Par-tay, Sasha style!

I continued, "And yeah, maybe Sasha fought back when whoever grabbed her, grabbed her." I shook my head as I looked around. "But nothing else in the room is knocked over. It doesn't make sense."

"Okay, so if Sasha didn't mess up the dolls, who did?" Calvin asked. "For the record, if I'm executing a home invasion with the intent to kidnap a child, I'm *not* gonna take the time to rearrange her freaking freaky dolls."

I agreed. But those haunting images from my dream popped back into my head. I thought about Sasha's eyes—how they'd looked empty as she'd leaned against the car window.

I rubbed a tired hand over my face and sighed. "Cal, I'm gonna tell you something, and you're going to think I sound crazy."

"Girl, I thought you were crazy from the jump."

I gave him the side eye. "I'm serious. I know it's going to sound completely unreal, but I can't *not* tell you."

Calvin nodded. "Okay."

"I had a dream this was going to happen." I frowned. "Sort of."

Calvin looked amused. "Like a premonition?" he said, and I could tell immediately that he wasn't taking me seriously whatsoever.

"I guess." I sat down on Sasha's bed, sighing. "It's hard to explain. Right before Carmen came to our door, I was having this nightmare. And Sasha was in it. She was walking down this deserted highway in the rain. I think—no, I *know* that she was in danger."

Calvin wheeled close and draped an arm over my shoulder, pulling my head playfully into his armpit. "You're like Old Mary One-Eye, the palm reader who lives underneath the highway overpass—but cuter."

"Dickweed."

"I love you too."

"I'm serious," I said, pulling free and looking up at Calvin. "Why would I have a dream about Sasha right before she disappeared? I feel like maybe I know more than my conscious mind will let on."

Calvin shook his head. "You had a bad dream. It's a coincidence."

I didn't quite believe that.

"Tell you what," Calvin said. "When they find Sasha—after you've gotten some good, uninterrupted sleep—we'll ask *her* if any part of your dream actually came true."

"Do you really think they'll find her, Cal?"

"I *know* they will," he said, his voice so rich with conviction that I almost believed it myself.

"I *so* hope you're right," I said.

CHAPTER THREE

The next two days were seriously surreal—and this was *well* before Friday's after-dark run to the Sav'A'Buck in Harrisburg. *That* fabulousness was still to come.

Calvin and I both took Tuesday off from school to search for Sasha in the daylight, while the rest of the neighborhood watch rapidly waned. It was creepy, seeing people who had been standing outside with flashlights and umbrellas just hours before as they bustled into their cars and SUVs for a normal workday as if nothing were different. Old Mr. McMahon, two houses down, whistled as he mowed his lawn.

Even the sun was shining again. It seemed, honestly, as though the entire world was giving Sasha the finger.

Wednesday meant it had been long enough since Sasha's disappearance that the police could finally become involved. My mom had delivered an exhausting number of diatribes about *that*. She could still remember the days when a missing nine-year-old got immediate attention from the local police. But it had been decades since anyone gave a crap—or had a fully staffed police force.

She remembered too when a thing called Vurp had been the major way people communicated. Phone calls had video, not just audio the way they did now. She could go a full *hour* on how the infrastructure in Florida had corroded to the point where we were forced to resort again to voice mails and text messages.

But she was the one who'd moved us here from Connecticut. (And I could go and on and on about the injustice of *that*.)

When my alarm went off at six thirty on Wednesday morning, I pressed Snooze once and stared at my ceiling, wondering if I could get away with another day of absence from school. I wasn't done searching for Sasha, even if everyone else was. I knew that even though the police could now be "involved," they wouldn't find Sasha, either.

"You're going to be late for the bus!" Mom called, rapping briskly on my closed bedroom door.

I exhaled heavily. Guess school was on my schedule. Reaching over to my bedside table, I picked up my old-fashioned alarm clock and pressed the off button on the back. I'd had the alarm set on the loudest ringer. Being a deep sleeper, I needed the equivalent of a fire drill to wake me, and this old clock was *loud*.

Throwing my legs over the edge of my bed, I resolved to continue the hunt for Sasha that afternoon. There would be time after school to keep searching. Calvin and I had at least four hours of decent daylight after our last class.

As I showered, thoughts of Sasha popped into my head.

She had been the only person who was kind enough to bring a welcome basket over to our house when Mom and I moved in.

I quickly towel dried my messy red mane of hair before shoving it into a ponytail.

Then, wrapping a towel around my body, I went back to my room and started the search for an outfit.

The jangling alarm from my clock cut through the air unexpectedly. I jumped, startled, and jogged over to the bedside table to shut it off again—I must have pressed the snooze button twice by accident—and stopped short.

The clock wasn't on my bedside table anymore.

Huh?

The ringing continued. I checked on the floor beneath my bed, and it wasn't there either.

Listening more closely, I realized with ever-growing confusion that the alarm was coming from my walk-in closet.

Heart beating hard, I opened the closet door and stepped inside. In the far left-hand corner were my pairs of sneakers and shoes. Opposite that was where I kept my dirty laundry in a messy heap. The ringing was coming from underneath that.

Scooping up jeans, T-shirts, and mismatched socks, I sifted through the clothes, and I found my alarm clock at the very bottom of the pile.

Turning it off, I crouched there in the silence.

Finally, I stood up, hiking my towel more securely around me.

"Mom?" I called.

Nothing.

I walked over to my bedside table and set the alarm clock down where I had left it earlier. Then I stepped out into the hallway.

I hadn't gone far when, on second thought, I backed up into my room to look, hard, at my bedside table.

The clock was still there.

Just checking.

"Mom?" I called again.

"Skylar!" Mom exclaimed. "What are you still doing in your towel?" She emerged from her room, clutching a mug of hot coffee in her perfectly manicured hands.

"Were you just in my room?" I asked.

Mom sighed. "No, I wasn't anywhere near your room, Sky." She fluffed her freshly styled hair anxiously with one hand, keeping a firm grip on her coffee mug with the other. "You're going to be late for school!"

I shook my head. "Why did you move my alarm clock?"

Mom looked absolutely exasperated. "Skylar Reid! I wasn't in your room! Stop with the crazy questions. Go get dressed! The bus is going to be here in"—she checked her silver watch—"three and a half minutes!"

I frowned. If Mom hadn't moved my alarm clock, then who had?

"Come on!" she prompted me. "Mush, mush! Let's go, let's go, let's go!"

I got outside just in time to give my mom the impression that I'd caught the school bus. Then I rounded the corner and hopped into Calvin's car.

"Question of the day," Calvin said, adjusting his rearview mirror and making a sharp right down Main Street toward Coconut Key

Academy. "Would you rather have one giant pimple on your face or a trillion tiny ones?"

I rolled my eyes. "Really?"

"It's the question of the day," he said insistently. "What would you prefer? Saying *neither* is not an option."

Calvin did this thing called "question of the day" whenever he knew I was bummed out or upset. It was a game that consisted of him asking a question starting with "Would you rather" and ending with two equally sucky scenarios.

I peered out the window, watching the trees filter by, and thought about the dream I'd had two nights ago.

"One big pimple," I said, sighing.

"Girl, you're *nasty!*"

"What?" I said, exasperated. "Why is that nasty?"

Calvin turned his radio down a notch. "Here's how I see it," he started, sounding as though he were about to discuss quantum physics with me. "If you've got a trillion tiny pimples, then you can probably just use cover-up and the world would barely ever know. There'd be a lot of them, but they'd be tiny as hell. Now, one big one on the other hand…" He shrugged. "Then you're basically a freak of nature."

I bit my nail and thought. "Maybe so, but one big pimple would disappear a lot faster than a trillion small ones."

"Not necessarily," Calvin said, wagging a finger. "This thing is, like, headlight sized. Basically, you gave birth to a second head."

"My lord, Calvin!"

He grinned. "You love me so much."

I looked at him and couldn't hide my smile. "I do."

We drove in silence for a moment.

"We're gonna keep looking for Sasha this afternoon," I finally told him. When he didn't answer, I glanced over to look at him. "Aren't we?"

"Uh-huh," Calvin said, but his expression was uncomfortable. He chewed on his lower lip.

"I'm not going to give up," I said. "She's out there somewhere."

Calvin nodded. "At least today the cops can get involved. Although it feels like a whole lot of *too little, too late*," he added.

I agreed. The system was screwy, but apparently things were so bad these days that even the wealthy town of Coconut Key didn't have enough money to pay for more than what my mom called a "skeleton crew" down at the police station. Because of that, now when a child went missing, there was a mandatory two-day waiting period. And even after that, a missing kid was more likely to be found by a neighborhood group or something called "citizen detectives."

Mom had muttered pretty darkly about that, saying that those citizen detectives probably took Sasha in the first place. When you earned your living finding lost children, the children had to go missing in order for you to find them.

I hoped that was the case—that Sasha would be brought home by someone demanding a reward. But I couldn't help but feel that was an unlikely scenario.

Calvin pulled into the Coconut Key Academy parking lot. All the handicapped spaces were empty. Lucky us.

"Do you think Amanda Green would go for me?" Calvin asked, as a group of girls walked by on their way to first-period class.

I glimpsed Amanda in the crowd. She looked scary, as usual. Rocking the faux-hawk hairstyle and piercings galore, she was the epitome of retro punk.

"I think she would eat you alive," I replied. "Anyway, you only like her because she's got your hairstyle."

"She's sexy," Calvin said, grinning. "I think she'd go for me."

I undid my seat belt and opened the passenger-side door. "Good luck with that," I said. "If you take her out on a date, just make sure to pack condoms and mace."

"You're stupid," Calvin replied affectionately. He opened his door and pressed the ramp to his car. He slid out sideways, the ramp depositing him, wheelchair and all, gently onto the sidewalk. Just as quickly, the ramp unhitched from his chair and slid back into the car.

"I wish I had a cool contraption like that," I said.

"Grass is always greener," Calvin mumbled.

———

School pretty much sucked.

With our rotating schedule, Chinese culture was my first class of the day, and I found myself in a new level of hell as I sat there listening to what was basically a fifty-minute infomercial. China was Coconut Key Academy's biggest corporate sponsor, and the class was mandatory for all juniors, with the idea that most of us would someday find ourselves employed by the former nation.

Of course, the number one job for American women was pregnancy surrogate, since the Chinese's one-child policy, combined with genetic manipulation, had yielded a population of pretty much all dudes. Yeah, they didn't think that one through.

Added to that was their complete lack of industrial regulation, which had turned corporate China into an environmental waste-land. It was much worse there than it was here, but Ms. Morton, the teacher, tried to bright-side it by pointing out that when we went to live in one of China's big cities—when, not if—we'd be amazed by the high quality of the Internet. And if we mostly stayed indoors, our risk of cancer wouldn't be *too* high.

Yay?

Yeah, no thanks—even though moving to Florida from Connecticut had been like time-traveling back to 2005 in terms of the reliability of the Internet. I mean, cell phone service was so sketchy here in the South that we often had to resort to texting. Talk about old-fashioned…

I got out of Chinese culture just barely alive and staggered through math and then stumbled into a popquiz in science class. I felt like I was dragging my brain cells through mud, and I must've failed the test. It was just too hard to concentrate when all I could think about was Sasha, missing and scared.

If she was even still alive.

That thought was horrible, and I quickly buried it. Sasha was alive. She had to be. I refused to believe otherwise.

Calvin met me in the hallway outside the music room. We both had fourth-period band practice.

"Where's your clarinet?" he asked, nodding at my empty hands as we trudged into Mr. Jenkins's class.

"Ask Mr. Jenkins," I replied darkly.

Calvin whacked me in the butt with his trumpet case as he wheeled through the open doorway. I flicked him on the ear and followed.

The bell rang, a final warning for us to find our seats. Calvin hurried toward the front of the U-shaped seating arrangement and parked himself next to the school's star quarterback, Garrett Hathaway, who was first chair for trumpet.

I moved all the way to the back, where Mr. Jenkins had assigned me for the rest of the school year. Grimly, I pulled a tambourine, cymbals, and a triangle out of a huge plastic bin. Kim Riley, master of the bass drum, nodded her hello. I nodded back.

"Okay, people," Mr. Jenkins said, tapping a pencil on the side of his music stand. "Let's get to work."

No one bothered to respond. Instead, the din of students became a tiny bit quieter as kids shifted their conversations into whispers.

"Let's have some quiet in here," Mr. Jenkins said, his voice only slightly louder. He tapped his pencil again. Today, his comb-over was especially horrendous, sticking up haphazardly as though a strong wind had managed to rearrange his follicles into some unique bird's nest.

I would have felt sorry for him if he hadn't taken me off clarinet and assigned me to the unbelievably super-duper lame task of playing percussion, comma, other.

"Quiet down, people!" Mr. Jenkins said again, his tone now insistent. Unfortunately, his big-boy voice carried quite an easily imitated whine. Calvin could do a mean Mr. J. I looked across the room at him, but he was busy listening to something Garrett was whispering in his ear.

As I watched, Calvin frowned and clenched his jaw before turning pointedly away from Garrett and rearranging the sheet music on his music stand.

"Okay, guys," Mr. Jenkins said, patting at his cumulonimbus hair. "I want to start off today with a new number: excerpts from Mozart's *Clarinet Concerto*."

Of course he did. It was my favorite piece—provided I was playing the clarinet solo.

"It's an arrangement I found, perfect for the instruments in our band. So, let's take it from the top. A one, two, three, four!"

The class started to play, and I laughed out loud because the tempo Mr. Jenkins had set was that of a Sousa march.

Even though the piece had a moderately fast tempo, lingering almost the entire time in a major key, it somehow still remained pensive—even melancholy. Leave it to Mozart.

But leave it to Jenkins to suck the soul out of old Wolfgang. Come to think of it, Mr. J. conducted *every* piece we played as if it were a Sousa march.

How on earth had he gotten the job of music teacher here? I'd had better musicality when I was six. Of course, when I was six, I was already playing the clarinet solo for this piece—which, in this arrangement, had been given to the trumpets.

Garrett and Calvin both were struggling to keep up, even with the abridged version of the melody. I, however, had sheet music that was filled with brick-shaped rests. I skimmed forward five pages and spotted two eighth notes. Oh, goody. There was a chance I'd get to crash the cymbals at least twice before the class ended. I didn't know whether to laugh or be horrified.

But then someone poked me, and I whipped around, startled.

Kim took her drumstick off my shoulder and used it to point to the classroom door.

It was Mrs. Diaprollo, the school guidance counselor. A tired-looking man in an ill-fitting tan suit stood next to her.

And they were pointing at me.

Mr. Jenkins frowned but didn't make any attempt to stop the band.

Mrs. Diaprollo's gesture to me was of the "Come with us, young lady" variety. So I set my cymbals on my seat before following them out of the room. As I shut the door, I could see Mr. Jenkins giving me the hawk eye. But the cymbals would have to wait.

Out in the hallway, Mrs. Diaprollo cleared her throat. "Ms. Reid, I'm sorry to interrupt you in the middle of your class." Her prim voice was authoritative and formal. It was the first time she had spoken directly to me since my first day at school. "But Detective Hughes needs to ask you some questions."

"Is this about Sasha?" I asked eagerly.

Mrs. Diaprollo's lips, pursed most of the time anyway, were puckered slits of pink. The creases in her face stood out deeply as she frowned and crossed her arms over her lace blouse. She looked to Detective Hughes, as if he might be better equipped to answer the question.

But the man in the tan suit merely nodded as if he was too exhausted to speak, and my heart sank. *This* was the man in charge of finding Sasha?

"This won't take very long, Skylar." Mrs. Diaprollo motioned for us to follow her down the hallway toward the teacher conference room, her sensible shoes clacking on the tile floor. I glanced over my shoulder at the detective, who trailed behind us. The man's face was gray and swollen. He looked like he hadn't slept in a month.

"In here, please," Mrs. Diaprollo announced, opening the door to the conference room with a flourish. Out of all the people in the world, the last person I would go to for advice was Mrs. Diaprollo. And yet she was the school's only guidance counselor.

"Skylar, you may take a seat," she said as Detective Hughes tossed a manila folder onto the table. As I watched, he went to the far corner of the room and got a can of Diet Splash from the soda machine. Hands shaking, he then pulled a chair out from the conference room table and sat.

I plopped down across from the detective. I was at least five feet away from him, but I swear I got a strong whiff of cigar smoke and stale booze. My stomach churned.

Mrs. Diaprollo sat next to the detective, primly smoothing down her calf-length skirt and placing her hands atop her lap. It was clear she had no intention of leaving the room—and I was oddly glad for that. She looked toward the man and nodded.

"Yes." Detective Hughes cleared his phlegm-filled throat. "I'm here to ask you some questions about the disappearance of Sasha Rodriguez."

He rubbed his hands over his face and then opened his eyes wide, as if working to stay awake. His hands were large and callused, and all of his nails had been bitten to the quick. They were still shaking. It was a small movement, but it was undeniable. He cleared his throat again.

"How long have you worked for the Rodriguezes?"

"About five and a half months," I said. "A little bit after my mom and I moved down here."

The detective nodded. "And how well would you say that you know the family?"

I shrugged. "Pretty well. I mean, I babysit for Sasha every weekend."

Mrs. Diaprollo tucked a stray hair behind her ear and then folded her hands, watching us both like she was observing a tennis match.

"Did you ever notice anything strange or unusual about Sasha?" Hughes asked, pulling a notepad out of his jacket pocket. He set it next to his soda can, but didn't make any move to write anything down.

Strange or unusual? "What do you mean?"

"For example, would she sometimes get upset or cry?"

I laughed once. "Well, yeah. I mean, she was nine. Nine-year-olds sometimes cry. You know?"

Mrs. Diaprollo looked at the detective, who nodded and then reached inside the same jacket pocket and pulled out a small circle-shaped packet. He ripped it open and poured it into the soda can. It was Gas-B-Gone.

The Diet Splash fizzled for a moment.

"What about Mr. Rodriguez? Ever notice anything unusual about him?"

"I…" I shook my head. "I don't understand."

Hughes took a long gulp of his drink and set it down shakily on the table. Without any explanation or segue, the detective launched into another question. "Did you ever observe Mr. Rodriguez punishing Sasha?"

"I guess," I said. "I mean, when Sasha broke the rules, Mr. Rodriguez would send her to her room for a time-out."

"Did Mr. Rodriguez ever go into Sasha's room with her?"

Mrs. Diaprollo repositioned herself in her seat like she was starting to get uncomfortable.

"Well, obviously. I mean, he's her dad." I shook my head, hoping I'd misunderstood. I felt my cheeks start to heat. "What does this have to do with anything?"

Hughes didn't bother looking up at me but simply plodded on with the questions, his voice almost mechanical. "When he went into Sasha's room, did Mr. Rodriguez ever close the door?"

"Oh, come *on*," I exclaimed. "Really?" I laughed, but it was a humorless sound. "You've got to be kidding me."

"Please answer the question," Hughes replied.

I tried to stay calm. "Yeah. And so did Carmen. And so did I."

"Did Mr. Rodriguez ever touch Sasha inappropriately?"

"No!"

"Did Mr. Rodriguez ever touch *you* inappropriately?"

"What? Absolutely not!" I laughed my surprise again, then looked at Mrs. Diaprollo, but she was busy staring at the tops of her nails.

"Did Mr. Rodriguez ever touch your leg?"

Okay, now he was really pissing me off. "Seriously?" I asked.

Hughes took another sip of his drink. "Please answer the question."

"No, he didn't touch my leg."

"Did he ever touch you on the rear?"

"My lord," I said. "I know what *inappropriate* means. He didn't touch me inappropriately. He didn't touch me anywhere at all—*ever!*"

Hughes nodded. "Did he ever touch your—?"

At this, Mrs. Diaprollo cut him off, slamming her hands down on the table with surprising force, as she sat up pin straight in her chair. "Detective, Skylar knows what inappropriate means, and her answer was no. I think this has been established."

And just like that, old stuffy Diaprollo earned some serious points in my book.

There was a moment of brief silence. Hughes sat back just slightly and retrieved a manila folder from his pile of paperwork. He opened it and slid the contents across the table to me. Tapping his callused finger on the glossy paper, he looked up at me, his eyes red-rimmed and serious.

I looked down. It was a picture of Sasha, Edmund, and me. Carmen had taken it one evening, right before the two grown-ups left for the movies. Sasha and I had just come out of the pool, and we still had our bathing suits on. Mr. Rodriguez stood between us, his arms slung loosely around our shoulders. I remembered the moment clearly, because Carmen had told us all to make funny faces. We'd laughed the first time we'd seen the photo.

I wasn't laughing now.

"Ms. Reid, can you please identify the people in this photograph?"

I shook my head, because, again, I knew where he was going. Yes, in this picture, Edmund was touching me. "This is effed up." Only I didn't say *effed*. I used the full f-bomb.

Mrs. Diaprollo groaned a little as if it had physically wounded her, but she kept her mouth shut.

The detective began to repeat himself. "Can you please identify—"

"I know what you're trying to do." I bit my lip. "You're making Edmund look like a bad guy, but he's not—"

Hughes interrupted me. "Did Mr. Rodriguez request that you address him familiarly by using his first name?"

I felt the room getting smaller and smaller. For everything I said to try to clear up the situation, the detective had a counter-question that made it sound ten times worse.

This time, I thought before I spoke. "Both Carmen and Edmund said it was okay to call them by their first names," I replied. "Ed…Mr. Rodriguez…is a nice man. He treated me like family."

Hughes finally took a pen out of his pocket and picked up his notepad. His chin was rough with stubble, and he scratched the side of his jaw with the closed pen before popping off the cap and scribbling something down. Then he rubbed his eyes and turned a page of his notepad. Throughout the entire string of questions, Hughes failed to make eye contact with me for more than a few seconds at a time.

He didn't care.

He was too tired to care.

I felt my face get hotter, and I swallowed hard.

"Are you aware of any problems that Mr. Rodriguez has been having lately? With money or…?"

"No!" I wanted to stop talking about Edmund! Sasha's disappearance had nothing to do with him! She was still out there, somewhere, and this idiot was just wasting everyone's time. "Why don't you ask him about that? I'm sure if you just talked to him for two minutes, you'd see that—"

"We're unable to talk to him," the detective informed me. "He's been missing since Monday night."

"What?" Edmund was missing too? Monday was the night Sasha had vanished! "Maybe he's with Sasha," I said excitedly. "Maybe…"

But my voice trailed off as Detective Hughes looked up at me. And I realized Hughes thought that Edmund had *kidnapped* Sasha. Or worse.

"No," I said. "That's *crazy*." My voice shook despite my attempt to stay calm. "Mr. Rodriguez loves his daughter. He would never do anything to hurt her."

Mrs. Diaprollo nodded, although I wasn't sure if she was agreeing with me or simply urging the interview forward.

Hughes clenched his jaw, deliberately not looking up at me. He scribbled something down and continued. "Did Sasha ever talk about monsters coming into her room late at night?"

I thought about the image I saw in Sasha's room, the night she turned up missing. And I thought about the nightmares that scared her—the ones that she talked about with me sometimes before I tucked her in. But I knew that wasn't what he meant. "No."

"Did you ever observe Mr. Rodriguez touching Sasha?"

Back to this again. I looked down at the picture of all of us making funny faces for Carmen. "Obviously, yes."

"Okay. That's all the questions we have for now."

I was livid, because I knew he was going to use my statement, my yes, as some kind of twisted proof that Edmund had done terrible things to Sasha. "You know if you do this, if you blame Mr. Rodriguez, then the people who really kidnapped Sasha will go free. We'll never find her, never get her back!"

Hughes looked up at me, and for a fraction of a moment I saw something in his eyes—sorrow, or maybe sympathy or regret. But it was gone as quickly as it had appeared, replaced by that defeated fatigue. He took a business card out of his pocket and slid it across the table to me. Then he took the picture and placed it back in the manila folder. "If you think of anything else that pertains to this case, please call this number."

I couldn't breathe. "You have to believe me," I insisted. "Edmund didn't kidnap Sasha! He would *never* hurt her!"

Hughes glanced at me again with raised eyebrows. I had called Mr. Rodriguez *Edmund* again.

This wasn't fair! This wasn't *fair*!

And then, just like that, from atop the conference desk, Detective Hughes's soda can launched into the air and exploded.

CHAPTER FOUR

"So let me get this straight," Calvin said, taking a bite of his peanut butter and banana sandwich. "You actually witnessed the dickhead cop get super-soaked by a can of soda as Mrs. Disapproval shrieked and moaned?"

I smiled wanly as I nodded. "More importantly, they haven't found Sasha," I said, picking at my granola bar, "and they're making the most ridiculous assumptions."

The midday air was unseasonably cool. Calvin and I ate our lunch outside at picnic tables by the quad, our faces warmed by the sun overhead. Birds chirped in the trees.

Calvin chewed and thought. "So according to Detective Inappropriate, Edmund is their main suspect."

I nodded. Calvin had special skills in finding the perfect nickname for just about everyone.

"What if this whole thing is one big miscommunication?" he asked me. "I'm sure when they talk to Edmund, they'll be able to clear this up."

"If they find him." I shook my head miserably. "It's like they're hell-bent on framing him. MF-ers," I added.

I nibbled a little at the granola bar, but my appetite had vanished back when Hughes had asked, "Did he touch you on the rear?"

Calvin somehow knew what I was thinking. "Did he touch you on the box? Did he touch you with a fox?"

I laughed despite myself as Cal reached around and grabbed his backpack from where it hung on one arm of his wheelchair. He rummaged through it and grabbed a water bottle from the bottom. Twisting the top, he took a sip, and then scrunched up his face.

"Ugh," Calvin said. "Lukewarm." He smiled sweetly. "Sky, would you pretty please with a cherry on top get me a soda from the cafeteria? I'll pay you back."

I dug in my back pocket for my debit card. "Yes, dear."

"Thank you kindly," he said, and worked more on his sandwich.

I trudged toward the lunchroom.

Since my first day at Coconut Key Academy, I had managed to avoid eating lunch inside. I always brought my lunch from home—Mom's crazy rule number 4008—and even on rainier days, I preferred sitting underneath the quad's gazebo rather than dealing with the lunchtime mob. Calvin had always opted for an outside lunch seat as well, and that's how we'd met on my first day last spring.

So when I opened the door to the cafeteria to grab Calvin's soda, I realized that this was the first time I had ever set foot in the crowded room.

And boy, did it smell! Not just pizza, fish, hot peppers, grease, stale juice. But also gasoline, baby powder, chlorine bleach, sour milk, burning plastic… And that terrible, unmistakable smell that only came from a bug frying in a halogen lamp.

The stenches bombarded me from all angles. I coughed a little, walking by tables filled with kids laughing and eating.

The soda and snack machines were in the far corner. I spotted Kim from band class. She was sitting at the same table as Amanda Green, Calvin's crush. Three other girls looked up at me as I walked by their table. They were all in similar garb…lots of eyeliner and piercings. The goths and misfits.

Next to them were four scrawny-looking boys, complete with acne and glasses. Rather than eat, they were all poring over a textbook, conversing quietly. I noticed them look up at me for a moment before returning to their studying. A brute-looking boy walked by in a Coconut Key Tornadoes jersey. He flicked the smallest nerd in the back of the head and then took a bow for all of his friends who were watching and laughing.

I turned to see who his friends were. The jocks. They were huddled together, a good fifteen or twenty of them, monopolizing the largest tables close to the windows. Every boy sitting there wore orange and black, the football team's colors. Some of the girls wore cheerleader outfits, while others were decked out in denim miniskirts, polo shirts, and way too much jewelry. There was a lot of long, blond hair going on.

Most of the gang glanced up for a moment and looked right at me as I went past. I spotted Garrett Hathaway. He had his arm around one of the tinier blond cheerleaders. He was wearing his Tornadoes jersey and laughing about something.

I honestly didn't know how anyone could stand the smell of this place. It was absolutely nauseating. I covered my mouth discreetly as I attempted to insert my debit card into the ancient soda machine. But it spat it right out. That was weird. I tried again.

A hand reached around from behind me and grabbed my card.

"This machine takes it ass backward," a male voice said, and I spun around.

Garrett Hathaway held my debit card and smiled at me.

I smiled back. It was a knee-jerk reaction. He *was* pretty disgustingly good-looking. Problem was, he knew it. *And* he was an asshole.

"Thanks," I said, watching as Garrett inserted my card into the machine. "What are you having?" he asked.

"Cola," I said, and Garrett pressed the button.

"For the prettiest lady in the caf," he said, grabbing the soda can as it bounced into the bottom tray and handing it to me.

"Thanks," I said again, as the machine spit my card back out. I put it in my pocket. It was time to escape, but Garrett was blocking my exit. He gave me a smile that was clearly meant to dazzle.

"I'm Garrett," he said, leaning in conspiratorially. "So, what happened today at band? I saw you go off with that cop and… It didn't have to do with that missing little girl, did it?"

I felt eyes on me now from every direction. It was like being in a fishbowl.

"Um, yeah," I replied, shrugging. "They're trying to find Sasha. I'm trying to help."

"Jeez, that must be really hard on you." Garrett shook his head. "I heard you used to babysit for her. I can't imagine knowing someone who just ends up gone like that."

"Yeah, it's been difficult," I said guardedly. I really didn't feel like discussing this with someone I barely knew.

Garrett put a hand on my shoulder and squeezed. "Poor thing. You've been through the wringer." He paused. "If you want, I could… you know…help. Too."

"Help," I repeated, a little surprised.

"Look for her," Garrett said.

Now I was majorly surprised. Was it possible that the asshole had a soul?

"I'll call you," he said, getting out his cell phone and flipping through his contacts list. "What's your number?"

I looked up right then to see Calvin watching us through the window, his eyes wide.

And maybe Garrett had a special homecoming-king sixth sense that let him know a rejection was coming, because before I could not give him my number, he shut off his phone and said, "On the other hand, I'll just stop by. Pick you up, so we can…you know. Search. Together."

"You know where I live?" I asked, surprised again.

"Well, yeah, down the street from the dead girl."

"Missing," I corrected him.

"Right," he said. "Maybe Saturday afternoon?"

I'd believe it when I saw it, but I wasn't going to discourage anyone from helping me find Sasha.

"See you then," he said with another smile, and walked away.

When I went outside, Calvin's "Oh no you didn't" was hanging in the air, as ominous as a storm cloud on the horizon.

"What was *that?*" he asked.

I popped the top of his soda and took a sip before handing it over to him. "Garrett wants to help us look for Sasha."

Calvin frowned. "No, he doesn't. He's a douche. In fact, he's a double douche. A super-douche."

"Well, that's what he said." I took a seat on the picnic table, resting my elbows on my thighs.

He ran an exasperated hand through his fro-hawk. "Maybe he wants to help you look for Sasha—in the backseat of his car."

I pretended to think about that, mostly to piss Calvin off. "He *is* pretty hot."

"So is Beth Randall, in theory, but I wouldn't touch her with a ten-foot pole."

Beth was the school's female Garrett Hathaway. In fact, they'd just broken up, noisily, last week.

The bell rang, and I gathered up my granola bar wrapper and lunch bag. Calvin took his soda can and put it in a cup holder on the side of his wheelchair.

"Still," I said, "if Garrett wants to help look for Sasha…"

Calvin tossed the sandwich bag into a nearby trash can. "He's douche-tastic. Take my word for it."

But all I could think of were the police detective's ugly questions about Edmund and how, if the investigation focused on an innocent man who would never hurt his daughter, they'd never find the real person who'd taken Sasha.

And we'd never get her back.

Wednesday afternoon was a waste of time.

Calvin and I drove around and looked at playgrounds, parks, and even the aquarium. No Sasha.

When I got home that night, I pulled my e-reader out of my backpack. As mundane as it seemed, I knew I had to keep up with homework. If nothing else, it would keep my mom from getting on my case too much.

I began a lengthy reading assignment about the Second World War, and even though history was one of my favorite subjects, I found my eyelids getting heavy. I cleared my throat and rubbed my eyes to stay awake.

But after reading just a few more paragraphs of what should have been a riveting story—Hitler had tried to bomb the crap out of London every night for months—I soon found my attention had wandered.

I was staring drowsily at the poster on my bedroom wall. It was a picture of a cat that my mom had given me for my tenth birthday.

I was allergic to cats, and since I couldn't have one, this was supposed to be some kind of lame substitute. I hated the picture and I'd long ago outgrown it, but I'd never been able to break that news to Mom. I'd tried to lose it in the move from Connecticut, but she'd found it and hung it here in my new bedroom.

The cat was clawing at a tree branch. Underneath it were the words "Just hangin' out."

Yeah. Calvin mocked me about it mercilessly.

I returned to my reading, vowing to stay conscious for at least another five pages. But gradually, exhaustion won, and I fell into a deep sleep.

The alarm was grating. I woke up with a yelp to see papers scattered everywhere. I had fallen asleep wearing my clothes and on top of my covers. And only half of my homework had been completed.

Crap.

Quickly, I hit the off button on the alarm clock—and then double-checked it, just to be sure. My eyes were cloudy, but I could clearly see that the clock was still securely on my bedside table.

Sitting up, I yawned and stretched my arms overhead. I felt rested for the first time in days. It was a welcome feeling, especially after everything that had been going on.

And then I remembered that Sasha was still missing, and Edmund was the police's prime suspect. The realization hit me like a punch to the stomach.

Things weren't back to normal just yet.

Sighing, I organized the papers on my bed and silently calculated the amount of time I'd need to complete all of my assignments before school started. It was no use. I would probably have to wing some of them or turn them in late.

I heard a sound in the corner of my room and looked up, startled again. But it was just the noise of the pipes creaking as my mom turned her shower on. I stared across the room at my blank wall, still working to wake myself up.

And that's when it hit me.

Blank wall.

Blank *wall.*

Where was my cat poster?

I stood up and crossed the room slowly, my mouth open. The sound of the pipes got louder, and I padded gingerly across my carpet, reaching out a hand to run my fingers across the wall space, as if touching it would confirm what seemed utterly impossible.

The poster that had been hanging there the night before...it was gone.

I *hated* that poster. I really did. But the fact that it was the epitome of tacky didn't make its disappearance any less weird.

I looked on the floor, even under my bed. No poster.

It had been set in a cheap black plastic frame. It would have been hard to miss.

But it wasn't there.

My heart was pounding again.

I stepped backward and looked behind me.

"Hello?" I said to the empty room, and then felt absolutely ridiculous.

I had a feeling, and the feeling told me to check my closet. I placed my hand gently on the doorknob before swinging the door open and lunging forward, fists clenched.

But there was no one there. I exhaled, relieved, and unclenched my fists. Yeah, right. Skylar the ninja.

I kicked aside my dirty laundry, but this time there was nothing underneath. Heart still pounding, I opened the top drawer of my old dresser. I'd put the piece of furniture in the back of my closet as a place to store junk I didn't want to throw out.

Nothing in the top drawer.

I paused…and then opened the middle one. I sifted through school assignments, a medal I'd received from my old school band in Connecticut, and a couple ancient paperback novels. Underneath them were four black pieces of plastic—the frame—and a rolled-up cylinder of glossy paper.

I took out the cylinder and unrolled it.

The cat stared back at me. I dropped it.

"*Mom! Mom! Mom!*" I sprinted out of the closet and down the hallway, tripping over a full basket of dirty laundry.

My mom came bounding out of the bathroom, her hair wrapped in a towel, turban style.

"What? What is it?" she gasped. Her ninja imitation was even more ridiculous than mine. I would have laughed if I hadn't been so freaked out.

"Why did you move my cat poster?"

Mom looked confused. "What cat poster?"

"The one from my room. You must have moved it. Right?"

She shook her head. "Sky, I haven't been anywhere near your room for the past two days. Not even to do laundry, which we need to play catch-up on, by the way."

I nodded impatiently. "Fine. Okay. But you didn't take down that *Just hangin' out* poster?"

"No, that poster is adorable. I know you love it. Why would I do something like that?"

I didn't understand. First my alarm clock and then my poster. Something was happening, but I didn't know what.

"Sky, are you okay?" my mom said, frowning. She shivered in her towel.

"I'm fine," I said. "Go get dressed. Sorry for the weird questions."

Mom stood there for a moment, staring at me. She opened her mouth as if to say something, but then shut it again.

"What is it?" I asked.

"It's nothing," Mom said. "Nothing important."

"I neeeeed coffeeee!" Calvin wailed dramatically as I buckled my seat belt.

"I haaaaave tiiiiiiiime!" I replied, grinning, as Calvin made a U-turn back toward Beach Street, one of the numerous CoffeeBoy locations on Coconut Key. But then he slowed. "Wait. When's your first class?"

"I'm free until second period," I replied.

"What happened to science with Wilson?" Calvin asked. Even though we didn't share all the same classes, we still knew each other's schedules by heart.

"Mrs. Wilson is out sick today," I said without thinking about it.

"Liar," Calvin said, grinning.

I looked at him and gasped, feigning shock. "Well, I nev-aah!" I exclaimed in a pretend British accent. I raised my hand to my chest dramatically. "Accuse me of lying? Despicable!"

Calvin grinned. "Mrs. Wilson was perfectly fine yesterday. I saw her rocking the pleated pants. What'd you do? Call her this morning and check?"

I realized that he was absolutely right. I had no idea why I thought Mrs. Wilson was sick. But I still knew it was true.

"Come on, lie-aah," Calvin said, pulling off an equally horrible Brit accent. "Let's get some coffee and scones!"

He parked the car in the closest space, which was just as good as the handicapped spot. Even though it was seven thirty in the morning, the place was dead.

I didn't know a whole lot about the state of the economy, but I didn't need to be a rocket scientist to figure out that things were getting worse. If a usually-bustling coffee shop wasn't ringing in morning customers on a weekday, there was a problem.

I hopped out of the car and waited for Calvin's nifty wheelchair ramp to let him out of the driver's side. "Scones?" I asked. "Do they even sell scones outside of England?"

My mother had once told me that back before CoffeeBoy, a chain of coffee shops right here in the States used to sell scones. But then England had gotten on the corporate government's blacklist and far more American donuts—with red, white, and blue jelly—had come into vogue.

"Crumpets too!" Calvin said delightedly as he closed the driver's side door.

This particular CoffeeBoy was looking pretty bleak. Inside the dingy place were three cheap-looking tables and a scattering of battered plastic chairs. Boxy TVs hung in each corner of the shop, tuned to various news channels. The din of reporters filled the almost empty room.

I absentmindedly tapped on the counter, an orange Formica rectangle stained with large *O*'s where people had set down their overflowing paper cups. A girl stood behind the register, looking simultaneously bored and despondent. She popped her gum as Calvin and I scanned the menu. There were no scones. At one time, there had been donuts available, but the word had been crossed off the menu with a bedraggled strip of masking tape.

Apparently there was coffee, or coffee.

"Hey…Amber," Calvin said, reading her name tag. Beneath her name was a little sticker that said "Ask me about my…" Amber had scrawled the word "schnauzer" in messy letters. "How's your schnauzer?"

"Dead," Amber said, and snapped a bubble.

"Right," Calvin replied. "Sorry to hear that. I'm going to have a large coffee, extra cream, lots of sugar."

"We're out of cream," Amber with the dead dog replied apathetically.

"Out of cream at a *coffee shop*?" Calvin asked disbelievingly.

Apparently Amber figured a lack of response would suffice for a yes.

"Okay, awesome!" Calvin said, his voice absurdly cheerful. My best friend was a clown.

"I'm gonna pass," I told him as I sat down in the least disgusting chair. I let Calvin continue to torture Amber and briefly thought about the homework assignments that I should have been working on, last minute. There was no way I'd be able to concentrate, though, with so much on my mind.

So I stared at one of the TVs and zoned out.

"…police continue to investigate the bizarre disappearance of both Coconut Key resident Edmund Rodriguez and his nine-year-old daughter, Sasha."

In a heartbeat, I was paying attention. I turned to search for the TV where the news anchor had just said Sasha's name, and found it. An image of Edmund Rodriguez appeared on the screen behind the blond news anchor, followed by a recent school picture of Sasha.

"In a breaking story, local law enforcement officials have identified Mr. Rodriguez's truck, which was found near an abandoned warehouse in nearby Harrisburg, just over the county line."

"Calvin!" I yelped. "Look!" I pointed at the TV.

"Can you turn that up, please?" Calvin asked Amber, who rolled her eyes and aimed a remote control toward the screen we were watching.

The image changed to a police lieutenant speaking into a miniature microphone atop a wooden podium. His expression was grim. I recognized Detective Hughes standing slightly behind him.

"Lab tests confirm that the blood in the bed of Mr. Rodriguez's truck was, indeed, that of his daughter, Sasha."

Blood?

Images from my dream three nights ago hit me like a punch to the head. I brought my hand up to my mouth and looked at Calvin. But Calvin didn't look away from the TV. The muscle was jumping in his jaw.

"…found another item, also stained with the victim's blood, which confirms our fears that this crime was of a…sexual nature."

"No," I said, and I shook my head as the picture changed back to the news anchor.

"We'll have the latest in sports and weather when we return," she said brightly as the station went to a commercial break.

Now Calvin was looking down at his hands, but then he turned and gazed at me. "You okay?"

"Am I okay?" I asked, laughing humorlessly, as on the TV children sang a song about toilet paper. "No, I'm so *not* okay! I'm furious!"

"I get that," Calvin replied quietly.

"I'm furious," I continued, "because I *know* Mr. Rodriguez didn't hurt Sasha!"

Calvin looked surprised at that. "Um, weren't you paying attention?" he asked. "They've got physical evidence. I'm just seriously glad that sick a-hole didn't hurt *you*."

"He didn't do it," I said, shaking my head adamantly. "I know he didn't do it."

"And how exactly do you know that?" Calvin countered. "Sky, I know you're upset, and I'm really sorry."

I bit a nail to the quick, frustrated. "Cal, you've got to believe me on this one. Remember when we went to Sasha's the night she went missing?"

Calvin nodded.

"And remember how I thought I saw something in her room?"

"The big, bad, vaguely witchy shadow that had her teddy bear?"

I nodded, ignoring Calvin's slightly mocking tone. "Well, when I was in that room... I don't know. It's like I could smell the fear—and something else too. That nasty sewage smell… I don't know how to explain it, but I felt this…I don't know, pressure. Doom or foreboding. And it definitely didn't have anything to do with Edmund."

Calvin stared at me. "Girl, are you playing with me?"

"Do I look like I'm playing around?" I asked.

He let out a steady exhalation and sat back in his wheelchair, folding his hands behind his neck. "I think you're losing it," Cal warned.

"Okay, so then answer me this," I insisted. "Why is it that the dolls in Sasha's room were all messed up? And why is it that things in my room are being messed with too?"

"What are you talking about?"

"Someone's been putting my stuff in weird spots. Like my cat poster."

Calvin snorted. "That jacked-up picture of the kitten hanging on a tree branch?"

"Yes!" I exclaimed. "When I fell asleep last night, it was hanging on my wall, and when I got up this morning, not only was it not there, but it had been removed from the frame, rolled up, and stashed in my closet!"

Calvin leaned forward and hummed the *Twilight Zone* theme. He wiggled his fingers in front of my face. "Whoever did it must be really tall to get into your room through the second-story window with no trees or ladders to climb."

"All right, fine," I said, crossing my arms over my chest. "Fine. Don't believe me."

"Aw, I'm sorry," he said, throwing his arm over my shoulder. "I know you're upset. I won't joke around anymore."

The news came back on with a completely different story. And we silently left the shop and got back into Calvin's car.

"I don't know, Sky," Calvin finally said as he pulled out of the CoffeeBoy parking lot. "Sometimes people just really suck. Plain and simple."

"I totally agree," I said, "but I don't think that Mr. Rodriguez is one of those people."

Calvin put his left blinker on, turning when the light changed from red to green. All of the disbelief was gone from his face, and now he just looked sad.

"I know I'm right, Cal." I'd just glanced down at my bitten fingernails, so I didn't see exactly what it was that made him hit the brakes so hard that the car came to a sudden, lurching stop.

The sound of our tires squealing was overpowered by the roar of a motorcycle engine. Apparently, we had narrowly missed hitting a bike.

"Damn!" Calvin hissed, and we watched as the motorcycle driver pulled away in a flash of red leather and an opaque helmet. "People need to learn how to drive!"

I watched the motorcycle get smaller and smaller as it moved farther from us, while I struggled to slow my pounding heart.

We were okay. The biker was okay. No one was choking on their own blood, gasping as they struggled to breathe...

And Calvin—who had only the vaguest idea why my mother had that stupid rule about my not being allowed to ride in a car with a driver who was less than thirty years old—had no clue that I was about to pass out from fear.

"All right. I think I've had enough almost-heart-attacks for one day," Calvin quipped with a laugh.

"Don't joke," I said sharply, unable to keep myself from glancing nervously at Calvin's chest, because I knew he had the heart health of a seventy-year-old man. "That's not funny."

He stopped laughing.

"Sky?" he finally said, watching the road as he drove—slowly and carefully this time. "Sometimes people suck. Things suck. A lot of it *really* sucks." He glanced at me, his eyes so serious I had to look down. "And when that happens, after you've exhausted all your resources, the only thing you have *left* is laughter." He pulled into the school and slugged his car into Park. "And in this life, I plan to laugh my damn ass off."

CHAPTER FIVE

And then it was Friday.

It was a normal enough school day, followed by more fruitless searching for Sasha, made worse by the fact that Calvin now believed what the police believed—that the little girl was dead, murdered by her own father.

I'd had a typically strained dinner with Mom, then escaped to Calvin's to watch a movie—after which we'd set off in search of chocolate to make those stupid s'mores. And we'd ended up taking that ill-fated trip across the tracks to Harrisburg.

To the Sav'A'Buck.

Previously, in Skylar's weirdly messed-up life, she and her bestie ventured into a grocery store in a super-low-rent part of town, where they were threatened at gunpoint by a large-bosomed female contortionist wearing designer shoes. Facing a hideous and somewhat embarrassing death-by-crazy-lady, they were rescued at the last second by a height-challenged super-girl with a blond pixie cut, a red leather motorcycle jacket, and an industrial-strength death glare.

Yeah.

And as if all that wasn't freakishly weird enough, after disarming and karate-chopping the crazy killer-clown-lady into submissive unconsciousness, Motorcycle Girl somehow knew my name.

"Way to protect Tiny Tim here, Sky," she'd said.

I looked at Calvin and he looked back at me, equally disturbed—so much so that the Tiny Tim insult didn't penetrate. Or maybe he was still too stunned to speak. I'm pretty sure I was in shock too.

"What were you waiting for?" the girl asked me, genuinely annoyed. "A sign from God? News flash! She's a little too busy with the real important shit to put in an appearance in this craphole."

She marched over to a stack of red plastic shopping baskets and yanked one off the top so she could...?

Grocery shop. Seriously.

There were quite a few things I wanted to do after nearly getting shot to death in the Sav'A'Buck by a murderous trophy wife from hell. Using the nearest bathroom so as not to add the awfulness of pee-pee pants to my swamp butt was high on my list. But food shopping?

Motorcycle Chick inspected a little box of tuna before throwing it into her basket. And then she stepped over the former Little Miss Sunshine before heading to aisle seven, her biker boots click-clacking on the industrial tile floor.

The rest of the store had completely cleared out by then, the shoppers and the store clerks stampeding through the front doors in a flurried panic. I could see people's headlights through the windows of the store as they peeled out of the parking lot in a hurry.

I still couldn't move. I *had* to be in shock.

Cal placed a shaky hand on my arm. "Dude," he said, staring down at the security guard and the crazy lady as they lay unconscious in front of us. At least the guard was unconscious. I could see him breathing. But Little Miss Sunshine was not moving at all. "Dude."

Motorcycle Chick reemerged from aisle seven and headed back toward us. Her basket was already filled to the brim. I spotted at least six huge jars of peanut butter as she walked past us on her way to the deserted registers.

"Hey!" I finally got my feet to move again as I followed her. I also managed to find my voice, but it sounded thin and tiny—as if I were Sasha's age. "How do you know my name?"

The girl looked up at me and said, "Oops," before taking a wad of cash from one of her many pockets. She threw it onto the register. The tinny music from the overhead speakers echoed through the empty store.

"Hey!" I said again.

She didn't pay attention to me as she swung herself over to the other side of the checkout counter. She picked off a couple of plastic bags and started packing her food. Only then did she say, "I'm in your class at school?" But she said it as a question, as if she knew I wouldn't buy it.

Cal spoke up from behind me. "If you went to our school, we definitely would have noticed you."

"Caught by the bullshit police," she said without looking up.

"And speaking of police, they're gonna be here soon. The real ones. You should go. Girl like you doesn't want to draw too much attention to herself."

"A girl like *me*?" I repeated. The heavy incredulity in my tone made me sound a little older now. Maybe twelve or even thirteen.

"Don't play games." She double-bagged the pile of peanut butter jars and then knotted the bag with deliberate, almost aggressive precision. "I saw what you did with that Taser."

"I didn't do anything with the Taser. I mean, I tried to tase the crazy lady, yeah. But it didn't work, obviously—"

"I'm talking about your abilities." The girl looked up at me then as she enunciated the word with four crisp syllables. Her eyes were the color of crystal, heavily rimmed with charcoal-colored liner, and I couldn't look away.

But then what she said sunk in. My *a-bil-i-ties*? The word made me uneasy. "I don't know what you're—" I started.

"Your powers." She nodded toward the woman on the ground behind me. "Tits McGee over there? She could smell it on you. Destiny addicts sense it sometimes, when they joker. Kinda the way one G-T can recognize another."

One G-T can *wha*…? I looked at Calvin and he looked back at me, equally lost. Clearly Motorcycle Girl wasn't speaking some kind of Floridian street code that I, a nonnative, couldn't decipher.

"Was that even a sentence?" Cal asked her. "When Destiny addicts *joker*? What does that mean? Can you try again, please, in American English?"

71

"I'm pretty sure that lady couldn't smell anything over the disgusting fish stank," I added, and now they both looked at me.

"Fish stank?" the girl repeated, as incredulous as if I'd just announced that I pooped rainbows and diamonds.

"And now *you're* freaking me out," Calvin said as he pointed to me. "First the weird sewage smell in Sasha's room—"

"You smelled sewage in Sasha's room?" Motorcycle Girl demanded, skewering me again with those odd blue eyes.

But I was the one who got up into her face—so much so that Calvin grabbed on to one of the belt loops of my jean shorts to hold me back. "How do *you* know Sasha?"

She looked away first, and when she met my eyes again, her expression was almost apologetic. Almost.

"I'm sorry for your loss," she said, and for the two seconds that it took her to say those words, I actually believed her.

But then she took a bite of an apple that she'd left out of her tightly tied bags. Like this was the perfect time and place for a snack. I wasn't sure I was ever going to eat again.

"I know about Sasha because she was all over the news for, you know, her fifteen seconds of fame," she said with her mouth full. "Hundreds of girls go missing every day, Red. I'm one of the few who cares enough to remember their names. That's how I know Sasha. And Betsy and Clarice and Lacey and DeNika and—"

"Did you take her?" I interrupted her, with all of the rage and grief from the past week making my voice quiver. "Do you have her? Give her back!"

"Oh, Bubble Gum," the girl said, shaking her head. "I wish it were that easy. And I swear to you, if I knew where she was, I'd tell you. But I don't." She sharply lifted her head then and said, "Police are on their way."

Only then did I hear it—sirens. But they were way, *way* in the distance.

"I'd love to stay and chat some more," she continued as she effortlessly lifted her two bags with one hand, apple still in the other, and started for the door, "but I gotta go. And I'll repeat, FYI, that you and Wheels definitely don't want to be here when the police show up. Not with your powers. That won't go well."

Again with the powers, and again with that uneasy feeling in my stomach. Still, I laughed as we followed her. "I really don't know what you're talking about—"

With lightning speed, she tossed her apple high into the air, then grabbed a heavy box of soup that was in a display right by the door, next to the ancient, broken Redbox machine, and flung it at Cal's head. I reached out instinctively, grabbing the box in midair, right before it hit him in the face. I mean, *right* before. I could feel the tiny hairs on my arms tickling Calvin's forehead. It was weird, because I was pretty sure I hadn't been standing that close to him before she'd grabbed for the soup.

"What the *Hay-ell*—" Cal started.

"Nuff said," the girl interrupted him matter-of-factly. She caught her apple before it hit the floor and took another large bite. "Don't worry, Scoot. Skylar's learning. You're not gonna die. At least not today."

"Are you okay?" I asked Cal even as I found myself thinking about the alarm clock and the cat poster, as the girl's crisp voice again echoed in my head. *A-bil-i-ties...*

Cal, meanwhile, had narrowed his eyes at the girl now walking out the Sav'A'Buck door before looking up at me. "I'm fine," he replied. "Except my cray-cray limit has maxed out."

I set the soup down on the floor before following the girl into the parking lot. I had to know more. "Hey! Wait!"

Calvin kept pace with me. "Really?" he was muttering. "We really want more of this?"

The girl had stopped next to a huge motorcycle—the only vehicle left in the lot besides Cal's car—but now she turned to face us. She was still munching away on her apple.

"I don't get you," I said. "So I caught the soup box. I can catch. I've always been able to catch. Big deal."

"It *is* a big deal," the girl said as she stuffed the bags into the small back trunk of her motorcycle, then tossed the apple core across the parking lot. She kicked away the stand and climbed onto the bike. It made her look even more petite, but no less of a badass. "It's a really big deal, Bubble Gum. If you're not careful, they'll come for you next."

And now it was the memory of that shadowy figure I thought I'd seen in Sasha's room that made me shiver.

Meanwhile, those distant sirens were getting louder.

"Gotta go," she said.

"Wait!" I yelled as the girl started the bike's engine. I could barely hear my voice over the roar. "Please!"

Motorcycle Girl revved the engine before leaning forward and glaring at me with eyes so intense that, again, I couldn't look away. "Listen to me. I'll be in touch. But right now, get into your car, both of you, and drive away. You need to get the hell out of here. *Now.*"

With that, the girl sped off on her motorcycle, leaving a cloud of dust and a whole crapload of unanswered questions behind.

At the same time, a different question was answered.

I looked down at Cal. He looked up at me and nodded. It was definitely Motorcycle Girl that we'd nearly hit and killed yesterday. Coincidence, or had she been following us?

Neither one of us said a word as we got into Cal's car. We "got the hell out of there" before the police arrived, because I'd had that little talk with Detective Hughes, and Motorcycle Girl was right. It *hadn't* gone well.

"I can't believe you couldn't smell that fish," I said, finally breaking our silence as we headed back home.

Calvin looked at me, his hands tight on the steering wheel. "Yeah. *That's* what you can't believe. A crazy lady with a gun, pulling out her own teeth, and *Destiny addicts sense your powers sometimes when they joker,*" he said in a very decent imitation of the motorcycle girl, "whatever the eff *that* means. Blondie knows both *your* name and Sasha's—and *you're* all about my clogged sinuses."

I reached for my bag, which I'd left on the floor of his car, and dug for my phone with its Internet access. Maybe we could answer some of these questions with a little help from Google. "Destiny addicts." I nodded as I powered up my phone. "And joker. And what else did she say? *G* and *T.* Let's see if we can find out what the eff at least *some* of this means."

What had Calvin said? That his cray-cray limit had maxed out?

Well, mine was now pinned. Plus that feeling of uneasiness had moved into my belly. Permanently.

We sat in Cal's car, pulled off to the side of the road and safely back in our neighborhood in Coconut Key, as we both used our phones and the intermittent Internet to attempt to understand what the blond-haired motorcycle girl had told us.

A-bil-i-ties.

"Destiny," Calvin read, the screen of his phone almost touching his nose, "is the street name for an illegal drug, quote, *a chemical compound called oxy-clepta-di-estraphen that has not yet been approved for use by the corporate drug administration.* Lobbyists claim it's safe, although expensive. Says here it was developed to treat people with terminal diseases. Cancer patients with a month to live. One article says *clinical trials have proven that it completely eradicates all traces of cancer in patients who've used it.*"

He looked over at me and there was something wistful in his eyes. "It makes users stronger, smarter, faster, literally *younger.* One doctor claims he gave the drug to a fully paralyzed patient, someone who needed a respirator to breathe after breaking her neck, and after a single dose, the woman was out of bed, breathing—and walking—on her own steam."

That was amazing. And now I knew what that look in Cal's eyes was about.

"What's the catch?" I asked.

"She died a day later," he said. "Patient number two—a man in a similar condition—lived a little longer, but he jokered and killed the doctor before he died too."

And there was that word again. "Jokered?" I asked.

"Urban Dictionary defines it as *to succumb to illegal-drug-induced insanity, complete with super strength, inability to feel pain or compassion, and enhanced mental powers, à la a comic-book super-villain,*" he told me.

"So the drug'll heal you," I deduced, "right before it drives you insane and then kills you."

"Details, schmeetails," Calvin said. "Destiny is also instantly addictive. On first use. You shoot up once, and you need to take it for the rest of your life. Or you die. It's also ridonkulously expensive. About five thousand dollars a dose."

I laughed. "Seriously?"

"According to the Internet," Calvin pointed out. "Which means all of it might be an urban legend." He smiled sadly. "Before I found the 5K-a-dose thing combined with the and-the-next-day-she-died thing, I was thinking, *Huh, I might want to try this.* You know, see if it could heal me."

"And be an addict for the rest of your life?" I asked, aghast.

He shrugged. "I take blood thinners because my heart was damaged. I have to take *them* for the rest of my life."

"That's different."

"Not really," he pointed out. "Or at least that's what I was thinking before I found that definition for jokering. Basically, when you take

Destiny, the drug changes your brain waves. It allows you access to more brainpower—it's called neural integration, and yeah, my eyes started glazing over too. In a nutshell, it sounds like Destiny eventually turns users into super-villains with—you're gonna love this—superpowers like telepathy, prescience—that's foreseeing the future—and telekinesis, which is moving shit around with your mind, right?

"According to the scientifically acclaimed website—and yes, that was sarcasm—Destiny Addicts R Us dot com, without proper training, the average person can't handle taking Destiny and suddenly having those kinds of enhanced mental powers, so their brains break and they go bonkers. Thus they joker. All of them. Always. Like Little Miss Sunshine at the Sav'A'Buck. All Destiny users eventually noisily self-destruct. The lucky ones just quietly drop dead without killing everyone else in the room."

We stared at each other.

But then Cal barked with laughter. "Telepathy?" he said. "Come on. That's nuts-balls. It's bad enough that Destiny is addictive and that it eventually kills you, no need to make up this comic-book crap to scare people away from trying it."

"If taking Destiny means you die, why would anyone take it?" It was really just a rhetorical question, but Cal answered me.

"Because people are stupid," he said. "And desperate. And selfish. And greedy. From what I just read, the drug's mostly abused by the uber-rich. And they don't take it because they've got cancer. No, they take it because they want to look younger, and the nipping and tucking's no longer working. That, and the fact that the very, very bad people who make and sell Destiny don't include a warning label on their product."

"God," I said.

"Rumor has it there's a plan in place to try to manufacture the drug more efficiently, to make it less expensive," Calvin told me. "Currently, there're two versions. The pure kind, sold in high-end nightclubs or passed along to patients in doctors' offices, and something called *Street D*, which is cut with things like antifreeze and sold to the addicts and the desperate. Chance of jokering from Street D is eighty percent higher."

I exhaled loud and long, but Calvin wasn't finished.

"Another side effect of the drug," he added, "even before the user jokers from his unbearable telekinesis or dies, or both, is this kinda intense feeling of superiority, which I guess makes sense. I mean, if you're sixty but you suddenly look and feel twenty? Wouldn't you feel superior? Cancer's gone, boom, here I am, world, stronger and smarter. Yeah.

"But there's also, allegedly, a lack of empathy that occurs with the use of Destiny. You stop being able to relate to anyone, even your own family. So even before you joker, you start exhibiting sociopathic, crazy-pants, psycho-killer behavior. But then when you joker, double boom, you do things like parboil and eat your grandkids without blinking, simply because you were hungry and wanted a snack."

"Oh, thanks," I said. "I needed that image."

"You're welcome." Cal looked at me. "So what'd you find?"

Predictably, Google had given me nothing from the letters *G* and

T, but I too had used Urban Dictionary to find that it wasn't *GT* or even *G* period *T* period, but rather *G* dash *T*. "G-T is short for something—someone—called a *Greater-Than*," I told him. "I don't know how real this is. Some websites are convinced G-Ts are urban legends, kinda like Sasquatch. Some sites think G-Ts are gods from above, and others say they're dangerous"—I read from my phone's screen—"*sociopathic megalomaniacs...*" I looked up at Cal. "A lot like a jokering Destiny addict, I think. The word *super-villain* was used a lot in what I read."

"So...a G-T or Greater-Than is, what?" Cal asked. "Another name for a Destiny addict?"

"Nope," I told him, popping my *P*. "Apparently, some people—mostly female people—have these...well, let me read this to you: *innate mental powers. G-Ts are born with access to more of their brains, and those powers can include*"—I glanced up at him—"*telepathy, prescience, and telekinesis.*"

"Innate means natural, right?"

"It means, baby, they're born that way, yeah," I told him, even as Motorcycle Girl's voice echoed in my head. *A-bil-i-ties.* "Apparently, having these weird superpowers can turn Greater-Thans kind of crazy too. Mean crazy. The words *feelings of superiority* came up a lot in my searches too. Along with *lack of empathy and compassion*, yada, yada."

"More comic-book bullshit," Calvin decided, and I wished I shared his skepticism and total disbelief. "SuperGirl from the Sav'A'Buck was just jerking our chain."

I nodded and didn't tell him how spooked all of this made me feel.

He'd call me Old Mary One-Eye again, and I didn't want to get mad at him and... No, I refused to think about any of this anymore tonight.

"What's not bullshit," I told him, "is the twenty missed calls from my mother." She'd started calling when we were back in the Sav'A'Buck, when I'd left my bag on the floor of Cal's car. I pointed to the lit-up numerals of the clock on his dashboard. "It's after eleven. I'm late."

I was so dead.

Correction: I was so *not* dead.

"You know, I think we should keep what happened tonight between us," I offered as Calvin started his car. We weren't too far from my house, thank goodness. Still, when I walked through that door, I was gonna get hammered by the wrath of Mom.

"I think that's a good idea." Calvin tightened his jaw as he turned onto my street. He laughed once, and his expression softened. "Hey, what do you call a knight in shining armor if the knight happens to be a girl?"

I knew he was talking about Motorcycle Girl. *A Greater-Than?* I kept that thought to myself. She'd scared me more than Little Miss Sunshine had.

Well, maybe not quite *that* much. Still, a shiver ran through me as Calvin turned into my driveway.

"Lights off!" I hissed, and Calvin quickly switched off his headlights.

"I seriously doubt your mom will be able to tell the difference between my car and my parents' car, especially in the dark," Calvin replied.

"I'm pretty sure she's got her own personal night-vision goggles," I said. "In a lovely shade of peach or maybe salmon."

Cal laughed, but more because he knew he was supposed to, and we sat there in the darkness of my driveway for a few moments before I turned to ask, "Are you going to be okay driving home alone?"

He made a dismissive *pssht* sound. "I'm good," he replied, but I didn't believe him for a second. He was still freaked out. How could he not be?

Still, I knew he wasn't going to cave. "Fine," I said. "Text me when you get home, or else it's on," I said as I stepped out of his car.

"I'm still racing you, so think of something good to bet, because I'm going to win it," Calvin replied, reminding me of the challenge he'd given me back in the Sav'A'Buck, pre-jokering Destiny addict.

"Oh, I will," I said, and leaned back in to give him a high five. We both felt better pretending everything was normal.

But when he rolled down the driver's side window as I walked up the steps to my house, I couldn't keep up the game. "I'm serious," I called out, quietly enough so that my mom wouldn't hear from inside. "Be careful."

Calvin nodded. "Yes, ma'am." And he backed out of the driveway, switching his headlights on again only after turning his car onto the street.

I was digging my key out of my purse when Mom flung the door open. "Skylar!" she gasped. "Thank God you're okay!"

This *would* have been the appropriate response for any mother to have—if she knew her daughter had just been held at gunpoint.

Unfortunately, this was how Mom acted all the time.

"Of course I'm okay," I replied casually, setting my purse down on the coffee table as I began my litany of FUVUs—frequently used vague untruths. "I'm so sorry I'm late. I don't know what happened. Cal and I were talking and I looked up and it was after eleven." I began to untie my pink high-top sneakers, hopping up and down a little to keep my balance as I worked on loosening the left shoelace.

My mom threw her arms around me, kissing the back of my neck feverishly, as if I'd just returned home from war.

Which was closer to the truth, I guess, than I preferred to admit.

The reality was that my heart hadn't completely slowed since we'd left the Sav'A'Buck. And yet somehow I was managing to go through all the motions I normally did after a night out.

Maybe I was still in shock.

But then my phone beeped, and I pulled back to read Calvin's text: Home safe. Heads up…Momzilla alert. She called my mom, looking for you, while we were out. Sry :/

Great, now Calvin was gonna be in trouble too, because *his* mother hadn't known that *my* mother didn't want me driving around in his car. Except she probably did now.

"Mom," I said sharply. "You called Calvin's mom?"

There was nothing she could say but *yes*, so she attempted to distract. "Do you have *any* idea how scared I was?"

I set my phone down on the arm of the couch. "Mom. Why in the world would you be so scared? I'm not *that* late."

"Because!" Mom's face looked contorted and pained, like she might actually start crying. Her usually perfect blond bob was even tousled as if she'd been running her hands through it. I realized that she was seriously upset. "Because what if…"

"What if…" I prompted her.

"What if…something happened to you? And I wasn't there? What if you got into a…another accident…or a…"

I sighed, trying to be calm despite my frustration at having *this* conversation again. *What if you get into another accident?* "Aren't you tired of talking about this? Because I am."

"No!" Mom was getting shrill. "I'm not going to stop talking about it until you stop scaring the crap out of me!"

Now I *knew* she was hyper-upset. Mom never even fake swore. Her manners were almost priest-like.

"Don't you get it?" she continued. "I'm trying to keep you safe! It's my *job*!"

"But I'm seventeen! I'm not *five*." I threw my hands up in the air. "So I get home at eleven instead of ten thirty. Big deal! I'm *fine*. Look! Take a good look!" I spun around, my eyes wide. "Alive! One piece. Congra*tu*lations! Job well done!"

Mom shook her head. "You're not seventeen until next Friday," she said, focusing on the least important thing I'd said.

"Uuuuggh!" I groaned. "Are you not getting my point at all? I'm not a baby anymore."

"I understand. I do," Mom said, her voice suddenly calm.

For a moment I thought that maybe I had broken through and we were going to discuss this like sane adults.

"You're upset," she continued, "because you just want to have a normal life. And that's what I want for you too. But you're not going to have that normal life if something absolutely horrific happens and you're raped and murdered or..."

I had spoken too soon. She was still bat-crap crazy.

"...mugged or *kidnapped*..."

Lalalalala, I sang to myself, blocking out my mother's insanity. If I kept listening, I was sure I'd have to break something, just to bring my blood pressure down. The possibility of steam escaping from my nose and ears was increasing by the second.

"...and then you stopped answering your phone while you were in that bad part of town..."

I looked up. "Wait. What did you just say?"

Mom paused. "I said..."

She'd said I was *in that bad part of town*. I didn't want to say it aloud, but we both knew what she'd said. How did she know where I'd been?

I looked at her, and then I looked at my phone.

Mom followed my gaze. She looked nervous.

"What do you have on here?" I asked, and lunged for the couch.

Mom tried to beat me to it, but I was faster. I grabbed my cell phone and shut it off.

From across the room, Mom's cell phone made a little beep.

I turned my phone back on. Mom's cell beeped again.

"Are you *tracking* me?" I exclaimed disbelievingly.

Her guilt was written all over her face.

"I can't believe you're spying on me!" My face got even hotter. I began to walk toward the stairs to my room, because I could not deal with this.

"Wait!" Mom called. "Sky, I'm sorry. I'm just…I'm doing it for your own good!"

"My own good?" I spun around, even more enraged. "How can you say you know what's good for me? It's your fault that we're here in this third-world land of the living dead. I hate it here," I continued, knowing that I was hurting her feelings but too angry to care. "I loved Connecticut, but you had to go and get a new job—"

"I loved Connecticut too," she said, but then took a deep breath. "You know that jobs are hard to come by in this economy, considering—"

She was an art investment advisor, which meant she spent about ten hours a week telling rich people how they should spend their next ten million bucks.

I cut her off. "And you couldn't find anything in Connecticut?"

Her mouth was tight. "No, I couldn't."

That was BS, and we both knew it, and I was furious because once again she was treating me like a baby and withholding information from me. There was a reason she'd yanked me out of school and hustled me down to Florida. God, she hadn't even told me about the move until the trucks pulled up to the house. I'd had to say good-bye to my friends via email. "You *ruined my life*! I hope you *know that*!"

I raced to my room and slammed my door shut. The rage boiling inside of me was too much.

"Aaaaagggh!" I roared as I dove onto my bed, then rolled and took my hairbrush off my bedside table and hurled it across the room.

It hit the opposite wall with an oddly unsatisfying *thunk*.

But then something really weird happened.

The brush didn't fall to the carpeting.

At least for a moment, it hovered there in the air before shooting back across the room and repositioning itself on my bedside table.

Uh

Bill

Uh

Tees.

Abilities.

"Oh, shit," I whispered. I grabbed my phone and texted Cal: U still up?

I rocked a little as I sat there on the edge of my bed, but made myself stop. Crazy people rocked like that. And I wasn't crazy. I wasn't crazy. I wasn't…

My phone beeped, but it wasn't Cal texting me. Calvin has lost phone privileges for the time being, it said. It was signed, Stephanie. Calvin's mom.

"Shit!" I took a deep breath to try to calm myself. I wasn't crazy. And I wasn't any more a Greater-Than than I was Bigfoot.

I picked up the hairbrush again and tossed it across the room. This time, after it hit the wall, it fell down to the carpeting. Down was a direction I was much more familiar with.

So why did I feel disappointed? This was a good thing, right?

"Sky?" Mom called from out in the hallway, and my face heated up. She was really going to continue this conversation tonight? After all the sneaky crap she'd pulled?

The hairbrush lifted off the ground and spun several times, like a cylinder in a car, before crashing against the ceiling. I watched, eyes wide, as it slid across the smooth surface with the fast precision of an object on ice.

Then it dropped into the air again and did a loopy figure eight before landing once more on my bedside table.

Whoa.

Whoa!

"I'm going to bed. Good night," Mom called, her voice weary.

Suddenly, I *wanted* her to piss me off.

Because I had a serious theory, and I needed her to help me prove it.

But I listened to her door shut and knew that she was spent.

Instead, I closed my eyes and thought about the argument that my mom and I had just had about the GPS system tracking me via my cell phone—about the way that Mom had belittled me, treating me like a child. I felt my face get hot as I became angry all over again.

I opened one eye just a slit. The hairbrush was still resting comfortably on the bedside table.

I closed my eyes again and moved on to more global issues. Things that really got under my skin…*bad drivers, cat ladies, mullets, world wars, racism, hate crimes, poverty, euthanasia in overcrowded dog kennels, corrupt politicians, liars, and cheaters…*

I opened my eyes. The brush was still on the bedside table, like a lead weight.

Keeping my eyes focused on the brush, I continued with my silent rant, willing myself into a state of fury...*bullies, homophobes, sociopaths, terrorism...* I focused... *cops who don't believe you, kidnappers, conspiracies, the monster who took Sasha, because that poor little girl might never see her mom and dad again—and I swear I will find those bastards and bring them to justice, and you better believe it!*

The hairbrush went vertical, and then it launched toward me, landing in the palm of my open hand with a smack.

Chapter Six

When I woke up on Saturday, I felt as if I'd been hit by a truck.

I rolled over stiffly in my bed, stretching my arms out to the sides and yawning deeply. Looking down, I realized I had fallen asleep in my clothes for the second time that week.

In fact, I couldn't even remember having closed my eyes.

For a moment I lay there, staring at the ceiling.

The hairbrush.

Last night I had moved my hairbrush with *my brain.*

I sat up quickly, but then just as quickly sank back down as a wave of nausea hit me, along with a dull ache in my back and legs. I felt as if… Oh, Lord, *really?* I was going to get my period *today?* It wasn't due for at least another week.

Before I could even begin to process what had happened last night, both at the Sav'A'Buck with the motorcycle girl and then after, I needed to do some damage control.

I rolled out of bed and, knees pressed together, shuffled awkwardly into the hallway toward the bathroom, shielding my eyes from the sunlight seeping through the front blinds. This morning, everything hurt.

From my bedroom, I could hear my cell phone beeping.

My thoughts shifted to last night's argument. My mom had attached a GPS navigator to my phone!

I moaned, realizing that getting angry was not going to help my current situation. I staggered into the bathroom and pulled a bottle of painkillers out of the medicine cabinet.

Taking two, I stuck my head beneath the faucet and clumsily gulped some water before tipping my head back and swallowing the pills. I rubbed my face and then glanced at my reflection in the mirror.

If I didn't take better care of myself, I was going to start looking like that washed-up police detective.

Mom was up. I could hear her moving around now in her bedroom. I pressed the lock button on the bathroom door, just in case, and then sat down on the toilet.

I looked down. Yes, I had my period. Fabulous.

The cabinet underneath the sink was just far enough away that I had to really reach to grab the tampons. I winced as I leaned over.

I had never been hungover, but it couldn't possibly be worse than this.

By the time that I had showered and started to move around a little bit, I was feeling better, the cramps down to a dull ache. Mom kept to her room, and I grabbed my cell phone-slash-*Where's Skylar?* spy system and headed downstairs.

I saw from my phone that it was nearly two o'clock in the

afternoon—I'd slept *that* late. And there was a new text from Calvin: U doin ok? Apparently he'd regained his phone privileges. I started to text him back, but then I wondered if my mom received all my texts as well. If she did, I'd have to start keeping things really vague. Better not to respond to Cal until I could tell him, in person, not to send me any messages about jokering Destiny addicts. Wouldn't *that* make Mom's head explode?

Leave it to my mother to turn my life into a Jason Bourne movie. She probably bugged my old teddy bears too. I picture myself tapping Morse code onto the arm of Cal's wheelchair. *Meet me under the highway overpass at oh-dark-thirty, dash dash dash, dot dot dot.*

"Skylar, I'm going to the store," Mom said, startling me as she stepped quietly into the kitchen. "Are you going to be okay?"

"Yeah." I deliberately turned away and poked my head into the fridge so that I wouldn't have to look at her. "You know where I'll be," I continued, and laughed humorlessly. I pretended I was deciding what to make for lunch, but in truth I wasn't hungry.

I knew, even without turning around, that my mom was standing there staring at me. I also knew that she'd been crying.

Imagine how she would've reacted if she'd known what happened last night, while I was breaking her rules out in Harrisburg. I was still a little surprised that she hadn't grounded me. Yet. That magic could still be coming.

But after a moment, she walked over to the kitchen counter and poured some coffee into her travel mug. "You know," she said, "your science teacher's in the hospital."

I turned around, leaning against the open refrigerator door. "Mrs. Wilson?" I asked.

"Yeah," Mom replied. "She has a terrible case of pneumonia. It came out of nowhere Thursday morning. It hit her really hard. You and your friends might want to send her a get-well card."

I realized with a jolt that Thursday had been when I'd gone to the CoffeeBoy with Calvin because I'd *known* that Mrs. W wasn't going to be in school. And sure enough, she'd been absent Friday too. How had I known that? I hadn't given it much thought before this, but it was *weird*.

Abilities...

No. If there was one thing I knew for sure, it was that I wasn't—*was not*—a Greater-Than. Whatever had happened last night with the hairbrush had been a fluke.

Please God, let it have been a fluke...

Mom took a sip of coffee. "All right," she said, moving forward to kiss me on my cheek. I shied away, and Mom nodded. "Okay. Be careful today. I love you."

"I know," I said.

I felt her lingering in the room for another moment, and then she left without grounding me.

Whoopee.

———

Trudging up to my room, I considered just going for a run and getting away from everything for a while. Maybe doing something normal would make me feel better.

I sighed and pulled out my red-and-blue racerback sports bra and a pair of running shorts. I slapped on some sunblock and tied my hair up into a high ponytail.

As I smoothed down a few flyaway curls, my gaze fell on the hairbrush on my bedside table. As far as I could tell, the brush—and the alarm clock and the cat poster—hadn't moved since I fell asleep last night. I halfheartedly tried to move my hairbrush again, but it just sat there like…a hairbrush. Of course, I was tired and crampy and not very angry. I sighed, wondering about my hairbrush theory. Another good theory was that maybe I'd dreamed the whole thing, but I knew that I hadn't.

I had a sudden vision of the clock, the brush, and the poster all dancing together in my room like something out of *Fantasia*, swooping and spinning over my bed while I slept. It was definitely disturbing, but way less creepy than another sharp vision I suddenly had. In this one, the shadowy gray creature I'd imagined in Sasha's room—the one who could've been a body double for the wicked witch from *Hansel and Gretel*—was climbing *into* the window.

And this time the window was mine.

The creepiest part was that the picture in my head was the mental equivalent of scratch-and-sniff, because I could smell it. That awful sewage smell from Sasha's bedroom. It was there, faintly, in the back of my throat like a visceral memory, nauseating and dizzying and awful.

The doorbell rang, startling me, and I jumped and squeaked. And just like that, it was all gone—the image, the smell, the sense of impending doom. Well, the sense of doom may have lingered, but I immediately laughed and made myself imagine that same gray witch-thing on my doorstep in the bright morning sunlight. In a Brownie uniform, selling Thin Mints.

I clattered down the stairs to the front door. I wasn't expecting anyone, but Mom did a lot of her shopping online, and we received packages pretty regularly. I opened the door and...

The front stoop was empty.

Frowning, I peeked my head out into the morning heat. Nobody was there.

"Hello?" I called. No one answered.

Across the street, a woman in a tennis outfit walked her three little dogs, all yipping gleefully on the ends of three long leashes. It was a beautiful, clear day, and the sun warmed the back of my shoulders as I stepped outside.

So why was a chill running through me?

I took another step toward the stairs so I could see down the street, all the way to the big palm tree in Sasha's front yard.

And that terrible, horrible stench of backed-up sewage—not distant and not a memory this time—filled my nostrils.

Gagging, I dashed inside and slammed the front door shut, locking it with one swift movement.

Why was I scared?

Because something evil was out there. Of that I had no doubt.

I sank onto the cool tile floor, dizzy and nauseated and needing to put my head between my legs so I didn't yuke on Mom's palm-treed welcome mat. But I grabbed for my phone, filled with an even stronger need to call someone for help.

But who? 9-1-1 was unreliable these days. And even if I got through, when I frantically claimed that a mysterious sewage smell was in my front yard, the operator would probably respond the way Calvin had. She'd laugh in my face.

Besides, when I accessed my phone, I immediately got the standard "Service is currently unavailable" message. Which meant I couldn't call anyone. I could only text.

I thought for a nanosecond about texting my mom, but rejected that instantly. She'd never leave me home alone again. Her imaginary fears were restricting enough without mine being added to the list.

Despite knowing that Cal would laugh at me, I'd just decided to text him, cryptically telling him to come over *right now* and then quickly turning off my phone, when someone banged on the door three times.

Boom boom boom!

And I screamed.

"Skylar?" The male voice was muffled through the closed door.

I scrambled to my feet to look through the door's small stained-glass panel.

Garrett Hathaway?

I flung the door open, as glad as I'd ever been to see him.

"Hey!" he said, looking confused. No doubt he'd heard my horror-movie-worthy scream of terror. "Are you all right?"

"I'm fine!" I said, forcing a smile and willing my heartbeat to return to normal. I gave him the age-old excuse. "Giant spider."

I took a tiny whiff of the air outside. No more sewage smell. Garrett's car was in the driveway—a little cream-colored roadster. Calvin and I had joked about those kinds of convertibles, calling them the *universal midlife-crisis car*. I wondered if this one belonged to Garrett's dad, or if Garrett was already in crisis at the tender age of eighteen.

Garrett, meanwhile, was looking at me. "Wow. You look hot!"

Oh, please. I didn't share the fact that the nasty-ass sewage smell had made me throw up a little in my mouth, and that if he kept up the BS, I might do it again—and this time not be able to keep it contained.

He must've sensed my disbelief because he added, "I'm serious. I've never seen you in anything besides jeans and a T-shirt. There is a *lot* of bare skin going on right now, and I am totally okay with that."

Ew.

"I'm about to go for a run," I explained, then asked, "What are you doing here?"

"I was in the neighborhood," he said, "and I thought you might want some help, looking for Tasha."

"Sasha," I corrected him.

"Right," he said, and gave me another of those meant-to-dazzle smiles. "So, can I give you a ride?"

He was seriously exhausting. I pointed to myself. "Going for a *run?*"

"Well, you're going to run on the beach," he said. "Right? I mean, how could you not run on the beach?"

You could totally not run on the beach if your crazy mother didn't let you get your driver's license and you didn't have an ultra-rich daddy to provide you with his midlife-crisis car. I stepped back inside to grab my keys off the table.

"We could look for Sasha while we're there." Garrett gave me another smile. "Let me help. I could also be your running buddy. Coach you, give you some tips. You know, I'd run cross-country if I wasn't the MVP of the football team."

I liked the idea of searching for Sasha down at the beach. Calvin and I hadn't done much more than drive by. Soft sand and wheelchairs didn't exactly mix.

Still, I couldn't help but think about what Calvin had said, warning me about Garrett's *douche-tastic-ness.*

Douche he might have been, but Garrett was a douche who was asking to help find Sasha.

I used my key to lock the door. "Okay. Thanks."

———

"I hope you're ready for some track lessons," Garrett said. "I've been running since I was, like, ten years old, so I can teach you a lot if you let me."

There was a double meaning in his words, and he leaned in as if he was going to kiss me.

So I got out of his car, hoping to avoid the awkwardness by pretending I was clueless. We were here to run, right? So let's run. I wanted to get this over with so I could get back to looking for Sasha.

"Usually," Garrett said as he followed me, "I like to go for a pretty long run. I'll head all the way down to the wall, which is three miles that way"—he pointed to the right—"and then back again."

I'd needed about point five seconds to recognize that getting into Garrett's car was an enormous mistake. Not only had I been forced to endure another fifteen minutes of really bad, really loud music and lots of engine revving, but I'm pretty sure Garrett checked himself out in the rearview mirror at least twenty times. I'd lost exact count around the third stoplight.

The icing on the already unappetizing cake was that Garrett had blown past the road leading down to the public beach, instead taking me here to this private strip of sand that abutted his dad's vacation "cottage," because it was "prettier and way less crowded out here." We'd look for Sasha, he promised, *after* we'd had our run.

It was true that the view was spectacular. I'd give him that.

White, immaculate hills of sugary sand coated an empty beach. Ahead, the glistening jewel-toned ocean expanded for miles. Behind us was that towering hulk of a mansion, its stone turrets jutting into the air like a castle. Vacation "cottage," my ass. Clearly, being pretentious ran in the family.

"So three and three makes six miles." Garrett was apparently unaware of my ability to do basic math. "Which is a decent distance for a run."

I didn't wait for him to lead the way. I plunged on ahead, down a set of wooden stairs. Garrett followed as I moved briskly toward the shore, our footsteps awkward in the unpacked sand.

"Now, since you're a novice runner," he continued, "you won't be able to go that far, or even keep up with me. So if I get way ahead of you, don't take it personally."

Seriously? Calvin was going to love hearing about this. "A douche, indeed," I said, and then realized I'd spoken aloud. "That's, um, Botsmanian for *great*."

There was no such place as Botsmania, but Garrett nodded. "Ah," he said. "Well, then… *A-douche-in-dee*."

I coughed. "That's actually the feminine version. It's more accurate for a guy to say, *Ama-douche*."

"*Ama-douche*," he repeated obediently.

I had another coughing fit. Somewhere, Calvin was already laughing his ass off.

"You ready?" Garrett asked.

I had never tracked my runs before, so I had no idea if six miles would feel long or short to me. Still, I nodded. "Whenever you are."

"*Ama-douche!*" Garrett took off, his feet pounding the sand as he ran.

I started running as well, slowed down a bit by another bout of coughing but warming up as I breathed in the beach air. It was salty and damp, and it actually refreshed me. I quickly caught up and set my pace with Garrett, staying at his side.

I had never tried running with a partner before. It was different. Garrett's pace was slower than I'd expected, and I really wanted to speed up. For the first few minutes, though, I felt obligated to stay with him, but then I remembered what he'd said… *If I get way ahead of you, don't take it personally*. Heart pumping, I began to feel really good for the first time in days.

So, I decided that if it was okay for Garrett to get way ahead of me, it was equally cool for me to run ahead of him.

Which is exactly what I did.

The breeze embraced me as I moved my legs across the solid sand

and tilted my face up to the sunlight. Forgetting everything bad, I just ran. My arms pumped by my sides, and I found myself repeating a mantra as my steps multiplied.

Everything-will-be-okay, everything-will-be-okay…

And then I looked up, and the wall that Garrett had talked about was right in front of me. I slammed my hand against it and turned around to start back toward where Garrett and I had begun our jog.

But when I turned, Garrett was nowhere to be found.

In fact, now that I thought about it, I hadn't seen him since I'd decided to speed up.

I couldn't even see a dot of an outline of him on the beach. And his dad's *vacation cottage*? Well, that was far enough away to look about as huge as my pinky.

Where *was* Garrett?

I felt energized. I wasn't tired at all. I touched the back of my neck and found that the very beginnings of sweat had popped through right around my hairline. Otherwise, I was completely cool and dry.

"Hey!" someone called from far away, up beyond the rolling hills of the sand dunes.

I turned to look, and…it was Garrett! He waved at me, one arm slung across the open door of his convertible, pulled to the side of the gravel beach road.

The road and the dunes were separated by a chain-link fence that had seen better days. I jogged up the hill and then stepped through a hole in the fence to get to Garrett and his car.

"Where did you go?" I asked, wiping sand off my hands.

"Where did *you* go?" Garrett said, and he sounded irritated.

"I was just running," I said. Now that I was standing right in front of Garrett, I could see how sweaty he was. His hair, usually spiked in the front, was stuck to his forehead. He had taken his sunglasses off and was wiping the perspiration from his chin.

Garrett shook his head. "Very funny."

"I'm not trying to be funny," I replied. "Why did you get in your car?"

"Because," he said snippily, "I looked down at the sand for a second, and when I looked up, you were gone." He shook his head. "There's no way you ran that."

"I totally did."

Garrett frowned. "You're seriously trying to tell me you ran three miles in…" He checked his watch. "…ten minutes?"

Was that fast, or was he just punking me? He seemed so serious. "I don't know. I didn't keep track. I just ran."

Garrett's frown deepened. "Fine. If you really ran that, then show me again. Race me. And this time, no cheating."

He *was* serious. "I didn't cheat."

Garrett made it obvious that he didn't believe me. He slammed his car door, leaving it parked beside the road, and followed me back through the hole in the fence. When we made it down to the packed sand by the water, he shook his head again and said, "You know the fastest mile ever run was in three minutes and forty three seconds?"

"Really?" I said. I didn't know that. I'd never really paid attention to things like the Olympics and world records.

"Yeah. Some dude from Morocco did it. But you just crushed his record."

"Maybe you miscalculated the time," I offered. I seriously doubted I had broken any world records today, considering I was still a bit crampy. I checked my watch instinctively, but it didn't provide any answers. I had no idea when I'd started running, or when I had finished.

"Maybe you're playing a joke on me. Did you have that gimp kid follow us and drive you out here to the wall?"

I narrowed my eyes at Garrett. "Gimp kid?" I repeated. "You mean Calvin? My best friend?"

Garrett shrugged. "I guess so," he said. "I've never really talked to him, so I wouldn't know if he was your best friend or not."

I'd seen Garrett talking to Calvin in band practice all the time. So with that, Garrett suddenly had officially become both douche-tastic *and* a bald-faced liar.

"Let's just do this," I said, angrier than ever. The faster we finished the race, the faster I could get away from Garrett. "How far are we racing?"

"We'll do a quarter mile. To that pile of seaweed." He pointed to a large mass of dark green mush, way down the beach.

"*A-douche-in-dee*," I said, wanting him to say it again.

He did. "*Ama-douche*."

Garrett and I lined up against the wall. I looked over at him, and he looked at me. "Wait a second," he said, and unpeeled his black tank top from his torso. His abs were six solid indentations—a total work of art that glistened in the sun. Too bad he was a douche.

I waited impatiently while he carefully rolled up his shirt, left it on the stone wall, and took a moment to stretch. Then he looked down at his watch.

"Okay. We start in three, two…"

And before Garrett said one, he sprinted forward, swinging his arms and legs wildly by his sides.

Double douche!

Rolling my eyes, I pressed my stopwatch button and took off after him, quickly catching up. As I passed Garrett, I saw the expression of disbelief on his face. And then I was ahead and looking only at the beauty of the ocean and the sky.

It wasn't long before I hit the pile of seaweed mush with one foot, hit my stopwatch button, and stopped running. Stretching my arms overhead, I yawned a little bit. The cool breeze felt nice. A single bead of sweat slid down my temple, and I caught it with one finger.

I turned around.

Garrett had only made it halfway. He'd stopped and was leaning forward, bending almost in half as he placed his hands on his knees.

"Garrett?" I called, even though I knew he was too far away to hear me.

It looked like he was starting to kneel down, right there in the sand.

"You okay?" I called out, and began to jog back toward him.

When I got closer, I saw that he was, in fact, kneeling. He then leaned over, bracing himself with his hands in the sand.

"Garrett?" I said again.

And that's when I watched the Coconut Key Academy star quarterback puke his guts out all over the sand.

"Oh, man," I said, running over to him. "Do you want me to get you some water?"

Garrett heaved a little more and then stood up, not looking at me. "Let's go," he said, wiping off his chin. "I'm taking you home."

I followed along beside him as Garrett trudged back to the car. Curious, I looked down at my watch. I'd run a quarter mile in forty-five seconds. Was that good? It seemed about right to me.

"Do you want me to run and grab your shirt?" I asked, pointing back down the beach. "You left it by the wall."

"Screw my shirt." Garrett coughed a little into the crook of his elbow. "You know," he said, "I was out partying pretty hard last night. Too much tequila—you know what *that's* like. That plus the heat... And I'm pretty sure I *did* miscalculate. This watch I use sometimes acts funny in the humidity. No way did you run a four-minute mile."

Garrett pressed a button on his keys, and the car beeped its acknowledgment. I glanced up at the otherwise empty road...and that's when I spotted her.

She was in the shade of a palm tree, her legs straddling her motorcycle, and she was far enough away so that I couldn't see more than the pale smudge of her face.

Motorcycle Girl.

I knew that *she* knew I'd seen her, because she shook her head at me, as if in warning.

"Hey!" I said to Garrett, who was busy making sure he hadn't thrown up on the front of his shorts. "Do you know that girl?"

Garrett gave himself one final brush-down before turning to face me. "What girl?" he asked, still breathless. He was drenched in sweat.

"That…" But when I looked up again, I found myself pointing to an empty expanse of road. The bike, and the girl, were gone.

CHAPTER SEVEN

I did the math—several times—and I had definitely run sub-four-minute miles.

And Garrett was definitely a douche.

As we drove home from the beach, I looked at my phone and realized that service was back, and that Calvin had been calling me off the hook. My mom, however, had not, which was both surprising and awesome.

"See ya," Garrett said, still not smiling as he pulled into my driveway.

"Thanks," I replied, Mom's years of training to be polite kicking in as I slammed his car door shut before jogging up my steps.

Garrett had promised we'd look for Sasha while we were out. And that hadn't happened. After the puking incident, I figured I wouldn't even bring it up and just wait until I got home to do some investigating myself.

Now it was almost four o'clock, and I needed to get my butt in gear.

As if on cue, my phone rang again. Calvin.

"Where the Jesus have you been?" Cal said before I could even spit out a *hello*. Garrett, meanwhile, pulled away with a squeal of tires.

"I slept late, then went to the beach for a run with Garrett," I told my friend.

"Excuse me, who?" Calvin said, even though I knew he'd heard me clearly. This connection was pretty good.

"He dropped by and said he wanted to help look for *Tasha*, but we went for a run instead," I reported. "For the record, you were right."

"Right about what?" Cal sounded annoyed.

"Garrett," I replied. "He's a douche."

There was a pause, and I heard Calvin sighing into the phone. "Man, Sky, I don't mean to be a drag, but could you please just shoot me an *I'm ok* on days like this? Maybe you've forgotten, but we almost got our asses *shot* last night."

Cal had a point. And I *had* almost forgotten. Until Motorcycle Girl appeared at the beach. Assuming, of course, that she wasn't a hallucination conjured up by my Greater-Than brain, God help us all.

"Sorry," I apologized as I opened the door with my house key. My mom wasn't back yet from shopping, which was good. That meant I could talk freely without fear of her overhearing. I quickly filled Calvin in on the GPS debacle and warned him to keep his texts vague.

I locked the door behind me after I went inside, remembering that awful sewage smell and the sense of evil it had carried with it.

Calvin had been appropriately silent for a moment, but now said, "Tasha?" as if what I'd told him about Garrett had just penetrated.

"That was the first douche-y thing he did." I laughed. "It wasn't the last."

"Garrett's douche-y-ness knows no bounds," Calvin agreed.

"Get over here," I commanded him as I went into the kitchen. "I just walked in. And I need to tell you about a trillion different things. I need to show you something too. Are you hungry? I could make some pasta."

I could hear Calvin as he shut the creaky door that connected his mudroom to his garage. "I am, but your mom's treating you to pizza in about forty minutes, so you should wait to eat."

I had already stuck my hand into a bag of corn chips. I removed it and licked salt off my fingers. "Wait. And how do you know this?"

"Saw her just a little while ago. I'll 'splain when I get there."

A few minutes later—time I spent online googling racing records—Calvin texted me: im here.

My house, unfortunately, was only partially wheelchair accessible with those steps leading up to the front door. When Calvin came over, he had to text or call when he arrived, so I could let up the garage door. At the back of the garage was a ramp leading to the main floor of the house.

I now hit the button on the inside of the garage, and there was Calvin waiting patiently. He pressed the little joystick on the right arm of his chair and moved himself forward and up into my house.

"Okay, lady, I know the topic is *how I spent my day*, and you've got a lot to tell me, but I'm going first. And I need you to sit down for this," Cal said.

"Good news or bad news?" I asked, thinking immediately of Sasha.

Calvin paused, and I could tell he was trying to decide. "Neutral?" he said uncertainly. "But weird. Let's go to your room."

My bedroom was on the second floor. It was a relative pain in the ass for Cal to get up there, but he knew that it was my sanctuary from my otherwise mom-charged house. I got behind the wheelchair and readied myself for the journey.

Calvin's chair was one of the best on the market, and it came with all of the newest technology—like the retractable ramp in his car.

When he'd first started hanging out with me, his parents not only installed the permanent ramp in the garage, but they also requested that I have the stairs up to the second floor measured so that they could install a special banister. Cal's chair had a retractable clip that attached it to the banister and slid him up and down, kind of like a makeshift escalator.

When we reached the top of the stairs, Cal pressed a button, and the clip disappeared beneath the arm of his wheelchair. "Take a seat," he said when we'd made it into my room.

I wondered what news could possibly be weirder than the things I was planning on telling and showing him. I hopped onto my bed and sat tailor-style next to my massive heap of pillows.

"So, I'm pretty sure your mom's bangin' Mr. Jenkins."

I nearly fell off my bed. "*What?*"

Calvin nodded somberly. "I'm sorry, Sky. I know that's really creepy, but I went to the CoffeeBoy this afternoon—the nice one near the mall? That's where I ran into them."

I seriously wanted to throw up. Mom…and my *band teacher*? "Wait," I said, "so they were in CoffeeBoy at the same time? That doesn't mean my mom is…" I shook my head in disgust, unwilling to complete the sentence.

Cal was insistent. "When I walked in, they were sitting in a corner together, huddled over a table. At first I just thought it was some random guy, which would be weird anyway, but then I spotted the comb-over."

"Oh my God, that is so gross." I bit a nail. "Seriously, there has to be some kind of explanation."

Calvin didn't look so sure. "I said hi to them, 'cause otherwise it would have been really awkward, and it was obvious they saw *me*. It's not like there are too many black kids in wheelchairs rolling through Coconut Key." He pressed the recline button on his chair, and the device tipped him back slightly. He crossed his hands comfortably behind his head. "Anyway, when I went over to their table, they both looked like they were hiding something."

I couldn't believe it. Even if they *weren't* doing…it, the notion that my mom would grab a coffee with the dorky band instructor was mind-boggling.

"Anyway, your mom played it off real smooth, like she hung with Jenkins on a regular basis and *so what, blah, blah, blah.* Jenkins turned red and said something like *Good afternoon, Calvin.* Before I left, your mom told me about the pizza, and would I like to join you." Cal laughed. "I'll pass, by the way."

"Thanks a lot," I replied. But I didn't blame him. My mind was racing. Was it possible that *this* was the reason we'd moved to Florida? Because Mom had a secret boyfriend? But Mr. J was new at Coconut Key Academy this year. I'd started school here last spring, and the old band instructor, Ms. Mackillop, had been awesome. But she'd really been old, and she'd retired at the end of the school year.

Leaving the position open for Mr. Jenkins to come in, move me to percussion from first chair clarinet, where I'd excelled, and then rub salt in my wounds by dating my mom.

Calvin shrugged. "Sorry to be the bearer of bad news. But I didn't want to keep it from you."

"No, it's good you told me," I said. "Can we change the subject?"

Calvin nodded.

I took a deep breath. "You're probably not going to believe this," I started.

"After the last couple days?" Calvin asked. "Try me."

"Okay. Well, first of all, I want you to look at my wall and tell me if you see anything different."

Cal glanced over to where I was looking and laughed. "Girl, really?"

"Tell me what's different," I insisted.

"There's no cat poster."

"There's no cat poster. That's right. I just thought I'd let you witness that yourself, in case you thought I'd been blowing smoke."

"Nah," Cal said, "I believed you when you told me. I just don't think the bogeyman is responsible."

"Neither do I," I said, agreeing with him. "And that's where it gets intense." I stood up and walked away from my bed. "Okay. Brace yourself." I paused. "*I* moved it."

Cal looked at me. "Okay…"

"But I didn't simply move it," I continued. "I moved it"—I paused dramatically—"with my mind."

Calvin's eyes got wide for a second. He was still looking at me. Several seconds of silence passed, and then Cal started to laugh.

"It's not funny," I said.

Calvin wasn't just laughing now. He was officially hysterical. "Oh," he said, holding his stomach. "Oh, Sky, you're killin' me!" He wiped tears from his eyes.

"Cal, it's not funny," I said again.

"I'm sorry, I'm sorry," he said, throwing his hands up in the air as if surrendering. "It's just...what? You're some kinda whatchamacallit? A Greater-Than?" His comment sent him back into hysterics.

"Yes," I said. "I think maybe I am."

That only made him laugh harder.

I'd expected this, and I even forgave him, because he had no idea how absolutely the idea freaked me out. I just sat down at my desk and waited for him to stop.

When he finally came up for air, I said, "Remember April? Not month-April, but girl-April. Crazy-girl April."

Cal nodded, looking at me with his *of course* heavy in his eyes.

He and I had met and become friends after a really scary incident where a girl named April brought a pair of handguns to school, with the intention of committing suicide-by-cop.

"She focused on me," I reminded him. "She kept saying *You're one of us*. Maybe she was a Greater-Than too."

But Cal was shaking his head. "Sky, she was messed up. Mentally ill."

"Yeah, but maybe that was because she was a Greater-Than." The online articles I'd read had said G-Ts were often driven crazy. That scared me.

Cal was not convinced. "So what was her power?" he asked. "She wasn't super-strong or super-smart."

"Maybe she was behind all those broken windows." Right when the police had arrived at the school, the cafeteria windows had shattered. One theory was that they'd been shot out by a trigger-happy cop, another was that some brave anonymous student had broken them as a diversion to distract crazy April.

"Yeah, because that's an awesome superpower," Cal scoffed, "if your superhero name is Vandal Girl."

"I'm pretty sure G-Ts don't have superhero names," I said.

"They absolutely don't," Cal agreed. "Because, sorry, G-Ts are *not* real."

"Sorry, you're wrong."

"Prove it," he shot back at me. "If you're a Greater-Than, wow me with your amazing powers."

"Okay." I got up, walked over to my bedside table, and picked up my hairbrush.

Cal's face grew solemn. "Sky, you actually believe this craziness," he said, and it was less a question and more of an observation.

"I do," I said with conviction. "It'll take me a second, though. So please just be patient and quiet."

I closed my eyes and repeated last night's litany of people, places, and things that really incensed me. My face began to heat up. That was good.

I opened my eyes and Calvin had the tiniest smirk on his face. It made me angrier. That was good too.

I stared at the hairbrush and focused all of my potentially Greater-Than brain cells on any unpleasant, anger-inducing image I could muster.

"What are you trying to do?" Calvin whispered.

I shushed him, focusing more, furrowing my brows together in concentration. I thought about my mom and Mr. Jenkins, and my face heated up even more.

But the hairbrush didn't move.

I thought about Mr. Jenkins coming over for family dinners, buying my mom flowers, and trying to offer me fatherly advice.

But the hairbrush still didn't move.

And then I thought about what it would mean if I really was a Greater-Than, like I'd googled and read about last night. The words I'd said to Calvin echoed inside my head: *Apparently, having these weird superpowers can turn Greater-Thans kind of crazy too. Mean-crazy.* I didn't want to become a compassionless, superior freak who was mean-crazy. And I wondered if the change would happen quickly, or more slowly and gradually. Either way, the idea made me *sick*. It *pissed me off!*

Calvin's wheelchair rocketed forward to the wall and then abruptly spun around three times in rapid succession before stopping.

The hairbrush, however, had not moved.

"Damn!" Calvin said, clearly ruffled. "I must have bumped the joystick."

"How could you have bumped the joystick," I exclaimed, "with your hands behind your head? That's just *stupid*." Uh-oh, I'd just called my best friend stupid. Was I already becoming compassionless and superior?

Calvin didn't seem bothered by it. "You're stupid," he said, but I could see something in his eyes that wasn't there before. "Sky, hello. You didn't move me with telekinesis. Really. I probably bumped the joystick coming up the stairs. A wire's probably loose. I'll take the chair in for a tune-up—"

"Cal," I said, determined to make him believe me, at least just a little bit. "There's more. When I went running, I raced Garrett."

Calvin looked up at me, and for a moment he looked kind of upset.

"And I won. I won by a *lot*." I paused. "I'm not saying this because I'm trying to brag or be superior in any way. But I looked it up online, and I ran something called a sub-four-minute mile today."

Calvin shook his head. "That's impossible. The last guy who did that was some Pakistani dude—"

"Moroccan," I corrected him. "And I know. It sounds crazy. I didn't believe it either. But Garrett clocked it. And then I did too."

"Sky, I love the hell out of you. I really do. But you're losing it." Calvin pressed a button on his wheelchair, and his position went from reclined to straight. I watched the machine gently bend his knees.

"I know," I said miserably. "I wish it were that simple. Then they could just send me to a padded room." I shook my head. "I guess maybe it *is* that simple. I mean, crazy people probably don't know that they're crazy, right?"

"I wouldn't know," Calvin said. "I mean, I don't think I do." He grinned at me.

"It's just so much at once." I paced around my room. "First Sasha, and then everyone started believing that Edmund would hurt her, and then the whole thing with the crazy gun lady at the Sav'A'Buck, and Motorcycle Girl, and…I'm just so tired. And sad."

Calvin's eyes got big.

"I know, it's a shocker," I continued. "Skylar Reid is officially talking about her feelings. Call Channel 540 News," I said. "I just…I've been so *angry* lately too. And scared. There. I said it. This Greater-Than thing really freaks me out and I just want Sasha to come home, and I'm so, so scared that she's dead. Phew." I blew air out of my mouth, suddenly filled with fatigue.

"Sky?" Cal said, and his eyes were even wider.

"I'm sorry if I'm overwhelming you. And I'm sorry I called you stupid."

"Sky!" Cal said again.

I stopped pacing. "What?" I said.

Calvin smiled nervously at me. "Um…your radio…is on strike… against gravity," he said slowly.

I looked in the corner of my room.

And, sure enough, my old pink satellite radio from grade school, the one that was in the shape of an antique boom box, was traveling back and forth along the wall—back and forth, swinging in the air—a good eight inches above the surface of my dresser.

I looked back at Calvin, who was staring at me. "Girl?" he said. "Whoa."

"Skylar?" Mom called. I heard her close the front door, plastic bags swishing in her arms.

I stared at Calvin, my eyes wide.

He stared back, and mouthed *OMG* silently at me.

"You here, hon?" my mom asked, her voice singsong as it carried up the stairs.

"In my room! Be right there!" I called back, eyeing the radio as it now swung through the air like a pink paper airplane—except it was a little heavier than paper.

Calvin looked at me, his mouth in the shape of a Cheerio. Then his face broke into a smile. "I'm not gonna lie. That's pretty awesome," he whispered.

I focused intently on the radio and willed it back to its place on my bureau. It remained in midair.

"I don't know how to get you down," I said shakily. I waved my arms in the air a couple times, as if pretending to cast a spell. Um, yeah. That didn't work.

"You're speaking to your boom box like it's a person," Calvin whispered gleefully. He kept his voice quiet, as if talking too loudly would somehow remind gravity that it was still an existing law of physics.

"Skylar?" Mom called, her voice louder as if she was coming upstairs.

I couldn't let her see this. "Wait here," I ordered both Calvin and the pink radio.

"We're not going anywhere!" Calvin crooned, and I slipped out into the hallway.

Mom was coming up the stairs.

"Mom," I said. "Hi."

As I closed the bedroom door behind me, the possessed satellite radio turned on with a blast of mariachi music.

"Skylar!" she chided. "I've told you that I don't mind you inviting Calvin over when I'm not here, but I'd still appreciate it if you kept your bedroom door open."

I rolled my eyes. As if Cal and I would actually hook up. Of course, Mom was just being Mom.

She frowned. "And what's with the music?"

Through the closed door, I heard a *thunk* and an "Aw, shee-it."

"Is he okay?" Mom asked, her brow furrowing with concern.

"I'm sure he's fine," I replied, trying hard to sound casual. "I just wanted to let you know we're here, we're studying, and…that's it."

Mom's expression was quizzical. "Oh…kay. Studying…opera?"

The music had switched to a bellowing baritone voice, the exaggerated vibrato executed jovially in Italian.

"Um, Cal likes listening to that stuff when he studies—something about his brain cells being stimulated." I shrugged.

"Settle down!" Calvin screamed from the bedroom, his words followed by another loud crash.

"Sometimes when he's trying to concentrate, he just yells at his brain to *settle down*!" I explained. "It's one of his…special studying techniques."

"*Ow!*" Calvin yelped.

"Along with vocalizations," I added.

Mom stared quizzically at my door. I waited, leaning my hand casually against the wall in an attempt to keep her from venturing any closer to my bedroom.

"Well…all right," Mom said. "I'm just going to put some groceries away, and then I thought we could order out for pizza. Whaddaya say?"

I hated it when Mom tried to get all buddy-buddy with me, almost as much as I hated it when she acted clingy and overprotective. But I wanted her out of the hallway A-SAP, so I could fix this radio situation before she heard—or saw—anything else. "Sounds good!" I exclaimed, feigning enthusiasm. The opera singer's voice cascaded through the hallway, interspersed with Calvin's *ow*'s.

"Great! I'll meet you down in the kitchen in ten!"

"Awesome!"

"And open that door, please. I mean it." Mom waved a finger, all cutesy, smiling at me as she sauntered down the stairs.

"Will do," I said, laughing nervously.

I waited until Mom was all the way downstairs before I went back into my room. When I opened the door, the radio shut off and fell to the ground with a thud.

Calvin was in the corner, holding his hands over his head as if he were fending off an explosion.

I shut my bedroom door behind me and ran over to him. "Are you okay?"

"Girl!" Calvin hissed. "Your satellite radio just assaulted me!"

"I'm sorry," I said helplessly. "I didn't mean to—it wasn't like I was trying to do any of that."

But Calvin wasn't really that upset. He lifted his hands off his head and grinned at me. "Dude!" he said excitedly. "We should go on tour! Like that magic guy who was around when my parents were kids. What was his name…David Blaine!"

"I guess you believe me now." I eyed the radio, making sure it was really going to stay put.

"I believe something just happened here," Cal said. "Does this mean you're some mythical superhuman called a Greater-Than? If I were you, I'd wait for a little more information before I monogrammed everything I owned with a *G*-dash-*T*."

"It scares me," I admitted. "I hate the idea of going crazy. Or even just being mean and compassionless."

"So don't go crazy or be mean or compassionless." For Calvin everything was always so simple. "You know, I'm serious about that tour thing," he said. "We'd be set for life!"

"You *are* set for life! Your parents have plenty of money."

Cal shrugged. "You're right. But being famous would decrease my chances of dying a virgin."

I laughed my amazement. "You're not going to die a virgin," I told him.

Calvin sighed. "I don't really know many girls who think the whole wheelchair thing is sexy."

"You'll find someone," I promised him, and I knew it was true.

"Hah!" Calvin said. "See? You have such a sweet and gooey inner center, it's impossible for you to *not* be compassionate. Even if this Greater-Than shite is real, you're gonna be fine." But then, because too much solemnity was a strain on his system, he again cracked a huge smile. "Girl, seriously? That shit was awesome!"

"Skylar?" Mom called from the bottom of the stairs. "Bedroom door stays open, please!"

I rolled my eyes. "All right, Mom," I called as sweetly as Cal imagined me to be, but then gave the finger to my closed bedroom door.

I promised Cal I'd call him as soon as my pizza fest with Momzilla was finished. After telling him my secret—that I might be a Greater-Than—I could finally breathe again.

Plus, I wasn't crazy. At least not yet. Knowing *that* was cool too.

My anxiety level about Sasha was still pinned pretty high, though. And I was twice as antsy since I hadn't had time yet today to continue looking for her.

And then, of course, there was the conversation with Mom that I was dreading. How, I wonder, would she bring it up. "So! Skylar! I've been boinking your band teacher!"

Mom was making a salad, cutting up cucumbers, as she greeted me with a cheery, "The pizza should be here soon. I paid a little extra for express delivery. And extra cheese!" She sang those last words like she was the one who was excited by that announcement.

In truth, I knew she'd eat only half a slice at best—with a knife and fork, no less. But whatever. If her guilt over having a secret boyfriend meant I got extra cheese, I'd take it.

I took a tomato off the windowsill, washed it, and got out another cutting board—all without Mom having to ask. She made a little happy clucking sound, and I rolled my eyes. I could feel her glancing over at me, but I kept my focus on the tomato as if my life depended on cutting it into equal pieces.

"So!" she said, and I braced myself, because here it came. "How's school going?"

"Fine," I said.

"Cool. Classes all right?"

I hated when my mom used words like *cool* or *sweet*. She was just embarrassing us both. "Yeah," I said. "Everything's fine."

I thought about band and how Mr. Jenkins insisted I play percussion, even though I could play the clarinet better than anyone in the entire school. I thought about the way that Mr. J didn't seem to know much about music. I remembered telling Mom that I couldn't figure out why the school had hired such an idiot.

I tried to remember how she'd reacted, but all I knew was that, at the time, she *hadn't* leaped to her feet and shouted, "That's my boyfriend you're disparaging! How *dare* you!"

Boyfriend was a weird word to use to describe a man who was at least forty.

Mom hummed a little bit, as if the silence I'd fallen into was too much for her.

"So," she said. "What about everything else? Things going smoothly?"

I thought about the last few days. *Smooth* wasn't the word I would have chosen to use.

"Everything's all right." I dumped the tomato pieces into the salad bowl. "Hey," I said, "I wanted to let you know something."

"Sure!" Mom's eyes lit up.

"Well, I just wanted to give you a heads-up that I'm going to be joining track. I went for a run today, and it made me feel really good."

Mom coughed a little, then of course washed her hands in the sink.

"It shouldn't be an issue," I continued, "'cause there's a bus that runs about an hour and a half later, after practice is out." I, of course, would get Calvin to give me a ride home, but Mom didn't need to know that.

"Actually," Mom replied as she dried her hands, "I was just thinking about after-school stuff too, and I found out that Maggie Jennings is offering a cooking class. She lives just two blocks down from us."

I laughed. "That's funny, Ma."

My mom didn't smile.

"You're *serious*?"

"It should be a lot of fun," Mom replied. "Look at how well you just cut up that tomato."

Seriously? "Okay," I said. "I'd rather stick needles into my eyes."

"Oh, Skylar, don't say such terrible things," Mom said, aghast.

"Well, it's true. I hate cooking. Plus I suck at it. I was just trying to be nice with the tomato—"

"All the more reason to take a class—so that you can improve."

I crossed my arms and leaned back against the counter. "But I don't have a reason to improve. I'm fine with frozen dinners. Or sandwiches. Cooking's not my thing. I'm gonna do track."

Mom shook her head. "Skylar, track is… Well, it's dangerous."

"Dangerous." I laughed. "Running is healthy. It's not dangerous."

"Well, haven't you heard the stories of long-distance runners dropping dead during a race?" she asked.

She was serious. "Mom," I countered, "I don't think we'll run marathons at school. I mean, they're twenty-six miles—"

"Even sprinters have died of heart failure," Mom said.

"But what are the statistics of that?" I asked. "Is it one in a million or one in a billion? I mean, people die of heart failure sitting on the john!"

She wasn't listening. "And then there's the damage to your ankles and knees. All those former track stars getting knee replacements at age twenty-five—"

"Mom."

"And the...the...athlete's foot from spending time in the locker room," she said, picking up the salad bowl and taking it over to the table.

"You don't want me to run track because I might get athlete's foot or drop dead." I followed her, trying to make her see how ridiculous she sounded.

But she just shook her head. "I'm sorry, Sky. I can't let you."

"Yes, you can!" I insisted. I couldn't believe we were actually having this conversation. It was like she was *trying* to make everything difficult. The person who should most enjoy seeing me succeed was keeping me from living my life. "Just let your neuroses go for a second and *listen* to how crazy you sound!"

"I'm sorry," Mom said quietly. "My answer is no." She cleared her throat. "Excuse me, I have to use the bathroom."

I knew she was going in there to cry. Well, it served her right. I hoped she felt as miserable as I did.

I sank into a chair and set my forehead down on the tabletop. I didn't feel like having pizza. I just wanted to go over to Calvin's and watch a movie and forget about everything for a while. My mom's BS was getting old.

Mom was still in the bathroom when the doorbell rang.

"That must be the pizza," she shouted through the door. "Sky! Would you use your debit card to get that?"

With a sigh, I pushed myself to my feet and trudged to the front door, debit card in hand.

The first thing I noticed was her tattoos.

The girl had full sleeves tatted across both her arms underneath the tacky red Pizza Extravaganza shirt. And although her cap was tucked low over her face, she looked up at me as she shoved the pizza box in my direction. "Take it," she demanded in a gruff voice.

We locked eyes. And my stomach did a somersault.

"Hey," I started. "You're…"

"Keep your voice down," the motorcycle girl from the Sav'A'Buck growled, "and take your effing pizza."

I took the cardboard box distractedly with one hand, holding the debit card out to the icicle-eyed girl with my other.

"Put your money away and listen carefully." The girl's voice was low and intense. "Tonight. Ten p.m. Coconut Grove Mall. We meet at the old twenty-plex." Motorcycle Girl cleared her throat and glanced over my shoulder before adjusting her cap so that it once again shadowed her eyes. "And come alone."

Just like that, the girl turned on her heel to leave. She was wearing the same steel-toed boots she'd had on last night when we'd almost gotten killed in the Harrisburg grocery store.

"Wait!" I hissed a little too loudly.

Motorcycle Girl turned around and placed an exaggerated finger over her lips, shushing me.

"I don't even know your name." I took a step outside, my own whisper as stern as I could make it. "You really think that I'm just gonna go to an abandoned mall to meet some random person whose name I don't even know…?"

"It's Dana," the girl interrupted me. "My name is Dana. Now be quiet and go inside. And get there tonight. Ten p.m. sharp. Don't be late. I don't like late. Late doesn't *work* for me."

I scowled and opened my mouth to respond. But before I could utter another word, Dana took another step toward me. "Bubble Gum, you're gonna want to be there. It's about Sasha."

Then, she turned and walked away.

"Ooh, that smells so good!" Mom said, startling me as she came to the door.

Motorcycle Girl—Dana—was already heading for the street, her boots clacking on the front walk.

"Did she deliver our pizza on a motorcycle?" Mom asked, as Dana started her bike with a roar.

"It's probably really energy efficient," I said as I handed Mom the pizza and shut and locked the door. She was still just standing there, so I took it back from her and nearly ran with it to the kitchen table, wanting to get this over with.

"Wow, you're hungry!" Mom exclaimed, her voice so cheerful again that I knew she was faking it.

"Yup," I said unenthusiastically.

Dinner was weirder than usual as I wolfed down the pizza. Mom sat beside me, dipping lettuce into her dressing and smiling sadly at nothing.

I made the mistake of glancing up at her, and she took that eye contact as an invitation to speak. "I can skip my mah-jongg game tonight, if you want."

What? No! "Why would you do that?" I asked.

"You usually babysit," she said, "and…"

And the little girl I babysat for was missing. "I was actually thinking Calvin and I could spend the evening searching for Sasha if you'd—" *Let me ride in Cal's car with him*, I was going to say, but I didn't get that far.

"Oh, honey," she said, putting her fork down. "I thought you'd heard."

"Heard what?" I asked.

"They announced it this morning," Mom told me, tears filling her eyes. "They've called off the search. The blood they found in the back of Mr. Rodriguez's truck was… Oh, honey, I didn't want to tell you like this. Let's not talk about this now."

"Why, because we're having so much fun?" I carefully wiped my mouth with my napkin and put it down next to my plate. My heart was pounding. "Just tell me. What *about* the blood in the truck?"

"The DNA tests were positive," she said, and she must've known that I didn't understand, because she added, "It was Sasha's blood. And there was way too much of it. She couldn't have survived…whatever atrocities were done to her."

Obviously, she could see that I still didn't understand, that I *couldn't* understand, and she put it into even plainer language. "Sky, the police have upgraded the case from a kidnapping to a murder investigation. There's no way Sasha could have lost that much blood and still be alive. I'm so sorry, sweetheart."

Sasha was *dead*?

I saw a flash of Sasha's empty eyes from my nightmare, and the slices of pizza I'd just wolfed down formed a sudden solid lump in my stomach.

I thought about Dana's brief message—Ten p.m. Coconut Grove 20-Plex. It's about Sasha—and I looked up at my mother, who still had those tears brimming in her eyes.

I pushed myself to my feet. "I'm really sorry, Mom, but I think I'm going to throw up."

Chapter Eight

In truth, I was fine.

Or at least as fine as I could be, having just received the awful news that the police believed that Sasha was dead. I refused to believe it. There must've been a mistake.

"Maybe I should call Dr. Susan," Mom said to me through the bathroom door. Her college roommate had become a doctor, and the rare few times I'd gotten sick, she'd made a virtual house call via our computer's intermittently working video-chat service. Come to think of it, the only time I'd ever seen a doctor besides Dr. Susan was last year's visit to the emergency room, after the accident.

"I don't need to talk to Dr. Susan," I groaned. "I think it's just food poisoning. Plus, I've got my period too, so... Ohhh, uhhh," I wailed.

Someone who heard me might've wondered if I was milking it just a little too much, but they didn't know my mom. I had to sell it, hard, so that when she checked on me tonight and I was just a lump in my bed, she'd believe I was finally sleeping and leave without checking further.

I didn't know how long it was going to take—my meeting with Dana, aka Motorcycle Girl, at the old cineplex over at the long-deserted Coconut Grove Mall. But I *did* know this: I *was* going to be there. If someone really had killed Sasha, then it had been someone who wasn't her father. I was determined to find out who and somehow make them pay.

I must've made another moaning noise, because Mom spoke again through the door. "My poor baby. I'll cancel my mah-jongg game."

"No!" I said, quickly opening the door, and Mom frowned. "I mean, please, *please* don't cancel anything. I'm going to take some of that pink tummy medicine and go to bed. I'll be fine."

"Are you sure?" Mom asked. "I hate to leave you by yourself when you're like this."

I wanted her to think I was ill, but not sick enough to make her stay home tonight. I was working on a very slippery slope here.

"It would make me feel even worse if you had to stay home," I told her, adding a trembling lower lip and puppy-dog eyes.

"Oh, honey." Mom reached to hug me, but I scrambled back into the bathroom.

"I'm so sorry. I'm gonna..." I said, slamming the door closed.

"That's okay, sweetie," she called after me. "Call me if you need me."

Speaking of calling... I took my cell phone out of my back pocket. Thankfully, we had service, so I quickly dialed Calvin's number.

"What's up?"

"Cal!" I whispered, turning on the water in the sink, in case Mom was still lurking outside the door. "I need you to pick me up at nine thirty."

"What's going on?"

"The motorcycle girl delivered our pizza tonight!"

"*What?*" Cal said.

"Yup."

"Damn it, I *knew* I should have stayed!" Cal said, disappointed. But then he perked up. "What's happening at nine thirty?"

"That girl—her name's Dana—she told me to meet her at the Coconut Grove Twenty at ten o'clock. I think she knows something about Sasha's disappearance. Her…" I closed my eyes and said it. "Murder."

There was silence on the other end of the line, for just a moment.

"Are you still there?" I asked.

"Yeah," Cal said finally. "Yeah, I'm here. I didn't know if you'd heard about…But you have so… I'm just really sorry."

"Skylar?" Mom called, and rapped gently on the bathroom door.

Crap! "I'm okay, Mom," I said, coughing a couple times for effect.

"Sky?" Cal said through the phone.

"*Hang on,*" I hissed back.

"Do you want me to get you anything?" Mom asked.

I took my toothbrush out of the mug shaped like a fish wearing lipstick—the shower curtain and toilet seat matched—and quickly filled it with water, shutting off the faucet, now *wanting* Mom to hear me through the door.

I dumped a little of the water out into the toilet as I made awful retching noises. It actually sounded like I was hurling. I was impressed with myself. "Oh, no, no, Mom. I just need to get this stuff out of my system."

"Dude, that's nasty," Cal said through the phone.

"Oh, sweetheart," Mom said.

"I'll be out soon," I insisted. "I'm already feeling *much* better. I'm just so tired now…"

"Okay, honey. I'm downstairs if you need me."

I coughed again and made my voice waver. "Thanks, Mommy."

I waited a couple seconds, and then turned the water back on and whispered into the phone. "Sorry about that."

"Man," Cal said, "why didn't you just puke and then call me back?"

"I wasn't really puking," I replied. "I'm faking sick. Otherwise, there's no way in hell I'm getting out of the house tonight."

"Well done," Calvin said. He must've been wearing his hands-free headset, because I could hear him applauding my performance. "Bravo. And the Oscar goes to—"

"Just pick me up," I ordered him. "Nine thirty. Don't be late!"

"If I end up getting hacked into a million little pieces tonight," Calvin told me, "I just want you to know that I will definitely blame you."

"All one million pieces of you?" I asked.

We'd driven all the way out to the unlit, hulking remains of the Coconut Grove Mall, where the twenty-theater cineplex had once been—and I quote—"the jewel in the mall's crown." This mega mall was still technically in Coconut Key, but it was close enough to the town's border with Harrisburg to have failed miserably when the economy quadruple-dipped.

In fact, it had closed for good when Mom and I moved down here last spring. And in the relatively short time since then, the greenery that had once decorated the formerly upscale parking lot had grown like mad, with weird fingers of out-of-control tropical plants reaching crazily for the sky.

It was spooky. And dark.

The town had put a huge chain-link fence around the entire abandoned property, just inside the road that encircled the mall complex. Cal and I had already driven the perimeter, and we'd found two separate gates in the fence, but both were securely locked with bolts and thick, heavy chains.

We were making a second pass around the place, Cal driving even slower now, because I'd thought I'd seen... "There!" I said, pointing.

Cal braked to a stop, angling slightly so that his headlights shone on the fence. Or rather, on the hole in the fence. Someone had cut the chain links to provide an upside-down V-shape that would allow access to a crouching person. Or one in a wheelchair.

It was conveniently close to the mall's main theater entrance, and I suspected it wasn't in that location by accident.

Cal looked at me. "Seriously?"

I was scared too, but I was also anxious to hear what this girl, Dana, had to say. What exactly did she know about Sasha? And what could she tell me about G-T's or Greater-Thans?

"Think about it this way," I told him. "If this girl wanted to hurt us, she wouldn't have saved our lives in the Sav'A'Buck."

"Good point," Cal said, but he didn't look convinced.

Still, he parked his car at the edge of the mall road. We got out, and he clicked the remote lock once, twice, three times before following me to that hole in the fence.

I bent over and slipped through, then turned, lifting back the sharp metal edges of the opening for Cal.

And then we were both inside.

The moon wasn't full, and the sky was typical Florida hazy, but the glow was still enough to light our way, especially when our eyes got used to the darkness.

The wheels of Cal's chair made a whirring sound on the pavement as we approached the silent, hulking building. An overloaded Dumpster sat near the doors, as if someone had started cleaning the place out, but then just given up and walked away.

"You ever go to the movies here?" I asked as we approached, mostly in an attempt to pretend this was just another normal evening out.

"Not in years," Cal answered. "It was too dangerous to come here, even after they hired security guards to walk you out to your car."

"Give me your phone," I ordered. There was some kind of lock on the huge plate-glass doors, but I couldn't see it clearly enough.

Cal turned on his flashlight app before he handed it to me.

He knew that I'd left my cell-phone-slash-tracking-device on my bedside table, next to the convincingly Skylar-shaped lump of pillows I'd placed beneath the covers of my bed. In case my mom peeked in to check on me, I'd also left my pink boom box on its white-noise setting, so she wouldn't hear me not breathing.

Still, if Mom discovered I was gone, I was going to be grounded until I graduated from college.

I shone the light on the doors, and although heavy chains were wrapped around each of the door handles, the chains didn't seem to be locking anything together. I gave the door a push, but it didn't give.

"I don't get it," I said, annoyed, as I gave Cal his phone back and tried the other doors with both hands. They didn't budge either. "Why would Motorcycle Girl tell me to meet her here if she knew it was going to be locked?"

From the darkness next to that Dumpster, a voice rang out clearly. "You gotta pull, not push."

I'll admit it. I screamed.

Calvin probably wouldn't admit it, but he screamed too, as he aimed his flashlight app at the Dumpster like the light was some kind of protective ray.

"Oh, I'm sorry. Did I frighten you?" The motorcycle girl—Dana—stepped out from the shadows and into the flashlight's glow, still wearing those steel-toed boots. "I thought I told you to come alone." She glared at Calvin as she scratched a gruff hand through the spikes of her platinum-blond hair.

I heard a faint click behind Dana and then an orange glow the size of my fingernail floated lazily in the darkness.

"You did," I said. "But I don't drive, so I couldn't have gotten here without Calvin. Calvin, this is Dana." I looked at her challengingly, despite the fact that my knees felt a little wobbly. "So who's *your* friend?"

"Forgive me," Dana said, sounding anything but sorry. "I'm being rude. My friend here"—she pointed behind her at the orange glow—"is Milo."

The glow became more prominent, and then a boy about Dana's age came into view behind her. His hair hung low and shaggy in his eyes, and he kept one hand stuffed into his jeans pocket, the other up to his mouth as he took a long drag on a cigarette.

"Ew," I said automatically, watching the smoke waft up toward the sky.

Dana turned back to Calvin. "Now that we're all properly introduced, I need you to scoot, Scoot. Go wait in the car like a good boy."

Cal looked at me, and I laughed a little even though nothing about this was funny. "Forgive *me*," I replied, "but just because you ride a motorcycle and have a bunch of crazy tattoos doesn't mean you get to call the shots. His name's *Calvin*, and he's not going anywhere, unless you want me to leave too."

With her chin tucked down, Dana glared at me. Her ice-colored eyes glinted through a thick shroud of dark eyelashes. Her blond hair stood out white, like a halo against the garish light from Calvin's phone. Behind her, Milo sucked on his cigarette. They were both silent.

I glared back at Dana, and the silence was tedious. I could hear the tick-tick of my watch as the second hand moved across its face.

And then, just as suddenly, Dana tilted her head up and let her mouth spread into a toothy grin. "Well, well, well," she said, leaning back to tap the side of Milo's shoulder with her hand, "the girl really *has* got some sass. I *like* it."

Milo nodded somberly. I watched him finally take the butt of his cigarette out of his mouth and drop it on the ground. He squashed out the few remaining wisps of smoke with his boot.

"What do you know about Sasha?" I asked.

Dana didn't answer. Instead, she nodded at Calvin, again keeping her eyes on me. "Does he know about you?" she asked. "Have you shown him yet?"

My pulse quickened, but I kept my voice calm. "Know about what?"

Calvin looked up at me. "Dude," he whispered, "how does *she* know about that thing you did with your radio?

Dana nodded. "Thanks, Cal," she said. "You just answered my question. Can I call you Cal, by the way?"

Cal opened his mouth to answer, but Dana interrupted him. "I guess you can stick around, Cal. Come on, let's get inside, away from these damn mosquitoes."

And suddenly the words she'd said back at the Sav'A'Buck made sense. *Kinda the way one G-T can recognize another.* I realized that Dana knew I was a Greater-Than because she was one too.

And just like that, I remembered her hurling that sharp-edged box of soup at Calvin, back at the grocery store. My brain played the memory in weirdly accurate slow motion, and in my mind's eye, I saw her toss her apple into the air—and make it hang there—the same way I'd done with my hairbrush and the radio in my room.

My eyes hadn't believed it at the time—and she'd really only defied gravity for a few short seconds before she'd released the apple from her telekinetic control, letting it drop back into her hand.

Here and now, my heart was in my throat, and I couldn't speak as Dana turned and pulled open the doors to the abandoned mall. Milo flicked hair out of his eyes, took an old-fashioned flashlight from his pocket, clicked it on, and followed. But he held the door open for the two of us.

I looked at Cal and he looked at me. I desperately wanted answers, and not just to my questions about Sasha. I knew he didn't want to go with them, but when I held out my hand, he took it.

And together we followed Dana and Milo inside the mall.

The graffiti in the cineplex's former lobby was really pretty amazing.

Milo caught me looking up at it and shone his flashlight along the decorated walls so I could see it better.

There were nicknames and messages so stylized that I couldn't decipher most of them, the letters and numbers in a beautiful rainbow of colors.

Dana was still leading the way—to a doorway marked theater six—when Calvin asked, "Are we really safe in here? I mean, if a guard comes—"

"Budget cuts have the security team doing a five-second drive-by, way out on the main road," Dana informed us.

This entrance was way around the back.

"And the serial killer zombies…?" Cal was making a joke. Partly. "Have budget cuts kept them away too?"

We followed Dana into the former movie theater. I could see from Milo's flashlight that someone had taken the screen off the wall and removed the rows of seats. Little metal bumps—places where those seats had been attached—dotted the slanting floor. And more graffiti decorated the walls and even the ceiling.

"Feel free to wait in the car," Dana told Cal as her buddy Milo put his flashlight on the ground, positioning it so that the light shone upward. Dana sat down beside it, and it dramatically illuminated her face. She motioned to me. "Sit."

I looked down at the dusty floor, and she laughed.

"Oh, come on," she exclaimed. "Really? I guess I was right the first time, Sunshine. You *are* a little diva."

I scowled and plopped down without any further hesitation. She wasn't going to call *me* a diva. "Tell me about Sasha," I demanded.

Dana laughed again, pulling something from her pocket as she glanced up at Milo. "Part diva, part pit bull."

I looked up at Milo too and saw that he was leaning back, one of his heels resting against the nearby wall. He'd taken a cigarette from behind his ear and was patting his pockets—for a lighter, I presumed.

"Ew," I said. "Seriously, could you not light that?"

He froze as he looked at me.

"Not only is it disgusting, but it's dangerous for Calvin." I pointed to Cal, who'd wheeled his chair between me and Dana. She'd started eating sunflower seeds and spitting out the shells. They landed, each with a click, on the slanted theater floor. "He has a stent in his heart from his accident, and it makes him really sensitive to secondhand smoke."

Cal shook his head—both at me and at Dana, who'd offered him some of her sunflower seeds. "Nah, Sky. It's cool."

"It's *not* cool," I insisted. Because of the damage done to his heart when the gas line to his house exploded, Calvin was going to be lucky if he lived to age forty, a fact that I didn't let myself think about very often. But I was determined that, with my help, he'd be a statistical anomaly and die while skydiving at age ninety-five.

"I was thoughtless," Milo said quietly. His voice was soft, with a gentle Southern twang. He snapped his unlit cigarette in half before putting it into his shirt pocket.

And before I could turn back to Dana to ask her again about Sasha, she said, "Before we get into the weeds, I need to know if you've told anyone besides Scooter here about your abilities."

"No." I shook my head as I looked back at her.

She looked...like a Greater-Than. Her hair, her eyes, her face. Even her clothes. She wore ripped skinny jeans tucked into those clunky black boots. Her shirt was white and tight against her muscles. Beneath, the black of her bra bled through the thin material. For a second, I thought about my own bra—how I had so little up top that I didn't even need to wear one. This girl was all curves and sex appeal, and I felt gangly and angular in comparison.

Yeah, if anyone here was something called a "Greater-Than," it was Dana, and not me.

"Today on the beach," she said, holding my gaze, "with Jock Itch."

Cal snickered at the nickname she'd given Garrett.

"Did he figure it out?" Dana asked me. "The reason why you run so fast?"

So running fast *was* one of my G-T abilities. I swallowed hard and shook my head. "No. He's clueless."

Calvin backed me up. "Garrett's douche-tastically self-centered," he said, then turned to frown at me. "Were you really not bullshitting me? I mean, how fast *can* you run?"

Dana answered for me. "Fast." She glanced again at Milo—who was still looking at me. "Well, that's good, at least. Keep it that way. No show-and-tell games at school or at a party. No more sharing cool tricks with 'special' friends." She made air quotes around "special" as she glanced at Cal.

"And while you're at it? Stay away from hospitals. Your personal boutique doctor might not give a damn about your unusual brain-wave patterns, but any large-scale medical facility will pop an eyebrow. As soon as you're tagged as different, the bad guys will know it, and before you can blink, you'll be dead. Your secret needs to be secret. Even Mommy can't know. Am I clear?"

I nodded. Unusual brain-wave patterns? "But...—"

"No buts. End of discussion. Keep your mouth closed, your running to a jog, and your inanimate objects on the ground."

Calvin giggled.

Dana glared at him, and Calvin stopped giggling.

"I have questions," I told Dana, "about the whole...unusual-brain-wave-patterns thing, but—"

She knew what I wanted. "Sasha first."

"Yeah." I nodded.

She carefully folded up her sunflower-seed package and put it back in her pocket as she said, "Police say her daddy killed—"

I cut her off. "He didn't. That's bullshit! Edmund would *never* hurt Sasha."

Dana smiled at that. I glanced up. Milo was smiling at me too.

"Why is that funny?" I asked.

"It's not," Dana said. "Funny. We're just glad you think that." She reached out a foot and kicked Calvin's wheel. "You're not convinced, though, are you, Scoot?"

"The evidence—" Calvin started.

"Is exactly the same as the so-called evidence that showed up when another little girl vanished, years ago, in Alabama," Dana said. "The two cases are virtually identical, and in both of them, the murdered girl's father is being framed."

Yes! That made sense to me. *That* I believed—that Edmund was being framed.

"But you said it yourself at the Sav'A'Buck," Calvin argued. "Little girls disappear all the time. It sucks and it's horrible, but it happens more often than most people think."

Dana shook her head. Her lips were pursed, like she was angry but didn't want to show it. I was surprised. Dana didn't seem to have a problem exhibiting anger. But she was holding something back. I could tell. "You're right, Boyfriend," she replied. "Girls do go missing, and it *is* horrible. But you're wrong about this. These two cases are connected." She looked again at Milo.

At her cue, he pushed himself off the wall and removed something from his inside jacket pocket. It was an old-fashioned manila envelope.

"What's that?" Calvin asked.

Milo leaned down to hand it to me, looking me in the eyes.

I opened the envelope. Cal moved forward a little and leaned over to peer down at its contents as I angled it slightly to catch the light.

It contained news articles from the Internet. A lot of them. They were old enough so that the cheap paper they'd been printed on had turned soft and yellow at the edges. I wondered if Milo's nasty cigarette smoke had contributed to their decay.

The headlines were all variations on the same theme.

Montgomery resident in custody for murder of seven-year-old daughter

Alabama Man Charged with Girl's Murder

I skimmed the top article. It was about a little girl named Lacey Zannino who had disappeared from her bedroom in the middle of the night. It mentioned her father, Ryan, and how he had disappeared the same evening that Lacey had gone missing.

The second paragraph was even more startling.

Police found Ryan Zannino's truck on the west side of Montgomery, thirty-five miles from his residence. Crime-scene investigators have determined that the bed of the truck contained large amounts of the victim's blood—enough for police to arrest Zannino for Lacey's murder without recovering the little girl's body.

I looked up, and Dana nodded knowingly. "Do you know if the police found anything else in Sasha's dad's truck? Besides the blood?" she asked.

Calvin pointed to the printouts, and I handed the entire packet to him. He leaned closer to the beam of the flashlight so he could read the rest of the article.

"Yeah," I said. "But I don't know what, exactly. Something made them think...awful things. But there *was* a truck, and it had Sasha's blood in it. Although I don't understand, if there's not a body, how they know—absolutely—that she's..." I had to clear my throat. "Dead."

"It's math, Sky," Calvin told me quietly as he flipped through the clippings. "The human body contains a set amount of blood. If you lose too much of it, you die. There's an expression called *bleeding out.*"

I cut him off. "I know what that means. I just... I feel like I would know it if Sasha was dead and..."

"Reality's a bitch," Dana said flatly. "Answer me this—did Sasha's dad work nights?"

"He was a security guard," I replied, nodding.

"Yup," Dana said. "So was Ryan Zannino. And have they found Sasha's dad yet?"

I shook my head. "No."

Milo crossed his arms over his chest. "If history repeats, he'll turn up soon," he said. "And he'll go straight into solitary confinement."

"Not if we find him first," Dana vowed.

Calvin shook his head. "Wait, wait, wait." His voice was tinged with irritation. He'd sifted through the articles and now pointed to one. "This says the Zannino dude was found guilty. They put him on death row *years* ago, for crying out loud. He's been in prison ever since." He looked up. "So how do you figure that he has anything to do with Sasha's murder?"

Dana gave Cal an impatient look. "You're not listening, Sidekick," she said. "I'm not saying that. I'm saying Sasha's dad is being framed, exactly the same way and probably by the same people who framed Ryan Zannino for Lacey's murder."

Dana was right. The similarities between the two crimes *were* remarkable. "Have you gone to the police—" I started to say.

She cut me off. "The cops and I aren't exactly on friendly terms."

Okay. "Then maybe *I* should—"

"You really need to start paying attention too, Bubble Gum. Last thing you want to do is attract the attention of the people who took Sasha and Lacey. You do that, and Cal's gonna be wandering around Coconut Key searching for *you*."

I was definitely missing something here, and not because I wasn't paying attention. "Why would they come after me?" I asked. "And I'm still not clear on why anyone would want to kidnap and kill these little girls."

Dana sat down again on the dusty floor as she smiled tightly. "Because they both had something extremely valuable."

I still didn't understand, and when Dana rolled her eyes, I felt stupid and incredibly less-than.

Dana leaned toward me. "Those girls were Greater-Thans too. Only they were too little to keep it a secret, and the wrong people found out."

Sasha was a... And suddenly, it made sense. Not the kidnapping and murder part—I still didn't get that. What made sense was Sasha's earnestly telling me that her dolls danced around her room at night.

She hadn't imagined it—they'd actually moved. She'd used Greater-Than powers like mine to make them dance.

I thought about the jumble of dolls on Sasha's usually orderly shelves and imagined her, in that awful moment when she was being abducted, delivering a telekinetic blast of fear and anger.

Cal, however, was still skeptical. "How do you know that Sasha had, you know, powers like Sky?"

Dana looked at Cal. "How do I know?" She laughed. Then, she closed her eyes and nodded three times.

With a swoosh, Cal's wheelchair lifted off the ground. The computer news printouts floated lazily in the air as Calvin's wheelchair spun in an elliptical pattern before cascading toward the floor and landing gently in front of Dana. Then, one by one, the pieces of paper dropped onto Calvin's lap, forming a neat pile atop the manila envelope.

"I know," she whispered, leaning in close to Calvin's astonished face, "because I know." She tapped the papers on Cal's lap. "So what do you think, Scoot? Are you ready to believe me yet? Or do you need more proof?"

CHAPTER NINE

Calvin didn't move for a moment. The theater was silent except for the sound of our breathing. Dana's breath sounded fast and labored, as if she'd just run a fast mile.

"Man, what's up with all y'all girls?" Cal finally said, peeking over the side of his wheelchair to make sure he was safely on the ground. "How did you learn to do that?

"It takes practice, practice, and more practice," Dana said matter-of-factly as she took the bottom of her tank top and lifted it up to her face. She dabbed at a few beads of sweat on her temples.

I caught Calvin staring at Dana's six-pack abs. "Okay," he replied slowly. "No offense, but I could practice my damn ass off until my brain pops, and there's *still* no way I'd be spinning shit around with my mind."

Dana nodded. "You're right about that, Boy Wonder," she said, pulling her shirt back down, as she gestured to me with her head. "I'm talking to the girl who's already got the gift."

From what I'd read on the Internet, I wasn't so sure being a G-T was a gift.

But Milo was smiling at me, so I managed to smile back.

"Okay," Calvin said. "Okay. All right. Let me just…process."

"Take your time, 'cause I've got all night." Dana squatted in front of me. She rested her elbows on her knees.

"You okay?" I asked, leaning down. She still seemed pretty out of breath.

"I'm just a little out of shape."

Calvin snorted. "Um, have you *looked* in a mirror lately? Girl, you're *swoll*."

"Swoll?" Dana replied, one eyebrow raised.

"Cal, you're stupid," I said, and laughed.

"Well, yeah." Calvin nodded his agreement.

I looked at Dana. She *was* solid muscle. Even though I towered over her petite frame, every square inch of her was tight and rippling. Her crystalline eyes were smudged on top and bottom with jet black eyeliner, and she had a shock of blond hair short enough to be a boy's cut. Yet, for every feature that would have normally been harsh—even masculine—she balanced it with curves and attitude.

If I had to picture a girl who could move objects with her mind, I'd picture Dana. Not skinny, freckly, red-haired little old *me*.

"Tell me about this so-called gift," I said. "Tell me why Sasha and Lacey were kidnapped and killed if their powers were supposedly so valuable." Even as I said the word "killed," I still didn't believe that Sasha was really dead. "And how come, if Lacey was seven and Sasha was nine, I'm only just now noticing my powers. I'm almost seventeen."

Dana nodded, and her expression was grim. She motioned for me to sit down again. Calvin leaned over, and Milo came forward as well. He took a seat next to me. I expected to smell smoke, but when he leaned close, I caught a whiff of vanilla instead.

"Some girls get their powers early," she told me. "Some, like you, are late bloomers. I don't know why that happens, but you should be grateful for that. Like I said, it's the little ones who aren't careful who get noticed. You'll catch up pretty quickly once you start practicing."

"Practicing," I echoed. I thought about how much effort it had taken to move my hairbrush.

"Skills like telekinesis take practice to hone," Dana said. "Same way little kids have to practice walking or using a fork. You have to work out your abilities just like you work out a muscle. You have to get your gifts *swoll*, as Boyfriend likes to call it. Truth is, I've never met anyone whose abilities are perfect from the get-go. Well, no one who's not on the verge of jokering anyway."

Cal and I looked at each other. There was that word again. Jokering.

"But that's a whole 'nother thing," Dana continued. "What we're talking about here—being a Greater-Than—is related to a science called *neural integration*. G-Ts can learn, through practice, to integrate more of our neural nets—aka our brains—and do all kinds of stuff that normies can't do."

"Telekinesis, telepathy, prescience…" Cal listed some of the things we'd found from googling Greater-Thans.

"Some of us can control electricity—cause blackouts or power surges," Dana said, nodding. "Some G-Ts can even deliver an electrical charge with their bodies. Some control fire or water or wind.

Some are just plain freaking-crazy empathic. The list goes on and on. Sometimes talents translate into normal-seeming things. An ability to play the piano or learn languages. And it's always an individual thing." She looked at me. "You won't develop the same abilities that I have—even with intense practice."

"So…how will I know what my skill sets are?" I asked.

"It's kind of touch and go," Dana replied.

"Minus the touching part," Cal offered.

"Stupid *and* cheesy," I muttered, and Cal blew me a kiss.

Out of the corner of my eye, I saw Milo run a hand through his shoulder-length hair. Dana looked at him. "Don't worry, I'm getting there. This is a lot for her." She smirked at me. "Milo got all excited when I told him what you'd smelled. The fish, the sewage."

Milo gave Dana an exasperated look. And all I could think was, *She'd told him about me?*

"Are you a Greater-Than too?" Cal asked him.

Milo shook his head. "I'm nothing special."

I caught another whiff of vanilla and wondered why I didn't believe him.

"It's all trial and error, Sugar Plum," Dana said. "Figuring out what you can and can't do. I got my powers when I was ten, and I'm still learning what I'm capable of. I wish the training was as simple as doing push-ups—you do the work, you get the muscle? But there are some G-T things—a lot of G-T things—that I just can't seem to do."

"Like what?" I asked.

"I can't read minds," Dana said. "God, how I wish I had telepathy.

But it's not my thing. I can tell you how many people are in a building as I approach, or how many rats are in this room. Two, in that corner." She pointed.

"Rats?" I said my voice going up an octave.

Milo flashed the light into the corner, and it caught the shining eyes of, yes, one, two rats.

"Ew!" I leaped to my feet.

"Begone!" Dana commanded, and they turned and ran away.

Milo followed them with the light, all the way out of the room.

"*That* was cool," Cal said as I slowly sat back down.

"If you don't mind, I wanted to ask you about those smells," Milo said as he put the light back. He had been so quiet until now that his voice startled me, and I jumped again.

Dana smirked at my display of nerves. "It's rumored that some G-Ts can actually smell emotions."

"I can do that," I said without thinking. Immediately I covered my mouth, shocked. *Could* I really do that?

Calvin was looking at me like I was crazy. "Girl, *what* are you talking about?"

"That sewage smell in Sasha's room," I said. "I smelled it—you didn't."

Milo nodded.

"And the fish smell in the Sav'A'Buck," I continued. "You didn't smell that, either."

"What good does it do to be able to smell emotion?" Cal asked. "No offense to your nose, Sky, but if I were a Greater-Than, I'd choose invisibility or maybe shooting lightning bolts from my fingertips."

"But it's not a choice," Dana said. "We don't get to choose. We are who we are. And Sky's apparently smell-sensitive." She turned back to me. "We've heard stories about girls smelling things like cinnamon, cloves, garlic, sewage"—she checked them off on her fingers—"vanilla, fish... And the reason it's a cool power to have, despite what Scooter thinks, is that it gives you insight into the manifest emotions of the people around you. Imagine being able to walk into a room and know with one sniff that the people in there want to kill you."

What kind of rooms did this girl walk into?

Milo cleared his throat. "Manifest emotions are the basics—love being the biggest because it covers so much ground."

"Maternal love, friendship and loyalty, attraction and desire," Dana listed. "Fear is the opposite of love, by the way. Most people think hatred is, but it's not. Fear and grief create the more complex anger and hate."

"The fish smell is fear," I realized. How did I know that?

But Milo was nodding. "And the sewage...?" he prompted quietly.

I answered with hesitation. "Evil."

Dana was nodding now too. "The smell of sewage *has* been linked to evil. For the record? Pure evil is completely devoid of all human emotion. So you're smelling a *lack* of humanity—without even the basic emotions present."

My head was spinning. But this seemed like the perfect time to ask: "Cal and I read about G-Ts online. That they—we—turn into sociopaths, that we lose our ability to relate to..." I didn't know what to call regular people.

But Dana did. "Normies?" she said. "Yeah, that's total bullshit. The few normies who know about G-Ts tend to be afraid of us, so they turn us into scary monsters." She made big claw hands, and her shadow behind her on the wall was actually kind of awful. "You don't have anything to worry about, Bubble Gum. In fact, you could use some toughening up."

I wasn't convinced, and Milo seemed to know that. "It's a big responsibility, but with the right training, you'll be okay," he told me with kindness in his eyes.

I thought about that vanilla smell I'd noticed when Milo had sat down, but I couldn't figure out what it meant. I also had no idea where I was supposed to go for *the right training*. It wasn't as if I could pop over to the local G-T Technical School for a class or two.

I looked at Cal, and I knew he was antsy because it was getting late. His mom was awesome, but even awesome had its limits. And I still hadn't gotten any real answers about Sasha. So I reluctantly changed the subject. "Back to Sasha. Are you saying that people—normies— kill G-Ts because they're scared of us?" It still felt weird saying *us*.

Dana shook her head. "It's way worse than that." She stared at the flashlight intently. The light flickered a little and then became brighter. "Okay. I don't know *exactly* what goes on in our bodies, but apparently we have some special enzyme in our blood that normies don't. You won't find it running through Milo's body or Scoot's, and probably not even your mom's. But there *is* a way to extract that enzyme from a G-T's blood and cook it along with some other *awesome* ingredients. The result is an illegal drug called Destiny," Dana continued.

"Seriously?" I said. "Destiny is made from…" It was too awful. I couldn't say it.

Dana could. "Our blood," she confirmed. "And I guess you already know what Destiny is."

"We know," Cal said grimly. "Addictive, deadly, expensive."

"Really expensive," she said. "And now you know why."

Again, I did the math. "So you think Sasha and Lacey were killed for this enzyme that's in their blood"—an enzyme that was in *my* blood too—"by the people, whoever they are, who make Destiny."

"Give the girl a prize," Dana said.

I shook my head, because it still didn't quite add up. "If they wanted Sasha's blood, then why was there so much of it in the back of her father's truck?"

"My theory," Dana said harshly, "is that they grab girls like Lacey and Sasha—and you—and they bring 'em to their lab to bleed 'em out, and then they dispose of their bodies somehow. I don't know how, but they make 'em disappear. Probably because if they showed up exsanguinated there'd be too many questions."

I swallowed hard, imagining Sasha's bloodless body tossed in some overflowing landfill, never to be recovered.

"They somehow extract the enzyme from the blood," Dana continued. "And after the enzyme's out, they use the blood to frame the most likely suspect—the girl's father. Whom they've kidnapped, so that Daddy mysteriously disappears at the same time the little girl vanishes, right?"

"Oh, my God," I said.

I smelled more vanilla, and I glanced at Milo. He was looking at me. He was always looking at me. I was starting to wonder if I had something stuck in my teeth or if I had my shirt on backward.

"When police are investigating a crime like this, their first suspects are always the immediate family members." Calvin finally seemed convinced.

"So it was an easy frame." I looked down at the manila envelope that Cal was still holding. "One they've done before."

"Yeah," Dana agreed.

"So your plan is to find Edmund—Sasha's father—before the police do." I looked from Dana to Milo and back. "I want to help."

"Whoa," Dana said. "Bubble Gum, I appreciate your enthusiasm, but you're untrained. You and Skippy would be more of a hindrance."

"So train me," I said, looking to Milo for support. For once, he was looking at Dana, one eyebrow slightly raised.

"No." Dana swiftly stood up. "I'm done."

I stood too. "Done following me? That's why you were at the Sav'A'Buck, right? Because you've been following me?"

She shrugged. "I thought you might know something. I knew you were Sasha's babysitter, and I could tell you were a G-T, but...I realized, back in the Sav'A'Buck when you didn't understand what I was saying, that you were clueless—and completely untrained." She looked over at Milo, who had slowly gotten to his feet too.

"Milo here made me reach out to you—to warn you to keep your powers on the DL. And I've done that. Consider yourself warned. Go home and lie low, Sugar Plum. When it's time for college, if you live that long, think about Boston. There's a super-secret G-T training center up there. They'd accept a girl like you in a heartbeat. As for here and now, I'm gone." She headed for the door, but Milo didn't follow her. There was impatience in her voice when she turned back. "Milo...?"

He just looked at her.

Cal spoke. "At least give us your cell numbers, in case we need to reach you."

"Yeah," I said, chin high as I glared at Dana. "In case we find Edmund before you do. Because I'm not going to stop looking—for him *or* for Sasha."

"You really think we have cell phones?" Dana scoffed. She looked at Milo imploringly. "You don't honestly want to babysit Goo and Gah here, do you?"

"She can smell evil," Milo said quietly. He was talking about me. "And if you train her, the way she wants? We won't be babysitting for very long."

And there we all were, in the silence of that old movie theater, as Dana and I tried to stare each other down. I was not going to be the one to look away, regardless of the freaky color of her eyes.

Cal broke the silence. "I kinda need to get home," he said to Milo as if he'd identified the boy as the only other sane person in the room. "Are you and Ms. Crazy Pants camping out here?"

"No," Milo answered him. "We tend to keep moving, never staying in the same place for very long."

Even though Dana and Milo weren't that much older than Cal and me—they both looked to be about eighteen, maybe nineteen at the most—it was clear that they didn't have a mom—insane or other—waiting for them at home.

It was also pretty clear from that *we* that Dana and Milo were together. *Together* together. But really, what did I expect—that Milo *wouldn't* be madly in love with a girl like Dana?

"So what's the best way to get in touch?" Cal asked.

Milo chuckled a little. "Would you believe me if I said all you have to do is want us to show up, and we'll show up?"

"I thought Hot Shot wasn't telepathic," Cal said.

"It's not quite the same thing."

"Coulda fooled me."

Dana blinked first. "Meet us tomorrow at noon," she finally said. "The Lenox Hotel, downtown Harrisburg. Bring pictures—printed photos—of Edmund Rodriguez. Wear shoes you can run in and a Kevlar vest if you have one. And don't be late." She turned and walked out of the theater, and I could still hear her when she added, "Jesus, I'm going to hate this."

CHAPTER TEN

"Would you rather," Cal said on Sunday morning as we headed into the heart of Harrisburg, "projectile vomit or develop sudden, uncontrollable Tourette's while on a blind date?"

I'd made it home last night and gotten into the house without Mom waking up. This morning as I'd nearly collided with her in the kitchen, I'd been tempted to ask her if the whole stacked-up-pillows-beneath-the-covers thing had really worked, but obviously that would have defeated the purpose.

As it was, she'd looked at my pink V-neck tee, skinny jeans, and pink sneakers and said, "Ooh, you look nice. Where are you heading?"

"Cooking class." I couldn't help myself, mostly because I was still smarting from seeing my reflection in the bathroom mirror. Yeah, I looked nice, but next to Dana, I was going to look like a "nice" twelve-year-old boy in a pink shirt and sneakers.

But Mom looked so sad at my caustic comment that I quickly relented. It wasn't her fault that I didn't have boobs. My father—he of whom we never speak—had to have been responsible for my height and coloring, so he was probably responsible for my less-than-generous physique as well.

"I'm walking over to meet Calvin," I told her. It was not quite a lie. I just left out the part where I was walking over to his car rather than his house.

Now, as I sat in his car, I realized I'd been in such a rush to escape that I'd forgotten to "forget" my cell phone at home.

"Dammit," I said as Calvin pulled onto the highway, heading for Harrisburg. I held up my phone. "I'm gonna shut it off. If she calls you, don't answer."

"Yeah," Cal said, "'cause I always answer, because I *love* the time I spend chatting with your mom."

I laughed, but then weirdly found myself defending her. "I think she seriously lost it after the accident. I mean, she was always overprotective, but..." I sighed.

"But you weren't even hurt."

I looked at Calvin, who as a child had survived his own near-death experience and ended up with a crappy heart and legs that didn't work. I didn't know what happened—what buttons my accident pushed—but when my mother came to the hospital, she acted like it was the freaking end of the world. I don't think it helped that the ER doctors kept rechecking me. They couldn't believe that I'd walked away from the totaled car without a scratch, while my now-former best friend Nicole was in the ICU, barely alive.

"My mother's crazy," I told Calvin as I tried not to think about that night more than six months ago in Connecticut, when Nicole had lost control of her car. We'd slammed into the median and started to roll…

I exhaled hard, pushing those images away, unwilling to relive it, unable to talk about it, even with Cal. It was over. I was alive and Nicole was too—although her parents had shipped her off to a special school in Switzerland.

Special school. Right.

"Well," Calvin said, bringing me back to the here and now, "I guess moms worry no matter what. Mine sure does." He looked at me. "Did you bring the photos Dana wanted?"

"Yeah," I said, pulling the printed snapshots out of my purse. Most of them were blurry, because Edmund was always in motion, always laughing at something. The two best included the just-out-of-the-pool shot that Detective Hughes had shown me, as well as a five-by-seven posed portrait of the Rodriguez family that Sasha had given me at Christmas.

Looking at the photos of Sasha made my throat tighten up. I missed her, and I wanted her back.

"So?" asked Cal. "Projectile vomiting or Tourette's?"

I considered the question, placing the photos carefully back in my bag. "Is the blind date someone I'd like to see again?"

Calvin took the same exit we'd taken to get to the Sav'A'Buck. "Absolutely. He's smart, funny, and super sexy. Basically, he's got all of my irresistible charm and more."

"Then Tourette's. Because dropping the f-bomb requires less cleanup than puking does."

"Good call," Calvin said, nodding. "I'm with you."

We passed the Sav'A'Buck on the right. Its neon sign was unlit in the daylight, and the place looked dingier than ever. I thought about the lady who had jokered in the store, and chill bumps popped up on my arms and legs. She'd willingly taken a drug made, at least in part, from the blood of girls like Sasha and Lacey.

And me.

The road we were on led directly into downtown Harrisburg. As we drove, the shops and homes became even more dilapidated and filthy. I stared at a brick building covered from sidewalk to roof with multicolored graffiti. Like the artwork in the old cineplex, it was pretty—but the mountains of trash piled up in what had once been a parking lot were not. The roof of another building had caved in, and its windows were boarded up. The next didn't even have boards in place—just a jagged rim of broken glass around gaping holes where the windows had once been.

You could practically smell the neglect, and truth be told, I was breathing through my mouth because the stink of rotting fish and burning plastic was so strong. The people here were filled with fear and something else. Despair? Whatever it was, it was awful.

"Dang," Cal whispered, slowing the car just a bit. "This is downtown?"

I'd thought I knew what Mom meant when she talked about the Second Great Depression, but the tired seediness of the CoffeeBoy or the Pizza Extravaganza in the less-well-off parts of Coconut Key was nothing compared to this.

A single hanging stoplight blinked red at a four-way intersection, and Calvin stopped for a moment. We both pressed the lock button on the door to make double sure it was engaged.

Across the street on the corner, a woman stood hunched over a brimming grocery cart full of garbage. She rearranged plastic bags, dented cans, blankets, and other miscellaneous objects, her face shaded by an oversized shawl. As Calvin and I drove past, the old lady turned to stare at us, revealing a horribly disfigured profile. Half of her chin was just…missing. One eye bulged almost completely out of the socket, while the other was swollen shut. She smiled—at least I think that was a smile.

I gasped and Calvin pressed the accelerator.

"Please tell me that's not the she-thing you saw in Sasha's room that night," he said, his tone light even though I knew he was spooked.

"No, that woman was homeless, but she wasn't evil," I replied.

"You say that like you know her personally," Cal said.

I shrugged. "No sewage smell."

"Oh, right," he said. "I almost forgot."

We kept going, further into the decaying center of Harrisburg, where more and more people were out on the sidewalks. Some of them pushed grocery carts; others huddled in the shade beneath the tattered awnings of stores, their knees drawn up to their chests. They looked defeated, as if they were already dead. The only other vehicle on the road was a pickup moving slowly in the opposite direction and ringing a bell like an old-time ice cream truck. It had a big, hand-lettered sign on it that read: *Human Corpses Only*.

I turned to look out the back as a man flagged down the truck.

He gestured back toward a building where two other men emerged, awkwardly carrying something child-sized that was covered with a dirty sheet. The first man sank to his knees on the sidewalk.

I realized that the hint of cinnamon that I could smell, even though the car windows were tightly closed and the recirculate button was on, was grief.

This was worse than I could have ever imagined.

"What are we looking for?" Cal asked. "I've forgotten the name."

"The Lenox Hotel. There, up on the right." I pointed at the looming brick building ahead. It was taller than the buildings around it, but no less dilapidated. It had a sign that said THE LENOX in block letters, in a style that reminded me of medieval knights, complete with a stylized lion.

"I hope for Dana and Milo's sake this isn't where they're staying." Cal pulled up next to the building.

I didn't answer, but I silently agreed. The hotel's front double doors had cracks in the glass that were covered by peeling duct tape. A faded and grimy black-and-white pinstriped awning hung overhead, part of it torn and hanging down almost all the way to the sidewalk.

"Should we go inside?" I asked uncertainly.

Calvin turned on his hazard lights. The only other car parked on the street was an abandoned two-toned hunk of metal with three of its tires missing. "Should we even get out of the car? The locals don't look too friendly."

An old man lingered below the hotel's awning, scratching compulsively at his scalp. He looked at Calvin's car and pointed a gnarled hand at us. Then he yipped like a dog.

A hand rapped on my window, and Calvin and I both screamed.

"Hey, Scooter! Open up!"

Dana stood on the sidewalk—where had she come from?—one hand on her hip. She was wearing the same knee-high boots that she'd had on last night, this time with black jeans and a black tank top. Her super-short hair was slicked back with a thick black headband. Pencil-thin red bra straps peeked out from underneath her shirt.

Calvin did as he was told. The yipping dog-man began to approach the car, but when Dana turned around and clapped her hands aggressively at him, he scurried away.

She hopped in the back, and Cal quickly locked the car again.

"You're late," she informed us matter-of-factly.

I frowned and looked at my watch. It was twelve oh two.

"Where's Milo?" Cal asked.

"We're gonna pick him up. He had to make a store run."

"He left you all by yourself?" Cal asked, astonished, adjusting his rearview mirror so he could see Dana while he drove.

Dana gave Cal what I'd come to think of as her dead-eye glare. "Don't you mean, *I let him go to the store all by himself*? Considering I'm a G-T and he's not?"

"Right," Cal said as he pulled gingerly away from the curb. "Sorry. Where to?"

"Dead ahead. The SmartMart's two blocks down." As Cal drove, Dana settled back in her seat. "I figured we'd start today's search over where Edmund Rodriguez's truck was found. And a heads-up, kids, because unlike this good part of town, where we're going is extremely dangerous."

I exchanged a look with Calvin. *This* was the *good* part of town.

"Coupla hard and fast rules to follow," Dana continued coolly. "Stay within sight of me at all times. And if I tell you to do something, you do it. You don't ask why; you don't hesitate. And if you have even the *slightest* suspicion that a jokering Destiny addict is in the vicinity, you get the hell out of there, double time. Am I clear?"

I looked at Cal again as we both nodded.

She laughed. "Although, sometimes there's no getting out. I once saw the aftermath of a joker who sent out such a blast of power that he turned every car in a two-block radius into shrapnel." She leaned forward to point out the front. "There."

The SmartMart was little more than a crumbled hut, the front windows opaque with overlapping posters. I noticed an ancient sign that read: "We accept food stamps." Someone had crossed out the words and written "Eat shit and die" over it. Posted next to it was a more current ad for Good Times vodka.

Milo must've still been inside, because although there were plenty of very large, scary-looking people hanging out front, none of them was him.

Cal pulled over as Dana continued her story about the cars-into-shrapnel thing. "Although truth be told, you can't outrun *that* kind of shit. Everyone in the area was turned into hamburger—including the joker." She laughed as if that was funny. "Joke was on him, huh? But dozens of people were all just completely chewed up. All that blood in the streets…" Now she sighed heavily as she sat forward to look out at the convenience store. "What the hell is taking him so long? Oh, my aching God. Milo seriously *had* to pick today to be a hero."

I had no idea what was so heroic about going to the SmartMart. I did have a suspicion, however, that Dana told that story to try to scare us into leaving. And I could tell from the expression on Calvin's face that she was at least half succeeding.

Cal was looking out the windshield at the bikers gathered in front of the SmartMart. I was more worried about the two tattered-looking men who stood across the street, talking to each other as they pointed at our car. Another creepy old woman stood on the corner, rocking back and forth. She held an old rag doll in the crook of her elbow. Each time she moved, the doll's head lolled limply back and forth.

"I'll find him." Dana sighed again as she reached to open the car door. But then she stopped and narrowed her eyes at the bikers outside the store and warned us, "Lock up behind me and don't open the doors for anyone. Y'understand?" She got out, then stuck her head back in the car to ask, "Your windows *are* bulletproof, right?" But she didn't wait for an answer. She just slammed the door and stomped her way toward the store.

Calvin clicked the lock a few extra times as we watched her vanish inside.

And then, it was like they all came out of the woodwork at once.

As if on cue, the bikers all turned and looked at us, more than one of them eyeing me through the windshield and licking their lips. Gross. One of them seemingly casually flicked open his jacket, and I spotted the glint of something metal in his waistband—a gun to test whether or not Cal's car had bulletproof glass?

But the bikers weren't the only potential threat. Across the street, a guy with a cane and a badly stained trench coat headed toward us. The old woman we had seen earlier with the horrible face approached with her grocery cart. She waved her fingers almost coyly at Calvin. The two old tattered guys started to cross the street as well. Everyone was heading in our direction.

"Chewy, I got a bad feeling about this." Calvin gave me his best Han Solo.

"Just…don't look at any of them. Heads down, we mind our own business until Dana and Milo are back." But it seriously *was* like one of those cheesy zombie movies Cal and I watched on TV. Everyone honed in on our car, all at once.

"What do they want?" Calvin asked. "I mean, besides to eat our brains."

"They don't want to eat our brains. I'm pretty sure this is just Dana testing us. Me. She's testing *me*. So just ignore them. Just *don't* look." But it was hard not to, and even I couldn't follow my own instructions. I looked up exactly as the old guy in the trench coat flashed us.

"Oh, my *God*!" Calvin shouted. "That is wrong. And disgusting! That is wrong *and* disgusting! Do *not* make me get out of this car, old man!"

"Don't you dare get out of the car," I told Calvin, squinting through my eyelashes as the old man, coat now closed, took his cane and whacked the driver's side window. "Dana told us to keep the doors locked."

"If this is a test," Calvin said, "that girl is messed up."

We were now completely surrounded. Some of the bikers had started rocking the car, and even I was starting to doubt my theory.

"Okay, that's it! Dana and Milo are going to get their butts kicked by these crazies, unless we do something," Cal announced. He shifted his car into drive and hit his horn repeatedly as he glared at the crowd. "Get the hell out of my way—I will not hesitate to run you down!"

He inched the car forward, revving the motor, and the crowd parted in front of us. He had a clear shot to pull out into the street and zoom away to safety, and even I was tempted to make a run for it. Instead he turned and drove right up onto the sidewalk, positioning the car directly in front of the SmartMart's door.

As we jerked to a stop, that door opened, and I had a front-row seat to Dana's astonishment. And I knew I was at least partially right. She'd expected us to run away.

Milo was right behind her, clutching a small plastic bag in one hand. He stuffed it into his inside jacket pocket as he locked eyes with me.

Neither of them seemed particularly worried about the crowd. In fact, Milo went over to the old man with the cane and whispered something in his ear. The man shrunk back and then sidled away.

One of the bikers nodded at Dana and she nodded back, and they all vanished too. And just like that, the street in front of the SmartMart went from completely crazy to completely deserted.

Calvin unlocked the car doors to let Milo and Dana in. "What the *hell*," he said. "Was Skylar right? What that some kind of test?"

Dana's eyes were cool as she looked at me. "Smart girl."

"Blood in the streets?" I tried to make my own eyes as chilly. "That was a little over the top."

"Just checking to see if you have balls."

"For the record," Calvin said, "we've got 'em. And so does Mr. Unfortunate, which, by the way, was something Sky absolutely did *not* need to see."

"Sunshine's gonna see a lot worse before we're done here," Dana countered sharply.

"So it was a test?" Calvin shot back. "Did you seriously pay that guy to flash—"

"No," Dana said. "The bikers were mine. Old Man Dempsey's just part of the local color. He's harmless. Mostly."

"Mostly," Calvin repeated as I chimed in with "The bikers *were* yours!"

"Yeah, mostly," Dana said. "Everyone in Harrisburg is dangerous. So yeah, the bikers happened to be friends of mine—this time. Next time? Who knows? Next time—"

"Did we *pass* your *test?*" Calvin asked, his voice heavy with attitude.

"Part one," Dana said. "Yeah. But part two is tonight, when you ask yourself, *Am I still alive?* If the answer is *yes*, then—"

"At this moment, you're arguing about irrelevant issues and wasting valuable time that should be spent trying to find Edmund Rodriguez before the police do. Because you know once they find him, we won't be able to get close to him, and we'll be back to square one." Milo's voice cut through Dana and Calvin's bickering. It was the most I'd heard him talk since meeting him last night.

Dana nodded but didn't stop glaring at Cal. "You're absolutely right."

Milo tucked his mop of hair behind his ears. He looked different in the daylight…The angles of his jawline were less harsh, and a five-o'clock shadow had begun to darken his chin. I didn't realize I was staring until he looked at me and smiled. Dimples popped out playfully on either cheek. I looked away fast.

"Let's start over on 80th Street, near the old Publix warehouse," Dana said, "where Edmund Rodriguez's truck was found." She gave Cal directions.

As he pulled his car down off the sidewalk, I stared out the window at the empty streets. I thought about how quickly Old Man Dempsey had adios-ed when Milo had opened his mouth. And how easily he'd brought Dana and Cal back on track. Impulsively, I asked, "You sure you don't have a gift too?"

Milo looked surprised. "Me?" he asked. Dana laughed.

"Yeah. I mean, what did you say to Mr. Dempsey? He was pretty worked up."

Dana shook her head and helped Milo answer the question. "He's just street smart, Sugar Plum. There's a big difference between street smart and Greater-Than, as you of all people plainly demonstrate."

"There's nothing wrong with not being street smart," Milo reassured me quietly.

"What I want to know," Cal said, "is why Harrisburg has such a large crazy-person population."

Dana and Milo looked at each other. Then Dana looked at Cal. "Sweetie," she said, "these days, half of the population is out of work.

The Haves don't want be reminded that they could be next to lose everything, so they hire guards to keep the Have-Nots out of their gated communities, which shoves them all together in neighborhoods like this one—which is the pimple on the sweaty ass of Harrisburg. That'd make anyone a little crazy."

She shook her head. "And then you show up in your Have-ie car and your little golf shirt and your pink sneakers—and they know that the bump in price that you paid for the pink ones instead of the white could feed their families for a week—and you stand out like lost baby ducklings in an alligator swamp. And some of 'em want to stick you with a shiv because you've still got what they lost, and some of them just want to stick you because they like it when people bleed."

"But no one's going to hurt you as long as Dana's around," Milo added.

"What, do you mind-control 'em?" Calvin asked sarcastically.

"Yeah, actually, I do," Dana said calmly.

"I thought you said you weren't telepathic." Calvin looked at her hard in the rearview mirror.

"I'm not," she said. "I can't read minds. I can only—strongly— influence them."

"Like, *these are not the droids you're looking for?*" Calvin asked.

"Yeah," Dana said. "Or…"

"This is where the police found Sasha's father's truck," Calvin recited, his head tilted at a slightly odd angle, as he pulled to the side of the road. But then he straightened up, shook his head, and made a face at me before he turned to glare back at Dana. "Holy crap. Did *you* do that?"

She spread her hands and shrugged. "I'll be here all week."

Calvin laughed his amazement, but his smile faded as he looked out the windshield. Since we'd stopped, the street had become crowded with more of the people that Dana had called the Have-Nots, most of them bedraggled and fidgety as they sidled closer.

Cal sighed. "Okay. I'm asking you this as a man with a sturdy, intact set of balls, Dana. From what you just told us about the locals, do you really think it's a good idea to leave my car here? I'm just saying."

Dana smirked. "Thanks so much for the mental pic. And I'll let you answer your own question."

Calvin's head tilted again. "No one's going to touch my car, either. If they do, Dana'll kick their ass." Again, he shook his head, adding, "God, that's creepy. Stop doing that."

"Just proving the point," Dana said. She quickly reviewed the rules she'd given us before she'd told that blood-in-the-streets story. But she added a caveat to her super-mind-control abilities: her powers didn't work on everyone. Oxycontin addicts, for example, were immune to her mental suggestions. Some jokering Destiny addicts were unreachable too.

So stay relatively close and always be ready to run.

I took out my photos of the Rodriguez family and handed one to Calvin. Milo reached inside his jacket pocket and pulled out a cheap printout from an online news source.

"Let's do this thing," Dana said.

As soon as I stepped into the outside air, my nostrils were bombarded by smells. More of that fish odor and burning plastic, as well as a grossly overbearing amount of garlic. I tried to detect any sewage smells, but couldn't find any. I wondered if I was overthinking it.

Milo smoothed his printout photo of Sasha's dad on the top of Cal's car roof. He paused for a moment and took a pack of gum from his pocket and popped a piece into his mouth.

"Ooh. Can I have some?" I asked, hoping the mint taste would somehow neutralize the awful stench of this city.

"Oh," Milo said. "Um. No. You, um, really wouldn't like this…flavor."

I think I was standing there with my mouth open. Who didn't share their gum? Of course he and Dana were probably on a more austere budget than I could even imagine. Still, "You wouldn't like this flavor" was kinda lame. If he didn't want to share, he should've gone with "Sorry, last piece."

"Sorry," he said again as he backed away.

Dana was already on the corner, talking to what looked like a group of soccer moms dressed up as prostitutes for Halloween. Except it wasn't October, which meant…

"Oh, God," I said, as Calvin beeped his car locked and took a moment to situate himself and his chair on the street.

Milo was now talking to a man who looked like Santa's evil twin. The bearded guy was selling something called "meat sandwiches" from an old hot-dog stand.

"What do you suppose kind of meat…" Cal started.

I shook my head. "Don't ask." Although it was hard not to notice the dearth of both dogs and seagulls in this neighborhood.

As if in silent agreement, both Cal and I turned and headed for the same group of ten-year-olds sitting on the front steps of what had once been a bank. They seemed a little less dangerous than the average Harrisburg-ite.

But they started shaking their heads as we approached, before we even showed them Edmund's picture—a trend that continued for the next several hours, regardless of whom we approached.

So that was our Sunday. Or at least most of it.

It might have been my imagination, but by midafternoon, people seemed to begin shuffling out of the woodwork again. The street was becoming more and more crowded with bodies. And nobody looked like they had anywhere else to be.

"We're popular around here," Calvin noted as we showed Edmund's photo left and right.

"Very," I said, as one after another of them shook their heads and shuffled away.

We didn't have to search out anyone at this point, because people just kept coming toward us. It was the same type of crowd one might expect on a street corner after a car accident had occurred—a little bit bloodthirsty and a whole lot of curious.

"Keep your eyes peeled for Edmund," I said. "You never know."

Calvin looked doubtful.

We walked into the crowd. The sidewalk narrowed significantly as hands and feet gradually began to impose on my personal space. It had to be twice as bad for Calvin. Even the shortest person towered above him.

Someone bumped clumsily into Cal's wheelchair. "Hey!" he said defensively. Watch it, will you?"

The woman who'd collided with him was a skinny little thing. She stared blankly at Cal, her eyes bloodshot and empty.

"What's your problem?" she asked, hands on her hips in an antagonist pose. As I studied her face, I realized she was really just a girl. She was definitely younger than both Calvin and me, but her stomach popped out underneath a sequined halter top. She was pregnant.

Calvin gave up trying to be defensive. "Um…" He paused. "Have you seen this man?" he asked, and showed the girl the photo of Edmund.

"What's it to you?" she asked, all attitude. People pushed her from either side to catch a better glimpse of Calvin and me, and she elbowed them dismissively.

"It actually means a lot," Calvin said. "The man in this picture? His daughter was murdered last week, and we're trying to track him down to ask him some questions."

As soon as Calvin said the word "murder," the girl froze and then backed away. She waved her hands in front of her face and shook her head. "Uh-uh," she said, "I don't know nothin' about a murder."

"It's okay. We're not with the police or anything," I said as reassuringly as I could. "We're just trying to find Edmund—this man— because we think he can help us figure out what happened."

But the girl had already turned on her heels. She pushed her way through the crowd, her hips swinging.

No doubt about it, the crowd was multiplying. Calvin and I waded through the dense cloud of people, showing Edmund's picture to no avail as it became next to impossible for us to move.

I've never been claustrophobic, but I was seriously having trouble catching my breath.

It probably had something to do with the fact that the fishy, garlic, burning-plastic smell was piercing my nostrils, now more than ever.

Every face I saw, every set of eyes, every pursed set of lips, seemed sinister and invasive. I held on to Calvin's shoulder. He was afraid to press forward, for fear he would roll over someone's toes. Downtown Harrisburg had turned into a flash mob minus the cool dance routine, and we were in the center of it.

"Sky?" Cal hollered, yelling over the din of the crowd, craning his neck to look up at me.

"I'm right here," I said, squeezing his shoulder, heart pounding. I could still see Dana and Milo, but they were way down the street.

I took a deep breath, but it felt like barely enough air entered my lungs. I needed space.

Everybody was pointing at us, moving closer and closer. Faces loomed above us, leaning over, the air thick and pungent with their foul breath.

"Calvin," I said, and I felt my face heat up as someone bumped into me, pushing me back and down onto my butt in the street. I had let go of Calvin as I fell, and we were immediately separated, the teeming humanity pushing forward and putting more distance between us.

"Where're Dana and Milo?" I thought I heard Cal say, although now I couldn't see him. I couldn't see anything except for faces and their shadows.

"Calvin!" I shouted, but he didn't hear me. A woman clutching a large bouquet of long-dead flowers loomed above me. She tried to tuck a crumbling brown rose into my hair, and I shied away.

"Don't touch me!" I said. But she didn't listen. "I said, *don't TOUCH ME!*"

And then there was water everywhere.

Not just a trickle, but a current of water sloshing and churning from the ground up, soaking everyone in its wake. I gasped, a sheet of the icy liquid slapping my face as I scrambled to my feet.

Everyone else gasped too and immediately shrank away.

"What the…" Cal started, as I lunged for him, grabbing his hand as the crowd vanished down corners and into alleys.

"Whoa." Dana and Milo stood across the street, gawking.

The source of the water was a fire hydrant. The thing had literally exploded. I grabbed Calvin's chair and dragged him away from the massive geyser of frothing water. Rivulets spilled past my feet, and as I pushed Calvin up onto the sidewalk, my sneakers squeaked wetly.

"Did you…?" Calvin started.

I nodded. "Yeah. I think so."

Dana started to clap. "Way to clear the area, Bubble Gum." It was clear she was frustrated. "Dammit, we were *so* close."

"Close?" I repeated.

As Dana and Milo crossed to our sidewalk, Milo stared at the fire hydrant as if he wanted to ask it some questions.

"Close," Dana said.

"As in, someone you talked to said they saw him?" I was frustrated too. "Because absolutely no one we showed our pictures to knew anything about anyone. Of course, they would've denied that the sky was blue if I'd asked them about it."

"No, no one admitted to seeing Edmund. That's not what I meant," Dana told me as Milo bit at a nail. I hadn't pegged him as a nail-biter, but he was really going at it.

"You okay?" I looked at him.

He stopped, mid-chew, and popped another piece of gum into his mouth. This time, I knew enough not to ask him for a piece.

Dana took a sudden deep breath, almost like a gasp. "We've got to stay put for a sec," she said, and closed her eyes.

Calvin looked around. "What's wrong now?"

I spotted sets of eyes peeking around corners and from alleys. The mob may have been temporarily spooked by my exploding fire-hydrant trick, but they were all still hovering close by.

"What is it?" I asked Dana. She stood with her chin tilted up slightly. Her eyes were still closed.

"We've got to stay put for a sec," Dana repeated.

Milo glanced at Dana, then waited. He didn't seem worried.

But she was standing there like she was waiting for a message from above or something. It was very strange.

Finally, she turned to me. "Over there," she said, pointing to an alley.

"What?"

"A boy over there. Wait for him."

I looked where she was pointing. A little boy peeked his head around the corner. He was probably only eight or nine, and scrawny. There was dirt on his face.

"He knows something."

Calvin scoffed. "Seriously?"

"Shut up, Boyfriend," Dana said, concentrating. "This doesn't happen very often, but when it does, I *do* take it *very* seriously." She closed her eyes again.

Dana seemed to imply that it was my move, so I walked toward the little guy. His eyes were wide and white against his sunburned skin. As I approached him, he cowered slightly.

"Hey," I whispered. "I'm not gonna hurt you."

"Yeah," he said. "I know. You got some food?"

I shook my head sadly and took the picture of the Rodriguez family from my pocket. It was soggy and the colors were starting to run, but Edmund's face was still clear. "Have you seen…?"

The boy nodded. "Yeah. He was here," he said, and tapped his tiny finger on the image of Edmund. "Why'd you make that fire thing explode?" He took his finger off the photo and pointed to the hydrant. The water coming out of it was down to a trickle now.

"I was angry," I said. "People were bothering me."

"Oh," the boy said, and nodded as if he understood. "Yeah. People bother me too sometimes. I wish I could make things explode like you do."

I thought about what Dana had said…how I couldn't ever tell anybody about my powers. "Well," I explained, "I think it might have just been a coincidence. I didn't really…"

The boy raised an eyebrow. It made him look much older, like a miniature grown man. "Uh-huh," he said.

"When did you see this man?" I asked, changing the subject. I unpeeled my wet shirt from my back where it was sticking to me like tape.

"Last week. He came here. He was crying. No one would talk to him. Then the old lady came in that van and gave him medicine."

I shuddered, and looked back at Milo, Dana, and Calvin. They were all huddled back a ways, staring expectantly at us. I turned back around and looked at the boy.

"What old lady?" I asked.

"The one with the really red eyes," the boy said, and scratched his head. "She gave him medicine," he replied again.

"What kind of…" I started to ask.

But a man came around the corner then, bellowing "Jeremy, get back inside, you little shit!"

And the boy sprinted away before I could ask him anything more.

CHAPTER ELEVEN

"I need a Valium," Calvin said as we drove toward Coconut Key.

"We need to go back," I said, shaking my head.

Calvin looked at me like I'd gone completely crazy. "We practically got stampeded by a mob of hobos. We are *not* going back! Besides, I gotta get home. I know you think my mom is the queen of permissiveness, but I know when I'm pushing it, and I've got to do the family dinner thing tonight."

I sighed. The scenery outside became much more pleasant as we left the slums of Harrisburg and reentered Touristville USA. I felt sick inside, as if by leaving I was somehow physically abandoning Sasha. "But that little boy knew something important."

"And that's why Dana and Milo stayed back there to look for him." Cal tapped his fingers nervously on the steering wheel. "Seriously, Sky? I think it's awesome that we're trying to bring justice to whoever killed Sasha. But there's a point where you just have to trust that the police will do their jobs."

"Listen," I said, biting a nail. "If this is too much for you, then just say it. I can do this alone if that's what you really want. If all this scares you, then you can bail, and I won't blame you."

"Yeah, you will," Cal said, gripping the steering wheel as he took the Coconut Key exit and headed for the bridge. "And for what it's worth, I'll tell you right now that I *am* one hundred percent crap-my-pants terrified. I'd be as crazy as those people back there in Harrisburg if I wasn't."

I looked at him. His face was grim.

"But if you think that I'm going to let you go at this alone," he continued, "then you're crazy too."

I reached over and squeezed Cal's shoulder. "Thank you."

Calvin dropped me off around the corner from my house before going back to his place to lie down. I expected Momzilla to be home and waiting anxiously for me—my phone had been shut off the entire time, after all—but when I got there, Mom's car was gone again.

I went inside and turned my phone back on before changing into dry clothes and plopping onto my bed. It was only five o'clock, but our trip to Harrisburg had worn me out.

Popping my earbuds in, I set my iPod to shuffle and leaned back, zoning out as the music lulled me to sleep.

The dream was different this time.

It started in that same field, and the sun was shining so brightly that my head started to hurt, right behind my eyes. I lifted a hand to my face to shield it from the glare.

Birds chirped in trees overhead, and I looked for them, but all I saw were leaves dancing in the breeze. That, and monarch butterflies weaving through the air. I sighed and sat down.

The grass was as green as emeralds and soft like a plush rug. I ran the palm of my hand over it and felt relaxed for the first time in a while.

The feeling of peace only lasted for a moment, because a dark shadow moved swiftly across the sky, blocking the sun. The horizon turned a bruised color.

I looked around me, and the field was gone. The birds were silent, their cheerful trilling replaced by the chirp of a hospital's heart monitor. I smelled rubbing alcohol.

And backed-up sewage.

"Don't look," a voice whispered, and I inhaled sharply.

"Don't look," another voice repeated.

I turned, and the highway was in front of me, stretching as far as I could see. The white dotted line dividing the lanes seemed to extend toward infinity.

Sasha was there.

Sasha was alive! She was standing there, clear as day, on the dotted white line, her back to me. Her hair was stuck to the nape of her neck, and her white-and-blue dress flowed urgently in the wind, pressing against her body and outlining her fragile legs.

"Sasha!" I called out, but she didn't turn around.

I tried to run toward her, but each time I took a step forward, she seemed farther and farther away.

When I woke up, my sheets were soaked with sweat, and when I reached up to touch my face, I felt tears on my cheeks.

But I brushed them away, my heart beating hard as I remembered the rush of relief, the sense of certainty that had filled me because I knew—I *knew*—that Sasha was alive.

What if the conviction I'd felt in my dream was real, and Sasha truly was still alive?

I reached for my phone, intending to call Calvin, but then I stopped. He wouldn't believe that Sasha wasn't dead. He was my best friend, and I loved him, but right now I needed someone to say, "Hell, yeah, Sky, you could be right."

Dana wasn't that person, either. It didn't take much to imagine her harsh, *Get a grip, Bubble Gum. The girl is gone.*

But Milo…

I found myself wishing I could talk to Milo, which was kind of weird because I didn't really know him—plus he'd made a point not to share his gum with me.

Of course, maybe my sense that Milo would offer the right kind of encouragement was as crazy as the idea that I should know—from a dream—that Sasha wasn't dead.

So instead of calling anyone, I had dinner with my mom—who didn't say a word about my phone being off, thank God. I did my homework, watched a little TV, and "celebrated" the end of the weekend by going to bed early.

I was starting to get really sick of Mr. Jenkins.

Monday was like jumping headfirst into the world of mediocrity, and band was proving to be the worst of it.

"Let's start again on the fourth measure of page nine," Jenkins said, patting the top of his head gently, no doubt double-checking that his comb-over wasn't too unkempt.

I still couldn't get over the fact that my mother and Jenkins had actually gotten coffee together. I prayed it had been a one-time deal, because the implications of their relationship being something serious were nauseating. Jenkins at dinner, Jenkins in our TV room, Jenkins at breakfast…

But sitting in the practice room with my triangle in my lap, I knew there were so many more important things to focus on, like finding Edmund Rodriguez. I hadn't heard a thing from Dana or Milo since yesterday—which made sense since neither of them had a cell phone, and if I wanted to talk to them, all I had to do was wish for it. Or something.

Yeah, and so far *that* hadn't worked.

I turned my sheet music to page nine and found the fourth measure. Fat, black rectangles dangled beneath the lines. Great. I had whole rests for at least three pages.

Kim Riley stood next to her bass drum and shrugged sympathetically at me.

I shrugged back.

Mr. Jenkins counted the class in with his usual *Let's Polka!* fervor, and everyone who wasn't me or Kim started to play the Beethoven piece we'd been working on for the past month. It would have been okay, even with Beethoven's trademark intensity, if Jenkins hadn't been a musical moron.

I looked over at Cal, who was concentrating as he played his trumpet. Garrett wasn't concentrating quite as much. When he spotted me looking in their direction, he smiled.

I looked away quickly.

I hadn't seen him since Saturday, but apparently he'd decided that we were on good terms. Maybe he was just excited that I hadn't told the whole school about beating him in that race—or the fact that he'd puked his guts out all over the beach.

Garrett turned and whispered something into Cal's ear. Cal glanced up at me and then looked down at his music and scowled. I wondered why Garrett was always so chatty with Cal in band practice...and why Calvin never told me what their conversations were about. It was pretty weird, considering Cal usually told me everything.

But then I thought about yesterday's dream and how I still hadn't mentioned it to Calvin, despite the fact that he'd driven me to school.

As I watched, Garrett slapped Cal congenially on the back and whispered something else, before Calvin hit Garrett on the shoulder. His smack didn't look quite as friendly.

Mr. Jenkins tapped his pencil on the side of his music stand and the band fizzled out. "Is there a problem?" he asked the two boys.

"Absolutely not, sir," Garrett said in a tone that was dripping with mockery.

Cal didn't answer.

"Well, then let's pay attention, please."

"Will do!" Garrett exclaimed enthusiastically. He was such a dick.

Jenkins squinted at both of them suspiciously before launching into a discussion of the Beethoven piece and what we all had to do to improve it.

I watched Calvin's jaw clench as he struggled to focus on what Mr. Jenkins was saying. There was something really wrong.

Finally, the bell rang, which meant it was time for Jenkins to shut up until tomorrow. I raced out of there as fast as I could, and then waited in the hallway for Calvin.

Two minutes went by, and he didn't show up.

The rest of the kids from band practice slid by me, laughing and talking with each other. Kim Riley waved silently on her way past.

I poked my head into the practice room, but it was empty.

That was beyond weird.

Cal never exited through the back, partly because he always walked me to the next class, but also because there was nothing outside the east band doors except the soccer field and some reserved parking spots for teachers and other faculty.

I walked through the practice room and peeked out through the windows of the east doors.

I spotted Cal's trumpet case on the sidewalk.

Quietly, I opened the door and stepped outside.

I heard voices and peeked around the corner. Sure enough, Calvin and Garrett were out there, but neither one of them had spotted me.

"...if you really think about it," Garrett was saying.

I heard Cal laugh a little, although the shake in his voice implied that he didn't think whatever Garrett was talking about was so funny. "I think I intimidate you," Calvin replied.

"You intimidate *me*?" Garrett scoffed. "Come on, man. You're black *and* you're crippled. I've pretty much got the upper hand."

I gasped, quickly drawing my hand to my mouth so I wouldn't make a noise.

"See, that's funny, because last time I checked, my skin color didn't really have much to do with anything. But it's cool. I know you can't help being an ignorant redneck."

Go Calvin.

Garrett laughed like that was the funniest thing he'd ever heard. "Man, my family's from New York. How am *I* a redneck?"

"*Man,*" Calvin said, mocking Garrett's tone, "you don't have to be from the South to be ignorant. These days, rednecks are everywhere. It's a state of mind."

"Well, if I'm ignorant, you're a little…bitch," Garrett exclaimed.

The bell rang. I didn't move.

"All right, Garrett. You win. Call me whatever you need to so that you can feel better about yourself and I can get the hell to class."

"Bro, I don't have to feel better about myself. I'm just grateful that I'm not stuck in a chair all day, and that I get to actually stand up to take a piss like a real man." Garrett chuckled cruelly. "Only bitches sit on the pot to piss. You know, maybe you should think about a sex change, considering you're already halfway there—because your dick is as limp as your legs."

Calvin didn't respond. For a moment, there was complete silence.

I realized in that instant that I'd never really thought about it. Could Calvin even…? I honestly didn't know. I was aware, just from reading, that some people who'd been paralyzed didn't have control over those parts of their bodies and sometimes even needed to wear an adult diaper.

But surely if that was the case with Calvin, I would have heard about it.

Or maybe not.

Garrett didn't seem to realize that he'd crossed a terrible line, because he laughed and said, "For all I know, it already got cut off in the accident. You know, *Calvina*, with enough estrogen, you could grow a really nice set of tits. Give you something to play with. Bigger than your girlfriend's, although that wouldn't take much, would it?"

"Are you done?" Calvin said, his voice tight.

"You know I screwed her," Garrett said. "She came to me, begging, because she wasn't getting it from you."

Calvin laughed. "It really pisses you off, doesn't it?" he said. "When I don't rise to your bait? I know exactly what happened when you took Skylar to the beach. She kicked your ass. Made you vomit like a little girl—"

"Fuck you!"

What I heard then sounded like Calvin's wheelchair clanking up against the side of the building, as if Garrett had actually *pushed* him.

I grabbed the door and flung it open so that it hit the outside wall with a crash, calling, "Calvin, are you out here?" as if I'd just come racing through the band room, and hadn't heard the last five minutes of Garrett's disgusting insults.

"I've got your trumpet case," I called as gaily as I could, as I grabbed the boxy thing by its handle. "Hurry up, we're already late to lunch and I'm hungry!"

Garrett must've lit out, escaping around the side of the building, because when I rounded the corner, Calvin was sitting there alone.

"You okay?" I asked him, mostly because it would've been weird not to say anything.

"Yeah," he said, forcing a smile. "I just needed to take a moment after, um, Jenkins's attempt to deafen Beethoven's ghost."

I made myself laugh at his joke, even though my stomach hurt. It was clear he wasn't going to tell me about Garrett's abuse as he followed me back inside. "Yeah, old Ludwig was definitely thrashing around in his grave today," I said as I wondered how long Garrett's bullying had been going on. I seriously doubted that today was the first time he'd been cruel to Calvin.

But from now on, as far as I was concerned, if Garrett was going to mess with Calvin, he was going to have to go through me to do it.

CHAPTER TWELVE

At lunch, I waited in vain for Calvin to say something to me about what had happened after band with Garrett, but he acted as though everything was absolutely normal.

"Question of the day!" he exclaimed, his mouth full of the leftover pizza his mom had packed for him.

I sat atop one of the picnic tables by the quad, my elbows resting on my knees. I didn't say a word. I just chewed my free-range and antibiotic-free turkey on gluten-free bread.

"Okay! Would you rather…have a long, hot make-out session with Mrs. Disapproval, or French kiss Mr. Kaspersky for ten minutes? Lots of tongue."

Mr. Kaspersky was our school principal, and he had the worst breath in the entire world.

"God, Cal, it always has to be while I'm eating!" I dropped my sandwich on top of my paper lunch bag and made a disgusted face.

Cal smiled, absolutely tickled with himself. "What'll it be?" he said.

I sighed. "Mrs. Disapproval," I replied.

"I didn't know you swung both ways," Calvin said gleefully. "That's pretty awesome."

"I don't!" I said. "Not that there's anything wrong with it, but it's just not my thing. I think Mrs. Disapproval probably has better dental hygiene than Kaspersky, that's all."

"What do you think about your friend with the steel-toed boots?" Cal said. "You think she's a girlfriend kind of girl?"

"Do you mean, do I think she's gay?" I shook my head. "No. Definitely not. I'm pretty sure she and Milo are a thing." I paused. "Why do you ask?"

"Just wondering what your thoughts were," Cal said, and took an enormous bite of pizza.

"Wait a second," I said, smiling. "You *like* her!"

Calvin scoffed, his mouth full. "Me?" He pointed to his chest and laughed.

"Oh my gosh, you *do*!"

He tried to play it super casual. "She is sexy, but in an extremely scary way," Calvin replied. "Like a dominatrix. And if you tell her I said that, I'll be forced to kill you."

"Good luck with that, me being a Greater-Than. Also? She probably wouldn't blink. She's probably used to having guys fall at her feet," I pointed out.

"You really think she and Milo are…" He pounded his fist into the palm of his hand.

I looked at him with unconcealed disgust. "What is *that*? Is that supposed to be…?"

"Banging," he said, doing it again.

"Banging," I repeated. "No, I do not think they are *banging*. I *do* think they make incredibly passionate, steamy, romance-novel-worthy love together, as often as humanly possible." This was the perfect segue into my admitting that I'd overheard his earlier conversation with Garrett, but I couldn't bring myself to do it.

"You got a problem with that?" Calvin asked. "With Dana and Milo?"

And I realized that I was frowning. "No," I said. "No, of course not. I was just thinking about your question of the day and throwing up in my mouth a little."

Calvin offered me a very self-satisfied grin. "You're welcome," he said.

School dragged for several more hours. I had so much crap on my mind that my brain actually hurt.

When the final bell rang, I almost fell to my knees and thanked whoever resides in the clouds. I was *that* relieved.

Instead, I waited outside in the front parking area, next to Cal's car.

He wasn't done taking the popquiz Mr. Daniels had so heartlessly surprised us with in history class today. I kicked at an empty soda can on the sidewalk and watched kids shuffle into their cars. The sun was out again today, and as a couple of jocks walked by, I heard them mention something about heading to the beach.

For a moment I wished that my life could be that simple again… just a normal high-school junior, getting through her classes so she could spend the afternoon at the mall, or maybe catch a movie or drive around with her friends.

For me, life had stopped being simple a long time ago. And it didn't show signs of letting up.

I wished... I didn't know *what* I wished, but I suspected it included Milo.

Just then, out of the blue, Dana rounded the corner on her huge-ass motorcycle, as if punctuation to my thoughts.

"Hey!" she called out to me over the roar of the engine, removing her white aviator sunglasses and stacking them on top of her head.

I stepped closer to the bike. Kids were looking at Dana, some of them pointing. I wondered if they thought she was a new girl or if they realized she wasn't high school material. Probably the latter.

"Hop on!" She pointed to the back of the bike.

I hesitated, because oh my God. She really expected me to just *hop on* that thing? She didn't wear a helmet, and I was one of those kids whose mom had made me wear protective headgear with my tricycle. And as much as I hated the fact that my mother's inner bat-crap-crazy alarm sounder could ever be right, statistics really did prove that even a minor accident on a motorcycle could be fatal without a helmet.

Add that math to the fact that it had taken me months to be able to ride in a car without holding on to the grab bar for dear life and...

I started to sweat.

"What are you waiting for, Bubble Gum? We've got work to do! You wanted training? I'm gonna train you. Now."

"I have to wait for Cal," I shouted back, trying to sound apologetic instead of relieved that I had a reason *not* to just hop right on. "We had a plan to go over to my house after school, to work on our math homework. I don't want to just, you know, ditch him. He'll be out soon."

Dana wasn't pleased. Her hoop earrings jingled against her neck as she shook her head. "Five minutes," she said, and tapped her wrist.

I nodded and relaxed, knowing that Calvin would save me.

Today, Dana was even more leather clad than usual. She was wearing the same tight black leather pants she'd had on that night in the Sav'A'Buck. Her black tank top was low cut, and the bra she was wearing pushed her chest up, resulting in some seriously admirable cleavage. Her red bomber jacket was form fitting and zipped only halfway up.

I glanced down at my plain, white T-shirt and jeans, and conceded I might as well be wearing overalls. I was that unsexy in comparison.

Dana placed her elbows on top of the handlebars of her motorcycle and made an impatient face. I looked around. A group of kids walked by, all of them dressed in black and orange—more jocks. And yes, Garrett was one of them.

"Hey, Skylar," he said, even as he looked Dana up and down. "Who's your friend? Nice...ride."

Just the sight of him made me so mad that I wanted to punch him in the face. Instead, I gave him a full-on ignore, turning to Dana and proclaiming, "I don't know what it is about Calvin. He's just so...*hot*. Don't you think?"

If she was surprised, she didn't show it with more than a single blink before she looked from me to Garrett and back. "Calvin," she said, loudly enough to be heard over the roar from her bike. "Yeah. Wow. I...really wish I'd met him first."

That stopped Garrett cold, but then Dana put the cherry on top by smiling directly into his stunned eyes and adding, "Move it along, Tic-Tac dick."

Garrett adjusted the collar of his team jacket and stalked off, his friends in tow.

And not a moment too soon, as Calvin rounded the corner just then.

He wheeled forward slowly, picking up his pace only after Garrett was completely gone. He looked at Dana and then at me.

"'Sup, Wonder Boy?" Dana said, and turned her motorcycle off. The parking lot got a whole lot quieter.

"'Sup," he said so casually that I wanted to laugh.

"Can I borrow your friend for a few hours?" Dana asked, and nodded toward me.

Calvin looked from Dana's motorcycle to me and back, and without missing a beat said, "Sorry. I'm not letting my girl ride that thing. Lock it up. I'll drive you wherever you're going."

"We're training," Dana informed him flatly. "At her request, might I remind you. You can't come with."

Calvin shrugged. "So, I'll drop you and leave."

"And pick us up afterward?" Dana scoffed.

"Your wish is my command," Cal told her evenly.

Dana turned to me. "You really gonna let Boyfriend here dictate—"

"He knows I'd rather go in his car," I admitted. "It's not what he wants. He just knows it's what I…want."

I expected Dana to blast me for being a coward, and I raised my chin against the proclamation of *chicken shit* that was sure to come. But instead she merely nodded and began taking several long chains from her saddlebags. "Let's do it, then," she said.

"Anything going on that I should know about?" Dana asked as Calvin's car pulled away. He'd dropped us down by the beach, near that same deserted stretch of road where I'd spotted Dana watching me run, last Saturday. She turned to look at me, her gaze sharp. "Scooter seemed…subdued."

No way was I telling her what I'd overheard. I shook my head as I shrugged. "We've got a math test coming up—"

"Don't BS a BSer," she interrupted. "If you don't want to tell me, don't, but don't *math test* me. Frankly, I think your loyalty to him is admirable, and vice versa. You're lucky to have found him, as annoying as he can sometimes be."

I sighed and admitted, "There *is* something going on, but it's private and…"

"You're not comfortable talking about it with an almost-stranger," Dana finished for me. "That's good, Bubble Gum. You're impeccable with your word. So how about I tell you what I've seen and what I think is going on, and you can either nod yes or no. Because maybe I can help." She didn't wait for me to respond, she just plunged ahead.

"Jock Itch, with the dark hair and the skeevy *I am God's gift* smile, has decided that you're his next girlfriend, which—understandably—is pissing Scooter off. You were naive enough to fall for some stupid line about helping you look for Sasha, but it wasn't until you were at the beach with him last Saturday that you realized he was trying to shoplift. You being you, you told Boyfriend what happened, and he probably got in JI's face, which resulted in Itchy showing his true ugly colors by saying something nasty back to Calvin—again probably dick related."

My mouth had dropped open, and I closed it. But then I opened it again to say, "Calvin's not my boyfriend. It's just…it's never been like that. He doesn't like me that way."

Dana actually looked surprised as I followed her through the hole in the fence and down the soft sand toward the water.

"Garrett—Jock Itch—has definitely been using me as some kind of pawn, though," I continued. "At first I thought he just wanted to be in the loop as far as what was going on with Sasha—you know, the curiosity factor. But after today…" I took a deep breath. "I'm pretty sure he and Calvin have been at war for a while. I'm a little freaked because, well, Cal never told me anything about it."

Dana nodded. "Yeah, he wouldn't." She glanced at me. "How long has he been in that chair?"

"Since he was really little. I don't know exactly, nine maybe?"

"Jesus."

"Yeah."

"If that was me, I don't think I could be anything but grim," Dana admitted, but then she exhaled and rewound a bit. "Wow, I was so sure you were a romantic unit. You guys are…really tight." And then she went and ruined what might've otherwise been a real bonding moment by adding, "I guess you *are* as shallow as you look."

I was tired of her condemnation and I got into her face. "How does being friends with Calvin make me shallow?"

"Tell me you wouldn't be all over him if he could walk," she countered.

That got me mad. "How dare you?" I said. "Has it occurred to you that *he's* the one who's not into me? Because news flash! He's not."

"Look at you. You're Little Miss Perfect. You honestly expect me to believe—"

I cut her off, stepping in even closer to her. I was much taller than she was, but she was stronger. If she wanted to, she could break me in half like a twig. But I didn't care about that as I said, "Yeah. I do. I expect you to believe me, to trust me—because I am currently spending a crapload of time trusting *you*. It can't just go one way."

There we stood, face to face, gazes locked, both with our hands on our hips.

Dana blinked first. She laughed. "You've got pretty big balls for a cream-puff debutante. I like it. It's good. But I still think you could wrap Scooter around your little finger if you *really* wanted to." She turned and pushed through the unpacked sand, heading closer to the water.

Shaking my head, I followed her again. "So what exactly are we doing here?" I asked.

"I told you already," she said. "We're training, like you wanted."

"We're not dressed to run."

"Yeah, we're not running—I'm not a runner," she said. "And even if I were, there's no way I could keep up with you. I don't have that particular gift."

"You seem to be able to disappear pretty quickly, from what I've seen."

"Oh, I didn't say that I can't move fast when I need to," she said, grinning a little bit.

"So…what else *can* you do?" I was extremely curious, and I have to admit I was still feeling a bit belligerent. "I mean, besides the not-telepathy mind-control thing."

Dana picked up a piece of driftwood and tossed it from her left hand to her right and back again. "Well, for one, I have 20/2 vision."

"You mean 20/20."

"No, I mean 20/2."

"Whoa."

Dana laughed a little bit. "I also have an eidetic memory."

"Isn't that like a photographic memory?" I asked.

"Yeah," she said, and threw the driftwood away. "It's exactly like a photographic memory. FYI, many G-Ts have some kinda enhanced memory."

"I'm pretty sure I don't," I said.

"Then why is it that you have an absolutely perfect grade point average?" Dana countered. "How does that happen? Do you spend every waking hour studying?"

I scoffed. "Um, no." I looked at Dana. "How do you know I have a perfect GPA?"

"Bubble Gum, I know more about you than you think. Answer me this: how many tattoos do I have?" Dana tipped her collar to make sure that her red bomber jacket was completely covering her.

The number nine popped into my head. I looked at her. "I don't know."

"Yeah, you do," Dana said.

I looked away.

"Name them," Dana said, her voice challenging.

I sighed heavily. "The tribal design on your upper arm," I said, sticking out one finger as I began to count. "The initials on the inside of your right wrist." I stuck out another finger. "The angel wings on your shoulder blades, the bar code on the back of your neck, the heart behind your right ear, the quote that runs across your upper back, the second set of initials below the angel wings, the rosary beads surrounding your left wrist, and the word *think* underneath your collarbone." I took a breath.

Nine. That I could see, anyway.

Dana grinned. "Point and match."

"Yeah, but what good is having an eidetic memory?" I asked her. "I mean, I get how it helps with a history test—*if* I've read the chapters..."

Dana walked down to the edge of the sand, where the water lapped back and forth. She glared at it, as if challenging it to surge and ruin her boots. "It helps a lot when you're trying to piece things together. It's also easier to keep track of people when you literally cannot forget a face."

My thoughts skipped back to yesterday afternoon in Harrisburg, and one small face in particular. "Did you guys ever track down that boy? Jeremy?"

Dana frowned. "We found him, but his dad wouldn't let him talk to us for very long."

"What did he say?"

"Same thing he said to you," Dana replied. "An old lady with red eyes came in a van and gave Edmund *medicine* and then took him away. I asked the kid what the van looked like, and he said it was a white one without windows in the back."

"Just like in my dream," I breathed.

Dana turned toward me so swiftly and with such intensity in her eyes that I took an involuntary step backward. "Did you just say like in your *dream*?"

I stared back at her. "Um. Yes?"

"Explain," she demanded.

"Okay. I know it sounds crazy," I started, "but I've been having these dreams about Sasha—"

"It's not crazy," Dana said. "You need to stop thinking of your abilities as *crazy*. And you need to stop looking so worried while you're at it. Being a Greater-Than makes you insanely special. Don't you get that?"

I suspected that I looked worried because I *was* worried. And I did totally get that being a G-T made me insanely special. But despite Dana's hasty reassurances on Saturday night, I was still worried that being a G-T would also make me insane.

Would it happen gradually? I wondered. My compassion and humanity slowly eroding until I was heartless and cruel? Or would it happen suddenly? I'd wake up one morning, just *boom*—with bulgy, crazed eyes and tangled hair, start dressing like Dana in leather, and call people things like "Bubble Gum" and "Scooter."

But I knew with a certainty that I couldn't quite explain that Dana was neither heartless nor cruel. She was rough and tough, and she had no patience for BS, but she wasn't anything like the monstrous descriptions of G-Ts that I'd found on the Internet.

"Dreams are a sign of prescience," she told me, "which is an absolutely *amazing* skill set. Combined with your smell-sensitivity and telekinesis? Seriously, Sunshine, you need to tell me these things—"

"How could I tell you," I countered hotly, "when I can't call you? Also, I thought they were just, you know, dreams. Bad dreams. Nightmares. FYI, I have bouts of gas, and I crave chocolate at certain times of the month. Are either of those things Greater-Than *skill sets*? How about my playing the clarinet and sight-reading music—"

She cut me off. "The dreams and music, yes; the farting and chocolate, no."

"Burping," I corrected her. "I burp. Not..."

She smiled at that, but it was far too swift. "Well, that's a relief, since we've got some significant car time together in our future. And you're right. How could you know?" She exhaled hard. "You'll have to excuse my impatience. Please, just tell me about your dreams."

I looked out at the ocean. "There's this one dream that I keep having—it started the night Sasha disappeared. And it's different from what happened when I was in her room with Calvin. Which was also kind of like a dream, but not really since my eyes were open and I was awake—"

"Oh, my God," Dana interrupted me again. "You have *visions* too?"

I stared back at her. "Maybe...?" I said.

"Right, how do you know?" She allowed me that. "Okay, here's how it works. Some of us, like me, are mildly prescient—very mildly. Like back in Harrisburg when that boy was there and I knew he had information. For me, it's just something that happens. Ironically, I can't predict *when* it's going to happen, and I can't *make* it happen. It just...does. Sometimes I just *know* things."

She nodded, her conviction absolute. "I *know*. But it's never anything big or particularly helpful like, *buy a lottery ticket with these five numbers*. Because for me, it doesn't have anything to do with something that's about to happen. Like, I don't *know* where or when lightning is going to strike. But—maybe—if we're looking for the tree that the lightning *did* strike, past tense, I can kinda charge through the woods and *know* where to find it. Are you following?"

I nodded.

"But a true prescient," Dana said, "can foretell the future. And I probably shouldn't say *the* future, but rather *a* future. Because if you know what's coming, you can work to change it, instead of just lying down and waiting to die. Lotta people who are prescient get scared by the idea that they can't change their fate, but it's totally flexible, so don't panic."

"Not panicking," I said, pointing to myself.

"Good," she said. "Most prescients see the future via their dreams, because the power is strongest when you sleep. It gets a little tricky, though, because the unconscious mind can add filler. Which can make the prescient messages kinda cryptic and challenging to decipher. But some powerful prescients also have waking dreams or visions. Although it just occurred to me that it's entirely possible you're not prescient, but psychic, which is also very cool. Prescient means your dreams and visions are about things that haven't happened yet. Psychic means you see events that have already occurred, or maybe even as they're occurring."

I nodded. "I think I might be psychic," I said, "because in my dreams, Sasha is alive."

"Start with the sleeping dreams," Dana said. "What happens in those?"

I told her about the highway—about how I had seen Sasha standing out in the rain and fog. I described the field and then the beeping sounds of the hospital heart monitor and the white-and-blue dress that Sasha always wore.

Dana nodded. "That's really good, Sky. Good detail. And I think you're right—that you're psychic, not prescient. When it happens again, make sure you write it all down, so we can all work together to figure out what it means. Okay?"

"Okay," I said.

"Now tell me about the other thing. The vision."

I explained to Dana how I'd seen the creature that I now thought of as the old lady in Sasha's room, on the night Sasha disappeared. I told her about the feeling I'd had when I spotted her—how it was almost like watching a low-res video online. I also told her how much it had scared me. And I reminded her about the sewage smell.

Dana looked grim. She nodded. "You have no idea how helpful this is going to be."

"So…you believe me," I said, and I have to admit, my tone was a tad challenging.

She smiled. "I do. About stuff like this? I'll always be the dead last person to doubt you."

I had to admit it: Having someone like Dana around felt good. Her lack of skepticism was refreshing. Nothing seemed to surprise her.

Or almost nothing, anyway.

"But you still don't believe what I said about Calvin and me?" I pushed.

She smiled again. "You *are* a pit bull, aren't you?" She sighed. "And no," she told me. "I believe you about that too. You were right. We have to trust each other—about everything."

But we didn't particularly have to like each other—she didn't say it, but I knew she was thinking it. Except as I stood there, looking back at her, I found myself…liking her. And wishing that she liked me too.

I focused on the conversation we were having out loud. "So do you think this old lady is the same one Jeremy saw with Edmund and the white van?" I asked, and shuddered a little at the memory of that pale skin and those scary eyes.

"What do you think?" Dana asked.

"I think it's not a coincidence," I said without hesitation. "Whoever she is, she's evil. And I think if we can find her…"

Dana finished for me. "We can stop her from stealing and killing the next little girl."

I watched waves crash onto the shore and swallowed. "Dana?"

"Yeah?"

"Do you think there's a chance that…maybe I *am* prescient, and… Sasha's still alive?"

Dana looked out at the water. Her eyes were glazed and unfocused. She looked profoundly sad.

Then she looked back at me, and it was as if she had snapped herself out of a trance. "No," she said. And her voice was solid with conviction. "The sooner you stop thinking that, the better off you'll be."

CHAPTER THIRTEEN

Today's lesson focused on telekinesis.

I sat with Dana on the sand. The wind had picked up, and I tucked my hair behind my ears.

"I was pretty little when I first started to move things," Dana told me, "It was…ugly. At first." She smiled. "Whenever I got angry or really upset, things would jump around the room." She laughed. "It used to scare the hell out of my dad."

"I'll bet," I said, thinking of my own experience with the hairbrush. I smiled as I imagined it chasing my mom around the house.

"This one time?" Dana told me, still laughing. "I blew out the dining-room window. Just *boom*! It was totally an accident. I had no idea I could do that. I was super pissed about something stupid—I don't even remember what anymore.

"When I was a little older, I realized that if I could channel those intense emotions, I could use them to move things intentionally. But it took serious practice," she continued. "And repetition. I learned to use specific mantras, and… Here's how it works: if you think about a stressful event, and go through the event in detail, your body will react as if it's literally reliving it. Especially if you have an eidetic memory and can focus on the details with as much precision as possible. Scientists have done studies. Your heart rate actually increases, and you even sweat and become breathless. It also increases the presence of adrenaline which, by the way, is your new best friend."

Adrenaline. Best friend. Got it. I nodded. But… "Rewind a sec to those windows breaking," I said, because something about Dana's recollection had struck a nerve. I swallowed hard. *Windows breaking. No explanation.* I'd been there, done that. Or rather, I'd been there while someone else had done that.

"Dana," I said. "You think there are other Greater-Thans around us right now? I mean, not here at the beach. But, just walking around, maybe at school or, you know, out there, in real life?"

Dana nodded. "Of course, Princess. There are plenty of us out there—although most girls don't realize their own powers. Some recognize that they're different and try to repress it. And keep in mind that there are varying degrees of G-T abilities. Some G-Ts can lift a pencil for a second. Big woop, right? They're on one end of the spectrum. On the other are the ones who can blow out windows when they get pissed off."

I nodded. "Last year I met a girl at school, and I'm pretty sure she was on the blow-out-the-windows end of the spectrum. Her name was April."

"Was?" Dana asked. As usual, she didn't miss a detail.

"She kind of…self-destructed." I told Dana briefly about that spring day in the quad when Cal's former friend April brought a pair of handguns into school and starting waving them around. She'd cornered me, and kept saying really weird and creepy things like, "You're one of us."

I'd been certain she was going to kill me and Calvin. But Cal, quiet hero that he was, managed to knock her down with his wheelchair, allowing me to kick her guns away and pin her in place until the police arrived. It had been a seriously crazy day. And that was putting it mildly.

"Just as April went down," I continued, explaining, "all of the cafeteria windows exploded." I swallowed. "It was never explained."

The police had insisted that no shots had been fired, but everyone in school was convinced they were lying, on account of all that broken glass. But if April was a Greater-Than, she definitely could've done it with a blast of her powers.

"I'm assuming the police took this girl away," Dana said grimly.

I nodded. "They shot her with some kind of tranquilizer gun." Right before April had lost consciousness, she'd begged me to kill her.

"Did she ever stand trial?" Dana asked.

"Not that I know of." I tried to remember the rumors that had flown around the school in the weeks following April's meltdown. "She didn't actually hurt anyone. It turned out her guns weren't even loaded. Calvin was pretty sure she just wanted…" It was so awful, I couldn't even say it.

Dana said it for me. "She was committing suicide-by-SWAT-team. She waves weapons around, everyone scatters, police make the scene, she won't drop the gun, so bang, she's dead. Or in this case, bang, she's tranked and delivered to some mental hospital, where they recognize she's a G-T and sell her to the nearest Destiny farm where she's tortured and bled dry. End result's the same. Another girl is dead." She laughed harshly. "A bullet to the head would've been more merciful."

Did April somehow know what was going to happen to her? *Kill me, Skylar! Kill me now! Please!*

I had more questions, but I wasn't sure how to ask. So I started delicately. "April was… Well, she seemed, um… Well, you said it was just a myth, but…"

"Whatever you're dancing around, Cupcake, just say it."

So I did. "Do you think that being a Greater-Than drove her crazy?"

Dana laughed. "Probably," she said. "There are times it drives me freaking crazy."

"I'm serious," I said.

"I am too," she countered. "Look, who knows why this girl tried to end herself? Whatever stresses she was under, did her G-T powers make things worse? Probably. You want a life lesson from her sad story? Learn to control your powers so they don't control you. And you start by giving yourself access to your adrenaline."

"My new best friend," I repeated her earlier words.

"Yup. And like I said, reliving a stressful event can actually produce adrenaline, almost as much as your body makes, living it in real time. Lucky you, we just pinpointed an event that was probably pretty effing stressful. Girl brings guns to school. Windows explode. *That'll* get your blood pumping."

I nodded. My heart was actually beating faster just remembering how scared I'd been.

"But you don't need to use that scenario. It can be anything you want." Dana held up another piece of driftwood. "If I wanted to move this telekinetically, first I'd focus on it and then relive a stressful, adrenaline-inducing scene from my past—but I've found out through trial and error that it doesn't have to be bad stress. Think about times when you've ridden on a roller coaster. You were probably smiling and screaming, but your body was producing adrenaline the same way that it would if you were really heated about something."

I nodded. "That makes sense."

"But it's harder to access those happier feelings," Dana told me. "It's easier, when you're starting, to let yourself get good and mad." She put the piece of driftwood on her lap. "Now. Once you've got that craptastic experience in your mind, which—again—means you've tricked your body into producing adrenaline, then you refocus your attention on the object you're hoping to move."

"Where does the whole mantra thing come into play?"

"Usually, while I'm trying to move something, I'll repeat two or three words. Like I'll pick the object, and then I'll pick the route I intend for the object to take. And I'll look at both and say *here, there; here, there* over and over again." She smiled at the expression on my face. "I know it's a lot to think about, but after a while, once you've practiced enough, it becomes second nature."

"Exactly how long do you think I'll have to practice before it becomes second nature?"

Dana shrugged. She placed the piece of wood on the ground and studied it intently for just a moment. The wood lifted off the sand and sailed into the air, landing several feet in front of us in the ocean. "I don't know. I'm sure it's different for everyone. It took me a few years to really hone it."

"A few *years*?" I watched the piece of driftwood as it dipped and bobbed.

"Who knows? Maybe it'll take you less time. I wasn't working on it twenty-four seven. It was more of a fun hobby than anything else, and I was also really young...a lot younger than you are now."

I sighed. "I hope it doesn't take that long."

"Let's try practicing," Dana said. "You up for it?"

Before I could answer, Dana had stood up. She wiped the sand off her leather pants and turned to look back at a trash barrel, where she used her telekinesis to extract a discarded water bottle. As I watched, she moved it all the way across the beach and into the ocean. She dunked it into the water, then—still not touching it—she unscrewed the cap and held it under the waves, filling it before she screwed the top back on. The bottle then sailed back toward me and settled gently in front of me in the sand.

"Focus on the bottle," Dana commanded. "And think about a moment in your life when your adrenaline spiked. Really think about details. What was the temperature? What did you smell? How did you feel that day? Was there music playing? People talking...?"

I don't know why, but for whatever reason the first images that popped into my head weren't about April. Instead, they were memories of that night seven months ago—the night of the accident. I thought about that narrow, winding New England road. I thought about the trees, and how the moonlight had filtered through the budding spring branches. I thought about the music that had been playing, an old hip-hop song with a driving beat. I'd never liked that song, but Nicole had played it ad nauseum.

I thought about Nicole's tears and anger, about how I'd shouted for her to slow down, about how quickly the road curved into an unexpected bend. And the squealing sound of tires on the asphalt as Nicole attempted to steer us away from the median.

But the more she'd tried to turn, the more the car spun out of control. And then the car had slid sideways, and Nicole looked at me with an expression of utter helplessness before she'd finally sucked in a thin burst of air. Then…impact.

Here on the beach, Dana was saying something to me, but her voice sounded hollow, like she was speaking at the other end of a tunnel.

"…going, Sky," I heard.

But I was on that road in Connecticut in that wreck of a car, next to my best friend who was now bleeding. God, there was so much blood. And I was fishing for a cell phone, but I couldn't find it…It was so dark.

She was gasping, gurgling, struggling to breathe, and I heard someone screaming and screaming and *screaming*, but suddenly it wasn't Nicole in the car; it was Sasha. She was covered in blood, and the terror in her eyes as she screamed was horrible to see.

"…keep going. Open your eyes…"

Heart pounding, I opened them, and I saw the water bottle in front of me, hovering slightly above the surface of the sand. But then, it zoomed up into the air, disappearing from sight.

Sasha's screams still echoed in the corners of my mind. But the beach was quiet, except for the lull of the waves and my labored breathing.

Then, with a *thunk*, the soda bottle fell from the sky and landed at my feet.

"Nice," Dana said.

And that's when I burst into tears.

———

It's important to take a moment here to note that I hardly ever cry.

I mean, seriously. It rarely happens.

The last time I'd let my emotions loose was after Nicole was nearly killed in the accident—and even then I'd made sure I was safely behind my closed bedroom door, where I was spared the embarrassment of anyone witnessing the event.

Last time I cried in public…? That was probably second grade, when Malcolm Murkoff lied to me in art class and told me I'd have to get my head shaved, because the paint that I'd accidentally gotten in my hair was radioactive.

But now I was on the beach bawling my eyes out in front of Ms. Bionic, of all people. *She* probably hadn't let out a wail from the moment her mother birthed her.

Fan-friggin-tastic.

But, try as I might, once the tears started, they didn't want to stop.

Nicole. I'd been thinking about Nicole, but then…I'd *seen Sasha*. Sasha, with blood on her face… She'd looked so scared.

But it was more than just a look. It was as though I'd actually *ingested* her fear…as if the same feelings she was experiencing had traveled into my psyche. I knew how she'd felt—*literally*.

It was a very specific sensation, that kind of conviction. It was more than a feeling—it was an absolute certainty.

I'd heard her voice in my core, and it had whispered breathily, *I'm going to die.*

"I'm… I'm… Oh my God." Gulping in snotty breaths of air, I collapsed onto the sand, pulling my knees in to my chest, sobs racketing through me. "I'm sorry," I managed, burying my face in my hands.

My eyes were closed, but I could feel Dana as she took a step in my direction and then, slowly, sat down beside me. I shook my head, digging the palms of my hands against my eyes as if manually redirecting the tears back where they came from.

"Hey," Dana said softly. I could feel her hand as she placed it gingerly on my shoulder. "Hey."

"I'm so—orry," I hiccupped again miserably.

"Sky, you don't have to apologize." Dana's hand on my shoulder was as much a comfort as it was a surprise. She wasn't exactly the hugging type.

But I couldn't stop crying, and Dana didn't do a thing other than rub her hand gently up and down my back.

Finally, after what felt like hours or even days, I had nothing left.

My sobs quieted, and I pulled my head up. Strands of hair fell into my eyes, and I slowly pushed them away. Staring out at the ocean, I tried to take some deep breaths. My nose was so frigging clogged that I had to open my mouth.

Dana probably thought I was such a loser.

"What did you see?" she asked when she was finally sure my little nervous breakdown had come to a close.

"It was... It was really awful." I forced myself to look over at Dana. Her face was grim. I cleared my throat and braced myself, because I knew once I said the words out loud, it would be even more real than it already was. "I think I just had one of those visions again. I think when I moved that bottle I saw..."

Dana kept her eyes locked intently on mine. "It's okay," she said. "Tell me."

"I think I saw Sasha getting killed."

And there it was.

Dana's eyes grew almost imperceptibly wider for only a fraction of a second. She took back the hand that she'd been using to rub my shoulder and leaned her elbows on her knees as she sat tailor-style in the sand. "I'm sorry you saw that." I could tell that Dana was dying to ask about the details, but she kept her mouth shut to allow me time to process everything.

"I want to catch these bastards," I hissed through gritted teeth. For the first time, I was honestly glad that I was a Greater-Than, because being a G-T was going to help me catch them. "I want them to pay for everything they've done."

"Believe me, kiddo," Dana replied, "we're on the same page."

"She was terrified," I blurted. "God, it was *beyond* terror. She knew she was going to die."

The corner of Dana's eye twitched as I spoke, almost like she wanted to wince but couldn't quite bring herself to show that much emotion.

"But I didn't see who she was looking at," I realized. "No! *No!* I should have turned around, but I wasn't thinking. It didn't even occur to me—"

"You might not have been able to see her killer," Dana tried to reassure me, even though I could tell that she was bitterly disappointed. "Visions are what they are—"

"But I didn't even *try*. What kind of psychic doesn't at least—"

"A beginner," Dana interrupted me again. "You're a beginner, so give yourself a break."

"I don't want to be a beginner," I told her. "I want to be like you! Please teach me everything. *Everything.*"

Dana studied me somberly for a few moments. Her crystal-blue eyes were almost the same color as the sky. "I'll do my best," she replied.

I looked at her and nodded, before turning away and gazing out at a distant pair of sailboats sweeping gracefully across the sparkling, sunlit water. It was difficult to believe that this beautiful world was a terrible place with terrible people.

But that was the truth. Innocent people like Sasha suffered at the hands of the evil and the greedy and then… Oh, God, I missed Sasha so much.…

Dana's voice jolted me out of my thoughts. "Bubble Gum, it's gonna take time."

I exhaled hard. "Still. There must be some exercises I can do while I'm at home—"

"I'm not talking about your training," she said. "I'm talking about…" She cleared her throat. "The way you feel. It's gonna take some serious time before it fades. And every second until it does is gonna suck. But it *will* get easier. One morning you'll wake up and you'll be able to breathe again. I promise."

Anyone else giving me that spiel would have been offered a swift eye roll. But it was Dana. And something about the way she spoke those words made me feel like she knew a thing or two about grief as well. Also, that cinnamon I could smell? It didn't lie.

"Come on, Bubble Gum," Dana said, standing up and brushing the sand off her leather pants. She offered me a hand and I took it, giving her permission to pull me up. "Let's get going. I think this is enough for one day."

"But I barely even—"

Dana shook her head quickly, dismissing my thought before I could spit it out. "Doesn't matter. You did more than you think. Remember—always do your best. Never more than that."

"Never more than my best?" I asked, laughing a little at the thought.

"Exactly." Dana didn't say anything else about it, so I just nodded. "Come on." She pointed to the road ahead.

We walked a little bit in silence. My head pounded from crying so hard, and I was exhausted.

"I think what you did earlier was really cool, by the way," Dana mentioned. "When you were honest about the fact that my bike made you uncomfortable. It's awesome that you admitted you were afraid. Not a lot of people are willing to do that."

I didn't know what to say, so I didn't say anything.

"The deal is," Dana continued, "that nobody can face their fear until they admit that they're afraid."

She must've sensed my skepticism, because she kept going. "Courage isn't being invincible, Sky. It's knowing that you're not, and taking risks anyway. It's knowing you're afraid, and taking action regardless."

I nodded.

"We'll get you on that bike," Dana promised, slapping me cheerfully on the back. "I promise."

Yay? I started to pull out my cell phone to call Calvin to come pick us up.

But Dana stopped me. "Don't call Scooter," she said.

"Why? He's our only way home."

"Not true," she said, marching back toward the main road. "You said you want me to teach you everything, right?"

"Right."

"Today, I'm going to teach you a little bit about public transportation."

And with that, I followed Dana to a nearby bench, where we sat and waited patiently for what would officially be the first public bus ride of my life.

CHAPTER FOURTEEN

After we made it back to the school parking lot, Dana took off on her bike and I started walking home.

I hadn't had a chance to look in a mirror, but I hoped and prayed I didn't look too swollen and miserable from all the crying. All I needed to make my day complete was the third degree from my mother when I got home. Although I realized that a little honesty would shut her down cold if I said *the reality of Sasha's death finally hit me*. And maybe, in sympathy, she'd let me stay out an extra half hour on Saturday night.

Yeah, dream on.

My cell phone rang and I fished it out of my pocket.

"How was training with GI Jane today?" Cal asked eagerly. "Did she make you yell *Sir, yes, sir!* and run down the beach carrying a telephone pole up over your head?"

I laughed despite myself. "She's not training me to be a Navy SEAL."

"Still…"

"I don't want to talk about it," I said. I kicked a branch across the sidewalk, remembering how I'd moved the bottle…and the vision of Sasha that had appeared in my mind as a result.

"Eh, you suck," Cal replied cheerfully. "Be that way. I'm really calling because my homework was killing me and I needed a caffeine infusion. So I came to CoffeeBoy and…"

He didn't need to finish. "Oh, no."

"Yep. Your mom's back. So is Jolly Ol' Jenkins."

I nearly choked. "Please tell me you're kidding."

"Wish I were," Cal said apologetically. "Man, they've gotta work on finding a different place for their little rendezvous, 'cause this is my damn CoffeeBoy. It's the only one around here that still has hazelnut."

"Are they *seriously* together together? I mean, maybe they just happened to walk in at the same time."

"Doubtful," Cal said quietly. "Wait a sec. I'm gonna try to see what they're talking about."

"Okay," I whispered back, keeping the phone pinned to my ear as I kept walking.

There was a moment of silence, and then Calvin's voice: "Hey, hey, hey! Ms. Reid! What's up?"

I heard my mom's voice, but couldn't quite make out what she said.

"Yeah," Cal answered her. "Just taking a break from the homework stuff."

Then Mr. Jenkins said something. His voice was as muffled as Mom's had been—but it was definitely Jenkins. His tone cut through.

"Oh, yeah," Calvin responded. "Practice makes perfect, right?" A fake laugh. "Alrighty, then. Have a good one!"

There was another brief pause, and then I heard Cal order his coffee. I waited for him to leave the shop.

"I'm back," Cal finally said into his phone.

"What happened?" I tried to prepare myself for the worst.

"Well, they were huddled in that same corner again," Calvin replied. "I tried to roll up quietly, but like I said before, I'm kind of conspicuous. Anyway, I only heard a tiny bit of their conversation."

"And?"

Cal cleared his throat. "Man, it was weird. It's like, I don't know exactly what they said. But they were definitely taking about *you.*"

"Me?"

"Yeah," Calvin replied, and laughed a little bit. "Talk about a parent-teacher conference, huh?"

"Ugh."

"So, I heard your name mentioned, and your mom was looking all concerned, like they were discussing something really serious. And… sit down for this. Jenkins had his hand on your mom's back, and he was rubbing her shoulders."

I stopped walking and stood in the middle of the sidewalk with my mouth hanging open. "What?"

"I know. It's nasty."

"Nuh-uh. It's *more* than just nasty. It's…*unacceptable!* Don't they have laws for that kind of thing?"

"Laws?" Cal asked.

"I don't know!" I sputtered. "It just seems so…*wrong* for a teacher and a parent to…do whatever it is they're doing. They must have laws for that."

I could hear Calvin as he started his car. "Unfortunately, it's not illegal. They jumped apart when I rolled up."

I shuddered at the very thought of Jenkins and Mom touching, kissing…having sex. I had this sudden awful, vivid image of my mom in her giant bathtub with bubbles up to her neck, and Jenkins in the doorway with only a towel around his waist, holding two glasses of champagne—and please, *please* God, let that have been my imagination and not some psychic vision.

"Anyway," Cal was saying, "you never know. He might have just been giving your mom some friendly parenting tips."

"Right," I retorted, "because he really strikes me as the parental type."

"Or," Calvin continued, "maybe your mom is trading sex to get you back into first-chair clarinet."

"Wow," I said, "that's even more awful than she's lonely and desperate—which is awful enough. Plus? If that is what she's doing, it's not working. And speaking of not working, you should really stop wearing that hat. It looks ridiculous on you."

"What hat?" Cal asked, his voice cautious.

"The hat that you're wearing. You know, the little navy blue one. It makes you look like a disgruntled train conductor."

Cal scoffed. "Girl, first off, I'll disgruntle your ass if you don't watch it. And second, how did you know I was wearing it? I just put it on."

I paused. "Wait, what?"

"The hat. I just put the hat on. I couldn't find it forever, but it was tucked in between my wheelchair ramp and the driver's seat. I don't know how I spotted that shizz. It blended in."

I closed my eyes and did what I'd done earlier when I'd counted Dana's tattoos from memory. I visualized Calvin's car, down to the last detail—the rosary beads hanging from the rearview mirror, the pockmarks in the steering wheel from where Cal had picked away at pieces of the outer lining, the cup holders... Right now, there was a CoffeeBoy cup in one, Cal's house keys in the other.

I focused, and I could see his e-reader lying on the floor, its screen saver flashing the message: *You are reading Modern Geometry, page 654.* Next to that was his unzipped backpack. A red sweatshirt stuck out from the largest pocket.

Tucked into the space in the car's dash, where there should have been a car lighter, were receipts of various sizes and colors. I honed in on the top receipt, closing my eyes and reading.

The print on the page was blotchy, as though the ink cartridge from the cash register was running on empty. But it was unmistakable. It was the CoffeeBoy logo, followed by today's date.

"That's insane," I mumbled, and opened my eyes.

"What's insane?"

"I can see you."

"Girl, quit playing. Where are you?"

"I'm walking to my house right now. Just left the school. But there are no cars around. And I can't *see* you see you. But I can definitely see you."

"Yup. You're definitely insane."

"I'm not joking."

"Well, I know that," Cal said, sighing. "And a week ago, I'd have

said that what you claim to be doing right now is impossible, but…
you have a tendency lately to prove me wrong."

I closed my eyes again, willing myself to envision more details about
real-time Calvin, but just as quickly it had appeared, it all vanished—
like I'd pressed the stop button on a DVD.

"Oh, man," I said.

"Would you mind telling me what's going on?" Cal asked.

"I just had another vision," I said. I giggled a little bit. "But I had
it in real time. Wow! It's like I just mentally vurped you!"

"Should I feel kind of violated?"

"Vurp," I repeated. "Like, video conferencing. They still have it
up north—"

"Vurp you," Calvin said. "I know what vurping is. I was making
a joke—"

I interrupted him. "I've gotta get in touch with Dana again, A-SAP!"

"A'ight," Calvin said. "But first can you puh-lease tell me where
you are so I can come pick you up? I've got an unfinished homework
assignment just waiting for you."

"I'm not doing your homework for you," I replied. "But if you
want, you can pick me up and I'll help you with it. I'm on Pineapple
Boulevard, two blocks down from the school."

"Dang," Cal said. "You really *did* have a vision. I'm nowhere near
you. All right, just hang tight and I'll be there in ten."

I hadn't been waiting long when a car slowed.

I was lost in seriously disturbing thoughts of Mom and Mr.

Jenkins, so I didn't notice it wasn't Calvin until after I'd scrambled to my feet.

"Hey, I thought that was you," Garrett said from his father's convertible. He was alone in the car. "Need a ride?"

"Nope," I said, feeling no need to add a polite *thank you* as I folded my arms across my less-than-voluptuous chest.

He hadn't bothered to pull over—he'd just stopped right there in the middle of the street, and cars rushed by, some of them honking, others slowing and sneaking around him.

But Garrett didn't seem concerned about inconveniencing anyone. "Seriously," he said, leaning over, pushing open the passenger door, and giving me what he no doubt thought was his sexiest smile. "Get in. I'll drive you home."

I had to step back to avoid getting bumped by the door. "Seriously," I said. "No. Calvin's coming to pick me up. So…move it along, Tic-Tac dick."

It was Dana's line, but I didn't think she'd mind my borrowing it.

Garrett's eyes got disturbingly cold, and there was something ominous and dangerous in his voice as he said, "What's *your* problem? I'm nice enough to offer you a ride, and all you can do is be *rude?*"

Rude? *I* was rude? Of course, he had no idea that I'd overheard him saying all those awful things to Calvin.

A white van with a ridiculous cartoon dog on the side lurched by, its tires squealing, startling me, and my heart started to pound.

Still, I swallowed my anxiety and stood there on the sidewalk, ready to give Garrett a serious piece of my mind.

But before I could open my mouth to speak, I caught a whiff of something as familiar as it was foul.

The sewage smell. It was back. With a vengeance.

I looked at Garrett. And smelled the sewage.

Garrett. Sewage. Garrett and *sewage*.

"Get away from me," I said, my voice low with emotion. I could feel my heart hammering a rhythm inside my chest, as my stomach heaved and churned.

And I couldn't stop myself. I turned and puked, right there on the sidewalk.

"Gross," Garrett said, reaching over to slam the car door shut. Without another word, he hit the gas and sped away.

By the time Cal pulled up, five short minutes later, I was fine.

"I need to go to the beach," I told him as he pulled away from the curb. "Can we go there?"

Calvin looked surprised for a moment, but then adjusted his ridiculous hat and nodded. "Okay, but could you fill me in, please? I'm feeling a little out of the loop here. And you look like you've seen a ghost."

I pushed Cal's backpack to the side so my feet had more room. His e-reader was still flashing that info about page 654 of his geometry text, and I shoved the thing into his backpack, pushing his sweatshirt down too and zipping the pack shut. "Okay. First of all, I just had a run-in with Garrett."

Calvin's expression didn't change, but I felt the tension in the air multiply exponentially.

"He stopped and offered me a ride. And you were right about him, by the way. Not that I need to convince you, but he's definitely douche-tastic. *Beyond* douche-tastic, actually." I rubbed a hand over my eyes. "Cal, I think he might be dangerous."

Calvin shot me a look that was steely. "Did he hurt you?"

"What? No! Of course not. I wouldn't let that happen."

Calvin nodded, his jaw clenched.

I glanced anxiously out the window. "But that awful smell came back. It was so bad that I threw up."

"On Garrett?" he asked hopefully, before he realized that probably wasn't the question he was supposed to ask. He reached down into a pocket in the driver's side door and pulled out an unopened bottle of water, handing it to me. "Are you okay?"

"*No*, to Garrett," I told him as I gratefully opened the bottle and took a long, refreshing drink. "And *yes*, to okay. I think the smell hit me harder than it did before, because of what happened during training." I told him about the vision I'd had of Sasha, and the muscles jumped in his jaw. "But you know what it means, don't you—the smell?" I came back to what had happened with Garrett. "Dana and Milo told us to watch out for it. The sewage. That smell represents *pure evil.*"

Calvin looked skeptical for only a moment. Then he pulled on the brim of his blue hat and sighed. I knew he had no choice but to believe me. "So explain how any of this calls for a walk on the beach."

"I think that Garrett spends most of his time over at his dad's house. It's waterfront property. He brought me there on Saturday when he was trying to impress me."

Calvin grunted.

"I just… If that smell was so strong when he drove up today… maybe there's a connection. Maybe Garrett had something to do with Sasha's murder." I glanced at Calvin. He was back to looking skeptical.

"I don't know, dude. Garrett as the homicidal, conspiratorial drug dealer slash kidnapper slash little-girl killer? I mean, he's douche-y to the max, but I think you're giving him a little too much credit. If that makes any sense."

Garrett was way too much of a himbo to be a criminal mastermind, even if he'd wanted to be. "It does. But it still doesn't explain why I smelled the nasty smell when I was talking to him today."

Calvin almost pulled into the public beach, but I motioned for him to keep driving straight.

"It's down this way," I said, remembering the route that Garrett had taken.

We drove past the long beach reeds before arriving at the end of the sandy path. The mansion loomed several hundred feet to our right. The late-afternoon sunlight reflected across its garish windows. Garrett's midlife-crisis convertible was parked in the semicircular driveway.

Calvin whistled. "Man, really?" he mumbled as he stared at the massive house. "I think we get it already. You've got money. You've got a lot of money. Shee-it."

I nodded my agreement. "It's obnoxious."

Calvin pulled to the side of the road and put his car into Park. We were far enough away so that if Garrett stepped out of his house or even looked out the windows, he wouldn't be able to see us lurking there. Calvin lowered my window. "Smell anything? And do lean out of the car if your answer is *ralph*."

But I shook my head. Unfortunately, we were also far enough away so that I couldn't detect the stench as I had earlier. "Nope," I said, popping the *P*.

"Do you think we should get closer?" Calvin said, sounding like that was the last thing he wanted to do.

"I don't know," I replied. I unclicked my seat belt so that I could have more room to bring my feet up beneath me on the passenger seat. "I mean, what if Garrett really is dangerous?"

Calvin tapped his fingers on his steering wheel and stared at the mansion. "Maybe we should wait and talk to Dana about this."

I exhaled my frustration. "So, now what? We do nothing until she feels like showing up again?"

"We could go into Harrisburg," Calvin suggested. "See if she and Milo are looking for Edmund—Whoa, wait. Sky. Look."

I lifted my head to see that someone had exited the house.

It wasn't Garrett. It was a man, probably in his late forties or early fifties. He had the same dark hair as Garrett, and he wore dark sunglasses and a black suit, and held a cell phone to his ear. With swift movements, he beeped open the BMW convertible before hopping into the car and pulling out of the driveway.

Calvin and I both realized it at the same time—he was heading straight toward us. We both ducked down in our seats as he went sailing past.

"Isn't that the car that Garrett drives?" Cal asked.

I nodded.

"So, that was probably his pops, right?"

"I'm assuming," I replied. "What about it?"

"Well," Cal said, his voice rising with excitement, "what if you really did smell what you smelled, but it wasn't Garrett who smelled?"

I looked at Calvin. "You mean…?"

"What if Garrett isn't the dangerous one?" Calvin asked, his eyes wide. "What if the person we have to worry about, the person who helped kidnap and kill Sasha, is Garrett's dad?"

CHAPTER FIFTEEN

It was no use. Calvin wanted to talk to Dana before we did any more *investigating.*

I couldn't help but be pissed as Cal dropped me off around the corner from my house.

"Call me if Momzilla announces her plans to marry Jenkins," he said, leaning over as I opened the passenger door and got out of his car. "I wanna be ring bearer."

"Oh my God," I said. "Don't even *think* about that."

"And don't do anything stupid," he added, urgency lining his playful tone. He didn't want me to try *investigating* without him, either.

"All right, Mom," I said sarcastically.

"Ouch!" Calvin said, and grabbed at his chest as if I'd just stabbed him.

I waved a dismissive hand at him as I closed the car door.

"Love you too," Cal called out the open window before he dazzled me with a smile and took off.

Meanwhile, Mom was home, which was another kind of bummer.

When I stepped into the house, she was already calling my name. "Sky? Is that you?"

"No, it's the neighborhood serial killer," I replied sullenly.

"Oh, good! You're back!" she called from the kitchen.

Oh, joy.

I pulled my cell phone out of my pocket. If she was still tracking me (why would she *not*?), Mom knew exactly where I had been. Not that it was a problem. I hadn't made any trips to Harrisburg that afternoon, so it's not like she had anything to gripe about.

"I'm cooking spaghetti and meatballs," Mom trilled. "It'll be ready in about twenty minutes."

I stepped into the kitchen. "Not hungry," I informed her.

Mom was leaning over a big pot on the stove. Her hair was swept up off her face, and diamond studs glinted on her ears as she stirred the pasta. I found myself wondering if she was wearing her good jewelry for Jenkins.

"But it's your favorite!" Mom protested.

Part of me wanted to challenge her and ask when she was going to tell me she was dating Jenkins. But a bigger part of me was hoping she'd just never bring it up. Ever.

My phone buzzed in my hand with a new text message from Calvin. FYI: Brooding sidekick was waiting at my door...wants to go for a car ride. You down?

I paused and then texted him back, glancing up at Mom. You mean, WITH your mom?

There was a pause, then Cal texted back: YES. He included a photo of himself that Mom would interpret as a silly face, but I knew was a silent *sorry*.

In the photo, over Cal's shoulder, I saw a familiar flash of dimples as Milo photobombed. And suddenly that "brooding sidekick" made sense. "Mom, I can't have dinner right now. I need to work on a homework assignment with Cal—it's due tomorrow. Sorry."

Mom looked disappointed and maybe even a little relieved as she nodded. "All right, sweetie. What time will you be home?"

I rolled my eyes and texted Calvin that I'd be over in ten minutes. After I looked up from my phone, I answered her. "I don't know. Couple hours. Ten thirty at the latest?"

Mom pursed her lips before forcing a smile. "Just please be careful. And bring your phone."

I nodded, making sure she witnessed the irritation written all over my face before I ran upstairs to change.

It took me a few minutes to figure out what to wear. I finally chose a black tank top and light denim jeans, with black sparkly sandals and a thin black headband. My earrings were little diamond hearts that my mom had bought me for my fifteenth birthday.

I raced out of the house, yelling *bye* and slamming the door before Mom had a chance to respond.

As I walked down our street, the breeze flirted with me. Strands of my curls drifted pleasantly against my neck. Another beautiful day was coming to an end on Coconut Key. I wondered why I was lucky enough to enjoy it…and why Sasha hadn't been as fortunate.

Mr. McMahon stood outside with a green garden hose, watering an already perfect emerald expanse of lawn. He waved to me as I walked by, his khaki pants worn high enough around his waist to graze his nipples. Old people.

I waved back and kept walking.

Further down was Sasha's house. The driveway was empty and the lawn was already overgrown.

I kept my head down the rest of the way as I walked silently to Calvin's house.

When I got there, Calvin's mom, Stephanie, was outside in jean cutoffs and a bathing-suit top, inspecting her tomato plant which had yet to produce any tomatoes.

When she saw me walking up the driveway, Stephanie came right over and hugged me. "Girl, where have you *been?*"

"It's been a rough couple of weeks," I said.

Stephanie nodded, her arm slung over my shoulders. "I know, baby. How are you holding up?"

I shrugged, afraid that if I opened my mouth I would cry again. I was on a roll today.

"I've been sending out prayers and more prayers that there's been some kind of terrible mistake, " she continued. "I'm pretty much stalking God, and he's starting to get all weirded out, but it's all I can do. I know you loved that little girl."

I nodded as we walked inside. Being around Stephanie was refreshing. She was more like an awesome friend than a mom type.

Calvin's house smelled like sugar and gingerbread. I inhaled appreciatively. Despite the hours of effort that my mom devoted, attempting to be Suzy Homemaker, Cal's house was more like a home than mine had ever been. And it was all so refreshingly effortless. When I was over here, I felt like I could move around without fear of breaking something.

"Sky!" Calvin called from the family room.

"Hey!" I called back.

"Water? Juice? Milk?" Stephanie asked as she let go of my shoulder.

"I'm fine, but thanks," I replied.

Stephanie pressed two fingers to her lips before planting the same fingers on my forehead. "Be safe when y'all go out with your ridiculously handsome new friend," she added.

"Will do," I said, but I think I blushed, because Stephanie laughed a little and said, "Hmm," as she went into the kitchen.

I headed down the hallway to the family room. Calvin was reclined in his wheelchair, fingers gripping the controller for his newest video game. He pressed buttons furiously as he stared at the TV screen. "You made it," he said without looking away from whatever battle he was fighting.

Milo was on the couch near Cal. He was leaning forward, elbows resting atop his knees as he observed Cal's video-game drama. When I stepped into the room, Milo sat up straight and looked at me, and Stephanie's words echoed in my head: "ridiculously handsome new friend." Milo *was* ridiculously handsome. But he was also Dana's boyfriend. "Skylar," he said.

"Hey, Milo." I was suddenly uncomfortably aware of the effort I'd made in changing out of my school clothes. Would I have bothered to change if I was just going to see Cal?

Calvin kept playing his game. "Okay, so apparently we're going to go pick Dana up at a super-confidential undisclosed location," he explained as he pressed a button on his controller. "Anyway, I'm going to let Milo explain a little more, 'cause I'm not following exactly why we're about to go play cat-and-mouse."

Milo's eyes were solemn as he gazed at me. "Dana told me about your dreams and psychic visions," he said, and somehow the statement was so profoundly personal that I blushed. "She thinks they're significant. And I do too. We want to try to locate the places that you've seen." He paused. "But first, Dana wants you to…find her."

"Find her?" I asked.

Calvin nodded, eyes on the screen. "Like the weirdest game of hide-and-seek ever."

The edge of Milo's mouth curved up into a half smile. "It's an exercise in something called *homing*. Dana is really excited about your ability. She wants you to explore it a bit. See exactly what you can and can't do."

"But I honestly don't know where she is!" I protested.

"I think you'll find that you do," Milo said as he gazed up at me with his pretty eyes.

I laughed as I forced myself to look away. "We'll see," I said. "But I have a feeling this is going to be a wild-goose chase."

"I second that," Calvin said.

Milo didn't seem fazed by my lack of confidence. "We should get going sooner rather than later. Although I'm glad that we're heading out as it gets dark, because the highway that you'd mentioned in your dream… You saw Sasha there at nighttime, correct?"

"Yeah."

Milo took a piece of gum out of his pocket and popped it into his mouth. "I think it's going to be easier for you to identify the location if all of the surrounding details are as similar to your dream as possible."

"Can you make it rain?" I joked. "Because it was raining in my dream."

"Ask Dana. *She* probably can," Calvin said, his tone deadpan as he finally shut off his video game. He looked up at me. "Did you remember to forget your cell phone at home?"

Milo raised a quizzical eyebrow.

"Actually, I remembered to bring it. But I'm going to deliberately forget it right here in your family room before we leave." As I said the words, I took my cell out of my pocket and placed it on the table.

Milo looked perplexed, so I told him about Mom's little GPS-tracking project as we left the house.

I heard Stephanie vaguely call, "Love y'all," before Cal closed and locked the front door.

I assumed that Milo would ride shotgun, since he was the new guy and all. But when we got to Cal's car, Milo opened the front passenger door and motioned for me to get in.

"A gentleman," Cal noted.

Normally, the little gesture would have resulted in an eye roll from me. But coming from Milo, there was something genuinely unpretentious and old school about it. I smiled at him for a second, until he smiled back. Those dimples creased on either side of his face, and I looked away fast as he closed my door for me. Dana's boyfriend. *Dana's* boyfriend.

"All right, Ms. Omniscient," Cal said as he waited for his wheelchair ramp to completely lock him into the driver's seat. "Right or left out of the driveway?"

"Left," I said automatically, and then covered my mouth with my hand.

"Left it is," Milo replied, leaning forward into the front seat, his hands draped over the backs of both headrests.

He was close enough that I could smell that vanilla aroma again, and I kept my breathing shallow, which only resulted in my heartbeat speeding up. Pretty soon my face was heating up again, and I coughed and swallowed.

"You all right?" Cal said, glancing at me as he took the left turn out of the driveway and down our street, back the way I had come.

"Fine," I said casually. We passed Sasha's, and my attention was temporarily diverted as I stared at the empty house.

"Girl, you better duck," Cal said, and I looked up just in time to see my mother standing out on our driveway. Her arms were crossed.

"Crap!" I said, and hunkered down quickly. "What is she doing?"

Calvin shook his head and zipped by. "It looks like she's waiting for somebody. She didn't see us, though. At least I don't think she did."

"Dammit," I said. "Why would I make us drive this way? I *knew* I shouldn't push my luck."

"Like I said, I think you're in the clear. Anyway, don't worry about it for right now. You won't have to deal with her 'til you get back."

"You're fairly frightened of your mother," Milo said. His observation was made into a question by the quizzical tone of his voice.

I didn't turn around to look at him. "*Frightened* is a pretty strong word," I replied. "It's not like she going to, you know, throw me in a closet and beat me with a belt or anything."

"I am immeasurably relieved to hear that," Milo said.

Calvin burst out laughing. "Man, you crack me up!"

But when I finally did look back at Milo, I realized that he wasn't being sarcastic. He really was *immeasurably relieved,* and I found myself wondering if maybe his mother *had* locked him in closets or beaten him with belts. But how exactly do you ask someone about something awful like that?

"A'ight," Cal said as he pulled up to a stop sign. "We're at a four-way here. Where should I be turning? *Should* I be turning?"

"Go straight," I blurted again.

Cal checked his rearview mirror, and Milo nodded at him.

The sun was beginning to set, and Coconut Key lingered in that ethereal dusk state. The light was almost unbearably bright as you headed west, but people heading east had already turned their headlights on, because the shadows were getting darker in that direction. We were driving south, which meant that the insistent glare whacked us from the right side.

I squinted and held my hand up to my window, watching as kids in a nearby yard ran through a sprinkler. Their little squeals penetrated the car, and Calvin smiled a little as we drove past.

My own heart filled with sadness as I thought about Sasha. She would never again enjoy a carefree moment like that.

"Take a left," I said, the sadness drowned out by an urgent pull on my brain—almost like a mental magnet.

"Left turn," Milo verified.

Calvin pulled out onto the main drag, and we picked up speed, traveling across town. He kept glancing at me, but the pull was telling me to keep heading straight, until it—and I—said, "Slow down. Take a right, up here."

This time Calvin didn't look back at Milo. He just turned down a smaller side street.

And then something really weird happened.

The sky opened up. And it started to pour.

"Huh. Well, maybe Dana heard what you said about making it rain," Calvin replied, switching on the windshield wipers.

I knew that Milo was watching me, and I didn't have to turn around to prove it. I could feel his eyes on me. I glanced outside at the darkening sky and the houses—most of them much smaller than those in my immediate neighborhood. It wasn't Harrisburg, but the people living in this part of town were obviously in financial trouble. "I've never been down here before," I pointed out, feeling a need to repeat, "Never."

"That's okay. Where should we go now?" Milo's voice was calm.

"When you get to the end of the road, take a right. Diner."

"Diner?" Cal asked.

I had no idea why I'd said that.

Until Calvin took that right and ended up smack dab in front of a little hole-in-the-wall restaurant with a neon sign out front blinking the letters *D I E R*. The *N* had fizzled out long ago.

"Diner," I verified with a shrug.

Milo smiled again and looked through the windshield.

I followed his gaze. Dana's motorcycle was parked out front.

"Marco!" Cal yelled out gleefully as he saw it too. He parked beside it.

"That's craziness," I said to Milo. "I've seriously never been here before." I turned to Calvin. "Do you believe me now?"

Calvin just shook his head.

"It's not craziness," Milo corrected me. "It's psychic. Like I said before, it's something called homing. You homed in on Dana, and you led us to her."

So this meant that I was psychic. I could see things that had already happened—or things that were happening at that moment. As opposed to being prescient, which would've meant I could see the future.

Which also meant that even though Sasha seemed to be alive in my dreams and visions, she was, in fact, already dead.

Unlike on the beach, this time I didn't burst into tears. But I wanted to. "Wait here," I told Calvin and Milo. There was no point in us all getting wet. "I'll get Dana."

But she must've been watching for us, because she was already coming out of the door and down the steps, heading swiftly for the car.

"Took you long enough," Dana commented gruffly as she climbed in, shaking off water as she pulled her red bomber jacket from her shoulders and draped it across her lap.

"Sorry I couldn't *psychic* my way over here any faster," I replied.

"I'm pretty sure *psychic* isn't a verb," Cal pointed out.

"It is now."

Dana's eyes widened slightly as she looked from me to Milo and asked, "Did she really...?"

"She did," Milo said, smiling at me.

"Well, hot damn, Bubble Gum," Dana said, slapping me congenially on the back. "Good job. Let's see you work that mojo again. If you can find me, you can find those places you've been dreaming about."

"I'll try," I said uncertainly.

"You'll do your best," Dana said, locking eyes with mine.

I nodded intently. "I'll do my best."

We hit the road, heading back to the main drag as Cal's car echoed with the rain's noisy drumming. I called out directions as I let myself be pulled again by that mental magnet.

"Take a right here," I said to Calvin after we'd driven for a while.

"That's I-75," Cal said. "You sure you want to get on the highway?"

"Just do what she says, Scoot," Dana answered for me, her voice impatient.

Calvin sighed dramatically and pulled onto the ramp. I looked around as we merged onto the four-lane interstate, heading north. But this wasn't the highway from my dreams.

Still, we drove in silence for about fifteen minutes as the rain poured down.

"No," I said finally. "The trees are all wrong. In my dream, there weren't any palm trees and…it was different. It felt different, it smelled different…" I searched for that same mental magnet that had led me to Dana, and oddly enough, I could still feel it faintly back there. "I mean, if I didn't have a curfew, I'd want to keep going in this direction, but…I really don't know for how long or how far."

"You're sure?" Dana asked, her voice intensely calm. "Dreams can be weird."

"I'm one hundred and fifty percent positive that this is not where my dreams have been taking place. This absolutely isn't it." As I turned in my seat, I could see that Milo seemed frustrated, but he didn't say a word.

"I'm sorry," I added. And I was. What was the point of being psychic if I couldn't use my dreams to lead us to the people who'd killed Sasha?

"It's not your fault," Milo insisted quietly. "It's not a perfect science."

"Whatever," Dana added as Calvin took the exit and looped over the highway to head back south. "It was worth a try. We'll just have to wait for you to have another dream or vision, and hope we get some information—"

"I had another waking vision," I told her. "It was right after our training session, after you left me at the school. I saw Calvin in real time."

"You what?" Dana's mouth dropped open. Milo stared at me too, looking surprised.

I explained what had happened earlier as Calvin nodded his agreement.

"Bubble Gum. *Please.* You gotta tell me things like that. Right away. Even if it doesn't seem that substantial to you."

"Oh, it was substantial, all right," Cal said fervently. "She could *see* me. If that ever happens again, Bubble Gum, like while I'm in the bathroom or—"

I shut him up with a hard look. That was all I needed—Calvin calling me *Bubble Gum* too. "I meant to tell you as soon as I saw you," I told Dana, "but the homing thing was, well, it took more energy than…" I gave up and just apologized, afraid if I kept trying to explain, I'd start to cry again. "I'm sorry," I said miserably. "There's just so much going on."

Dana sighed and ran a hand through her rain-dampened hair. "It's all right. Just please mention these things to me from now on, okay? Remember. I can do a lot of things, but reading your mind isn't one of them."

Cal shot me a knowing look. "You should also tell her dot dot dot…"

I nodded. "I smelled sewage again."

Dana looked like she couldn't decide whether to look extremely excited or gravely pissed. She tried for an expression that combined the two.

It worked.

I went on to explain our suspicions about Garrett's dad. Then I explained how Cal and I had driven to Mr. Hathaway's beach house to sniff out more clues.

"But I didn't think it would be a good idea to keep investigating without you there," Cal added. Way to suck up to Dana.

"So," Dana said, folding her arms over her chest and sitting back in the seat. "Obviously we need to get ourselves over to Garrett's beach house for a little sneak-and-peek. And soon. But tomorrow Milo and I have something more pressing on our schedule."

Milo spoke up. "That can wait."

She looked at him, annoyed. "No, it can't."

"Dana wants to break into the police evidence locker," Milo told us.

She rolled her eyes at him. "You make it sound both harder and more dangerous than it is. All I have to do is mind-control some weak-willed cop and get him to give me a private tour."

"Merely walking into a police station is dangerous for you," Milo said as he reached into his pocket for a piece of gum. He looked at me and his face was grim. "We don't have NID cards."

I didn't think my eyes could get any wider, but I'm pretty sure they did. NID stood for National ID. Everyone over age twelve was required, by law, to carry their card at all times, and parents were required to carry cards for their kids. Just venturing out of your house without your NID card was dangerous—let alone walking into a police station.

"What's in the evidence locker?" Calvin asked, glancing at Dana in the rearview mirror, and I turned to look at her too.

She'd pushed her arms into the sleeves of her jacket, backward, so that most of the leather material was covering her front like a blanket. It made her look younger and kind of vulnerable. Then she leaned back again, and the moment was gone. Dana was back to being a bad-ass chick.

"That's exactly what I want to find out," she shot back.

Cal smiled and tried again. "What do you *think* is in the evidence locker?"

Dana hesitated. But then she said, "Back in Alabama, when they found Lacey's blood in the bed of *her* dad's truck, they also found a kid-sized dog collar. The kind with metal spikes that you put on your pit bull before a dogfight. Or something you might use as an S-and-M sex costume. It was covered in her blood too."

"God," Calvin uttered.

"God had nothing to do with what happened to those girls," Dana replied darkly.

"You think…" I started.

"I think there's a serious possibility that the cops found a collar in the bed of Mr. Rodriguez's truck as well. And I also think that it was planted there."

Milo sighed a little. I could tell, even from that small noise, that he was profoundly saddened by all of this.

"I remember hearing on the news, when the story about Sasha first came out, that the crimes were possibly of a *sexual nature*. Remember that?" Cal asked, glancing at me as he drove.

I nodded and waited to speak, because the lump in my throat was humongous. I couldn't help but think about both my dreams and my visions, and the utter fear that I'd seen in Sasha's eyes. I didn't know what awfulness Sasha had endured before her death. But I did know one thing: Her father hadn't been the one who'd hurt her.

"Does it really matter if a similar collar was found in the back of Edmund Rodriguez's truck?" Milo asked Dana quietly.

"Yeah, it matters," she said. "It's proof we're on the right track and not wasting our time again. If the bastards who killed Sasha are the same ones who killed Lacey, they should've already leaked the news about the dog collar to the press. That detail should be all over the news—drive the public into a frenzy so that there's no sympathy when Edmund reappears. If the killers are lucky, he'll be found by a mob who strings him up—no need for a messy trial."

I cleared my throat. "How about if I go to the police and pretend I have more information for that detective who interviewed me at school? Detective Hughes? While I'm talking to him, I can ask him what the awful thing was that they found in the back of the truck."

Dana was already shaking her head. "I don't want you anywhere near the police."

"I have a NID," I pointed out. "Plus Detective Hughes gave me his card." I looked from her to Milo to Calvin. "Everyone knows how much I love Sasha." I cleared my throat and corrected myself. "Loved her." I pushed, feeling more confident. This *was* something I could do to help. "I'll keep my abilities on lockdown."

Dana was wavering, I could tell, especially when she exchanged a glance with Milo.

"At least let me try," I said as Calvin pulled up to the diner where Dana had left her bike, "before you risk getting shipped off to wherever they ship people without NID cards."

"I'll think about it," Dana said, and climbed out of the car without so much as a good-bye.

Milo made up for it. "Cal," he said with a nod before giving me a smile that didn't erase the sadness in his eyes. "Night, Sky."

We watched Milo and Dana as they trudged back to the motorcycle. The rain had begun to let up a bit. My eyes hurt from crying earlier, and my brain hurt from all of the *training* Dana had put me through for the day.

"Home?" Cal asked, looking at me.

"Home," I said with a sigh.

CHAPTER SIXTEEN

I had never been inside a police station before, but the image I'd conjured up in my head was far more glamorous than the reality.

Tuesday after school, Dana and Milo showed up as Calvin was pulling out of the Coconut Key Academy parking lot. They waved us over to the side of the road.

Dana hopped in like she owned the car. "I'm gonna let you try this," she told me, before turning to Cal. "You know where you're going, Scooter?" she asked, apparently deciding to completely skip "Hello" or "How are you?"

"Downtown?" Cal asked uncertainly. I knew he was just as clueless about the police station's location as I was.

Milo edged in next to Dana in the backseat. "Hi, Skylar," he said, and smiled at me.

I blushed for no reason. Then I blushed because I was embarrassed about blushing. Sighing, I turned to face the front before offering a "Hey."

"Downtown...sort of," Dana replied, crossing one leg over the other. Today, in the especially hot weather, she'd succumbed to wearing jean shorts for the first time since we'd met. Of course, she still had on her knee-high boots. "Take a right up here. I'll direct you."

Calvin nodded. "Your wish is my command."

"Okay. Let's review," Dana addressed me, all business. "You're going into the station, and you're going to find the cop who interviewed you. You're not going to speak to any other person about any details of anything. Do I have to state the obvious? I guess I better: you're not going to reveal *anything* about yourself or your gifts." Dana chewed at a cuticle. "You got that so far?"

I nodded.

"Go straight here," Dana mentioned to Cal. She was still looking at me. "Let's role-play. What are you going to say to the detective?"

I paused. And then I laughed.

"What's so funny?"

"I'm nervous," I said. "I feel like I'm about to audition for the school play."

"Um, yeah. Get over it. If you're nervous practicing with me, you're gonna be super nervous when you have to do it for real."

Milo leaned forward. He was wearing shorts too—cargo shorts, with a really cool pair of sandals on his extremely nice-looking feet. He had a tank top on, with a short-sleeved plaid shirt open over it. "It's okay. I know it probably feels silly, but if you just go through it a couple of times, you'll feel more confident when you speak directly to the police officer."

"Thanks, Milo, 'cause it really looks like little Miss Princess needs another good sugarcoating," Dana remarked.

Milo didn't respond, but her sarcasm didn't seem to particularly bother or surprise him.

"All right," I said nervously. "I'm ready."

"Okay, go," Dana said. "You start."

"Hi, Detective Hughes," I said in a ridiculously pleasant voice. I wasn't much of an actress.

Calvin giggled.

I socked him in the shoulder and continued. "Remember me? I'm here because I wanted to follow up on that interview you conducted with me last week. I just...wanted to know if there was any news about Sasha or Edmu—"

"Okay. Stop right there," Dana demanded. "First of all, you cannot walk in and start asking questions. Nobody cares if you want to know what happened to Sasha. They're not a news station. They're working crazy hours for pathetic pay so that they can hopefully *gather* information—not *divulge* it."

I swallowed hard. "Okay," I said. "Do over."

"Take two," Calvin agreed.

Dana slammed her hands down on the tops of her legs. "There will be no take two when you walk in there!" she exclaimed. "So let's get this right!"

Milo started to say something, but I cut him off. "Hey!" I said to Dana, my tone sharp. "I'm trying my best here! Isn't that what you asked me to do? So sue me if I don't know what to say to a detective in a murder case! It's not exactly par for the teenage-suburban-girl course!"

Dana cleared her throat uncomfortably. "I apologize, Bubble Gum. I just really want this to work."

"Me too," I said a little softer.

"Okay," Milo intervened. "Why don't we figure out exactly what information Skylar is providing that gives her a legitimate reason to talk to the detective again."

"Good call," Calvin said, and followed Dana's lead as she continued pointing out directions to the station.

"Yeah," I agreed. "I'm going to do better if I have at least a rough-draft script to work from."

Dana nodded. "Why don't you tell the detective that you saw a white van driving around your neighborhood on the evening of Sasha's disappearance?"

I stared blankly at her. "But I didn't," I said.

Dana threw her hands exasperatedly into the air. "I *know* that, Princess. But that little boy from Harrisburg saw Edmund getting *medicine* from an old lady in a white van. So we know there's a white van involved. And there very well may have been a white van driving down your street at some point that night. We don't know. But I'd bet my ass whoever took Sasha didn't walk out of your neighborhood carrying her in their arms. There must've been *some* kind of vehicle and *white van* is as good as any."

"So I'm going to walk into a police station and lie, bold-faced, to a detective who is conducting a homicide investigation."

It was Dana's turn to stare blankly. Apparently that was *exactly* what she wanted me to do.

Calvin kept driving. "I have an idea. What if Skylar says something like, *I remembered that I saw a really creepy old lady near Sasha's house on the night she was kidnapped, and then I was talking to a little boy who said he saw the same lady in a very suspicious-looking white van*"—he pitched his voice higher in a terrible imitation of me—"and that way you won't be lying, and then you could say, *I thought it might be important information.* And then, once you've got the detective's attention, you sneak in the question about the dog collar."

"How would I ask that?" I wondered out loud.

"Just say, *I heard there was a dog collar found in the back of Edmund's truck. I was wondering if you found any leads connected to that evidence.*"

I looked at him in exasperation. "That's not what I sound like."

He glanced back at me. "Yeah, it kinda is."

"Is *not*—"

"Wow," Dana's voice was monotone, and we both looked back at her. "Way to sound completely incriminating. Ask the detective about evidence that hasn't been announced to the public. That's genius, Boy Wonder."

"What?" Cal said defensively. "I don't see you offering suggestions."

"Well, if we want Sky to walk out of the station without handcuffs on, she'd better avoid asking any specific questions about dog collars."

If this little *practice session* was supposed to make me feel more confident, it had served to do the exact opposite in record time. Beads of sweat popped up on my forehead.

"Everything is going to go just fine," Milo reassured me, as if reading my thoughts.

"Unless there *wasn't* a dog collar in the back of the truck," Calvin countered. "And frankly, I really don't see the problem in *asking*. I mean, wouldn't they be more likely to think there's a leak somewhere in the department? All we really have to do is make an anonymous online post to some crime-stoppers' message board, say we heard a rumor about a dog collar in the back of Mr. Rodriguez's truck, and Sky can say—honestly—that she read about it online."

Milo looked at Dana. "That could work," he said. "Leak the news ourselves."

She looked back at him. "Can you make it happen?"

"I can," he said, then held out his hand, looking at me. "May I borrow your cell phone?"

Dana caught his arm. "Better not use hers."

"It won't be traceable," Milo assured her. "Not even by the police."

"My phone's still turned off," I said apologetically. "I've been turning it off while I'm in class—and whoops, I keep forgetting to turn it back on when school gets out."

Dana snorted. "Laudably sneaky, BG. Milo told me about your mom being insanely overprotective." She looked at Milo. "One would think that any prospective boyfriends might want to ponder long and hard before signing on for that BS."

"Calvin, may I use your phone?" Milo asked.

"But of course," Calvin said, passing his phone over his shoulder and into the backseat as he continued to drive.

"I don't want a boyfriend," I told Dana as Milo used Cal's phone to access the Internet. But as I said the words, they seemed to ring with a touch of desperation, kind of the way, when my mom was trying to eat healthy, she would say, *I don't want that donut.* I turned back to face the front, away from Milo's dimples. He was Dana's boyfriend, anyway. "I don't need that kind of complication right now."

"Pull in here, Scoot." Dana pointed to an ugly, poop-colored building with yellowed, rusty-looking front doors. "This is the police station," she said. "Park around the side, where we won't be as conspicuous."

"Nice digs," Cal said.

I swallowed and my heart started to pound.

"Now that you know what you're saying, you want to run through it?" Milo glanced up from Cal's phone to ask. He didn't wait for me to respond. "I'll be the lady at the desk." He cleared his throat and spoke in a very silly falsetto. "May I help you?"

It was so ridiculous that I had to laugh. And as he glanced up at me again, his eyes smiling, I knew he'd done it to get me breathing again. "Yes, please," I said. "I need to talk to Detective Hughes. I have some information about the Sasha Rodriguez case."

"I'm Detective Hughes," Calvin contributed in a very stupid-sounding, deep, booming voice. "Have you come to tell me all of the many places where Edmund Rodriguez touched you inappropriately?"

I laughed again, and because Milo was looking at me questioningly—even as his thumbs raced across Calvin's phone's keyboard, I said, "When he interviewed me, almost all of the detective's questions were about inappropriate touching—"

"Stay in character," Dana barked.

So I said, "Actually, no, Detective, but I do have information that I thought was important. I remember seeing an, um, older woman with gray hair near Sasha's house. And a…friend—a little boy I know—said he saw the same woman in a white van—"

"He's probably walking away from you right about now," Dana interjected. "Because he's got four million other, more important things to do."

"I'm sorry, Detective," I said quickly, "but can you tell me if it's true…? The news I heard online at…" I looked at Milo.

"Citizen Detective dot com," he provided.

I repeated the website URL, adding, "There was an anonymous post that said an S-and-M dog collar—in Sasha's size—was found in the truck, covered in her blood." Just saying that out loud made me feel sick to my stomach.

"You'll have to watch him closely for his reaction," Dana advised. "And don't be afraid to add the violins. Tell him how much you loved the girl, how important it is that you know the truth, how you've been having nightmares—"

"I will," I said.

"You're going to be great," Milo said quietly as he handed Calvin back his phone.

"You want me to go in with you?" Calvin asked me.

"You can't," Dana said. "Really, Scoot, I know you want to, and God knows I want you to go in there with her too, but…" She looked at me somberly. "You have a better shot of getting real information if you go in on your own. Trust me on that."

I did trust her, and with a deep breath, I reached for the door handle.

"Dammit," Dana hissed, and I turned around quickly to look back at her. She was making a face, her eyes squeezed tightly shut. "*Dammit!*"

"What's the problem?" Calvin also glanced at Dana in his rear-view mirror.

Now Dana was shaking her head and breathing hard. "Something's wrong."

Milo looked curious too, but he didn't ask Dana what she meant. He waited patiently for her to elaborate. While he did that, he also turned to gaze at me.

"Something's really wrong. Everyone be quiet!" Dana demanded, even though none of us had spoken again. She scrunched up her face and leaned forward, rocking a little in her seat. Finally, she opened her eyes. "Shit! This isn't going to work."

"How do you know that?" Cal asked.

"I just…it's like back in Harrisburg when I knew that little boy had information. I can't do this on cue," she said, clutching her forehead, "but when it happens, it's always accurate. We're wasting our time."

"If Skylar goes inside, will she be in danger?" Milo asked as he reached into his pocket and pulled out his packet of gum.

Dana didn't hesitate. "No. There's no danger. Just…I don't really know what I'm feeling here—it's very strange. I think…the detective isn't here. Or something." She shook her head again.

"Always accurate, huh?" Calvin said. "*Or something…?*"

"You should go in," Dana said to me, ignoring Calvin. "At least find out when he'll…be back…?"

My heart was pounding again. "Can I please have a piece of that?" I asked Milo, knowing his answer would probably be *no*, but I was now completely freaked out and didn't want to go inside the police station with seriously bad fear-breath.

"Not unless you want a dose of nicotine," Dana said as she yanked the gum packet from Milo's hands. She handed it over to me.

It was something called Smok'B'Gon—a type of gum specifically used to "aid in smoking cessation."

Milo had quit smoking? I looked up at him questioningly.

The edge of his lips curved up into an almost imperceptible smile. But his eyes were uncertain, like he was embarrassed or nervous.

"That's so awesome," I said, beaming. "Good job!"

Milo actually blushed. It was unbelievably charming. He turned and looked out of the window, his grin widening.

"All right, Sunshine." Dana yanked the gum packet back. "It's showtime, ready or not. Do your thing."

The smell was what hit me first.

As soon as I stepped into the station, my nose burned. Stale booze, cigarettes, and…garlic. Yes, garlic and onions. And burnt coffee. And the old, familiar fish-of-fear smell. It was pretty disgusting. And sad. The large open lobby smelled *desperately sad.*

I bucked up and shook off the urge to gag. I needed to pull myself together if I was going to get this done.

The entire place was dingy and hot. A tired ceiling fan revolved drunkenly overhead. Printers beeped. Cheap-looking cubicles divided the room into cluttered sections. Some people looked up at me from their gargantuan pile of paperwork. Others didn't bother.

A counter stretched across, separating visitors from the main part of the room, and even though individual lanes were roped off with signs overhead labeled *Information*, *Processing*, and *Cashier*, only one woman was there. She sat at an unmarked part of the counter, in front of a computer where she typed furiously. She was enormously heavy, with a furrowed brow and chin-length dyed-red hair that had started to turn gray at the roots. Her mouth was open slightly as she worked, and she breathed heavily, as if just the exertion of moving her fingers across the keyboard was too much for her.

As I approached, I read the little plaque on her desk. It was engraved with the words: *Desk Sergeant Olga Moran.*

I stood there for a moment, but she didn't look up from her computer screen.

"Excuse me," I tried, but then jumped back, startled at what sounded like the woman kicking the counter, rapid-fire, with both feet. *Ba-dah, ba-dah, ba-dah, ba-dah, ba-dah, bahm!* And yet she still hadn't looked up at me. Nor broken a sweat. It was beyond weird, and I stifled the urge to laugh as I pictured her wearing tap shoes and rushing to dance class after work.

I couldn't see what she was wearing on her feet because the counter was solid, all the way down to the rather disgustingly grimy tile floor.

And instead of falling onto that floor in hysterical laughter, I spoke even louder. "Excuse me. Um, I'm here to speak to the detective who interviewed me last week at my school...?"

The desk sergeant finally turned her giant head and gave me an apathetic stare. Her hot-dog-like fingers slipped off the keyboard as she leaned back, placed a pensive hand on her chin, and gathered the energy necessary to speak. "Case number?"

"Excuse me?"

"What's the case number?" Her voice was a monotone, and I realized that instead of looking at me, her eyes were focused somewhere on the back wall, over my head.

"I…there was never a case number given to me." I stood up on my toes, hoping for eye contact. "Like I said, a detective came to *me* and asked *me* questions. I'm here because I have information that I believe will help solve the case?" I knew I had to stop phrasing my sentences in questions and start sounding more absolute, or I'd never get to talk to Hughes.

"If you want to talk to a detective about a case, you need to know the case number," the woman droned. She opened a pack of cough drops and stuffed one into her mouth before immediately cracking the candy with her teeth and resuming her typing.

A rush of menthol filled my nostrils, and combined with the other terrible smells in the room, it made me need to sit down. But there were no seats on this side of the counter, so I lifted my chin and tried to breathe through my mouth.

"And I told *you*," I said, trying to keep my voice calm, "that I didn't get a case number. Detective Hughes didn't give me one when he conducted the interview." There. I'd managed to make that a statement.

Sergeant Moran stopped typing. Something I'd said had finally caught her attention, because this time when she lifted her head from her computer screen, she actually looked at me. Her beady eyes were like two question marks as her lips formed the shape of a Cheerio. She worked the cough drop around in her mouth. "Hughes?" she repeated.

"Yeah. He came to my school—Coconut Key Academy—last week to ask me about the missing little girl. Sasha Rodriguez. Do I really need a case number to talk to him again? I'll be quick."

The sergeant closed a manila folder and leaned forward, weaving her fingers together as she placed her large forearms on top of the counter. The exertion made sweat trickle from her temple down to where her earlobe connected to her jaw. She shook her head, and the bead of sweat plopped onto her arm. "Little girl, you can't talk to Detective Hughes—whether you have a case number or not." She cleared her throat. "Nobody can talk to him anymore. I hate to break it to you, but Hughes? He's dead."

Ba-dah, ba-dah, ba-dah, ba-dah, ba-dah, bahm!

She was kicking the counter again, and it was so bizarre that as I took a swift step backward, I nearly tripped over my own two feet. When I caught myself, I realized that, clearly, I hadn't heard her correctly.

I mean, for a second there, I actually thought this woman had told me that the detective I'd seen last week was *dead.*

"His funeral was this morning," Sergeant Moran announced, and I realized I'd heard her quite well the first time.

And yet I couldn't stop myself from repeating, "Dead?"

"Heart failure," she intoned, and for a moment, I actually saw something human in her eyes. She had liked Hughes.

I exhaled. "I'm really sorry to hear that."

"We all are. He was a good detective." *Ba-dah, ba-dah, ba-dah, ba-dah, ba-dah, bahm!* "Carrots! Stop that! Right now!"

She'd barked that directly in my face—and I had no idea how to respond. Was it some kind of weird nickname she'd assigned me because I had red hair? Except I wasn't making that banging sound, so I couldn't stop.

But then she awkwardly bent over and directed her words beneath the counter, speaking in baby talk that would've made me crack up if I wasn't so stunned by the news of Hughes's death. "Is my widdle puddy-tat hungry? Does my widdle Cawwots want din-din?"

As I watched, Sergeant Moran put a can of cat food and an opener on the counter, the exertion of reaching for those items causing her to wheeze.

I sniffed the air, suddenly aware of more than just the odors of menthol, fish, and garlic.

It was faint, but unmistakable. The sewage smell was back.

I coughed into my elbow as a ringing started in my ears. I tried to breathe shallowly, but that didn't help. The sewage smell was getting worse and worse by the second.

"Anyway," the woman continued, grunting with each turn of the crank as she opened the can of cat food, "if you really feel like waiting, I can page Detective Sparks. He's in charge of delinquent files, and—"

"No!" I said, remembering even in my shocked state that Dana had said not to discuss the case with anyone else.

She looked at me with her head cocked, as if observing a rare specimen.

And then it hit me like a freight train.

Like ten freight trains, bound for my nose.

The sewage smell. It was back, and it was nasty. I looked wildly around the room. But the apparition of the old lady from Sasha's room hadn't just drifted in the door. In fact, there was no one else in that front area of the building—just me, Olga, and Carrots—*Ba-dah, ba-dah, ba-dah, ba-dah, ba-dah, bahm!*—who must've been scratching to get free, which made his or her crate rattle against the base of the counter.

Meanwhile, the sewage smell was getting worse. It completely drowned out the desperate sadness of the room, filling it instead with...terror.

And evil. An awful, corrosive, insidious evil.

I gagged. And I looked for a trash can to puke into.

But there wasn't one in sight. Without another word to the desk sergeant, I staggered out of the station, bursting through the doors and back around the corner of the building into the parking lot.

Where, for the second time in two days, I puked my guts out onto asphalt.

My eyes watered and my throat burned and my hands did too, and I realized that I'd dropped onto my hands and knees—and the blacktop was hot. I was also vaguely aware of the sound of Milo and Dana getting out of Calvin's car, of the two of them arguing after Dana's voice demanded, "What happened in there, Bubble Gum?"

"She can't answer your questions. She's a little busy right now."
Milo sounded more annoyed than I'd ever heard him.

Dana: "But I need to know—"

Milo: "You need to back off. Give her a break. Come on, get back
in the car before you start sympathy-vomiting. Let me handle this."

When he spoke again, his voice was closer. "Sky, are you okay?
How can I help you?"

I shook my head as I threw up again, and it was hideous. I wasn't
able to keep myself from crying—I was a bodily liquids fountain. In
fact, snot was also pouring out of my nose. And yet Milo was reaching
for me anyway, moving into splatter range.

"Oh my God, don't touch me, don't touch me!" I moaned, and he
immediately backed away. Of course, like an idiot, I felt the need to
immediately apologize. "I'm so sorry," I sobbed. "I just have to...get
it all out of my system. This happened yesterday, and then I was fine."

"I just wish you would let me help you," Milo said. "You're so
much like Dana—always thinking you have to go through crap like
this alone." He raised his voice. "Calvin, you got any water in the car?"

"Sorry, I don't," I heard Calvin call back to him.

Milo sighed. "Well, okay," he said. "Sky, I'll be right back."

"Milo! Don't you dare!" I heard Dana shout from the car, and
when I lifted my head, I saw him disappear around the corner of the
building. He was going into the police station.

I was already starting to feel a little better. By the time Milo came
back, carrying a couple of bottles of water that he'd gotten out of a
machine in the lobby, I'd pushed myself away from the puddle of puke

and was leaning against the side of the building. I was digging through my purse, looking for a tissue, but of course, I couldn't find any.

Except then Milo was there, crouching down beside me. He took off his over-shirt, and then he pulled off his tank top, and I laughed in surprise at the sudden display of smooth, tan muscles—six pack included. Had I really thought, at one point, that Milo was skinny?

He was not.

As I watched, he opened one of the bottles of water and doused his tank top with it, then offered it to me, so I could use it to wipe my face.

The kindness in his eyes made me tear up a little again. "Thank you," I whispered as I took it.

It was cool and soft, and it smelled like vanilla. And I was getting puke and snot all over it.

"You okay?" he asked me as he slipped his arms back into his over-shirt. He picked up the bottle of water, opening it and holding it out to me. "Better just rinse and spit until you're certain the fireworks are over."

I laughed at *fireworks*. "They're over," I told him, but I did as he suggested, just to be safe.

He, meanwhile, had taken his tank top back as if he wasn't grossed out, and was using the other bottle of water to rinse it. He gave the shirt back to me, and I used it to wipe my face again.

"I smelled it again," I told him. "The evil."

He nodded. "I figured." He sighed as he looked at me. "Dana's got a lot of questions for you, but if you need to take another minute—"

"No," I said, taking another sip of the water, this time letting it slide down my throat. "I'm…back." I pushed myself to my feet as Milo hovered nearby, ready to catch me if it looked like I was going to fall.

"You want to make a bet," he told me, "that the first thing Dana's gonna say when we get back into the car is *Milo, you effing idiot.*" He smiled at my confusion as we headed for the car. "I'll let her explain."

"Milo, you effing idiot!" Dana said, only she used the real f-word. But then she turned to glare at me as I slid into the front seat alongside Calvin. "Do you have *any* idea how *dangerous* it was for him to go *into* the police station like that?"

"I needed water," Milo said evenly.

"Drive! Get us out of here!" Dana ordered Calvin, and he pulled out of the police station parking lot.

"I do know," I answered Dana. "Without a NID card—"

"Miles doesn't just not have a NID," she told me. "There's an outstanding warrant for his arrest."

That was news to Cal and me, and we exchanged a wide-eyed glance that Dana, of course, made note of.

"Yeah, don't get your panties in a twist," she said. "The charges were theft, but the money was his, and the so-called victim was our allegedly loving foster father, who'd just locked me in the closet for two days with no food or water." She turned back to Milo. "You could've been pinged by their face-recognition software! If they'd ID'd you, you could have put *all* of us in danger!"

"I kept my head down. No one even noticed I was there," Milo told her.

"That you know of," Dana pointed out, heavy on the attitude.

"No one's following us," he countered calmly. "It's over, so let's move on."

"It's over," Dana scoffed. "Yeah. Right. Like it's a one-time thing, like you're not a guy who's obviously started thinking with his—"

"Stop." Milo's voice was tight. "I'm willing to have this conversation with you, Dana, you know that I am, but we'll do it later. Not now."

I looked over to meet Calvin's eyes. I'd once gone with Nicole's family to an amusement park, and her parents had argued heatedly during the entire forty-minute drive. This felt a little bit like that.

In the backseat, Dana exhaled a very long, very beleaguered-sounding sigh. "So what happened in there, Bubble Gum?"

"Well, to start with," I said, "Detective Hughes is dead."

"*What?*" Calvin, Milo, and Dana all exclaimed at once.

"I *knew* something was really wrong," Dana added.

"How did he die?" Calvin asked.

"The desk sergeant told me it was heart failure," I reported.

Dana blew air out of her mouth, making a raspberry sound. "Yeah, right. Heart failure, my ass. Someone murdered him because he knew too much."

I frowned. "You seriously think…?"

Dana's face was grim. "The people who killed Sasha don't mess around, Sky. If they thought Detective Hughes stumbled onto something that would exonerate Edmund Rodriguez and point attention toward them, killing Hughes would be as inconsequential to them as ordering a latte with lunch. And about as easy to do. A man his age? Make it look like he'd had a heart attack? *I* could do that. With the right drugs…?"

Calvin looked the way I felt. His face was a little gray, and he shook his head. "Man, I don't know about y'all, but this is starting to get to me. I mean, if you're saying this dude got killed because he knew the truth…? The truth that we're trying to uncover here…?" His grip on the steering wheel was so tight that the edges of his chocolate-colored knuckles had whitened. "I'm just saying we might be in over our heads."

I took a deep breath and told Cal and Dana what I'd already told Milo. "That sewage smell came back when I was in the station." I crinkled my nose. "It was worse than any other time I've smelled it."

"Any chance that Garrett Hathaway's dad works for the police?" Calvin asked. "I mean, you didn't see him in there, did you?"

I shook my head. "Wow, I didn't think of that. I wasn't looking for him," I admitted. "I guess I could…"—I took a deep breath—"go back?"

"You don't have to do that," Milo said.

I turned to look at him. "Maybe it won't be as bad, now that my stomach is empty." As if on cue, it rumbled.

"I don't want to go back there today," Dana said. "Not after Milo's foolishness. But maybe in a few days, if we don't find any other leads."

"Just let me know in advance," I said, managing to sound braver than I felt, "so I can skip lunch."

"Next time I'll go in," Calvin volunteered. "I won't be able to smell Garrett's dad, but I remember what he looks like."

"We don't have to go back for that," Milo said. "If you drop me at the library, I'll hop onto the Internet, see what I can dig up on Mr. Hathaway. If he's a cop, it'll be public record."

"A cop who owns beachfront property?" I wondered. "It doesn't make sense."

"Or it makes too much sense," Dana said darkly. "If he's working for the people who make Destiny..."

"Dude, you don't have to go to the library. You could use my phone," Calvin offered Milo.

"No," Milo said. "Thanks. I might have to dig deep, and it's too hard to do that and keep it untraceable. If I go to the library, I just need to switch computers every fifteen minutes and I'll be fine. Plus I can take a shower while I'm there."

There were so many homeless people in this part of Florida that the church-run library had opened a soup kitchen, a laundry, and a locker-room setup for the less-fortunate to use. To access their services, you had to attend a mandatory church program in their chapel or show your local church punch-card to prove that you'd gotten some God within the past week.

"You could take a shower..." *At my house*, I was about to say, but I substituted, "At Calvin's."

Cal looked at both Milo and Dana in his rearview mirror. "Absolutely," he said. "Any time. My mom is cool."

"Thanks," Milo said. "But as long as I'm going to use the computers at the library..."

"I'll take you up on that shower, Scoot," Dana said. "The church library gives me a rash."

"So...to the library, where we drop Milo," Calvin said, "and then home?"

I turned around to find Milo watching me again as Dana nodded.

"Regardless of what Miles finds out about Garrett Hathaway's father," she said, "I want to get into that beach house." She looked from Calvin to me. "And I want to do it soon."

CHAPTER SEVENTEEN

"It's kind of like the Cold War détente," Cal said.

"What in the world are you talking about?" I asked.

It was Wednesday morning, and we were walking through the school parking lot, getting ready for another day.

Milo had come over to Calvin's house after his library research session, and he'd reported that Garrett's dad, Richard J. Hathaway, did *not* work for the Coconut Key police department. He was a doctor—a plastic surgeon.

We'd also found out that the seeds that Milo had planted online—about the dog collar being found in the back of Edmund Rodriguez's truck—had borne fruit. The police had confirmed the rumor. It was all over the news, so Dana now had the proof that she'd needed.

"I'm talking about you and Garrett," Calvin said now. "Of course, he's obviously the Soviet Union."

"Obviously."

"What I'm trying to say is that he saw you puke, after you saw *him* puke. And now there's an agreement between you two, even if it's unspoken."

Calvin was right. We had both seen the other person upchuck. And now we both had dirt about an embarrassing incident. If one person leaked info about said embarrassing incident, the other person would go down too. In flames.

"Détente," Cal said again, and grinned.

"I suppose," I said. "Although I'm really not worried about people knowing I threw up. It happens."

"Okay, I know you're Miss Humble and all, but you can admit it. It was exceedingly embarrassing. I mean, if it was anything like what you did at the police station…"

I shook my head. "Whatever," I mumbled. I really didn't want to have to think about any of that right now.

But, as if on cue, Garrett pulled up in his dad's zippy little car.

"Shee-it," Cal muttered. I instinctively grabbed the arm of Calvin's wheelchair before pointing to the band building.

"Come on," I said. "Let's just go."

"Hey!" Garrett called, slamming the door shut before striding toward us. I purposely didn't look back as we walked. I was also breathing through my mouth just in case he smelled like sewage.

"Hey!" Garrett tried again, louder this time. "Did you get the e-vite to my party?"

I sighed. "What?" I asked, turning halfway around. I refused to actually have a conversation with the lamest asshole on the planet. But then I realized what he'd said—party—and I made myself turn all the way toward him. And smile.

Garrett smiled back at me. "I just wanted to know if you were coming to my party Friday night. Pops is out of town, so I'm having a little shindig at the ol' beach house. It's pretty exclusive, so... You're welcome."

I laughed out loud at his arrogance, and then played it off like I was coughing into my sleeve.

Cal slapped me on the arm. I knew what he was thinking, because I was thinking it too.

This was our ticket into Garrett's house. No B and E necessary.

We'd spent more than an hour with Dana last night, first learning that B and E was short for "breaking and entering," and then planning a *Mission: Impossible*-style caper. I knew Calvin was as relieved as I was that we wouldn't have to scale the outside of the house to the porch off the third-floor master bedroom to get inside. This way, we'd just waltz in through the front door, which was more my speed.

I smiled again at Garrett. "Yup," I replied. "*We'll* be there. All of us. I've got a coupla friends visiting from out of town too."

Garrett's grin didn't drop, but his eyes got cold as he looked from me to Calvin and back. His teeth were gritted. "Oh. Okay. Awesome. I'm looking forward to it."

"*A-douche-indee!*" I said gaily, hoping that he remembered.

He did. "*Ama-douche!*" Garrett responded. He looked at Calvin, whose mouth was open. He leaned in close to Calvin and lowered his voice, but my hearing was excellent so I heard him say, "It's Botsmanian for I'm gonna steal your girlfriend, asshole."

But Calvin just laughed and said, "I'm sorry, could you repeat the...Botsmanian, was it?"

"*Ama-douche*," Garrett said. "Skylar taught it to me the day we went to the beach." He winked at me and swaggered back to his car.

Calvin's mouth was still open. He turned to look at me. "He honestly doesn't realize that, phonetically, what he's saying is…"

"Apparently not," I said, watching as Garrett sifted through his backseat, no doubt organizing the homework assignments he'd bought and paid for online last night.

"You are my goddess," Calvin told me.

"I'm your super-goddess," I corrected him. I'd just agreed to spend the night of my seventeenth birthday at a super-douche-arama event.

Although, on second thought, Milo would be there.

"Heads up!" Calvin called out suddenly, interrupting my thoughts. He grabbed my arm, pointing at the school parking lot.

A delivery truck had rounded the corner, and somehow it had lost control. I watched in disbelief as the big, gray vehicle slid and spun, the driver clearly making an admirable attempt to stop the screeching tires from spinning.

And then I looked up to my right and realized that Garrett—completely unaware of the impending disaster—was directly in the out-of-control vehicle's path.

"Garrett!" Cal yelled.

But as Garrett looked up and saw the coming danger, he had nowhere to go. The truck was sliding sideways toward him and his dad's car. He was going to be sandwiched between two very large, very heavy pieces of metal in about a second and a half.

Without hesitating, I focused on Garrett and thought about how much I absolutely despised the things he'd done and said to Calvin. I let myself get really rip-roarin' pissed, as I dug deep and seethed and raged and…

A nanosecond before the truck would have crushed him, Garrett was lifted up off the ground. He hurtled sideways into the air, over three parked cars, before landing with a not-so-graceful thud on the cement sidewalk.

And the truck slammed into Garrett's dad's BMW, rendering it two-dimensional, with a hideous screeching of metal on metal.

Teachers and students alike ran outside to gape at the wreckage. The driver of the truck was utterly disoriented but seemed mostly okay as he stumbled out of the driver's side of his badly crushed vehicle.

Mrs. Iccavone, who taught first-year Latin, spotted Garrett on the sidewalk and screamed, "Someone call 9-1-1!"

"Garrett?" I was already on my way over to where he'd landed as Calvin followed me.

"Oh my God!" Mr. Tanner, the soccer coach shouted. "Is he okay?"

As I knelt beside Garrett, I could see his chest rising and falling. He was definitely knocked out—but he was also clearly alive.

"Everyone back up! Give him room!" Mrs. Iccavone used her outside voice, but no one listened to her. The crowd swelled around still-unconscious Garrett, pushing Calvin and me back, away from him.

"Ho. Ly. Crap," Cal finally managed. He looked up at me. "What just happened?"

Dazed, I watched as an ambulance came barreling up the school driveway, its lights flashing and siren wailing. "I don't know," I said. "Can we find a place to...sit down? Or..."

"Sure," Cal said, grabbing my arm and wheeling away from the crowd.

When we were far enough away, Cal looked at me. "You saved his life, dude."

I nodded, stunned. I'd saved his life.

I had saved a *life*.

Cal held out his fist for me to bump. "Huge respect for saving the ungrateful douche-master. I don't know if I would have been so generous."

"You know you would've," I replied. "So don't pretend to be such a hard-ass."

"Ah, crap!"

"What now?" I asked, looking around wildly—for what I wasn't sure. Maybe a crashing private jet or stampeding elephants escaped from the zoo...

"Well, if Garrett is hurt," Calvin said, "he most likely won't have that party on Friday."

I answered him without a pause. "Sprained ankles. Mild concussion. No worries."

Cal raised an eyebrow. "And I win the lottery. Please say that I win the lottery?"

"No, but Garrett'll be back to school by Friday. The party's still on." I pressed my hand against my stomach as we went into the school. "God, I'm having really bad cramps."

"Saving douche bags'll do that to you," Calvin said. "*Ama-douche*," he repeated. "You might have crazy-ass, lifesaving superpowers, but girl, getting him to say that…? It was the highlight of my decade."

"*A-douche-indee*," I agreed.

CHAPTER EIGHTEEN

You were right. 2 sprained ankles and a mild concussion. G'll be back in school 2morrow. Dang.

I got the text from Cal later that evening around eight o'clock, while I was sitting at my desk zipping through another math assignment.

I set the phone down and ran my hand through my hair. I was on edge. Okay, I was beyond on edge. I was frazzled. After school, Calvin and I had tried to conjure Dana by wishing she would appear, but that didn't work. We even tried homing in on her, but my mental magnet weirdly pulled me to I-75 south, and after a few miles, Cal turned around.

What was even more rattling tonight was the fact that, even though I never knew *when* it was going to happen, Dana had managed to meet with me daily since that first night at the cineplex.

But Wednesday was almost over. I sighed again and picked up my phone and typed: Still no word from D.

I redirected my attention for a moment to my homework until the phone beeped again.

M just stopped by.

Okay, so I'd be lying if my stomach didn't do a mini-somersault. Which I completely ignored. Mom was at some PTA meeting so I wrote back: Great! Let's do that HOMEWORK. Be there in five.

Before I even had a chance to stand, though, my phone rang. I answered it.

"Girl, if you seriously think I would let you waltz around in the dark alone right now, then you really are stupid." Service was bad, and Cal sounded like he was calling from the moon, all distorted and echoey.

"Fine. Come get me," I replied, "but do it fast. I don't know how much time I have before Momzilla gets back."

"Bow chicka woww-woww!" Calvin mocked porn music into the phone.

"You suck," I said.

"Um, I am definitely not the one sucking," Calvin started.

"Argh! Stop! Earmuffs! Lalalalala, not listening!"

Calvin giggled. "I'll see you in a sec."

I hopped away from my desk and raced to my closet. Sifting through my clothes, I found a pink V-neck T-shirt. I rummaged through my drawer and pulled out my favorite comfy white cotton bra. Then, reconsidering, I threw it back and opted for a black lacey push-up I'd bought back in Connecticut. Not that I had much to push. I had never worn it. In fact, Nicole had bought it for me. According to my former best friend, every woman, at some point in her life, needed the help provided by a good piece of lingerie.

My skinny jeans were dirty, so I grabbed khaki capris—the ones that made my butt look curvier than it actually was—and shut the closet door. Glancing again at the ridiculous lace bra, I wondered if, with the help of good lingerie or not, I would ever be sexy.

As I dressed, I looked in the mirror. My hair was especially unruly today, red curls springing defiantly around my face. I attempted to smooth them down, but they popped back up. Frowning, I pulled my shirt over my head, and then took a banana clip and pulled all of my hair back. The flyaways were still there.

Plus, the bra was horrible and lumpy underneath the shirt.

Sexy. My ass.

Calvin texted his arrival with another porn-themed message: Good evening, miss. Did you order a pizza? Chicka-bow-bow!

Sighing, I concluded that the outfit would have to suffice.

I ran downstairs, refusing to acknowledge the fact that my heart had picked up some serious speed. I took a deep, calming breath, draped my oversized bag over my shoulder, and then flung the front door open.

And immediately collided with Milo's very broad chest.

"Oh!" I heard myself exclaim as I hit him hard enough to make him lose his balance, and he grabbed on to me for a second. As we teetered there on the landing, I should have been thinking with dismay about the way my bag had exploded off my arm, its contents spilling all over the front steps.

Instead, oddly, an image popped into my mind—big and clear, like a high-def, 3-D movie. I was in it, but it took me a second to recognize myself.

I was in a room I'd never seen before, a room that was filled with flickering candlelight and flowers—gorgeous roses. My hair was down and it looked really great. And when I smiled, I seemed to glow. I'd never thought of myself as pretty, but suddenly I was.

But the weirdest thing was that I was naked, and I wasn't at all self-conscious about my body, even though—holy moly—I turned to see Milo standing right there beside me. He was wearing jeans, but the top button and part of the zipper were unfastened. He didn't have a shirt on, and as he smiled and pulled me into his arms, his skin felt so smooth and cool against mine.

He leaned down to kiss me, but before our lips touched, I returned to sanity, probably because I'd hit the concrete landing with my butt.

Milo had definitely softened the blow, hanging on to me so that I landed in slow motion, but now he'd let go as he attempted to gather up the miscellaneous mixture of junk that had exploded from my bag.

"I'm so sorry," I stammered as I scrambled to help. "I didn't see you…"

"My fault," Milo said, even as we both moved to grab my hair-brush, and my elbow made contact with his nose.

"Ow?" Milo said, wincing a little bit. Even his exclamations were polite.

"Oh, no! I'm so sorry!" I said again, both of us crouched down and facing each other. Gum wrappers, lip balm, and old receipts lay scattered around us.

Milo gathered up three tampons and quickly handed them to me. Fan-freaking-tastic. The only thing that would be more embarrassing was if I were to blurt out the fact that, apparently, just seeing him again evoked pornographic fantasies. Although maybe that was Calvin's fault with his *bow-chicka-bow-bows*.

"Thanks," I said, stuffing the tampons back into my bag. We were silent then, both working on retrieving what proved to be mostly a whole lot of crap that I didn't need.

When I finally stood, he did the same. We were still facing each other. I had never noticed how much taller he was until now...and being taller than me was no easy feat, considering that I measured a *statuesque* five foot eleven. My perfectly petite mother had, of course, come up with the description. It was supposed to be a positive word, but everyone knew it was a synonym for gargantuan. Gigantic. Ginormous. Godzilla-esque.

But next to Milo, I felt normal.

"Thank you," I said again, and I knew that my face was the hue of a beet.

Milo's smile was concerned.

"I hope I didn't hurt you," I said, remembering the elbow to the face that I'd given him.

"No! No, you didn't." Milo frowned. "I thought maybe when you slammed into me, I'd hurt *you*. I was thinking about...something else when I came to the door and...I shouldn't let myself get distracted." He tapped on his nose and then grinned. "I'm fine, though. See? Still intact."

I forced a smile and then gave up, instead confessing, "It's been a weird couple of days, and...I'm kinda exhausted."

He nodded. "Calvin told me about Garrett. What you did. That was pretty amazing, for you to be able to tap into that kind of power."

But I shook my head, no, even as I said, "Yeah, it was pretty great, but…I'm not sure I want…this. Any of this."

"I know." Milo's eyes locked onto mine. As I gazed back at him, there was a moment of silence.

Which was cut short by the honk of Calvin's car horn. "Guys!" he yelled out of his open window. "What the heck are y'all doing?"

Milo was *Dana's* boyfriend. What the heck *was* I doing?

"Sorry!" I said. I flew past Milo and jogged toward the car, opting for the backseat instead of shotgun. I didn't give Milo a chance to open or close the car door for me.

He paused for a moment as if he was considering offering to switch places with me, but then he climbed into the front passenger seat and rolled down his window. I noticed that his T-shirt—green—was snug today, revealing those muscles I'd admired in the police station parking lot as we'd sunbathed beside Lake Puke.

I'd also admired those muscles with both hands in my little fantasy—which was still freaking me out. It was then that I realized—more oddness—that Milo was wearing his hair pulled back in a ponytail, which was exactly how he'd worn it in my imagination or vision or whatever it was. No, it couldn't be a vision because it most definitely wasn't happening at the moment I was seeing it, nor had it ever happened in the past.

I would have remembered that.

Yeah.

I focused on getting my seat belt buckled, unable to keep myself from glancing into the front of the car.

Where Milo reached into his pocket and pulled out a piece of smoking-cessation gum. And then he looked back at me as he reached into another pocket and handed me a stick of MintyMintyChew. "Here. I got you the kind that doesn't taste like crap."

I took the piece, and emotion clogged my throat. Oh my God, was I really going to start to cry because Dana's boyfriend had just given me a piece of gum? I managed to squeeze out a tearless "Thanks" as I quickly stared out the side window.

"So, what's the deal?" Cal said as he backed out of my driveway. "Where's Dana tonight? Are we playing freaky hide-and-seek with her again?" A fly had somehow gotten into the car, and Calvin swatted at it impatiently.

"No," Milo replied. "Dana's not going to be with us tonight."

"Is it her day off?" Calvin asked smartly. He backed out of my driveway.

Milo laughed a little, quietly. He spotted the fly and waved it away from his face. "I guess you could say that."

"What exactly are we doing tonight? Isn't Dana in charge of our little army?"

Milo nodded. "She is." He scratched at the nape of his neck, where his hair was gathered loosely. I'd never liked the whole dude-in-a-ponytail look, but somehow he made it look good. "But we have an errand to run that doesn't require her presence."

Calvin drove purposely slowly down the street. "So what are we doing? And where are we going?" He glanced at me in his rearview mirror. "Or are we going to rely on Skylar's instincts again to determine that? And I'd like to take this opportunity to point out that the girl is tired after her Captain America impersonation today."

"We will not be tapping into Sky's unconscious this evening," Milo told us both. But then he dropped a bomb. "We're going back to Harrisburg."

"Oh, *hay*-ell no!" Cal immediately exclaimed.

"Why do we have to go there?" I said at the same time, leaning forward between the two front seats. The last thing I wanted to do right now was spend another hour or two with creepy drug addicts—*especially* if Dana wasn't around to protect us. I spotted the fly on the back of Milo's T-shirt, and I brushed my hand quickly against his shoulder.

The fly lifted off Milo and flew out of the open window as I heard Milo say from the front seat, *I won't let anything happen to you.*

I looked at him. "How can you know that?"

Milo turned around, surprised. "Sorry?"

"You said you wouldn't let anything happen to us. But without prescient powers, how can you be so absolute? I mean, I know you'll certainly try to keep us safe, but…"

It was Calvin's turn to look surprised. "Sky, he didn't say that. He didn't say anything."

I shook my head. "Yeah, he did. You did," I said to Milo, "just now. I heard you, clear as day."

Milo stared at me, his eyes solemn. I didn't pull away when he placed a fingertip on my knee and told me, "I didn't open my mouth." *Is she really able to do that?*

"Do what?" I said, and then my mouth dropped. "Whoa. *Whoa.*"

You can hear me? And Milo pursed his lips a little bit, as if to prove that the words weren't escaping from his mouth.

"Yes…?" I breathed.

Milo let out a triumphant sound, similar to a laugh but louder, and I looked at him with my eyebrows furrowed.

You're reading my mind, he told me, again without speaking the words aloud.

"Oh my God!" I looked down at his finger, still lingering on my knee, and then I looked back up into Milo's eyes, and then back at my knee, his finger, his eyes—over and over again. And I made the connection. Literally. *I can hear your thoughts when we touch,* I realized. *Can you hear me?* I added silently, and Milo whooped and pulled his hand away to dance a bit in his seat.

"I can hear you, Skylar!" he yelled. "I most certainly can!"

"All right, seriously? I'm beyond lost," Calvin warned. "Like, maybe I should be skipping the trip to Harrisburg and just bring y'all to the hospital with the padded room instead."

I laughed. That was *incredible.* And it was obvious that Milo thought so too. If he'd tried to smile any wider, his jawbone probably would have broken.

"Wait," I said. "Let's try it again." I held my hand up, and Milo did the same. Our palms touched, and I laughed at how the ends of my fingertips barely made it to his bottom knuckles. I was that much smaller. *Like baseball mitts.*

Milo laughed. "I'm not really a big sports guy," he said aloud, "but it's a good metaphor."

I pulled my hand away and squealed. "Holy mackerel!"

Calvin looked positively fed up. "Whatever it is y'all are smoking, please don't offer me any, 'cause it's making you both ape-shit crazy."

"I can get in Milo's head," I blurted to Cal. "I am literally able to hear his thoughts. And he can hear mine."

Calvin frowned into the rearview mirror. "Really?"

"Really," I said. "Wow, I wonder if I can do it with you."

Milo turned around, and he was frowning slightly. I wondered if I was imagining things, or if he actually looked a bit jealous. But just as quickly, he shot me that grin again and said, "It's worth a shot. We'll want to know how far your powers extend."

That was enough of a green light for Cal. He took a right-hand turn and parked quickly in a gas station lot. Then, after swiftly pushing the car into park mode, he swiveled around in his seat. "Okay, what do you need me to do?" he asked.

I shrugged. His guess was as good as mine. "I think it had to do with physical contact," I offered.

"Fine," Cal said, reaching quickly for my hand. I took it.

And we stared at each other.

And stared.

Finally, Calvin busted out laughing. "Girl, seriously?"

"Wait," I insisted. "I'm trying my best to concentrate…"

"I don't know how your mental wavelengths are doing, but mine are pretty much white noise."

I waited for a few more moments, but the car's idling engine was the only sound. Plus, I couldn't *feel* Cal the way I had *felt* Milo. It sounded absolutely insane. But it was the only way I knew how to describe it. I'd felt Milo inside of my head, warm and calm and lovely.

Milo had propped himself forward, his elbows leaning against the tops of his legs. Without warning, I let go of Cal's hands and grabbed Milo's shoulder…

…*eyes are prettier than music, but she doesn't know that, I can tell…*

…and then I let go, because my hand had gotten unbearably hot, or maybe it was my brain that had heated up. Either way, the sudden connection was so intense, so intimate, that I inhaled sharply.

Milo jumped a little too.

"I'm sorry," I said. "I didn't mean to…" It felt as if I'd walked in on a stranger using the bathroom; it seemed that rude, and just as embarrassing. Had he been thinking about Dana? "Oh, God. I really need to ask before I do that, don't I?"

But Milo shook his head. "You don't have to ask. I was just surprised. I can feel you—when you're there."

I nodded. "Same here. I can feel you." And I blushed at my own words.

Calvin tapped his hands on the steering wheel as he put the car back in gear and pulled out of the gas station. "Tell me this isn't the Ouija board trick."

"What is the Ouija board trick?" Milo turned away from me to ask.

"You know," Cal said, waving his hands in the air. "The Ouija board trick. When two people conspire to move the dial, and they both act equally surprised, but they're pushing it in the same direction at the same time. And nobody else knows it because the two tricksters act so excited, but they've actually planned it out hours in advance."

I shook my head. "No conspiracy here," I replied.

Milo nodded his agreement.

I resisted the temptation to touch Milo again. I caught him looking, and I didn't need any special power to figure out that he was thinking the same thing.

I sat back in my seat.

Milo turned around so that he was facing forward, but he spoke loudly so I could hear him. "We're going to need to tell Dana about this, after she gets back."

I nodded. I couldn't wipe the dopey smile off my face. I was telepathic. But only, at least so far, with Milo—who was Dana's freaking boyfriend. Thinking about *that* got me to stop smiling.

And then I *really* stopped smiling as I remembered my little naked fantasy from before. Oh my God, I'd been thinking about kissing Milo when he'd bumped into me. Had he picked up on that? Had I sent those crazy thoughts sailing into his mind? Had he seen me naked?

Except, as far as being naked went, it was a pretty awesome naked me that I'd imagined.

Still…

"Am I really driving to Harrisburg, people?" Calvin asked, slowing down as he approached the interstate.

Milo nodded, glancing back at me as he said, "We're not going too deep into the city this time. We'll be safe. I know a guy who lives right on the border. A forger. We're hiring him to make us some fake IDs."

Calvin looked uncomfortable, but he didn't say anything as he turned onto the highway.

I managed to push my wayward fantasy out of my head, but I was unable to stop thinking about what had just happened between Milo and me. I concentrated, trying to figure out what we'd both experienced, trying to come up with a reason why I could read Milo's thoughts and not Cal's.

"Milo?" I asked. "Are you sure you don't have…gifts? Like Dana and me?"

Milo looked back at me and shook his head, adamant. "Dana and I have done a lot of tests, and I'm definitely not a Greater-Than." The edge of his mouth turned up into a smile, and he shrugged. "I'm really nothing special."

Oh, I had a very hard time believing that. "Then how could you feel—hear—what I was thinking?"

"You let me," Milo replied. "It was all you."

Calvin drove in silence, glancing up into the mirror every once in a while to look at me as I sat there in the backseat. I had a difficult time reading his expression. He seemed annoyed—or maybe he was just nervous about going back into the crappy part of town.

It seemed ridiculous. Here I was, trying to decipher what my best friend was feeling, even as I could recite back a virtual stranger's thoughts—just by placing a fingertip on his skin.

"So are you able to do…what we just did…with Dana?" I asked.

Milo shook his head as he looked back at me again. "Dana's not telepathic, although she'd really love to be. She's tried everything she can think of to develop those skills, but that's not how it works. You are what you are. And while you can hone your talents—like, she's taken her telekinetic skills and trained herself to the point where she can use them in some pretty amazing ways—most G-T's have only one or two things they can do." His eyes studied me somberly. "You're proving yourself to be extremely exceptional."

"Yeah, but I can't control any of it yet," I pointed out. "I mean, I'd like to be able to touch you without forcing my thoughts down your throat." I felt my face heat as I realized what I'd just said. *I'd like to be able to touch you.* "I mean," I stammered. "What I meant was, what if I accidentally bump into you, and then, boom, everything I'm thinking, and everything *you're* thinking is—"

"It's okay," he interrupted me. "I don't mind."

"Well, you should," I said. "What if you're having a…a…private-thought moment?"

Milo smiled at that, and there was something in his eyes that I couldn't quite define. It was more than amusement, though. And God, it was similar to the way he'd looked at me in my little daydream, right before he'd kissed me. "You're right," he finally said. "That could be awkward."

Calvin cleared his throat. "So tell me where I'm going here," he said a little sharply.

Milo turned back around. "Sorry. I'm…distracted again. Take the next exit. It's the same one we took into Harrisburg last time. But at the end of the ramp, you're going to turn left. So we won't pass the Sav'A'Buck. We're actually heading back toward Coconut Key."

"That's cool with me," Cal said.

It was definitely cool with me too.

"So why, exactly, do we need fake IDs?" Calvin asked.

"We need to find out more about the drug problem in this area," Milo answered. "Dana thinks it might lead us to the people who killed Sasha."

Calvin sighed. "Man, what do you mean *find out about the drug problem?* I thought we were going to pass, this time, on hangin' with the creepy peeps."

Milo's profile looked sad to me as he looked at Calvin. "The addicts in Harrisburg are not what we're looking for. We need to find the richie-riches, as Dana calls 'em. The people who can afford to buy Destiny."

"So if these Destiny addicts aren't in Harrisburg," Calvin asked, "then where are they?"

Milo chewed on his nicotine gum. "Everywhere," he said. "But mostly where there's a lot of money."

"Coconut Key," I muttered as Milo nodded.

"And we need fake IDs because…?" Calvin asked.

"A lot of Destiny users spend their time in nightclubs and high-end hotel bars—the *beautiful people* locations," Milo explained. "We'll need fake IDs to get in."

Calvin made a noise. "Man, no one's going to let me into a club, with or without a fake ID! Look at me!" He waved one hand in front of his legs as his other gripped the steering wheel. "Who wants to let someone in a wheelchair through the gate? Bouncers won't let you in if you're not sexy enough, and last time I checked, my chair has a sexy rating of negative ten."

"Dana's going to help you with that," Milo replied.

"Help with what? Making me sexy?" Calvin laughed.

Milo shook his head. "Wait until Friday. She'll show you."

Calvin looked at him with disgust. "She'll *show* me. That's the best you're going to give me?"

"I think you're going to need to see it to believe it."

"Okay, oh mysterious one," Cal said with a laugh. "Be that way."

As we exited off the interstate, I could see the lights of the Sav'A'Buck in the distance. Other than that, everything was dark.

"Turn here," Milo said urgently, and Calvin pulled a sharp right, his tires screeching slightly down the narrow street.

I looked around. The area was mainly residential, but the houses were dilapidated and sallow. On either side of the road, the few remaining streetlamps cast a flickering and feeble light onto the pavement. The front lawns were either overrun by crabgrass and weeds, or comprised completely of ground-up shells.

"We're going to number 3111," Milo said. "Fourth house on the right-hand side."

Calvin pulled up to the place. It was a rundown single-story building, the paint on the shutters peeling off like old snakeskin. The front porch sagged slightly, and a hanging wind chime whistled and clanged with an ominous sound as the breeze blew through it.

"And how well do you know this…friend of yours?" Cal asked skeptically.

"He's a friend of a friend of a friend," Milo specified.

"Oh, good."

Milo placed a reassuring hand on Calvin's shoulder. "It's okay. I'm certain that you're safe here."

Calvin was clearly not convinced. "Let's just get this over with."

I leaned over to open my door, but this time Milo beat me to it. I thanked him quietly as he shut it behind me.

"I'm not gonna be able to go inside," Calvin noted. The steps up to the front porch were steep, and rickety to boot. "You guys better get this done fast," he added grumpily.

But just as I was about to offer to wait outside with Calvin, a huge dude with tats and a trucker hat opened the front door to the house and marched down the steps to meet us.

He was a burly guy with a thick, ratty beard, and I'd assumed at first glance that he was at least thirty-five, if not older, but as he got closer I realized that the facial hair had thrown me way off. He was actually only a few years older than Milo—just seriously weather-worn. He was, himself, pretty much a walking fake ID.

"Y'all can't come in, 'cause Becka's feeding the baby and her tits are out."

Lovely. Apparently Milo had some really classy friends of friends of friends.

"You must be Nicholas," Milo said. "Renfro sent me."

"Renfro, huh?" The trucker dude crossed his arms belligerently, as he hacked a loogie to the side. "If he sent you, he told you how much it was going to cost."

Milo ignored the drool missile and nodded, unperturbed. "Nine hundred. Each."

"Dollars?" I asked, my voice squeaking a bit as the word popped out of me almost involuntarily.

Nicholas glanced at me. "Cash," he told Milo. "Paid up front. Non-negotiable and nonrefundable. If the IDs don't work 'cause your girlfriend's twelve, I don't want to hear about it."

"I'm not twelve," I said indignantly. "I'll be seventeen on Friday."

"Well, yee-hah," Nicholas said with absolutely no inflection. "Thus endeth the jailbait phase."

"She's not my girlfriend," Milo said a little too quickly—as if the idea were horrifying to him—as he took what looked like a bank envelope from his back pocket and held it out.

Nicholas took the envelope with a hand that was almost completely tatted, and opened it to reveal a thick, healthy-looking stack of bills.

Calvin's eyes got huge as Nicholas counted the money.

I touched Milo's arm, needing to ask, *Where did you get that?*

"Eighteen," Nicholas said, looking from me to Calvin to Milo, even as Milo took my hand and squeezed it. His own hand was dry and cool and really nice, which made me realize that mine was sweaty. *Yuck.*

It's okay, Milo told me, and I realized I'd broadcast that entire thought.

"I'm assuming," Nicholas said, "this is for the Mouseketeers and that you're good."

Dana's really good at finding…things of value and selling them on the black market. "I'm good," Milo told Nicholas pleasantly. "But I'd be even better if you showed just a *little* more respect for my friends."

Finding, I asked him a tad anxiously. *You mean, stealing?*

"By all means," Nicholas said, heavy on the sarcasm. "Please. Step right this way, sir and ma'am." He led the way toward a separate structure that was half garage, half Quonset hut, turning on the light inside and opening the metal door so that Calvin could roll right in.

Milo held onto my still-sweaty hand as we followed. *No, I mean finding.* And it was weird, because instead of him telling me with words, I saw a very clear, very sharp picture in my head of Dana and me—and Calvin too—at the Sav'A'Buck. And I saw Dana take the gun that the jokering woman had brandished, and tuck it deftly into the back of her pants.

And I knew, from seeing that, that the money Milo had used to pay for our fake IDs had come from Dana selling that gun. I also knew... *Catching Sasha's killer really matters to her.*

It does, Milo agreed.

A camera flashed, and I flinched, looking around and realizing that this hut was part computer lab, part photography studio, and it was my turn to step in front of a green screen and get my picture taken.

For my fake ID.

I let go of Milo's hand and moved into position.

"On three," Nicholas told me, but the camera flashed right after he said *one*.

"Hey," I said. "That's gonna suck."

Nicholas was in a rolling chair, and he zoomed across the room to the computer station. "The pictures have to suck," he said. "If they're too good, they'll get looked at, and you don't want that."

And sure enough, up on his computer screen was a picture of me, mid-blink. I was smiling, but my eyes were almost entirely closed.

"Wow," Calvin said. "You look stoned."

"And yours is so much better," I countered as Calvin's face appeared next to mine on the screen.

Milo took one look at it and cracked up. It was the first time I'd heard him laugh out loud with genuine amusement. I smiled. I liked the sound. It was deep and warm—a lot like the way it felt when I was inside of his head.

"What?" Cal said.

Milo caught his breath. "You look…"

"Constipated," I finished for him.

"That's my sexy face," Calvin protested.

"It looks like you're due for a stool softener," Nicholas said bluntly. "It'll definitely do."

Milo and I lost it. Cal scowled, but then he laughed too.

"This is gonna take a while," Nicholas said. "Three hours at least. You wanna come back to pick 'em up?"

"No," Milo said. "I'm gonna stick around while you work. Just let me get my friends on their way home."

He was already herding us toward the door, but I took his hand again. *I don't want to leave you here alone!*

"I'll be fine," he said aloud as he closed the hut's door behind Calvin. *That friend of a friend told me that Nicholas is brilliant but kinda irresponsible. It's best to wait while he does the work. Eighteen hundred dollars is a lot to gamble.* "You need to get home."

"We can wait with you," I said, but I was thinking, *God, three hours from now it'll be after midnight, and if something goes wrong and my mother finds out, I'll be grounded for life.*

I felt Milo smile. *We definitely don't want that.* Gently, he disengaged himself from my hand so that he could open the car door for me.

Calvin was already getting in the driver's side, and I knew that he was more than ready to leave.

"How will you get home?" I asked Milo.

"Actually," he said as I got into the car and opened the window. He bent down to talk to me. "Dana and I are camping not too far from here."

And I was glad, then, that he'd let go of my hand. Dana. I'd completely stopped thinking about Dana—his girlfriend. I felt simultaneously jealous and terrible. What was *Dana* going to think about my ability to read Milo's mind? If Milo were *my* boyfriend and some other girl could see and feel his thoughts? I would not be happy.

"Still," I managed to say. "You don't really know this guy."

"Yeah, but like you said, we don't want you grounded," he pointed out.

"But she didn't say that," Calvin started, but then looked from me to Milo and back again. "I still think you guys are pulling the Ouija board trick."

"Cal," I said calmly. "You know me pretty well. Do I seem like the type to play a practical joke on you?"

Calvin squinted his eyes suspiciously. Then he relaxed. "Yeah. You're right. But I'm still having a tough time buying it. In fact, *all* this shit is hard to swallow. Up until the past couple of weeks, I was a firm believer in basic laws of physics. Like, gravity? Call me crazy, but it was a principle that I'd sort of accepted."

There was sympathy in Milo's eyes. "I had a tough time wrapping my brain around all of it at first too," he admitted quietly.

"Oh yeah? And how long did it take you to finally feel like your life wasn't some long, drawn-out, very strange dream?"

Milo paused to think. But then he grinned. "Calvin, I don't think I've woken up yet." He glanced at me. "It gets stranger every day." He straightened up then, backing away from the car. But then he bent down again to add, "Go straight back to Coconut Key. Don't stop for anything. Get home safe."

I nodded as Calvin pulled away.

Milo stood in the dim light outside Nicholas's crummy house and garage, and I watched him until he faded and blended in with the darkness of the night.

And all I could think was, was this it? Was it happening? Was I turning into more of a compassionless sociopath with every breath I took?

I know Dana said it was a myth—that being a Greater-Than didn't mean I would automatically lose my empathy and my humanity and my ability to be a good person.

But a good person wouldn't have spent the past ten minutes clinging to her friend's boyfriend's hand.

Or fantasizing about him kissing her like that.

Or—worst of all—wishing, at least a little, that she was prescient, which would mean that kiss she'd imagined in such glorious Technicolor was yet to come.

Friendship with Dana be damned.

CHAPTER NINETEEN

I was back on the highway again. This time, the rain had let up, but the fog hadn't, so it was really difficult to see even a few feet in front of me.

I had a pretty massive *holy crap* moment when I realized that I was dreaming again. And that thought was immediately followed by the idea that if only I could get my hand on my phone, I'd be able to take notes for Dana. But since my phone with those notes would inevitably be left in my dream world, there was really no reason to try to record anything. Once I woke up, none of this would be tangible.

Kudos to me for trying, though.

I tried to concentrate and at least make *mental* notes about what I was seeing. The trees on either side of the interstate were blowing in a fairly strong breeze. Oh, yeah, and I was back in that mystery car, wearing that mystery dress. I looked down at my lap and studied the pattern of the fabric. It wasn't exactly high fashion. In fact, the cheap-looking blue-and-white diamonds looked a lot like the design on a hospital gown. I reached around and felt the back. Sure enough, the material was tied in the back twice—once between my shoulder blades, and another right above my butt.

Okay, so it didn't just look like a hospital gown. It *was* a hospital gown. But why?

And then, talk about *holy crap* moments. *Milo*, of all people, tapped on my windshield. I screamed a little, or I think I did. It definitely startled me. But Milo's smile calmed me as I unlocked the door.

He didn't make a move to get into the car, though. I motioned for him to walk around and jump into the passenger side, but he motioned just as adamantly, insisting that I get out.

I paused. In the very first dream that I'd had, I'd gotten out of my dream car to try to chase Sasha down the highway—and, in the blink of an eye, had found myself alone in the middle of a field with the creepy she-thing.

Milo was insistent, so I reached to open the door.

But then I hesitated, double-checking, just to be absolutely *certain* that it was Milo out there.

And, yeah, nobody else in the world had dimples like that. Even in that crazy fog, I could tell that much.

I stepped out of the car.

And I instantly realized my mistake. My butt had to be hanging out of the hospital gown!

But when I reached around to close the opening, my hands grazed denim. Jean shorts. I hadn't been wearing them in the car, had I?

Milo shrugged like he didn't know.

So I guess in dreams you don't have to touch me to get inside my head, I said without opening my mouth.

Guess not, Milo answered, his lips pursed as he watched me intently.

And then something *really* crazy happened.

Milo took a step toward me, put his hands on my hips…

And he kissed me.

I'm not talking peck on the cheek, either.

I'm talking full-on, passionate, head tilted to the side, hair blowing in the wind, tongue-touching, heart-pounding, I-want-your-body kiss. And I did something really crazy.

I kissed him back.

Pinch me, because I think I'm dreaming, I told him as I melted against him, as his arms tightened around me.

Very funny, he said, and when he pulled back slightly to look down at me, his eyes smiled. But it was a smile that was laced with heat, which totally took my breath away, because I knew he was going to kiss me again.

Except, the heart-rate monitor sound was back, and even through the fog, I could see her over Milo's shoulder.

Sasha.

She was running toward us down the long, straight road, waving her arms over her head as if trying to get our attention.

At first I thought she was wearing a mask, because her face was the color of a fire engine, the whites of her eyes startlingly bright against the shiny contours of her forehead. But, as she got closer to us, I realized that the girl was horribly, gruesomely covered, head to toe, in blood.

Milo grabbed my shoulders and tried to bury my face in his chest, as if instinctively attempting to shield me from the awful image. But it was engraved forever in my mind, and even though I knew I was asleep, I also knew that when I woke up, this terrible, bloody picture of Sasha would still be there. Because it was the same image I'd seen in my vision when I was with Dana down on the beach.

But when I looked again at the girl's face, she wasn't Sasha anymore. Suddenly, she had turned into Nicole, my best friend from Connecticut, but then, just as suddenly, both Nicole and Sasha were lying on the highway, bloody and desperate and needing my help.

Sasha! Nicole! I called out, but when I tried to speak, no sound came out.

Milo heard me, though. Without opening his mouth, he pressed his hands against my face, and I felt him respond. *They can't hear us, Sky. They're not really here. They're somewhere else.*

Frantically, I screamed and screamed, calling their names, even while knowing that there was nothing I could do to help them. I pulled myself away from Milo's protective embrace, and my world faded to black.

———

When I woke up, my mother was humming an old Celine Dion song and rustling with clothes on my floor as she sifted through them, trying to find the dirty laundry.

Somehow, despite the fact that I'd simultaneously had the best dream and the worst nightmare of my entire life, I managed to sit up slowly in bed, while not shouting, *Oh my God, what are you doing in here?*

Mom turned to look at me. "Good morning, sweetheart," she said pleasantly. Today she was wearing gray linen pants and a sleeveless turtleneck sweater. Her hair was poufy and side-parted, with a thick headband. It reminded me of pictures I'd seen of 1950s housewives.

"Morning," I croaked as I attempted to wipe a glob of sweat from my hairline. I was completely soaked with fear-induced perspiration. I hoped my mom couldn't tell.

"Sorry I got in so late last night," Mom replied. "The parent-teacher prom committee ran over, and a few of us ended up stopping at CoffeeBoy afterward." With two fingers, she picked up a wrinkled sweater that probably hadn't seen sunlight in months and added it to the dirty laundry basket.

Somehow this whole conversation was almost as surreal as my recent dream. It seemed almost...disrespectful to chat about prom committees, of all things, after what I'd just witnessed.

Still, Mom hadn't been in my head. I played along. "It's okay. I went to bed pretty early." All of the relentless lying to my mother was starting to leave a bad taste in my mouth, despite the fact that it was necessary. And to be fair, it wasn't as if she were being completely honest, either. Prom committee, my ass. Unless, of course, Jenkins happened to be working on the school dance, which was kind of scary to consider.

"I'm glad you did that," she replied, her voice singsong as ever. "You need the sleep. It's been a rough couple of weeks."

"You can say that again," I mumbled. My heart was still banging against my chest, but somehow I managed to sound calm. And Mom still hadn't seemed to notice the fact that I was perspiring like I'd just spent an hour in a sauna.

Mom picked up the overflowing laundry basket. "I just wanted to put a little bug in your ear about that cooking class," she started.

I covered my face with my hands. This woman was seriously exhausting.

"Skylar, hear me out," Mom continued. "It's a six-week thing—two times a week. You get to be around other kids your age, the instructor's nice, you bake cookies, you mingle…"

I kept my hands over my face while I shook my head slowly. The last thing I felt like doing these days was *mingling* with anyone.

"Please, Skylar? It would mean a lot to me."

I dropped my hands and stared disbelievingly at Mom. "Well, it would mean a lot to *me* if you'd let me do something I actually liked—like track. And, just to clarify one more time, I *did* say track. I know when we talked about it the other night, you heard *Russian roulette club*."

Mom laughed a little, but I glared her smile away.

"Seriously, Mom, the last time I checked, most people really don't die at track meets. You know, the whole running in a straight line thing? Not too risky." But even as I said the words, I knew a very sad truth. That even if my mother was suddenly possessed by the Friendly Ghost of Permissive Parenting, I *couldn't* go out for track. As soon as I ran my first race, I'd reveal myself to be a Greater-Than. I might as well walk around carrying a sign saying *Come and get me, very bad people who killed Sasha and Lacey.*

But Mom took the matter out of my hands. "I'm sorry, but my answer's still no," she said quietly.

"Forget it," I muttered.

Mom gazed at me with sad, deer-in-headlight eyes.

"Um, could you leave my room now?" I asked impatiently.

Mom flinched as if I'd slapped her in the face. "Sorry, sweetheart. Yes, I'll leave you alone." And with that, she quietly closed the door behind her.

Great. Just fantastic. As angry as she made me, it was even worse when Mom did things like apologize and act super sad.

"Ugh," I said, and threw off the covers. Enough wallowing in self-pity. I had more important things to worry about.

Like using my psychic-powered dreams to find Sasha's killer and keep the bastards from hurting any other girls—myself included.

As I organized my backpack and got ready for school, I thought about the details of this most recent dream. The trees, in particular, stuck out. They hadn't looked like typical Florida palms or banyans. But they didn't look much like the lush forests of Connecticut, either.

It occurred to me that, even though Sasha had been kidnapped in Coconut Key, the likelihood she was still in town—or even in Florida—was pretty iffy. I made a mental note to talk to Dana or Milo about that next time I saw them.

Milo.

Oh, yeah. *That* whole thing.

I mean, it was kind of hard to not focus on that part of the dream. I could still remember every detail. Milo had smelled like vanilla again, and he'd tasted minty, without even a trace of cigarette smoke.

Guilt hit me solidly in the chest as I thought about how vivid that kiss had been. It was, without a doubt, the most romantic kiss of my entire life. Which was not to say there were a lot of kisses to compare it to in the *Skylar's Romantic Moments* subfile of my important memories. But there *were* a few that rated, the big kiss with Tom Diaz, sophomore year, holding first place. Until now, that is, when a kiss—from a dream, no less—knocked it down to a very solid second.

And I sighed as I realized what that probably said about me—that out of the two most romantic kisses of my life, one had been with a guy visiting from California—a guy I knew was going home the next day. And the other had been, yes, in a dream, with the boyfriend of a girl whom I not only wanted to be friends with, but who could soundly kick my ass if I pissed her off.

I grabbed a towel and headed to the bathroom to shower.

Of course, Milo and I hadn't really kissed. And we weren't going to.

Like he'd even want to. I remembered how quick he'd been, last night, to tell Nicholas the forger that I wasn't his girlfriend.

Except, God, if he could read my mind every time we touched, I was going to have to be extra careful about what I was thinking. It would be unbelievably embarrassing if he brushed against me while I was fantasizing some fairy tale where he played Prince Charming to my naked Cinderella.

I sighed as I turned on the shower. It would be nice if *some* part of my life could be easy or simple. For a long moment, I closed my eyes and wished everything could go back to the way it had been before Sasha was kidnapped.

Mom rapped on the closed bathroom door. "Sky, I forgot to tell you. The toilet in there is clogged, so don't flush it! I have to call the plumber."

Yuck. "Okay, Ma." I raised my voice to be heard over the sound of the running water. "What happened?"

"Don't know," Mom called back through the closed door. "It was fine last night. But it's backed up this morning. So no flushing, please."

"Got it." I loved how Mom had to repeat everything she asked of me at least twice, as if she didn't have faith I'd catch on the first time.

I felt her presence as she lingered in the hallway for a moment, and then I saw the shadow of her feet underneath the crack in the door as she walked away. I couldn't believe I was saying this, but I really hoped Mom had another date with Jenkins sooner rather than later, so she could continue to stay out of my hair.

I showered quickly and dressed just as fast. I could hear Mom moving stuff around downstairs in the kitchen. I really had to pee, so before I grabbed my backpack, I ran back to the bathroom and used the toilet.

Without thinking, I flushed the damn thing.

Of course, the toilet made a pathetic, watery noise, without that ending *clunk-cluh-clunk* of the water going all the way down. I hopped up and looked in.

"No," I said quietly as the water in the bowl began to rise.

"No!" I repeated, louder this time, as it got higher and higher.

"Skylar?" I heard Mom call from downstairs.

So I tried something kind of whacked.

I thought about the dream I'd had, and the way I'd felt when I had seen Sasha and all that blood. And I let myself get upset.

Her face, with those wide, little girl eyes looking to me for help. But I'd been able to do nothing. *Nothing.* Those little arms. She'd been waving for me, imploring me. And I couldn't save her.

My heart pounded. I thought about Sasha and stared at that stupid toilet and thought about the water turning around and going back down, taking whatever was blocking the pipe with it. And I let my heart beat really fast.

And then…

…eff me if the toilet didn't make a huge burping sound before it just sucked all the water down, flushing it quietly and efficiently, as if it had never been clogged.

"Ha!" I exclaimed.

Okay, so Dana probably wasn't talking about fixing the plumbing when she'd told me that my *gift* would come in handy. But it was a pretty convenient bonus.

"Skylar?" Mom called again.

"Fixed the toilet," I called back, still breathing heavily.

"What?" Mom yelled.

"Nothing," I hollered. And then I smoothed down my hair in the mirror, grabbed my backpack, and raced out the front door.

Of course, I'd forgotten that track tryouts were today.

But the oversized orange-and-black banner stapled across the front of the school gym was more than happy to remind me that not only did I have a mother who was insane, but that I too was not normal, and would never be normal again.

Girls Winter Track Tryouts! Bring sneakers and a smile! 3–5 p.m.
GOOOO, TORNADOES!

I scowled at the banner as I passed it yet another time after science class.

"Hey, what's your problem?" Cal said, speeding up to match my pace.

"Sorry," I said as I turned around and waited for him. "I'm pissed off." I fussed with my ponytail and nodded toward the banner. "Track tryouts are today."

Calvin didn't need to take more than a few seconds to do the math. He said, "No way can you join track. Your life would be in danger."

"I know." I sighed dramatically.

"That sucks," he said sincerely. "I'm really sorry."

I looked at him.

Like me, Calvin would never be able to join track. But unlike me, he couldn't run record-breaking speeds or move his boom box without touching it or read Milo's mind. Unlike me, he was stuck sitting in a wheelchair, destined for an early grave. *And* unlike me, he was not complaining.

"This morning, your mom called my mom about that cooking thing," Calvin told me. "I'm signing up to take a class with you."

"Oh my God." I winced. "I'm so sorry."

"No, it's actually really great," he said. "My mom talked yours into letting us take a class called Twentieth Century Film, instead. It's held over at the community college, in their auditorium."

I must have still looked blank, like I didn't understand the really-greatness of what he was telling me, because he added, "Their really large auditorium where they don't take attendance, so they don't know who shows up, and they screen really long movies that we can stream and watch online at a more convenient time so no one will know we're cutting class? And the first class is Friday—tomorrow night—and my mother not only negotiated us an extra two hours to go out for ice cream to celebrate your birthday after the class ends at ten thirty, but she got your mom to give permission for me to drive you there and back."

I had to repeat it because it was just too amazing. "So, tomorrow night, I can not only get into your car with you without having to hide, but I don't have to be home until twelve thirty?"

"Double bonus: first movie on their list is *Rear Window*," Cal told me with a grin. It was a movie we'd already seen—one of Hitchcock's thrillers, with a hero who was in a wheelchair. "So when you get home and your mom goes, *How was the film?*"

"I can tell her that it rocked," I finished for him, and we high-fived. "I am so buying your mother flowers."

"She likes tulips," Calvin told me.

"Oh, by the way? We need to get back in touch with Dana and Milo," I told Calvin. "I had another dream last night." I glanced at him. "And? I fixed my toilet this morning."

Calvin looked at me like I had just grown a second nose. "Um, that's cool?"

"No, I mean, I fixed it with telekinesis. Isn't that kind of ridiculous?"

Calvin scratched his chin and stared at me. "More than kind of," he said, "but I guess I should start getting used to it. It seems like you and Dana both come with buckets of ridiculous. I'm talking craploads of ridiculosity."

I raised an eyebrow.

"It's a word," Calvin assured me.

"Anyway," I said as we walked to band practice, "I was thinking about it, and I figured it might be really important. I mean, if I can move both solids *and* liquids—that's a really cool gift to have."

"Yeah," Cal replied. "You should work on moving gases too. Take the oxygen out of the killer's room or something. That'd be awesome."

"Wow!" I exclaimed. "I hadn't even *thought* about that!"

Calvin frowned. "Girl, I was kidding."

"I'm not!" I said, clapping my hands. "Consider the possibilities!"

"Okay, don't go all mad scientist on my ass, pretty please," Calvin said, and his words stopped me. "Maybe you should consult with the boss before you start any experiments. Call me crazy, but I actually enjoy respiration."

He was still laughing, but I felt a little sick. "You don't really think I would…" I couldn't say it.

"Whoa," Cal said, and his tone shifted so quickly that I touched his shoulder, concerned.

"What is it?" I asked.

"Whoa," Calvin said again, even more quietly. "Check it out." He pointed at the entrance to the band practice room.

At first, all I saw was a group of faculty and teachers, including Diaprollo and Jenkins. The principal and vice principal were also standing there, as well as a few other staff members I didn't recognize.

I almost asked Cal what he was talking about, but then Mrs. Diaprollo took a step to the side.

"Holy crap!" I exclaimed.

"Holy crap is right," Cal murmured, his mouth hanging open.

Holy crap indeed.

Garrett Hathaway was in the middle of the circle. The teachers were bending down to talk to him.

And the reason why they were bending down was because Garrett was seated. He made eye contact with Calvin for a very brief second, and then quickly looked away. But Cal didn't stop staring.

The teachers stepped back, and then Garrett pushed himself toward the band room, just in time for Cal to catch up.

"Hey, Garrett," Cal said, nodding to the quarterback as he rolled by. "Nice wheelchair."

CHAPTER TWENTY

The rest of the school day was basically a blur.

And understandably so. It was pretty freaking difficult to concentrate after seeing Garrett Hathaway, of all people, in a wheelchair.

I do remember the color of Garrett's face when Mr. Jenkins worked to clear a larger space for the quarterback in the front row of band practice. Moving everybody's music stands three feet to the left was a tedious process—and it involved a lot of stares and whispers from the rest of the class.

Of course, I was equally focused on my menstrual cramps—which were back in full force today, which was beyond annoying.

As Chinese culture class—my last of the day—dragged on, I looked at the clock. The bell was going to ring any second, which was a good thing, because I needed a tampon switch soon. *Sooner* than soon.

The bell finally rang, and I grabbed my backpack and booked it out of class, speed-walking toward the nearest girls' room.

Was it possible for anything to go right these days? A little reprieve from the relentless drama and mishaps would have been heaven. But that was apparently just a pipe dream at this point in my life.

I went into a stall and slammed the door shut and inspected the damage.

It was bad.

I thought about tying my sweatshirt around my waist, which would have been great if I hadn't left my hoodie at home that morning.

I dug into my backpack for a tampon—and came up empty.

And, of course, I didn't even have a lousy dollar to feed to the community dispenser, and the old-fashioned machine didn't take debit cards. Only coins.

"No!" I wailed miserably.

I heard the bathroom door open. Peering under the crack at the bottom of the stall, I caught a glimpse of familiar white sneakers. Kim Riley. Had to be.

I heard Kim cross to one of the sinks and turn the faucet on.

"Hey," I called out impulsively. "Is that you, Kim?"

She turned off the water, listening and no doubt wary of who might be calling her name. There were a lot of mean girls in our school.

"It's me," I told her. "Skylar. From band? Hey. I'm in a little bit of a bind here…" I yanked my pants back up before opening the stall and poking my head out to offer her an embarrassed and toothy smile.

She knew exactly what had happened. "Bummer," Kim mumbled as she tossed her paper towel into the trash can with rather extraordinary aim.

"Yeah," I said. "You wouldn't happen to have an extra tampon…?"

Kim shook her head. But she dug in her baggy, ripped jeans and pulled out a tiny Yoda-shaped change purse. She extracted a dollar coin from its open mouth, stuck it into one of the slots of the dispenser, and turned the knob. *Clunk.* It was the sound of salvation.

"Oh my gosh, you're a lifesaver," I said as she handed the tampon to me. I grabbed it and shuffled back into the stall.

"Here," Kim said, digging into her backpack before I closed the door. "Take these." She tossed me a pair of old, wrinkly gym shorts.

"Oh, thank you!" I exclaimed. "I'll get them back to you, A-SAP."

"Eh," Kim said, slinging her backpack over her shoulder and trudging out of the bathroom. "They're too small. Keep 'em."

With that, she was gone.

Okay, so sometimes life didn't completely suck.

I tugged Kim's shorts on, grateful that I'd chosen to wear sneakers today. Platform sandals and gym clothes would've been quite the fashion statement. I carefully rolled up my jeans and stashed them in my bag.

Then I jogged out of the bathroom and into the hallway, throwing my backpack over one shoulder. I picked up my pace as I rounded the corner—and collided straight into an extremely distraught-looking Jenkins.

"Skylar!" Jenkins said, adjusting his tie as I took a step—more like a leap—back from his chest.

"Sorry, sir," I replied. "I didn't mean to bump into you."

"No, it's all right," he said, glancing uncomfortably at my outfit. "Will you... Is that... Are you really...?"

Jenkins didn't provide a verb or otherwise end his sentence. I waited for a moment, because he didn't make a move to get out of my way, either. But he didn't say another word.

Awkward.

"Ooo-kay," I said, glancing around him anxiously. "Well, I guess I'd better get going…"

Hopefully Cal was still waiting for me in the parking lot. But I'd disappeared as soon as school had ended, and it had taken me at least twenty minutes to clean up. He probably thought I'd taken off for more training with Dana. Which meant I was doomed to walk home.

"Where are you headed in such a hurry?" Jenkins finally asked, his tone just a bit strained. He stared at my sneakers as if they could answer his question, before looking up into my eyes. "Going for a run, it looks like…?"

Where I was going was none of his business. "I've got some stuff to take care of. Is that a problem? I mean, school's over and all."

"Calvin is looking for you!" Jenkins blurted out. "He says it's incredibly urgent. You mustn't waste time!"

"What?"

Jenkins nodded adamantly. "It's imperative that you find him now!"

Calvin? Urgent? That didn't sound good.

"Where is he?" I asked.

Jenkins looked absolutely miserable. "I'm not entirely sure, but he left in a huge hurry, and I think it would be best if you were expedient in finding him."

I turned and started to run toward the parking lot.

"Not *that* expedient," Jenkins called out as I left. "Don't run in the school!"

"I'm just walking fast," I hollered back, even though I didn't slow down.

When I got to the parking lot, Cal's car was nowhere in sight, as I'd expected.

"Crap," I said, and pulled my cell phone out of the front pocket of my backpack. I swung my bag over my shoulders again and began to jog as I dialed Cal's number.

It went straight to voice mail.

"Crap. Crap!" I picked up my pace. Coconut Key Academy wasn't too far from our neighborhood, but I didn't want to waste a moment.

I tried his phone again. Voice mail.

It wasn't like Cal to shut his phone off. With a growing sense of urgency, I began running.

I picked up my pace. My backpack bumped irritatingly against my back with every step I took, but I chose to ignore it. I needed to get to Calvin's house fast.

In a few minutes, I'd made it onto Peachtree Lane, which meant I was close to Cal's. I tried his number again.

"Quit blowing up my phone!" Cal exclaimed after the first ring.

I stopped running. "Cal? Oh my God, are you all right?"

"Girl, I'm trying to download a movie on my phone right now, and you're messing up the connection!"

My breathing was ragged as I choked back impending tears. Dammit. These days I always felt as though I was about to cry.

But he was okay! He was okay!

"Sky, what's going on?" Cal said. "Where did you go after school? I looked for you, but you were ninja-stealth after band ended."

"Calvin!" I couldn't help it. I lost it again and burst into tears. "I love you!"

There was a pause. "Sky, you're freaking me out."

"I just… You're my best friend, and if something happened to you, I don't know how I could live with myself!"

"I'm fine," Cal said. "What made you think I wasn't?"

"Jenkins," I said, walking as I talked. "He told me that you needed to talk to me, and that it was urgent. He made it sound like you were in danger."

Cal made a scoffing sound. "Man, Jenkins? I haven't talked to him about anything." He laughed a little bit. "I mean, yeah, I asked him if he'd seen you, but… Dude, the way you sounded, I thought there was some serious emergency. Are *you* all right?"

"I'm fine," I said, rubbing my eyes. "These, um, allergies are getting to me."

"Pollen's really bad this year." Like a good friend, Calvin politely cosigned my BS. "Come on over. We'll watch a movie."

"Okay," I replied quietly. "I'm almost there anyway."

"Hey," Cal added, "have you heard anything from Milo or Dana?"

"Nothing yet," I said.

"After you get here, if they haven't appeared—if you're up for it—we can see if your homing skills are working today."

"Okay," I agreed.

I sniffled back the last of my stupid tears as I pushed the cell phone back into the pocket of my backpack. Embarrassed, I glanced around to see if anyone had witnessed my little outburst. A few cars drove by. An elderly lady watered some plants. A little old man walked toward me with his dachshund. The dog's bedazzled collar shone in the sunlight.

I smiled politely as I walked past them, hoping that I didn't look as if I'd been crying. I worked to slow my heartbeat by breathing deeply…

And just as I turned onto Cal's street, I caught a giant whiff of that sewage smell.

"Oh," I said, the odor hitting me like a right hook to the nose. I covered my mouth as my stomach churned, looking around wildly. But I was alone.

Except, all of a sudden, I *did* see someone. He was at least twenty feet away, and he'd been hidden behind the bushes in Mr. McMahon's yard. But as I watched, he pushed himself to his feet and began stumbling toward me.

He was bald, with a head that seemed almost to shine in the afternoon sunlight, the pale crown contrasting with the weathered tan of his face, as if, until recently, it had been covered with thick hair. He was also wearing clothes that were filthy and stained with what looked like…blood?

"Oh my God," I managed. And just as quickly, the sewage smell vanished.

But the man didn't. He was still trudging in my direction. "Hey!" I called out as the man continued to stagger down the road. He lifted his head at the sound of my voice.

And, even with the newly shaved head and the ragged clothes, even from so far away, I knew exactly who he was.

I stopped in my tracks and held out my hands in a gesture that I hoped was nonthreatening. "Don't run! Please, don't go anywhere! It's going to be okay!" I tried to keep my voice steady. "Everything is going to be okay, Edmund."

I've heard people talk about experiences that seemed like a whirlwind because they happened so fast, and I never really knew what they meant until that moment when Edmund Rodriguez looked up at me with those blurry eyes and that bloodstained face. Because I didn't get the chance to spit out one more word before five cop cars rounded the corner with sirens blaring and loudspeakers booming.

"Down on the ground! Don't move! On the ground! NOW!"

I hit the ground *fast*, my hands sprawled out on either side of me. The street looked curious so close to my cheek, and I spit out bits of sand that had gotten stuck to my mouth when I'd landed.

But someone scooped me up in their arms as effortlessly as if I were made of feathers and carried me to the side of the street. I looked up and saw a cop in full uniform staring down at me. "You're okay, miss," he said.

I wanted to tell him that I knew that already—that I was much more worried about Edmund—but once again there was no time for words.

Because Edmund wasn't listening to the cops. He was still lingering, as if in a trance, in the middle of the street with his hands raised slightly, while the cops continued to holler through their crackling speakers.

"Down on the ground! NOW!"

And then the policeman who'd carried me to the sidewalk set me down abruptly. He joined the other nine officers, who all drew their weapons and pointed them directly at Edmund.

"You've got to listen to them, Edmund," I whispered. And there's no way he could have heard me, because the cacophony from the cars' sirens and the numbing feedback from the speakers was so overwhelming. But he did raise his hands a little bit higher before bending down and landing on one knee, and then the other.

The policemen rushed him all at once, taking him down to the ground where he landed on his face with a *thunk*.

And I hit the sidewalk too, my face again against the concrete, and it was the weirdest thing—as if my bones had turned to mush or as if my muscles had completely ceased to work. I couldn't have pushed myself up off the ground if my life depended on it. And yet I wasn't afraid. I was watching Edmund, who was looking back at me, his eyes hollow and empty. It was like his soul had completely died.

And I knew this was my chance to ask him about the old lady in the white van, to ask him who'd killed his daughter, and I also knew that I wouldn't have a chance to ask him more than one question before the police took him away.

But when I opened my mouth, it was like back in the car when I'd said "Diner," or after the accident in the school parking lot, when I'd rattled off that list of Garrett's injuries. And the words I spoke were "Where's Sasha?"

As I heard what I said, as a part of me thought *No, what a waste of this chance to get answers*, I was hit by the briefest flash of a vision—of Sasha clutching the very teddy bear that was missing from her bedroom. Unlike my other recent visions, her face wasn't bloody, and she wasn't terrified. Instead, she was sleeping, exhausted, her eyelashes long and dark against the softness of her tear-streaked cheeks.

As my vision cleared, Edmund let out an exhausted breath, his body like a lax piece of plastic as the cops molded his hands behind his back and clipped cuffs onto his wrists.

Still, I waited with almost unbearable excitement, certain that he was going to tell me something important, something vital, something that would prove that I wasn't crazy or naive or even just guilty of wishful thinking, and that Sasha was unquestioningly still alive and out there, somewhere. Somehow...

Frowning, he spit a piece of gravel out of his mouth before he spoke.

And said, "Sasha who?"

CHAPTER TWENTY-ONE

I don't remember walking to Calvin's house.

I remember that the police left as quickly as they had arrived, taking Edmund away with them.

You would think that at least *one* of them would have checked to see if I was okay, considering the fact that they were bringing Edmund into custody under the assumption (albeit false) that he had kidnapped and murdered a girl.

But they all pulled youies in the middle of the road and raced away, sirens blaring, leaving me alone and disoriented on the sidewalk.

Next thing I knew, I was letting myself into Calvin's house and walking toward the sound of video games coming from the family room in the back.

It wasn't until I was standing there, swaying slightly as I stared into the shocked faces of not just Cal, but Dana and Milo too, that I realized Dana's motorcycle was parked out in the driveway.

"Skylar, what happened?" I heard Dana ask.

I dropped my backpack onto the floor with a thud as she and

Milo both rocketed out of their seats, practically throwing themselves at me. And I must've still been both freaked out and overwhelmed, because my backpack launched itself up off the floor and orbited me in a quick, tight circle, as if protecting me from impending attack.

Dana and Milo both stopped short.

"Are you all right?" Milo asked, as Dana said, "Breathe, Sky. Just breathe."

"And maybe you should sit down," Calvin added. "Or go into the bathroom, pronto, if you smelled the smell again. Are you going to—"

I cut him off as I sank down right there, onto the tile, grabbing my backpack from the air and hugging it close as it struggled to get free. "Edmund came back. The police arrested him."

"Ah, shit!" Dana sat down on the floor next to me.

"I'm sorry," I said. "There was nothing that I could do. I saw him, and I was trying to talk to him, but he was…acting really weird and… Someone must've seen him and called the police because there were all these cop cars, and…" Maybe Calvin was right, and I was going to throw up. I swallowed hard. "It happened so quickly."

Dana followed her own instructions and breathed deeply, in and out several times, as if willing herself to be calm, even as my backpack stopped fighting me and became fully inanimate again. "Okay. This isn't the end of the world. We can still—maybe—get to him. Ask him questions. We're just going to have to get creative. *More* creative."

But I shook my head. "Even if we do manage to visit him in jail to ask him questions, he's not going to be able to answer them." I told them what had happened—my vision, my oddly worded question, and Edmund's disappointing answer. "He doesn't even know who Sasha is."

I could feel Milo's eyes as he watched me will myself not to cry. "You're bleeding," he said.

I looked down, afraid for one horrifying second that I'd leaked through Kim Riley's gym shorts, but he was looking at my knee. It was a mess—I hadn't skinned it that badly since I fell off my bike back in sixth grade.

It didn't hurt—until I noticed it. "Ow," I said, but then added, "I'm fine. It's okay." I looked at Dana, who was quietly grim. "I'm so sorry."

"You did your best," she said gruffly.

But I wasn't sure of that.

Dana looked impatient as she ran her hand through her hair. "What did he look like?" she asked me. "Edmund. Was he in bad shape?"

"Yeah," I said. "It was really bad. His clothes were torn and filthy—bloodstained. And he was bald—his head was shaved."

Milo looked at Dana, who nodded.

"Exactly like Lacey's dad," she said. "The shaved head. All of it."

"Really?" Calvin said. "Well, damn. That's eerie."

"The worst part," I said, "was the look in his eyes. It was like someone had wiped Edmund out—like he was a body walking around, but there was nothing inside. I don't know. It's hard to explain."

Dana was quiet as she nodded.

"I'm making sense?" I asked.

"Yes," she said.

"That's exactly what happened with her—Lacey's—dad," Milo said.

"So did he ever remember…anything?"

Dana looked horribly sad. "Yeah," she said. "Eventually he did. Remember his daughter, that is. Beyond that, no memory whatsoever, starting the night she was taken, the night he went missing. It's like those few weeks just got wiped clean."

"Doesn't that happen when people experience really traumatic events?" I asked. "I've heard of that before."

Dana scoffed. "Please, Bubble Gum. You really want to chalk it up to PTSD?"

"I don't know," I said. I knew from the shrink that Mom had sent me to after the accident that PTSD, or post-traumatic stress disorder, could happen when a person had been through a horrible event. It was a coping mechanism, and it sometimes involved memory loss. I didn't have it—at least not that particular symptom. I remembered the accident a little too clearly. "What else do you think it could be?"

"The drugs they gave him," Dana said. "Or some kind of memory wipe."

Calvin was skeptical. "Like in *Men in Black*?" he asked. Will Smith was one of his favorite old movie stars.

"Like, I'm going to trespass into your mind and erect a bunch of blocks so that you can't access certain memories," Dana told him. "They're still back there, but you can't reach 'em, so it's as effective as a wipe."

"Come on," Milo told me, holding out a hand to help me up. "Let me help you clean that out."

Without thinking, I reached for him, even as Calvin asked, "You can do that?"

…never let you get hurt again, I promise you that.

"Whoa!" I said, because Milo was suddenly there, deep inside my head. His hand was warm and solid too, and as he pulled me to my feet, he was looking directly into my eyes, and I suddenly felt much, *much* better.

It was impossible not to smile at his ridiculously bold statement as he pulled me into the wheelchair-accessible bathroom that was right off the playroom, even as I heard Dana answering Calvin. "No, but I've heard rumors about Greater-Thans who can. I've been trying to learn how to do it."

"Oh, really," I said out loud to Milo. "And how are you going to pull that off?"

Milo smiled too and hit me with, *I know. It's an ambitious goal. But I grew up watching* Star Wars, *and that whole "Try not. Do or do not" thing resonated.*

"The word *try* is not in your vocabulary, huh?" I said, even as Dana spoke over me, saying, "With relentless training."

She and Calvin had joined us in the huge bathroom, and she was answering my question because of course she thought I'd been talking to her.

Milo and I both turned to look at her at the same moment, and I realized that I was standing there, grinning foolishly up at him as I held his hand.

I let go of him, fast, suddenly feeling a whole lot worse again as Dana narrowed her eyes at me. "Okay. What the hell."

"Milo was just being nice," I started, because the last thing I wanted to admit was that I had a crush on Dana's boyfriend.

But then Milo spoke up from where he was now rummaging in the linen closet, getting out a towel and a washcloth. "I didn't tell her."

I looked at him in surprise. "You didn't…?"

"Tell her," he said again. He set the towel on the sink counter as I realized Dana's WTF hadn't been about my holding her boyfriend's hand, but rather her astute awareness that Milo and I had been having a partially telepathic conversation.

"Why didn't you tell her?" I asked as Milo turned on the sink faucet and washed his hands before soaking the washcloth.

"Tell me what?" Dana exclaimed.

"Milo and Skylar can read each other's minds when they touch each other," Calvin interjected.

Dana took a deep breath and laughed it out. "Are you serious?"

"I'm serious," Milo and I said at the same time. But then he looked from me to the toilet and added, "Close that and sit."

"Or it's the Ouija board trick," Cal added. I glared at him as I sat, reaching up to take the washcloth from Milo. I could clean out my own skinned knee. I wasn't a five-year-old.

"I wanted you to have a chance to explain it," Milo said to me. "You know more about what goes on than I do. I don't share your gift."

My knee stung, so I pressed the washcloth against it as I looked at Milo and then at Dana. And I shook my head. "*I* don't know what goes on. I just know that I've never been able to hear anyone's thoughts before, but I can hear Milo's."

"And he can hear yours too?" Dana said. She looked pissed that Milo had waited to tell her about it—and equally amazed that it was even possible to pull off what we had done. "That's freaking... Wow. I mean, that's something."

I frowned. "I think I have to work harder, maybe practice more, because I tried to get into Calvin's head too, and I couldn't. For some reason, it only works with Milo."

Milo was hovering, and I knew—even without reading his mind—that I wasn't scrubbing at my knee with sufficient force. But as I lifted the washcloth to look beneath it, it was red with blood.

"The fact that it could work at all with a normie," Dana said, "is pretty unbelievable." She held out her hand to me. "May I?"

Milo took the opportunity to take the washcloth from me and rinse it in the sink, as I grasped Dana's hand and...

Nothing.

The silence was broken only by Calvin's heavy sigh of weary long-suffering, and I shot him a warning look. This was *not* the Ouija board trick, and I knew exactly how to get him to believe us.

"I got nothing," Dana finally said, letting go of me.

Milo was there with the rinsed-out washcloth, and I took it from him again.

"There's soap on it," he said, which of course made it sting even more.

"Turn on the water," I told him, "and then go out of the room with Calvin and let him whisper something to you, and then come back in and..." I looked at Cal. "Milo and I will do our *not*-Ouija-board trick, and I'll tell you what you said."

Calvin gazed at me. "Turn on the water—and sing," he countered. "Loudly."

I rolled my eyes. "Fine."

Dana watched as the water went on, and Milo followed Calvin out into the Williams's family room. She shut the door behind them, turning to look at me as, from the other room, Calvin shouted, "Sing," adding, "Loudly!"

I sang the first song that popped into my head, which was, oddly, an old nursery rhyme that my mother used to sing to me when I was little. "Ring around the rosie, a pocket full of posies. Ashes, ashes, we all fall down!"

Dana was looking at me as if I'd grown a second head. But instead of berating me for being remarkably uncool, she said, "You *do* know that song is about catching the plague or some kind of violently awful disease and dying, right?"

I didn't know what to say to that, but then I didn't have to say anything, because Cal and Milo came back into the bathroom.

And Milo was going to come over and touch me, which made my heart beat harder—one, because I was an idiot, and two, because the last thing I wanted him to do was to get hit by a slew of uncontrolled and giddy *I'm crushing on you* thoughts. Or—God forbid—have him catch a whiff of that dream I'd had about him last night.

The one where he'd given me that Hollywood-blockbuster-worthy kiss.

So I braced myself, forcing a smile as I held out my hand in much the same way Dana had held her hand out for me. But Milo was still all about cleaning out my knee, and instead of taking my hand, he knelt next to me and took the washcloth.

He looked up, watching me through thick-lashed eyes, and placed a hand around the back of my calf to steady me. I inhaled at the sudden, abrupt contact. But then I laughed, because the words that he'd thought at me were... "Beam me up, Scotty?" I repeated.

"Holy shit," Calvin said.

Dana looked confused. I guess she didn't watch much ancient cult TV. "What does—"

"It's from *Star Trek*," Calvin said. "Captain Kirk actually never says it in the show, but it's... Never mind."

"Are you satisfied?" I asked him.

"I am," Dana said. "It's freaking impressive to be able to establish a telepathic connection with a normie...? I've heard it's been done with two Greater-Thans, but..."

She kept going with her explanation, but I didn't hear her, because Milo was thinking at me, things like *This is gonna hurt. I'm so sorry, but I gotta get the dirt out. ...and skin is so soft, lips were even softer... Don't think about that, don't think about that, don't think about—*

He pressed down with the washcloth on part of the scrape that still contained grit and dirt, and a tiny sound of pain escaped from me—I couldn't help it. He looked up at me, his eyes filled with apology, and right at that moment, I must've lost what little control over my subconscious that I had, and I flashed—in brilliant and vivid Technicolor—into a memory (eidetic, of course) of part of last night's dream.

The part where I was kissing Milo.

He pulled his hand away from my leg—fast—as if I'd burned him.

"Oh my God," I said aloud, because we were no longer connected. "I'm so sorry!"

"No, no, that was my fault," he countered, even as he scrambled farther away from me, nearly leaping to his feet. "I had this...crazy dream last night, and I'm so sorry."

He'd turned away to rinse off the washcloth in the sink. He was focusing intently on the task. And he was turning red.

He had a dream last night?

I took a step toward him and, in a moment of impulsive courage, grabbed his shoulder, because God knows I wasn't going to ask this question out loud in front of Dana. *You had a dream about...me?*

He looked up at me, his expression one of desperate embarrassment, and I felt more than heard his reply. He was unable to form a coherent thought other than *God, I'm so sorry.*

But I saw, without a doubt, that somehow, someway, we'd had the same dream last night. The *exact* same dream.

Oh God, I asked him, *did I make you kiss me?*

And Milo looked mortified, which made me feel even more mortified. But I kept my hand on his shoulder as he gazed at me and...

Sky, you didn't make *me do anything.*

I sighed. And I studied his face. *But you remember it? Last night, with the fog and the—*

...highway, he finished for me. *And that silly hospital gown you were wearing. Why were you wearing that thing?*

"Holy crap!" And I must have said *that* out loud, because Dana and Calvin both said "What?" at the same time.

"Do you want to tell them or should I?" I asked Milo as I took my hand off his shoulder.

But Milo touched my arm and silently said, *It was just a dream. You don't have to say anything that will make you uncomfortable.*

He let go of me and I took a deep breath. "I had another dream about Sasha last night," I told Dana and Calvin, "and Milo had the same dream."

"You're dream projecting," Dana said, and it was more of a statement than a question.

"I'm not sure what it is that I'm doing," I said.

"Dream projecting is when a telepath is so powerful that her unconscious essentially forces her dreams on anyone who might be susceptible." Dana looked from me to Milo and back.

"So it *was* my dream," I concluded, unable to meet Milo's eyes. I *forced* my dreams on him?

"And therefore, it contained psychic elements," Dana concluded. "How many times has it happened?"

"Just once," I replied.

"Five, er," Milo blurted at the same time. I glanced over at him, confused. "I mean, I'm not sure." He looked absolutely horrified. "I've had several with... Skylar has entered a few of my dreams before. Two or three. Or five." He cleared his throat. "Five total. Give or take."

"Wait, wait, wait," Dana said, her eyes glinting. "So Miles, you've had a total of five dreams in which Skylar was present, but Sky, you only remember one, which happened last night?"

Milo nodded miserably. I stared at him, but he wouldn't meet my eyes. So I turned to Dana. "That's correct."

Dana stood and rolled up the sleeves of her fitted white T-shirt, creating an impromptu tank top. "Okay. I'm only going to say this once. And Milo knows it already, so more shame on him than on you, Sky." She sniffed. "Nature loathes a vacuum. And I. Loathe. Secrets."

Milo studied the contents of the bathroom's medicine cabinet, pulling out a box of gauze pads and medical tape.

"And when I think about things that I loathe, I get angry," Dana continued. "And you don't want to see me angry. Believe me."

Calvin giggled a little bit. He couldn't help it. It's what he did when he was profoundly uncomfortable.

"Scooter, something you wanna share with the group?"

"No, ma'am," he said quickly, and used massive amounts of effort to force the corners of his mouth down.

Then there was an extremely awkward silence that lasted far too long.

Milo alone was busy—opening a paper-wrapped gauze pad and digging back through the cabinet to find some antibacterial gel.

But then Calvin raised his hand and said, "I've had dreams with Sky in them before…but that doesn't mean that she planted those images in my brain, right? I mean, I also have a say in what I dream about, right?"

"That's right," Dana said.

"You have dreams about me?" I asked Calvin.

"Usually they're nightmares," he replied. "Like the recurring one where you show up at my house with bedhead and dragon breath and I have to hide under the covers until you go away."

"Lovely," I said as Milo finally turned back to me with the gooed-up gauze pad and tape. I reached to take it from him, to apply the bandage myself. That way he wouldn't have to touch me again. Although, if I could force my dreams on him while we both slept, he was kind of doomed. I could smell his embarrassment mixed in with his ever-present vanilla, but I suspected that what he was really feeling was enormous embarrassment *for* me. And I felt my face heat.

"What about you, Milo?" Dana said, ignoring Calvin's joke. "What are your dreams about?" And there was something challenging about the way that Dana was staring Milo down as she asked him.

Milo glanced at me. "Well, they're all pretty vague. Except for the last one that I had…so I'm guessing the others don't really matter. Especially since Skylar doesn't remember them."

"Come on," Dana said, clearly irritated.

"He's right," I said before Milo had a chance to respond. "He's never been in any of my other dreams—psychic or regular. It would be a waste of time dissecting every one of his."

"All right, Madam Freud," Dana said snootily, but she moved the discussion forward. "Then at least tell me the details about the dream that you imposed on Milo."

I didn't like the way she'd phrased that, and I must've looked pained, because Milo shot me an apologetic look as he mouthed an "It's okay."

I told her the dream in detail. Okay, so maybe it wasn't one hundred percent detailed. I left out the whole make-out session, but everything else was accurate and thorough—down to the types of leaves I'd noticed on the trees. Deciduous leaves on decidedly non-indigenous trees.

"I noticed them too," Milo said.

Dana looked pleased, for once. "Okay, this is good," she said. She turned to Milo. "Do you think you could identify the type of leaves if you saw them in a picture?"

"Definitely," Milo said.

I nodded too. They'd had a very distinct shape.

"Cool. Let's get on that quick," Dana decided. "Calvin, can Milo use your computer to do that research?"

"Of course," Calvin said, leading the way out of the bathroom and over to the table where his Internet computer was set up. "But aside from our little science project, what's the next step here?"

Dana blew out a frustrated breath as she followed him. "I'd say Plan B is all about figuring out why Skylar gets whiffs of the sewage deal around our good friend Quarterback McDouche with the stupid car, so…"

"I love you," Calvin mentioned.

Dana rolled her eyes. "Whatever, Boyfriend. But we need to get into his potentially smelly-ass house."

Milo and I were engaged in an awkward little dance to leave the bathroom, each motioning for the other to go first. This was not a battle I could win, so I gave up and went out the door.

"He's having a party tomorrow," Cal replied. "A sunset luau on the beach—whatever that means. Skylar scored all of us an invitation because Garrett totally wants to do her."

Milo tugged at a cuticle with his teeth before reaching into his jeans pocket and pulling out his pack of gum.

"What time does this fabulous shindig start?" Dana asked.

"Five thirty," Calvin said.

"How…early bird," Dana said. "But we can use that to our advantage if we come up cold. There are a lot of places in Coconut Key to search."

She looked from Milo to Calvin to me. And I knew she was talking about the club scene. I still didn't know—even with a fake ID—how Calvin and I would ever get into an over-twenty-one hotspot.

"We'll meet—right here—tomorrow at five," Dana continued. And then she smiled as if she could read my mind. "Don't worry about what to wear. I'll bring clothes. For both of you."

"Oh, boy," Calvin deadpanned. "I can't wait."

Dana snapped her fingers. "Bubble Gum," she said. "You're with me for some serious discussion and then a little training. Riding the Bus 201, followed by Storing Calories 202. Let's do it. Let's move."

I jumped to follow her—and tripped over my own backpack that I'd left in the middle of Calvin's very hard marble tile floor. I braced myself for my second skinned knee of the day, but I didn't hit the ground.

Because Milo leaped forward and saved me.

He caught my arm and kept me from going full horizontal, instead slamming me hard against the broad expanse of his very solid chest.

And an image coursed through me with the precise rhythm of a heartbeat, filling my brain and sending heat waves into the core of my body.

Milo, his hands traveling up my waist, my own hands dug into the thick of his gorgeous hair, his lips brushing mine as our tongues touched…

"Oh my *God*!" I said, and jumped back away from him.

"Shit!" Milo exclaimed, and I realized it was the first time I'd ever heard him swear. But he immediately apologized. "I'm sorry. I'm so sorry."

And there we were, staring at each other, wide-eyed and both breathing hard.

"What's going on?" Dana asked, glaring at us.

"Nothing," we both said quickly. Except I was still waiting for my heart to stop thumping in my chest.

Dana stared us both down for another moment before finally dismissing Cal and Milo. "Come on," she said to me. "Let's go."

I didn't look back, but I could feel Milo's eyes on my back as I followed his girlfriend out of Calvin's house and into the humid heat of the late afternoon.

CHAPTER TWENTY-TWO

Pizza Extravaganza was almost entirely empty, so Dana and I gravitated toward the window booth.

I watched Dana as she slid into her seat. Every move she made was smooth, almost stealthy. Even doing something as mundane as finding a table at a pizza place had the charismatic strategy of a cat burglar.

No wonder she was Milo's girlfriend.

I tugged self-consciously at Kim Riley's gym shorts as I sat down, feeling hopelessly unsexy compared to Dana and her sleek leather pants.

"So what did you need to talk to me about?" I asked politely. I had some things that *I* wanted to talk about—like the distinct possibility that Sasha was still alive—but I wanted to wait until Dana had said her part. And I was fervently hoping that her part didn't include a *hands off my boyfriend, bitch* speech.

I swallowed hard, thinking about the incredibly R-rated vision I'd had of Milo and me just a few minutes ago. Had Dana sensed it?

I wasn't a boyfriend thief! And yet I couldn't *not* notice how my pulse rate picked up when Milo was near. Ugh. I needed to get a grip, and fast. He was Dana's. She surely loved him—how could she not? So, game over. Or at least that's how it should go—unless Dana was wrong and the Internet was right, and I was spiraling into some sort of G-T-power-induced moral abyss, slowly but surely moving toward a monstrous humanity-free zone where I truly didn't care about ridiculous conventions like boyfriends and love and the difference between right and wrong and oh my God....

Dana took her sunglasses off, and then crossed her hands on top of the table as she looked at me. "We need to get even more serious about your training," she announced.

"I know," I said, dropping my eyes to the surface of the table to hide my relief. This was something I *wanted* to talk about.

But Dana couldn't smell emotions the way I could, and she read my body language as discouragement. "Hey." She knocked on the table in front of me until I looked up to meet her gaze, and her usually icy eyes were filled with kindness and empathy. "I'm not putting you down. You're doing awesome. I just think that if we talked a little bit more about strategy and coping mechanisms, you'd get more done—and maybe even avoid the unpleasant side effects."

I didn't say a word.

Dana decided my silence was an invitation to clarify. "I'm talking about your reaction to what happened today with Edmund, not to mention your professional-grade puking."

I smiled at that. "Thank you *so* much for reminding me."

Her lips twitched, as if she were holding back her own grin. "If it makes you feel any better, I've been there, done that. It was years ago, but it happened." Dana's smile grew and then turned wistful, as if she was rewinding a memory. "Believe it or not, I didn't make it to a bathroom, either. I puked right in Milo's lap."

I felt my eyes get huge. "Really?"

Dana nodded. "Eh," she said dismissively. "You know him, though. He's a rock. Nothing bugs him. Well, almost nothing."

"I can tell," I replied warily, afraid we were entering the boyfriend-warning zone.

"You've only seen the tip of the iceberg, Bubble Gum." Dana played with a packet of sugar. "Milo's been through it."

I raised an eyebrow, not understanding.

"He's had a rough life," Dana continued. "You know about the warrant. Imagine having to steal money that's yours from someone who's supposed to take care of you, someone whose idea of *taking care* of kids included frequent use of their belt—and then having that follow you for the rest of your life."

I couldn't imagine.

"I met Milo in that foster home," she told me. "He'd been there for a while." I could tell by the way Dana said the words *a while* that she was talking years. "He'd been through the typical shit-show. You know, dead mom, wino dad who ended up in prison...all that loveliness."

"I'd guessed it was bad," I whispered, "but I really didn't know how bad."

"Well, how would you?" Dana shrugged. "Anyway, you have to understand something." She focused her eyes on mine, gazing at me with an intensity that made my throat turn dry. "Milo hasn't met many girls like you. So just take that information and file it somewhere useful in that big brain of yours, and back the hell off."

I leaned across the table, because it was so important to me that Dana understand. "I would never," I said, shaking my head. "I mean, yes, he's great, he's amazing, he's..." I tried to make it into a joke, of sorts. "Mere words cannot describe the wonder that is Milo." But Dana definitely wasn't laughing, so I quickly added, "But he's my friend, and *you're* my friend, and I would never, *ever* do anything to come between the two of you."

Dana blinked, once. Other than that she didn't move a muscle.

"Never," I added for emphasis.

"Well, good," Dana finally said. She glanced toward the door to the kitchen as if looking for our waiter, but there was no one in sight. "Milo and I have been..."—she cleared her throat—"together for years. I'm glad to hear that you respect that."

"I do," I said.

"Good," she said again, and then she sat there, just looking at me as if she was maybe going to say something else, or as if she were waiting for me to say something else to her.

I didn't know what there was to add, maybe an additional reassurance that I'd understood her message—back away from my boyfriend—but then I didn't have to say anything because an absurdly cheerful waiter approached our table.

"Hi! I'm Mike! I'll be your server today! Can I start you off with something to drink?" Mike chuckled a little, as if he couldn't contain his own jubilance.

"We're ready to order," Dana replied, not bothering to check with me.

Mike nodded eagerly, his pen perched above the pad and ready to write.

"We're gonna need a large pepperoni pizza, extra cheese, sausage, mushrooms, and stuffed crust. Two baskets of bread, two large colas, and a lot of napkins."

The waiter's hand moved furiously across his notepad. He punctuated the order with an expressive pop as the pen hit the paper. Then he looked up and nodded. "Be back soon!"

"Wow." I asked Dana, "Are you trying to fatten me up?"

"Who said I ordered anything for you?"

I frowned.

"I'm kidding." Dana grinned. "But I'm not kidding about you needing to eat more. You're skinny as it is. And if we really do train the way I want to, you're going to be burning a seriously huge amount of calories. The telekinesis is an enormous drain. I bet the telepathy is too. And, believe it or not, the more full you keep your stomach, the less likely you'll be to…regurgitate the contents."

"I'm not sure about that," I said skeptically.

"Just try it and see. It can't hurt to try, right?"

I nodded cautiously.

"It's a nourishment thing. If you don't provide the fuel, your body starts to, well, kind of cannibalize itself. You don't just burn fat, you burn muscle, and that weakens your entire system. Keep yourself fed, and you're less likely to have nasty-ass side effects."

Swiftly, she grabbed a clean napkin off a nearby table. "You got a pen?" she asked me.

I started to dig through my bag as she added, "Anyway, I'm serious about taking this training thing to the next level. And I want to make sure that things go more smoothly tomorrow when we're sniffing around McDouche's house looking for clues."

I was still searching when Mike came back to our table with the sodas. As he leaned over to place the drinks on the table, he made eye contact with Dana. His head tilted abruptly to the right. "I would love, very much, to give you my pen," he announced almost robotically, and pulled a blue ballpoint out of his shirt pocket.

He presented it to Dana as if it were the Hope Diamond, and she took it from him just as gravely. "Why, thank you, Mike."

It was the same thing she'd done to Calvin when we were all in his car, driving around Harrisburg. *Mind-control*, Cal had called it.

I laughed out loud as Mike walked back to the kitchen. "That's so crazy."

Dana didn't reply, but moved our soda glasses out of the way, leaned over the table, and motioned for me to do the same.

"All right. Let's get organized here." Dana scribbled my name at the top of the napkin. Underneath that she made a vertical column of dashes, as if she was planning to write a list. "Okay. I want to review your talents—everything that you know about so far."

I thought for a moment. "Well, the most obvious one is the telekinesis."

Dana nodded and jotted it down.

"Then there are the smells. I don't know if that's something that's becoming more pronounced, or if I'm just more aware of it now that I know that I have that skill…"

"Probably both."

"And then there's the whole psychic thing," I continued. I almost wanted to laugh; our whole conversation sounded so ridiculous. And yet it was all true. I was psychic.

"Psychic abilities," Dana said, nodding as she wrote.

I thought about the most recent vision I'd had of Sasha…the one that had appeared in my mind so clearly, right before Edmund's awful arrest—and how I'd asked him "Where's Sasha?" instead of "Who killed Sasha?" Hope rose in my chest like a tidal wave. I knew this was my opportunity to argue my case. "Dana, I'm not sure that my abilities are only psychic. You know, with my dreams and…visions?" I took a deep breath and just said it. "I think I might be prescient too."

Dana looked up from the list without moving her head.

"I just… When Edmund showed up this afternoon, it was terrible. I mean, it was as awful as it gets. I had another vision when I spotted him. And it was strong. And powerful. And when I spoke to him? It was like that time when I just knew you were in that diner."

Dana waited for me to continue.

I dropped the bomb. "I think Sasha's still alive."

"No." Dana dropped Mike's pen and took a long sip of soda from her straw. Swallowing, she shook her head. "No. I understand you want to believe that. But there's no way."

I placed my hands on the table for emphasis. "But I *saw* her! She was asleep! She wasn't dead. And it wasn't a…a past-tense image. I really think it was happening *in that moment*. Like with Calvin in his car, with the hat."

But my words didn't convince Dana. She leaned over the table, and with eyes brimming with sympathy, she covered my hands. "No, Sky," she said again.

I pulled my hands free as I scowled and opened my mouth, more than ready to argue my point.

"And if you want to tell me why you disagree, Bubble Gum, I'm all ears—*after* we finish reviewing this list. Because whether Sasha's dead or alive, we need to keep working."

I could tell she was just humoring me. Sighing mightily, I crossed my arms over my chest. "Fine."

"Okay," Dana said. "So we were talking about your psychic slash prescient abilities."

On the napkin, Dana placed the word *prescient* between two very large and imposing sets of quotation marks. She didn't believe me.

So I'd just have to show her. But right now, I moved on. "I have an eidetic memory," I said.

"'Kay. What else?"

"I can run really fast."

Dana shook her head. "Man, I love that one. It is so freaking cool to watch you do that." She smiled as she wrote it down.

"And recently…" I cleared my throat, feeling my cheeks heat up. "I found out that I can get into another person's head by…touching them. But it's only that…one person. Milo. I don't know why," I added almost apologetically. "Ditto with the dreams."

"Contact telepathy and projection dreams." Dana nodded. She didn't look upset at all, which was a good thing. If I were Milo's girlfriend, I'd be way less cool with another girl invading my boyfriend's brain—but I guess Dana was just super confident. Of course, how could she not be? She was the epitome of sex appeal.

"I think that's it."

"You forgot to mention your musical abilities."

I blushed in spite of myself. "Oh, yeah," I said. "But that's not something to fluff my feathers about. It's not like it would ever help us out." I tried to make it into a joke. "*Excuse me, creepy old lady who steals little girls. What's that you say? Listening to Mozart melts your brain…?*"

Dana studied my face, and I looked down at my fingers nervously. Finally, she spoke. "A few years ago, I went to a bookstore." Dana took a sip of soda. After an appreciative *aah*, she continued. "I couldn't afford to buy anything at the time. Not even a cheap paperback. And my e-reader had just gotten run over by a very angry trucker in a neon-orange semi—long story. Long and very disappointing. Anyway. I missed the whole sit-read-and-relax process, so I picked up an old hardcover from the bargain bin. It was sixty-eight cents." Dana smiled. "The book was called *Learn French in 24 Hours*. Well, I read it in two. And when I was done, I had learned French."

I laughed. "You're kidding."

"Nope." She took another sip. "I remember thinking, *Well, that was easy*. So I found another book called *Master Japanese*. I read that too."

"And?"

"I mastered Japanese."

"You're kidding me."

Dana shook her head. "Nope." She played with her straw. "I'm not trying to…fluff my feathers, either. But I know that there's something about the way that you and I can use a greater percentage of our brains that makes us…unique. Different. Special."

"Greater than?"

"You can call it that if you want. But my point is that you can't take any of this"—she waved the napkin—"lightly. And you can't take it for granted. But you also can't start thinking you're better than anyone else, just because you got lucky and you won the genetic crapshoot that allows you to integrate more of your brain than the average normie can. Because thinking that you won is just one way of looking at it. The other way says that you lost. Big time."

I knew exactly what she meant and I rubbed a hand over my face. "It's tiring sometimes."

"I know," Dana said almost tenderly. "It's a gift, but it's also a frickin' heavy burden." She smiled, and I smiled ruefully back at her.

Of course, Mike the waiter interrupted the moment. "Pizza time, ladies!" he exclaimed, sliding the ludicrously enormous tray of piping hot pizza onto the table between us.

"Thanks?" I was skeptical because the thing wasn't cut. But then Mike put an enormous pizza cutter with a huge, round, dangerous-looking blade onto the table, along with the bread baskets and a huge pile of napkins.

Dana looked at Mike, her gaze deliberate.

Mike's head tilted to the side. "I would love to bring you some red pepper," he said, his automaton voice back again.

I coughed a little into my sleeve, watching as Mike quickly scurried toward the kitchen, but then stopped and grabbed a container of red pepper from another table. He ran back and handed it to Dana, before his head returned to an upright position and he waltzed away.

"Man," I said, picking up the pizza cutter. "You really are a pro at the Jedi mind-screw."

Dana shrugged. "Practice makes perfect," she said nonchalantly. "Here. Let me help you with that."

The pizza cutter was pretty dull, despite its horror-movie, implement-of-torture look, and I was having a hard time getting the pie to slice. Dana tried to yank the thing away from me, but I was holding on too tightly. Somehow, the circular blade grazed the side of Dana's palm, proving it to be sharper than I'd thought.

"Shit!" she hissed, and I looked up, wide-eyed, as she started to bleed.

"Oh my gosh! Are you okay?" I asked.

"I'm fine," she replied. She took an extra napkin and applied pressure to the cut. It didn't look like it was terribly deep—but there was a lot of blood. The napkin quickly turned red and soggy.

"I'm so sorry!" I managed.

"Don't be. Let's use this as… Well, just watch." Dana pressed the napkin firmly against the wound.

"What am I watching for?" I asked. But Dana quickly quieted me with a stern glance as she removed the napkin.

At first I thought it was my imagination. It looked like the cut was a lot smaller than I'd originally perceived it to be.

But then a few more seconds passed, and I realized that the cut was getting smaller—in front of my very disbelieving eyes.

"Whoa," I whispered.

And then, it was gone. Just like that.

No scar. No nothin'.

"Access to the self-healing centers of your brain is a pretty standard and basic G-T skill," Dana told me. "A small cut like that is pretty easy to disappear. Bigger injuries take more time. But you have to be very specific and focused when you use this talent, or all your tats'll vanish. Your body'll read 'em as something that needs to be healed and…" She looked at me and came to the correct conclusion. "No tats. Of course. Still, you should try it on your knee, while we're eating."

She paused as Mike came running out of the kitchen, his head tilted to the side. "I would love to cut your pizza for you!" he announced, and we sat back as he did just that.

"Thanks, Mikey," Dana said.

"It's a new thing that isn't going over very well. But our manager thinks it's a way to get our customers more involved with the Pizza Extravaganza experience, whatever that means," he told us cheerfully. His head tilted again. "I would love to tell my manager that you ladies think it's kinda stupid."

"You go do that, Mike," Dana said, and he rushed off. She grabbed a slice and took a bite and told me, with her mouth full, "Focus on your knee, and as you breathe, send each inhale toward your injury and picture it healing."

I did just that, and two slices later, I took off my bandage and found a scrape that looked like it had happened two weeks ago, instead of two hours.

"Dana, this is freakishly awesome." I gingerly touched my knee, but it no longer hurt. At all. I looked up and smiled at her. "Seriously, if they could bottle and sell this, people would be very rich."

"They can, and they are," Dana replied. "Don't you see now?"

I actually did. "So *that's* the reason people take Destiny."

"That's *one* of the reasons why people take it." Dana grabbed another slice of pizza. "But not everyone has the patience to learn how to control the healing centers of their brain. You can't just take the drug, and presto, you're cured of the cancer that's eating your lungs or your prostate or whatever. You have to take the time to learn to harness the power it gives you—and it gives you way more than just self-healing abilities." She waved the napkin at me again. "Anyone who takes Destiny could find themselves saddled with a variety of skills, which makes them dangerous when they have adverse reactions to the drug. And it's definitely a *when*, not an *if*.

"But whoever is in charge of making and distributing this stuff doesn't really care about that." She put her recently healed hand up and rubbed two fingers against her thumb. "It's about money. That's all they care about. If they had even half a conscience, they wouldn't be harvesting little girls for the product, for Christ's sake."

I thought about Sasha—who was out there, still alive. I believed this more and more with every moment that passed, with every breath I took. But I kept my opinion to myself as Dana slid another slice of pizza onto my plate.

I took a large bite as she waved the napkin at me again and said, "Not to freak you out, but my experience has been that G-Ts are more like me. I have a few things that I can do really well. But this list? This is crazy. Without any training? Plus, you're only sixteen."

"Seventeen tomorrow," I corrected her through my massive mouthful.

"Seventeen, sixteen, whatever," she dismissed it. But then what she said nearly made me choke. "I don't think there's ever been a girl with as much raw talent as you, Skylar. If I'm a so-called Greater-Than, you're a holy-shit-what-the-hell. So eat up. You need your strength, because I'm going to train you. Together we are going to sharpen and hone your skills, so you can totally kick ass and defend yourself. Because until you can? There are some badass mofos out there who would like nothing better than to strap you to a table and bleed you dry."

Dana and I took the bus as far as we could, then walked the last quarter mile to the former public facility known as Coconut Key Memorial Park. It used to be a huge, tree-dotted mix of lush gardens, playgrounds, and sports fields, before the city had shut it down this year.

It had another one of those chain-link behemoths around it, but Dana knew exactly where that fence had a hole.

As we went in, pushing past the overgrown plants and shrubs, I breathed in the humid air, which was salt-filled despite the fact that we were miles from the beach. It was almost six o'clock. Mom was probably wondering where I was.

Luckily, my cell slash GPS tag was still at Calvin's house.

"So what are we doing?" I asked, already exhausted from my emotional day.

"I want you to move something large today," Dana replied as she led me to the toddlers' playground. "The beach would have been tricky, because there really isn't a whole lot to manipulate. But here"—she waved her arms in a grand *ta-da* gesture—"we've got options."

"Large," I repeated as I looked around. Once lovely, this part of the park had large rope-like trees that created a canopy overhead. Sunlight flirted through the intertwining branches, the bark peeling off in curlicues. But the playground had been thoroughly vandalized in the months since it had closed. The statues of two little kids running with a dog had been knocked over, and the poor girl was broken in half. The swing sets were twisted and bent, and what had once been whimsical rocking animals now listed crazily on their springs. A flagpole had been broken off about a dozen feet up. It was splintered and split, as if a giant had come along and snapped off the top to use as a toothpick.

That top part of the pole, stripped of its ropes or rigging, lay near a pair of forlorn portapotties that had been left behind.

"How large?" I asked.

But Dana had already gone over to kick at the top of the flagpole. She looked up at me. "This'll do."

"Please," I scoffed. "There's no way I could—"

"Yes, you can," Dana interrupted me. "And you can start by losing the negative attitude."

"But that thing is huge!"

"Yup," Dana said. "So get ready to use a serious amount of your mojo." She was dead serious.

I blew a breath of air upward. My hair caught the breeze, and the bangs I'd been trying to grow out stood up on end, fluttering around my face.

"Come on," Dana said. "Concentrate."

With another heavy sigh of exasperation, I closed my eyes. Remembering what Dana had told me the last time we'd trained together, I began to review the instructions out loud. "I am now going to…think about an experience I had which raised my heart rate." I wracked my brain. At first, I couldn't come up with an especially good example, which was absurd, considering what I'd been through the last few weeks. But then, just as quickly, an image of Milo popped into my head. It was from last night's dream. And, yes, it was the part where he was kissing me.

My heart started to pound, and I tried to push it away, but I couldn't.

Somehow Dana knew that my pulse rate was up, because she said, "Good. Whatever you're doing, it's good."

I wanted to stop her, but I didn't know what to say, what to do.

She kept coaching me. "Think about the details. Bring yourself to that moment again. Soak in what you can see, hear, smell, touch. Take a moment and bring yourself back to that place."

Milo's chest, rising and falling so close to mine, and those lips—those *lips*... They had taken my breath away...

Thump, thump, thump.

...and the way his tongue had touched mine, the way shivers had run all the way down my entire body...

Thump-THUMP, thump-THUMP, thump-THUMP.

...and he smelled like vanilla, oh God, it was happening, it was happening...

Thum-thump-thum-thump-thum-thump.

...and my heart was beating so fast, it was pounding a hole through my chest, and I thought briefly about that stupid flagpole, and then I thought about Milo, and I thought about how I wanted—desperately—for that moment between us to be real, but God, I didn't want to hurt Dana, and I was so afraid, not just that I would, but that I'd stop caring about hurting her, because the truth was that I wanted, I wanted, I *wanted*...

And *CRRRRAAAACCCKK! Pss-pss-pss-pss-pss-pss-pss*...

God, what was that smell?

I opened my eyes and the first thing I saw was Dana, dancing to get out of the way of the sprinklers from the park's irrigation system. Somehow I'd activated them, and they were spraying out muddy-looking water. But they quickly fizzled, as if there hadn't been all that much in the pipes to begin with.

She didn't mince words. "Wow, that went *really* wrong!"

The top of the flagpole was exactly where it was when I'd started. But I saw that the portapotties—both of them—had been split in two. They lay there like cracked eggs, with the nasty blue liquid from their holding tanks oozing out.

"Oh, gross!"

And that wasn't my shame at total failure that I was smelling, because Dana was covering her nose too.

Together we backed away from the awfulness.

"It's okay," Dana reassured me. "In fact, I'd be a little freaked if you got it right the very first time. Tell me what you were thinking about."

I froze.

She didn't notice. "Or maybe I should ask what you were *feeling*. When I was first starting, fear was a biggie. If fear was involved, I could get completely blocked."

"I was afraid," I admitted, and it wasn't a lie.

She continued to deconstruct the exercise as we hiked back to the hole in the fence. "Of course, it's possible that telekinesis is just not your thing—and I mean major TK, not the parlor trick move-a-pencil crap."

That didn't make sense. Yes, I'd mostly moved small things—the hairbrush, my radio, the cat poster, my backpack. "But I'm pretty sure I used it to save Garrett."

"Hmm, I forgot about that. Well, maybe you need life-or-death stimulation," she theorized. "Or maybe your telekinesis is like my psychic powers. Sporadic. It happens when it happens, and you just got lucky that day."

That made me unhappy. "Out of all the G-T powers," I admitted, "that's the one I want when we catch up with Sasha's kidnappers."

Suddenly I was back to attempting to defend myself—and Calvin and Milo—with a clarinet sonata or maybe a little forced psychic dreaming. Yeah, *that* would hurt those hardened criminals *real* bad.

Dana smiled at me. "Don't sweat it, Bubble Gum. You are what you are. And remember that massive list on the napkin? What you are is pretty freaking fantastic, whether this kind of large-scale TK is in your toolbox or not."

Would she say that, I wondered, if she knew that I'd gotten my heart rate up and spiked my adrenaline by thinking about kissing her boyfriend?

CHAPTER TWENTY-THREE

That night, I slept like a rock.

It was a welcome change. As helpful as the dreams probably were, they were also exhausting. Oblivion was relieving, and when I woke up the next morning, I felt like a million bucks.

And then, I remembered.

It was my birthday.

As if on cue, Mom burst into my room.

"Oh, *birthday girrrrl*," she exclaimed, her voice lilting and singsong.

And God help me if she wasn't wearing one of those pointy, paper party hats. Oh, lord.

"Wake *up*, sleepy*head!*" Mom cooed, dancing over to the side of my bed. She had kazoos. Oh, shoot me now, she actually had kazoos.

But then I remembered that film class was supposed to start tonight, and that Cal's mom had negotiated a twelve-thirty curfew. Since I was scheduled to go right over to Cal's house after school, that meant this was it. This too-early, oh-my-God, do-you-really-have-a-hat-and-kazoos moment was my mother's only chance to celebrate my birthday with me.

"Yay," I said, mustering as much enthusiasm as I could.

"Get out of bed, Miz Seventeen-Year-Old!" Mom took my comforter and briskly uncovered me. I wanted to curl up into a ball, my pajama-covered knees tucked up to my stomach. Instead I sat up and gave her jazz hands. "Yay."

She loved that, blowing gaily into one of the kazoos. "Come on downstairs and celebrate! There's a pile of presents with your name on them. And I cooked you a big, ol' special breakfast!"

I gave her a third *yay* as I tried not to laugh at that terrible hat. The glittery letters across the front read: *mom o' bday grl.* "I'm just gonna shower. I'm right behind you."

"Sounds good!" Mom exclaimed. She planted a kiss on the back of my head and danced out of the room, closing the door behind her.

The room was still dim, even though all my curtains and blinds were now open. A crash of thunder reverberated through my bedroom.

It was pouring outside.

Yay.

————————

School was predictably lame, although the rain let up around noon.

Despite Cal's attempts at keeping things light for my birthday, I could tell as we ate lunch that he was freaked about tonight. I couldn't blame him. He would be walking into the home of his enemy. Garrett had been so terrible to Cal, and I doubted he was going to let up, especially after a couple of beers—and in front of an equally buzzed crowd.

I did my best to get through the day without feeling nervous myself.

As much as I didn't want to admit it, as disappointed as I was that I hadn't moved that flagpole, I was still pretty spooked about my ability to crush a pair of porta-potties, simply by thinking about kissing Dana's boyfriend. So much was weird and wrong about that—I didn't even know where to start.

Calvin and I went back to his house after school and played some mindless video games to kill time and take our minds off the big, pink party elephant in the room.

As I worked on level five of some shoot-'em-up-'til-their-brains-fall-out game that I'd never played before, I felt Calvin's eyes on me.

"What?" I said, keeping my own eyes locked on the TV screen.

"Would you rather…"

"Oh my sweet Jesus, Calvin."

I could feel Cal grinning. Meanwhile, my avatar did a backflip and then cut off a zombie's head with a machete.

"Would you rather…" he started again, "be forced to get a tattoo of yourself across your entire abdomen, or a nose ring that connected to a tongue ring that connected to two nipple rings by a chain?"

"I'm speechless," I said, pressing a button and blowing up a car before annihilating two zombie women with a machine gun.

"Come on, this one's not that difficult," Calvin said. "The piercings, of course. At least you could take them out."

"I seriously think that the piercings would hurt more, though."

"Girl, for a second! But the tattoo? That's some permanent shit!"

Not if you were Dana. Or me. I'd woken up this morning with my knee almost completely healed. I finished level five and handed the video-game controller to Calvin. "Maybe I *want* a tattoo of myself on myself."

Calvin didn't have time to respond, because the doorbell rang.

"It's open! Come on in!" Calvin shouted, and I gave him my best WTF look. "What?"

"What if it's some nasty-ass serial killer out there?" I asked him. "Or a vampire—you just invited him in."

"Vampires don't exist," Calvin scoffed.

"How do you know?" I asked. "A week ago you would've said girls with telekinetic and telepathic powers don't exist."

"Good point," Calvin said, adding, "Holy shit."

"Holy shit" was right, even though it definitely wasn't vampires who'd walked into Calvin's house.

It was Dana and Milo, dressed to the nines.

"Wow," I said, and Calvin nodded his agreement. "You guys look…"

Well, they both looked amazing. It was the truth. Either my eyes were playing tricks on me, or Dana's hair seemed to have grown since the last time I'd seen her—which was absurd, since it had only been twenty-four hours ago. But she'd managed to put her blond locks into two spiky pigtails by the base of her neck. Dark cat-like liner framed her icicle-colored eyes, and her cheeks were glowing with color.

And that was just above her neck.

Her outfit was amazing. She was wearing a slinky, silver halter dress, her ample chest busting out of the top. Even though she was short, Dana's legs looked extra long tonight, probably thanks to the astronomically tall knee-high boots she was sporting.

And then there was Milo.

His hair was just messy enough to look undone without seeming sloppy. Five-o'clock shadow flirted across the expanse of his jaw, but it wasn't dark enough to cover the dimples that popped when he smiled. The button-down shirt he'd chosen was a light blue, its sleeves rolled up. The contrast of blue against the tan skin of his forearms was absolutely impossible to keep from staring at. He looked like a male model yanked from the pages of a fashion e-zine.

They were basically the hottest couple alive.

Dana was carrying a duffel bag, and she plopped it onto the leather ottoman and quickly unzipped it. "We're running a little late, so you should hurry and get dressed. I want to get going ASAP."

Calvin was looking like a dog in heat as he stared at Dana and her slinky dress. I slapped him on the shoulder.

"Um, I don't know what kind of house parties y'all go to in whatever town you're from, but Coconut Key isn't exactly black tie." Calvin looked at me with disapproval and rubbed his shoulder dramatically.

"Good to know," Dana said. "But we're not dressed for your stupid party. We're going straight from there to the clubs."

I looked at Milo. He'd carried a bag in too, but it was smaller than Dana's. He set it down next to his feet as he smiled at me. I looked away. "There's no way we're going to pull off this look," I said, pointing to Dana's dress.

Calvin tugged at the front of his shirt and pretended to be offended. "Hey, speak for yourself, Sky."

Dana didn't look up as she sifted through the pile of clothing she'd brought. "Here," she said, throwing me something pink and something blue. "That'll look hot."

The something pink was smaller than the something blue. Actually, both were pretty freaking small. "Wow," I said. "Um, okay. You don't think I'll be arrested for wearing this?"

Calvin's eyes got huge as I held up a pastel halter top and jeans that would seriously hug my hips.

"I think that you're going to get into a very elite club for wearing that. And I think that's the only thing we're concerned with right now."

It might have just been my imagination, but I seriously felt as if Dana gave me more attitude when Milo and Cal were around than when it was just the two of us.

Still, I didn't talk back to her. "I'll go put this on," I said instead, heading into the bathroom to get changed.

As I walked past Milo and caught a whiff of his now-familiar vanilla, my stomach did somersaults. I swallowed hard and kept walking, purposely not meeting his eyes. But then he said, "Happy birthday."

I couldn't not look at him when he said that, and as I smiled back into his extremely pretty eyes, I felt the world tilt. "Thanks," I said.

"I wanted to get you a present," he told me quietly in that almost unbearably sexy Southern drawl, "but I kinda ran out of time. See, I spent most of the day trying to track down some really effective black-market antinausea meds. I thought you might need them tonight, but…I didn't score. I'm sorry about that."

He gestured to his bag, which was about the size and shape of one of those mommy bags that women carry filled with things like diapers and snacks and bottles. "So I packed some extra water and towels. And I found some surgical face masks at the drugstore, thinking maybe, you know, if you smell the sewage smell you can slap one on and…" He shrugged. "It's stupid, I know. It probably won't help."

"It might," I said, and what was stupid was that I was on the verge of tears at the idea that he'd gone to so much trouble for me. "Thank you." I bolted for the bathroom, locking the door behind me.

It really was ridiculous. The outfit, that is.

I checked myself out in the mirror from different angles.

First off, my stomach was showing. I *never* wore outfits that revealed my midriff—partly because my mom would have keeled over from a heart attack, and partly because it wasn't really my style.

Still, I had to admit it. The jeans fit me pretty perfectly. Even though I was lanky, my curves were being hugged with a serious vengeance.

I wondered if I should put some makeup on to complete the outfit. But I didn't have anything with me in my backpack besides an old tube of lip balm.

The makeup-free look would have to do.

Quietly, I exited the bathroom, feeling slightly absurd. The halter was tight enough to show off what I was seriously lacking upstairs. It was embarrassing.

But it wasn't about me. This was, ultimately, about finding Sasha, who was not dead.

I slunk over to my backpack with the intention of stashing my clothing inside, when Dana, Cal, and Milo all turned to stare at me.

Calvin's jaw dropped. "Dude. I seriously feel weird saying this, but…you're hot."

"Shut the front door," I told him.

Dana's gaze flitted back and forth between Cal and me. "You look good, Bubble Gum."

Milo didn't say a word. But he also hadn't stopped staring at me from the moment I'd come back into the room. I both wanted him to stop—and to never stop looking at me, ever again.

"What do you think, Miles? Can she pull off the look?" Dana eyed Milo intently.

He nodded. "Um. I…Well, the short answer is yes."

I tried my best to keep from blushing. And I failed miserably. And I started to get a little mad. What was he doing staring at me, when Dana was standing right there looking the way *she* was looking?

"All right, Scoot," Dana replied. "It's your turn."

"What, did you get me a pink halter too? That's really nice of you."

Dana made a huffy sound, as if she didn't have time for him. "You're wearing this," she said, and shoved a pile of clothes onto Calvin's lap. But then she cleared her throat. "You…need help?"

"Sadly, no," he said. "I'll be right back for my photo shoot." He wheeled himself into the bathroom with a flourish.

I looked at Dana, who was now busy pulling a smaller bag out of the duffel. She took a seat on one of the couches. "Come here," she ordered me, patting the cushion beside her. "Let's get you made up."

I sat and Dana spread foundation across my nose, cheeks, and chin.

"Hold still," she commanded, and began working on the bottom lids of my eyes with a liner pen. "And try not to blink."

I blinked.

Dana looked at me with barely contained disapproval.

"I'm doing my best," I told her.

I glanced across the room to find Milo smiling at me. I smiled back, but then jerked my gaze away—and found myself staring into Dana's icy eyes.

"Sorry," I said.

She narrowed her eyes at me and said, "You're lucky you're working with a pro."

She finished my eyeliner, then used a thick wand to swipe mascara on both my top and bottom lashes. She also pulled out a palette of different colors of eye shadow and used the pads of her fingers to spread and blend shades across the arch of my lids.

I tried to ignore the fact that I could feel Milo watching me from across the room, even though I wasn't looking.

Finally, Dana brushed a little pink blush across my cheekbones and added a dab of tinted gloss to my lips.

"You're good to go," Dana replied.

"Can I see?" I asked.

"Sure," she said. She pulled out a miniature mirror and handed it to me.

I looked at the reflection. And the reflection didn't look so bad.

"Dang," Cal said as he coasted back into the room, "every time I turn around, Skylar gets hotter and hotter. It's, like, *Twilight Zone* shit."

Milo, meanwhile, walked up to Calvin with a grin on his face. "You don't look so bad yourself," he replied.

I looked at Cal's outfit. His T-shirt was snug and a cool shade of green, and his jeans fit perfectly. On his feet were his favorite green and black sneakers, and they matched the outfit well.

"Yeah, you look really awesome," I had to agree with Milo.

"Okay, okay," Dana interrupted us. "We've established how good we all look. So let's do it. Let's go."

CHAPTER TWENTY-FOUR

It was raining again as we piled into Cal's car, boys in front, girls in the back. And I wondered what we looked like. If one of Cal's neighbors, glancing out their window, happened to see us, what would they think? *There go four attractive young people, heading out to have fun.*

Hah. Fun. What a concept. Especially considering how much fun I'd had last time I had been to a party. Lord knew I couldn't possibly have a night as bad as that one had been.

Still, fun wasn't top priority tonight. The main mission here was to get to Garrett's father's beach house and sniff every nook and cranny for clues. Literally.

Cal hadn't forgotten where to go. He drove to Garrett's place like he was on a mission, his expression grim.

Milo chewed thoughtfully on a piece of gum. I could see little drops of rain on his forearm that hadn't dried yet.

"So you know what you're doing here, right?" Dana asked me.

"I'm looking for the sewage smell," I said, yanking my gaze away from Milo, hoping Dana hadn't noticed I'd been staring at him.

"Correction. You're looking for *any*thing, including the sewage smell. It doesn't matter if it's just a hunch or a feeling. You've gotta tell me right away. Deal?"

"Deal."

Milo turned around in his seat. "You'll do great."

I tried to smile. Failed. If this went really right, I'd be puking in Garrett's yard, in front of my entire high school, sometime in the next half hour. Oh, and if it went *really* really right, the boyfriend of my G-T trainer and friend would get a brain full of a fantasy make-out session when he attempted to help me.

Ultimate, extreme worse-case scenario had me morphing into a full-blown G-T monster and not giving a shit about any of that as I simultaneously stole Dana's boyfriend and destroyed the world.

Yeah, I was gonna do great.

"Is there anything else that you'd like me or Milo to be doing while we're inside?" Cal asked. "I mean, we're pretty much just going to be hanging around."

"That's exactly what I want you to do. Hang around," Dana said. "We're here supporting Sky. And—no one needs to know this, of course—we're also here to distract people from what Sky'll be doing."

"Yeah, 'cause you did a really good job of making her inconspicuous," Calvin retorted smartly, glancing in his rearview mirror at me and my pink halter top.

Dana didn't get a chance to respond because, as she opened her mouth, Calvin pulled up to the beach house.

The place was absolutely packed. Cars were strewn haphazardly across the driveway, and most of the junior and senior classes stood outside laughing and pushing each other across the lawn. Some of them were smoking cigarettes. Others tilted their heads back as they chugged cans of beer.

"Wow. This looks awesome." Dana's voice was monotone.

"Yeah, this is what you get from Coconut Key," I replied. No one else could hear it, but my heart had begun to pound. I took slow breaths. I honestly didn't know if it was because I was anxiously anticipating finding clues that would lead us to Sasha—or if the whole scene reminded me a little too much of that night in Connecticut, all those months ago.

"We good?" Dana asked, and it was a less a question of how we were doing and more a *let's get out of the freaking car already*.

"Yeah," I said, and opened the passenger door and got out. The boom of a bass-heavy song thumped through the front yard. I looked around at the crowd of people.

And I sniffed the air.

Salt water, stale alcohol, cigarette smoke, fish, a mixture of perfumes, body odor, garlic, roses, Milo's vanilla…and no sewage smell.

"Anything?" Milo had basically snuck up behind me, and his voice was so close to my ear that I jumped and shivered simultaneously.

"No!" I exclaimed. Calming myself quickly, I added, "I can smell lots of stuff, but with the exception of the fear-fish smell and the garlic, which means I'm not sure what, I think it's everything you guys can smell too. The usuals."

Dana cupped her hand around her ear as if to say *speak up*. Then she pointed to Calvin, who was wheeling himself toward me and looking a little out of the loop.

I hollered over the music. "I was just saying that I didn't smell anything yet."

Dana nodded and motioned for all of us to gather in a huddle. She placed an arm around me and another arm around Milo. Calvin leaned forward, his ears perked.

"We need hand signals," Dana said. "Otherwise, Skylar's going to be screaming weird stuff about smells and sewage and God knows what else. Let's do a fist pump if there's nothing and a head scratch if she detects something."

I looked at Dana incredulously. "A fist pump? Really?"

Dana shrugged. "What's wrong with a fist pump? Just carry a cup, pretend you've been drinking, and no one will look at you twice."

"Ooh, ooh!" Calvin said. "I have an idea! How about if the sewage smell's not that bad, you throw up on Garrett once, but if it's terrible, you ralph on him twice."

I gave him a first pump, right into his shoulder.

"Ow," he said. "I just think that would be funny."

"I'm not throwing up," I told him. *Please God, let that be a prescient statement…*

"The signal needs to be big enough so we'll all see it," Dana interjected. "It's a fist pump. Get over it." She looked from me to Milo to Calvin. "If one person gets the message, make sure to keep it going. Eyes peeled at all times. And if it's possible, let's all try to stay in the same room."

She dismissed our little huddle, and the four of us headed to the front door. As we walked through the swarm of kids, people turned to check us out. It could have been because we were dressed like club rats. It could have been the fact that Dana and Milo were new faces. It could have simply been the sight of Calvin coasting up to a party at Garrett's house.

Whatever the reason, dozens of eyes followed us from the end of the driveway to the front door. Which was opened, before we could otherwise knock or ring the bell, by a cheerleader named Jackie, who no doubt had nominated herself as official hostess.

"Whoo!" Jackie said, almost falling on her ass. She caught herself just in time, hanging on to the doorframe for dear life as she laughed. "Oh, wow! It's the new girl and wheelchair boy and…two people I've never seen before, including a *really* hot guy!"

"Thanks," I said. "We'd love to come in."

Jackie blew a few strands of hair off her face, but they landed sloppily again right next to her mouth. She then tried to use a hand to fix her hair, and instead spilled the contents of her red plastic cup all over the marble tile.

"Oh, doo-doo!" she squealed, and ran off, presumably to get another drink.

"The kind of girl you'd take home to meet Mother," Dana commented, using care to step over the spill as she entered the mansion.

I looked at Calvin. "You need help?" There was a half step between the house and the landing, just large enough to pose a problem for a wheelchair.

Calvin looked pissed off that I'd asked. "I'm fine," he said gruffly, and revved the power on his chair before attempting to rocket over the hump.

He got halfway, and then slid back again.

Dana turned from inside the house and watched Calvin struggle. Milo, meanwhile, walked up behind Cal, intending to lift his chair inside.

"Don't touch it," Calvin growled.

My heart was in my throat. It was painful to watch Calvin when he got prideful and stubborn.

He tried a few more times, but the wheels just wouldn't make it over the step.

Inside, I could see people in crowds of threes and fours, talking and laughing. Some couples were making out. A group of jocks stood around a pool table, knocking back shots and roaring victoriously like frat-boy wannabes.

No one seemed to notice us yet. Thank God.

Dana approached the doorway again. "What's the issue? The fricking step is the issue?" She sounded angry and impatient. And somehow angry and impatient was far better than sympathetic and kind. It was like Dana was speaking Cal's language.

Cal's shoulders relaxed a little as he nodded at her.

"Screw that," she said. "Do me a favor, Scoot, and rev the power again."

Calvin did, and the wheelchair went airborne before doing a half spin and landing inside the house—quite conveniently missing Jackie's spilled drink by at least a foot.

I looked at Dana. Who looked at me. "Shut the hell up," she said, and marched into the house.

The three of us followed Dana as if she were our tour guide. More people began to notice our presence, and the staring started again in earnest.

Dana pointed to the first room on the right. A massive-sized TV was hanging on a wall next to an ornate fireplace. Kids were sprawled across every couch, chair, and love seat in the room. In the far corner was an open liquor cabinet the size of my walk-in closet.

The driving beat of the music was persistent and deafening. Dana looked irritated. She locked eyes with me, her expression one big question mark.

I scowled before I fist-pumped.

Milo led us to the next room. It was actually set up very similarly to the last, minus the television and the love seats. Everything else was virtually identical, including the liquor cabinet.

I made a circuit of the room, weaving my way through the boisterous crowd. And then I fist-pumped.

A group of girls had gathered in the doorway, and we had to push past them to get back into the hallway. One of them whispered something about how Jackie was right—the new guy *was* cute.

I looked at Milo, who seemed completely oblivious to the fact that every girl at the party was absolutely googly-eyed over him.

Of course, Milo wasn't the only one getting the attention.

I had never seen so much tongue-wagging in my life as I followed Dana into the room with the pool table. The football players snapped to attention.

"*Damn!*" A dark-haired senior I'd seen a few times before whistled. He nudged a few of his buddies, who all turned and ogled Dana.

She gave all of them the finger.

379

The funny thing was, the rude gesture didn't deter them. A few of them clutched at their chests, as if manually slowing their heartbeats. One of them, a handsome boy named Vince who was in my Chinese culture class—who was actually kind of funny and nice when he wasn't caught up in the mob mentality of his teammates—dropped to his knees before Dana. "I will die a happy man if you give me your phone number," he said, looking up at her with the kind of blue eyes usually reserved for Hollywood movie stars.

I glanced at Milo, but he was completely relaxed. He was even smiling a little as he watched Dana—who gazed down at Vince expressionlessly.

"I lack both a phone and a give-a-damn," she said before looking over at me, her perpetual question in her eyes.

I sniffed a few times, but all I could smell were hot peppers and warm beer. I wondered if the pepper smell was linked to the inordinate amount of teenage lust bouncing around in there.

Calvin looked at me too, and I did a quick fist pump.

"Let's keep moving." Milo leaned close to my ear to suggest it, and that was fine with me.

Next up was the kitchen, which would have been absolutely stunning—if it wasn't completely trashed with beer cans, bags of potato chips, and red plastic cups. Every appliance was shiny silver metal, each countertop an elegant marble pattern. Rowdy partygoers crowded around the island in the center of the room, where a row of red cups were lined up between two determined-looking senior girls.

"Beer pong. Gotta love it," Cal said.

"Or not," Dana shouted grimly.

Milo leaned in close to me. "Anything?" he asked.

"I don't think so," I said, sniffing the air.

There was more of that pepper smell…although now it was a little fishy as well, which was gross.

But, besides those two things, nada. Why didn't I smell anything? I'd been bracing myself for it all day. I'd imagined us identifying Garrett's father as the insidious leader of a Destiny drug ring. Dana would use her mind-control powers on him and get him to tell us where Sasha was being held, at which point we'd leave him tied up in the trunk of his car as we raced off to rescue her.

But it was pretty clear that Mr. Hathaway wasn't here tonight. Nor was there a sewage smell.

"This is bullshit," I exclaimed, frustrated.

Calvin shook his head. "Nuh-uh, 'cause bullshit would smell like something."

"Hilarious," I said as I fist-pumped again, adding an unenthusiastic "Whoo-whoo!"

Dana briskly led us out of the kitchen and back into the foyer, where a set of stairs led to the second floor. But as we rounded the corner, Garrett came careening toward us from the family room. He was still in a wheelchair.

"Well, looky, looky!" he exclaimed, his voice thick from the effects of alcohol as he shouted over the music. "It's Super Sky and her boyfriend—and her hot, hot friend." He frowned as he looked at Milo. "Who are you, Homes? I don't know you."

I lifted my chin as I gazed back at Garrett, my eyes challenging. "These are the friends I told you about. They're visiting from out of town."

Milo leaned forward, and I couldn't hear him but I could read his lips as he told Garrett, "The name's Milo. And I'm definitely not your homeboy."

I caught a massive whiff of fish from Garrett, and I knew that Milo scared him—which was kind of ridiculous, since Milo was one of the gentlest people I'd ever met. Except...maybe he wasn't. He was tall. And pretty solid. And the look he was giving Garrett held an unspoken promise of an ass-kicking, if provoked.

And then, as I watched, I saw Garrett look at Calvin, and like the bully that he was, he attacked. He pivoted his wheelchair slightly, so that he was facing Calvin. "And what up wit you, nigga?"

I swallowed a gasp and both Dana and Milo bristled. But Cal was calm, just staring Garrett down. "I'm glad you finally bought the *Learn Ebonics* books-on-tape," he said.

When Dana laughed, Garrett got even more petulant. "You think you're so funny, don't you, Williams, but you want to hear something really hilarious? In a week, week and a half, I'll be out of this fugly chair for good. But you'll be sitting down to piss for the rest of your life."

There was a moment of silence—or deafening music as it were—and then Dana kind of laughed again and muttered, "Well, hell."

She turned to look at me, and then she looked over at the stairs, and I got the message and swiftly headed up them. This situation was on the verge of escalating, big time. Because no way was Dana going to stand there and let Calvin get treated like that. Except, that kind of escalation was going to result in the four of us being asked to leave.

And if we were going to get evicted from this party, I'd better finish searching the house first.

I hesitated on the top landing, but then turned to see that Milo had come upstairs with me. "This way," he said.

And truth be told, I wouldn't have checked the second and third floors as thoroughly if he hadn't been assisting. There were a lot of shut bedroom doors that I didn't particularly want to open, but Milo just led the way, popping the locks and pushing them ajar.

I closed my eyes, stuck my head in and simultaneously took a sniff, and apologized.

"Sorry!"

"Sorry!"

"Sorry!"

"Sorry!"

The third floor held Mr. Hathaway's huge home office. Milo was laughing at me as we snuck in there. He sifted cautiously through paperwork on the top of the massive mahogany desk, while I worked on sniffing the walls and built-in cabinets.

"He's a doctor," Milo reminded me. "A plastic surgeon." He held up a couple of patients' charts.

I inhaled the smell of leather and cigars. No sewage.

"Doesn't that mean he might be connected to the production of Destiny?" I asked. Lucky for us, this room was far enough away from the rest of the party that we didn't have to yell over the music anymore. Still, we kept our voices barely above a whisper, just to make sure no one found us snooping in here.

"Could be," Milo said as he looked at me. "On the other hand, if the drug catches on, cosmetic surgeons are going to be obsolete. So you'd think he'd be heavily anti-Destiny."

"Good point," I said, opening a closet and sniffing a collection of white lab coats.

"Anything?" Milo asked.

"Nothing. Completely sewage-smell free," I said. I fist-pumped once more, just to drive the point home.

He smiled at that.

I wasn't as amused. "This is a total waste of time." I sighed as I flopped down in an overstuffed leather chair. "I don't know why I thought this would be easy. But now that we're here, it's just…" I tried to explain. "It's wrong. It feels wrong."

He took me seriously, half sitting on the edge of Dr. Hathaway's big desk as he asked, "What feels right?"

He asked, so I told him. "I feel her. Sasha. I want to try homing in on her, the way I did with Dana when she was at that diner."

Milo looked down at his feet as he sighed, and I knew with a burst of sadness that, just like Dana, he didn't believe Sasha could possibly still be alive. "Sky," he started.

I cut him off, pushing myself to my feet and heading for the door. It was time to leave this party. "Forget it."

He stood up too, intercepting me, blocking my path. "Look, I've never had a vision, but if it was anything like your dreams—"

I held out my hand to him. "I'll show you what I saw."

Milo's eyes were somber. He took my hand, and as our

now-familiar contact switched on, I focused on exactly what I'd seen yesterday afternoon.

Sasha.

Asleep.

Breathing.

Alive.

But that's what being psychic means, Milo thought at me as he held my hand in both of his own. *You see what* happened. *Past tense. Whoever took Sasha kept her alive for a while. That's what you saw.*

No, I tried to tell him. *This is more than that!*

I know that's what you want to believe, he sent back to me as he put his arms around me and held me close. I could smell his sympathy and his own deep sorrow as he told me, *I'm so sorry, Skylar.*

And then—God, what was wrong with me?—those images from that dream were back, and the Milo in my head was kissing me, and I was kissing him back.

I jerked myself free from his arms and I stared at him, wide-eyed, as he stared back at me.

"Sorry!" We both said it at once.

And then I turned and bolted for the door.

"Sky, wait!" I heard him say. I clattered down the stairs, and oh, crap, this was too weird, because Dana was sitting on Calvin's lap, right in his wheelchair, kissing the bejeezus out of him.

But I knew right away that Dana was doing it either to piss off Garrett or to allow Calvin to save face—or both.

Still, I could smell Garrett's jealousy, which probably kept me from smelling Milo's, since he was right behind me.

"Time to go, lovebirds!" I announced brightly to both Cal and Dana, and just as I expected, Dana came up first for air. Cal was no fool. As long as Dana was kissing him, he was going to milk that situation for all it was worth.

And sure enough, he kept Dana on his lap as he wheeled them both toward the door.

Leaving Garrett both slack-jawed and toothless. He tried though, saying, "You're a total loser, Williams." Except Cal looked nothing like a loser with Dana's arms around his neck. So Garrett went for pompous and dictatorial and intoned, "I think it's time for you and your friends to leave."

"Come on, baby," Dana said to Calvin, kissing the side of his face. "We got places to go and far better things to do."

I met Cal's eyes when his wheelchair launched up and over that troublesome doorjamb, and as he held tightly to Dana, I knew that his smile was one I would never forget.

He looked like he'd just hit the lottery, watched Tupac come back to life, and won the Olympics, all at the same time.

I followed them out, with Milo on my heels.

At least one of us was having a very, very good night.

CHAPTER TWENTY-FIVE

I could feel Milo watching me as we drove north on the interstate.

Our destination was a club called Pretense.

Calvin was still ridiculously happy, dancing like a fool to the radio, right there in the driver's seat.

Dana was sitting up front next to him, and I watched her make a concerted attempt to not laugh. Her face contorted as she held back a smile that poked through regardless of her efforts.

"Are you seriously doing the robot?" she scoffed.

Cal nodded and sang along: "*My anaconda don't want none unless you got buns, hon! You can do side bends or sit-ups, but please don't lose that butt...*"

Dana scowled. "What *is* this?"

"*What?*" Calvin offered Dana a look of mock devastation. "Girl, this song's a classic. This is Sir Mix-A-Lot." He shook his head, astonished. "You've never heard Sir Mix-A-Lot?"

"No," Dana said.

Calvin mouthed the word "wow" exaggeratedly as he glanced back at me in the rearview. It was impossible to not smile at him, but at the same time, I couldn't shake my feelings of frustration. We were wasting time. I *knew* we were wasting time.

"Oh, before we forget," Dana said, turning in her seat to look at Milo. "You have those IDs? We're gonna need 'em."

"Yeah, right," he said, digging into his jeans pocket and pulling out a thick wallet.

"The fake ones," Calvin verified.

"The fake ones," Milo replied, nodding. He held out one to me and handed the other to Dana.

"Wow," I said, reading mine. "Skylar Macmilton?"

"You have to take what they give you," Milo said with a shrug. "Trust me when I tell you that Nicolas knows what he's doing."

I checked the birth date. "Huh. So this would make me..." I did the math in my head. "Twenty-three years old."

"Twenty-one would look too obviously fake," Calvin reasoned.

I scoffed. "Yeah, but twenty-*three*? I can't even get into an R-rated movie without getting the evil eye from the ticket lady. Twenty-three is pushing it."

Calvin took his ID from Dana and glanced at it as he drove. "Whaat?" he scoffed. "I'm twenty-seven! Nuh-uh. There's no way."

"There's a way," Milo said quietly.

Cal answered his own question. "Dana'll use her mind-control mojo. But then why spend all that money on something we won't even need?"

"You need to show something," Milo told him. "It's better not to push it, have Dana's *mojo* convince the bouncers to forget to read the dates."

That made sense.

But then Dana turned to look at both Milo and me, and her eyes were somber. "My mojo might be in remission," she said.

I sat forward. "What do you mean?"

Her lips tightened. "I mean that when I tried mind-controlling Quarterback McDouche, back at his party—it didn't work."

I remembered her quiet "Well, hell," before she shot me the unspoken message to go ahead and search the house's top floors.

"Maybe it was because he was drunk," I offered.

She shot me a disgusted look. "Seriously? Alcohol makes the brain more compliant."

"What about Percocet?" Calvin suggested. "A total wuss like Garrett was no doubt given big-gun painkillers for his ouchy boo-boos." He snorted. "Like he knows what pain is. Still, I could tell just from looking at him. Dude was definitely stoned."

Milo reached forward to touch Dana on the shoulder in a reassuring gesture that seemed so sweetly intimate that I had to look away. "I bet it was the painkillers," he murmured.

"I hope so," she whispered back.

"You want to test drive it on me?" Calvin asked. "Your mojo mind-thing?" And then, just like before, his head tilted to the side and he said, "I will take the next exit and then, because we're nearly at the club, I will turn down the volume on the radio and sit quietly while Dana discusses our strategy." His head straightened back up. "Wow, that's so weird." He glanced at Dana as he turned the radio down, then signaled to exit the highway. "But in an awesome way, because it worked."

She smiled at him. "It did. Thanks."

"So what's our strategy?" I asked as Calvin caught the off-ramp and pulled out onto an urban-looking street with buildings and lights on either side. I wanted to suggest that we shelve Dana's so-called strategy and use this time more productively—by letting me see if I couldn't home in on Sasha. I wanted to follow the pull that I felt and see where it led us. But I knew that Dana would be as frustrated by that idea as I was at hers. We each thought the other's approach was a serious waste of time.

"Why do we need a strategy?" Calvin asked. "We're going to a club to pretty much do the same thing we were doing at the party. Let Skylar sniff her way around, hope she smells the smell."

"We're going to this club," Dana said, shaking her head as she corrected him, "because we're trying to track down Destiny pushers and users. I'm gonna find them, and yes, Sky's gonna sniff them, and if and when she smells the funky sewage smell, I'm gonna move back in and have a little talk with them. If we get more than one stank hit, then we'll gather as much information as possible and try to figure out what they all have in common."

"And if I don't smell anything?" I asked, my frustration giving a challenging edge to my tone. "Kinda the way I didn't smell anything at Garrett's?"

"We'll do the best we can," Dana said.

That was my invitation to suggest a Plan B. "If we fail, can we try something else? Like let me use my homing skills to lead us to Sasha."

Dana sighed heavily, so I added, "Or maybe you're right and she's dead, and I'll be leading us to her body—but that would be good to find too, right?"

"I'll think about it," she gave me, then said, "While you're inside, stay close to Milo. He's going to be keeping an eye on you."

Oh, good. Wasn't that just dandy?

"That's not a problem," Milo said, and I bit back my *Speak for yourself.* It wasn't his fault that I mentally jumped him every chance I got.

Dana continued. "Calvin. Since you like to dance so much, you're going to do your surveillance from the middle of the club. Dance floor."

Calvin's expression turned panicked for a second. He opened his mouth to protest.

But Dana interrupted him before he got a word out. "I know what you're thinking. But you won't have to worry about the wheelchair getting in the way."

"Oh, really," he said. "I mean, have you seen how big it actually is?"

Dana laughed. "Just trust me on this one."

Calvin drove past bars and restaurants, the lights garish and flashing neon. He bobbed his head to the music, although he wasn't fooling me. I could tell he was nervous again.

It was then that a sports car came shooting out of a parking lot, engine roaring, tires screaming, and rubber burning. Calvin burned off a little of his own tires as he braked hard and squealed to a sudden stop.

My seat belt bit into my chest, and I heard myself shout in

alarm, "Watch out!" The panic that consumed me was familiar—it took far less than a bona fide near-miss from a serious idiot to set me off. I closed my eyes and tried to slow my ragged breathing and push away the images that always, always flooded my mind when this happened.

Nicole. Her face was ivory white, rivulets of blood trailing down her temples, pink frothy bubbles of blood-stained spit rising from her lips. She was trying to breathe, gasping, and she looked at me, frantically begging for help...

Help I couldn't give her.

And then—*oh God*—it was as if my inadvertent thoughts about Nicole had conjured up a vision of Sasha, because I saw her again. She too was covered with blood, only she was screaming and screaming and *screaming....*

"Skylar." I heard Milo and then I felt him inside my head as he touched me. *Sky.*

Help me, I begged him. *Please...*

I was trying to look around, to *really* look, hoping to see where Sasha was, but it was dark and her fear was suffocating. It was hard not to give in to those feelings of panic.

And somehow Milo knew. I realized that I didn't need to form a coherent thought to make him understand—I just had to blast him with everything I was thinking and feeling.

He held tightly to me, both in the backseat of Calvin's car and inside of my head. I could feel him, steady and solid and warm. It grounded me and I was less afraid.

I strained my eyes to see what Sasha saw—to see what was making her scream like that, and although the darkness lifted enough so that I got a glimpse of the menacing outline of a man—a big man—I couldn't make out his face or where we were.

Then, as quickly as it had started, it was over, leaving me out of breath, on the verge of tears, and extremely aware that Milo was still holding me crushingly tightly in his arms.

I wanted to cry, and he knew that and told me, *It's okay if you do.*

But it wasn't. It wasn't okay, and taking a moment to catch my breath and close my eyes as I leaned back and absorbed Milo's solid strength wasn't okay, either. Besides, I was more convinced than ever that Sasha was alive, but I knew that he didn't believe me. And somehow *that* was the worst thing of all.

So I sat up and pulled away, and he immediately let me go.

Dana was staring at me from the front seat, and Calvin was glancing at us in his rearview mirror. Milo quietly told them what we'd both just seen—leaving out Nicole and the accident—while I adjusted my halter top and tried to smooth down my hair.

As I looked out the car window, I saw that we'd reached our destination. A lit-up sign read *Pretense* above a striped awning. A long line of people stood outside the door, shifting their high-heeled weight and fluffing their hair.

Without Dana and her mojo, we would've had to wait for hours.

Milo removed a fresh piece of gum from his pocket and popped it into his mouth. He pointed to the right. "There's a parking lot behind the club, if you just turn down this way."

Calvin did as he was told. The one handicapped space was, of course, vacant.

"Pays to be a cripple," Calvin muttered under his breath as he parked and cut the engine.

"Don't get out of the car yet," Dana said. I paused, my hand on the passenger door handle. "No, *you* can get out," she specified, looking at me and Milo. "In fact, it'll be better if you do."

Calvin was confused, but he played up the funny. "I'm pretty sure she wants to kiss me again," he quipped.

I glanced back at Dana one more time before leaving Cal's car and shutting the door behind me. She looked tense—sick, almost. Her face was scrunched up just slightly, and she pursed her lips.

"Is she okay?" I asked Milo.

He dug in his jeans pockets and then stopped, as if remembering that what he was looking for was no longer there. He chewed furiously on his gum. "Yeah. She just needs to concentrate."

"What is she doing?"

"If I told you, you wouldn't believe it."

"Try me," I said. I pointed to myself. "I'm the one who can read your mind—and let you read mine—by touching your hand. I think I'm likely to believe just about anything you tell me."

Milo smiled at that, but didn't get a chance to respond.

Because before he could open his mouth, the driver-side door to Calvin's car swung open. And Cal took one leg and swung it onto the pavement.

And then, with awkwardly locked knees, my paralyzed best friend got out of his car and marched resolutely past Milo. He stopped in front of me, both feet planted firmly on the ground as he stood there, sans wheelchair, his thin legs shaking beneath the weight of his upper body.

"Holy," he said, his voice quavering. "Effing." He smiled down at his wobbly legs. "Shee. It."

CHAPTER TWENTY-SIX

It was a miracle.

Calvin was standing on his own two feet in front of me, without any assistance from his wheelchair. He wasn't even hanging on to anything.

I was speechless.

But, once again, Milo didn't look all that surprised.

"Calvin!" I whispered, reaching out a hand to touch him, as if what I was seeing wasn't actually real.

"Ho-ly shee-it," he said again. And, for a moment, I thought he was actually going to cry.

Instead, he whooped. It was the sound of someone overcome with pure, unadulterated joy. "Oooooh-hoooooo!" he cried out, and those little underused legs of his marched in place. "This is…"

"Awesome!" I finished for him, my voice low with a mixture of disbelief and excitement. Dana was doing this. Dana had the telekinetic power to make Calvin stand up and walk around.

She kicked open the passenger door to Calvin's car and stepped out onto the blacktop, dropping the f-bomb under her breath like she was keeping the beat to a song. Bullets of sweat popped off her. I could see the sheen across her forehead, even from several feet away.

"Are you okay?" I asked her. She was doing this, but from the look of things, it wasn't easy.

She grimaced and slammed the car door shut behind her. She trudged toward us, all her movements slow and labored, as if she were wading through mud.

"I'm 'kay," Dana verified.

As if to prove just how okay she was, she made Cal do a jumping jack.

And then she marched him back and forth in front of us. He swung his arms by his sides, as if attempting to create a more natural-looking stride. It made him look even more absurd. I didn't say anything, though, because he was grinning his ass off.

"Let me see if I can…" Dana said, and marched Calvin over to a nearby bench. She frowned as she moved him. His lower body pivoted before his knees and hips bent, the movements jerky and almost militaristic. Calvin being Calvin, he snapped off a sharp salute right before Dana sat him down.

She immediately relaxed, all the air leaving her in one long sigh.

It was amazing, the kind of control she must've had to be able to maneuver him that way. "Have you done that before?" I asked "How long did you practice before you…"

"I didn't," Dana snarled. "Practice. This was my first try."

"Wow," I said, even as Calvin chimed in with a "Ho shit!"

"*Ho shit* is right," Dana replied. "It's a little harder than I'd anticipated."

"Do you want me to try to help?" I asked her.

"*No!*" Both Dana and Calvin exclaimed at the same time.

"I mean," Cal continued, "that's nice of you and all, but it's not like you've had a lot of experience with this stuff. I think maybe you should practice a little bit more on inanimate objects before you start pulling the full-on Jesus moves. Please. I love you, but no, thank you."

I couldn't argue with that. "Are you going to be okay?" I asked Dana.

"I'll be fine," Dana insisted. "It's gonna be a workout, but I've got this." She looked at Calvin. "Just, don't be offended if I sit you down at the bar every once in a while."

Calvin grinned up at her. "You are my queen. Do whatever you want with me, Your Majesty."

———————

We walked right into the club. All four of us. No problem.

We all flashed our IDs as Dana leaned close to the bouncers who stood behind a maroon-colored velvet rope.

Their necks were as thick as my waist and their arms were crossed across their chests, noses pointed to the air. I could practically see their blood pumping through the bulging veins in their Popeye-esque forearms. And whatever Dana said to them, they didn't blink. But their heads tilted slightly to the side as they waved us in.

Calvin turned around to grin at me as he walked through the narrow entryway of the club and into the main room. He mouthed the words *Jesus moves* to me.

Or maybe he said it, and I just couldn't hear him over the relentlessly loud throbbing of music that wasn't particularly interesting. Again, like at Garrett's, it would be impossible to speak and be heard in here, and as Dana turned to look back at me, I gave her an unenthusiastic fist pump.

No sewage smell here. Not yet anyway.

Overhead, chandeliers dangled and twinkled against the dim light of the dance floor. The place was packed. Everywhere I looked, people danced and moved, the patterns of their skimpy outfits gleaming against tanned, hard muscles.

I felt rude at first, pushing against strangers as I attempted to find a space with some elbow room. But I quickly realized that attempting to apologize or say "excuse me" every time I nudged someone was both tedious and unnecessary.

No one cared.

I breathed more deeply, and beneath the gallons of perfume and cologne, I got garlic and peppers and some kind of cloyingly sweet smell—and of course that relentless, ever-present fish. I hated—*hated*—that smell, and come to think of it, I hated just about my entire birthday so far.

And then I smelled vanilla.

I turned, and sure enough, Milo was right behind me. Unlike Dana, his eyes didn't hold that same-old question. He probably figured that if I smelled something nasty, I'd be barfing, and since I wasn't... He smiled reassuringly and mouthed the words *Want something to drink?*

I shook my head, because I was already well on my way to needing to pee. And I turned away fast, because I found myself wanting, with a sudden fierce desire, to close my eyes and make a wish and turn myself into a far more normal seventeen-year-old who'd gotten a fake ID to come to this club to *dance*, not sniff people for traces of evil, like some kind of glorified rescue dog.

And as long as I was wishing for the impossible, I wished that Milo was here with me, and not just in a *Milo, you get to babysit Sky* way.

I wished he would dance with me.

Of course, right at that moment someone bumped into me. I stumbled slightly, and Milo reached out to steady me, his hand electric against my waist.

Our connection clicked on, and ohmygodohmygod, everything I was thinking was right there, front and center for him to see, hear, feel, know—and I tried to shut it all down. But I knew there was no way I could make my mind go completely blank, so I grabbed at that last thought, and I aimed it at an almost impossibly handsome dark-haired man—boy, really, because he wasn't that much older than me—who was dancing with a bored-looking girl in a red minidress. And I focused on his mocha-colored skin and midnight brown eyes so that Milo would interpret my previous thought as *I wished he would dance with me.*

Come to think of it, he looked kind of like Tom Diaz, of super-romantic-kiss fame, although he couldn't possibly be. Tom was back in California and…I suddenly found myself missing Tom with an intensity that rolled through me like a surging high tide—and Milo took his hand from my waist as if he'd been burned.

Which was a good thing. Although, in all honesty, it was the *idea* of Tom that I truly longed for—the idea of having someone in the same way that Dana and Milo had each other.

Because if I had someone like Tom, I wouldn't be standing here in this noisy, crowded, smelly room jonesing for Dana's boyfriend.

Misery filled my throat, and I glanced back at him. He said something to me, which of course I couldn't hear.

He said it again, and again I shook my head, and, with frustration on his usually patient face, he held out his hand for me to take.

So I did.

I really hate it here too, he told me. *I'm sorry you're having such a crappy birthday, Sky, I really am. Why don't we just find someplace to sit and wait for Dana? Unless…I know you want to dance. And I know I'm not Tom, I mean, I didn't even realize you had a boyfriend—*

He's not my boyfriend, I admitted, but then added, *I mean, yeah, I wanted him to be. He was really nice. I met him at a party about a year ago and… You know how you meet somebody and everything just clicks?*

He did know. He didn't say as much, but I could feel it.

And then—amazingly—they're equally into you? I continued.

Yeah, I guess. Milo's smile was rueful as he pulled me to the side of the room where there was a café table—one of those high ones—with a single empty stool. *Sit.* Before I could form the *What about you?* thought into words, he added, *I'll stand. I'm good.*

So I climbed up onto that chair as he thought, *So Tom moved to California?* He held my hand atop the table, loosely caught between both of his as he gazed out at the dance floor, as if standing guard.

No, he was only in Connecticut visiting his cousin, I told him. *He went home. He wanted us to do some kind of crazy, long-distance thing, thinking we could see each other on vacations, but when we looked at our calendars, we didn't both have the same week free for the next two years, so…we just kinda let it go.*

I'm sorry, Milo said, and I knew that he meant it.

Still, I shrugged. *I'm glad I met him. And you know, I was only sixteen. It's not like I'm not going to have another chance to meet someone equally great who's equally into me, right? Although, to be honest, I've met a lot of guys, and the first thing I usually think is, "Well, he's no Tom Diaz."*

Milo glanced at me with those eyes. *Maybe you should plan to go to California after you graduate. Does he live in L.A.?*

Sonoma, I told him. *His family owns a…restaurant, I think it was.*

It's beautiful out there. Dana and I spent a coupla months in San Francisco, which is not that far from Tom-Diaz-land.

You've been with her—Dana—for a long time. It wasn't really a question, and I didn't wait for him to answer it. I just plunged on. *I really like her. Dana. I value her as a teacher, as a mentor, and a…a role model. And a friend. I think of her as a very close friend. She's very important to me.*

He blinked at me. *That's…good. I'm sure she'll appreciate knowing that.*

And you are too, I added. It was a little heavy-handed, but I wanted to reassure him that, in case he picked up even just the smallest whiff of my crush on him, he'd understand that I had priorities and a well-developed sense of right and wrong—please God, don't let that change. As long as my G-T-ness didn't turn me into a sociopathic monster of selfishness, I would never, ever jeopardize my friendship with Dana.

Important to me, I added. *I'm really glad that you're my friend too, Milo.*

He pulled his hand away to get his pack of gum from his pocket and to unwrap a piece. Part of the paper had glued itself onto the piece, and he frowned at it, glancing up to roll his eyes and smile at me. He leaned close to my ear to say, "I'm honored that you think of me as a friend."

I touched his arm. *Where* is *Dana?* I asked, but then said, *Never mind*, and took my hand back, as I saw her over by the bar. She was talking, heads close together, to a stunningly handsome but undeniably dangerous-looking man.

Milo touched my shoulder, his hand warm against my bare skin. I looked up at him as he pulled his hand away fast. "Sorry," he said. "I should probably just…" He reached out again to touch me with a single finger against my elbow. *Look out on the floor.*

I turned and looked out where the crowd was thickest. At first I could only see a mass of moving limbs, but when I looked more closely, I noticed that Calvin was in the center of it all, doing the infamous robot, undeniably in the spotlight.

As if my thoughts had cued it, a literal spotlight came out and focused its beam on Calvin.

The crowd went crazy, and I laughed out loud. Milo was grinning too.

But the weird thing was Calvin didn't look like he was having a good time. In fact, he seemed to be waving his robot-like arms to catch Dana's attention. As I watched, he tried to leave the dance floor, but then Dana turned to glare at him, and he spun on his heel before doing a half split on the floor and then jumping into the air.

The crowd whistled and clapped.

I reached for Milo's hand. *Oh, man,* I told him, still giggling. *I'm glad he couldn't feel that, 'cause it looked like it would have hurt.*

But then I stopped laughing because Dana had left the bar and was heading for us, the gorgeous man just a few steps behind her.

I pulled my hand free from Milo's, because that would've been just a little too weird—my sitting there like that in full view—but Dana didn't slow down as she approached. She *did* touch her nose and widen her eyes at me as she breezed past us, so I knew enough to take a deep breath when her new friend followed after her.

But he was sewage-smell free, and I broadcast that by fist-pumping into the air. "Whoo!" I said. "Whoo!"

Out on the dance floor, as if it was a call-and-response, Calvin gave an answering "Whoo-whoo!" and then pulled a *Saturday Night Fever* move, followed by a backflip and then something that looked like an extremely manic fox-trot. Of course, that was really Dana who'd choreographed that.

"Girl, please!" I could see Calvin's lips move as he implored Dana, his eyes indignant as his feet moved beneath him.

But she ignored him, even as her new friend introduced her to a group of equally gorgeous women. Destiny users, all of them. Had to be.

Out on the dance floor, Calvin was laboriously performing something I'd previously seen mastered only by Russian men in fur hats. He squatted down, jumped up, and then lifted his knees. Then, without warning, he switched to an extremely elaborate *Riverdance* rendition.

I looked from Calvin to Dana, who was sitting with her new friends, plural now, at a table over by the dimly lit hall that led to the bathrooms. And then I looked at Milo. I held out my hand, and as our connection clicked on, I asked, *Ready for a field trip?*

He smiled. *Always.*

He helped me down off the stool—not that I needed help.

I know. But I don't want you to fall.

Thanks, I thought back at him. We went past the table where Dana was now sitting, and I took several deep, deep breaths. Nothing. As I fist-pumped, my frustration inspired a jumble of thoughts containing words that would have made a sailor blush. I never would have said any of that aloud, except—oh great—Milo's hand was on my elbow. He'd had access to all of it, and now he was laughing.

I felt myself flush. *Shit, I mean shoot! I keep forgetting that everything I think is now public.*

Not public, he told me. *Not really. And don't worry. I can keep a secret.*

He took my hand again, weaving our fingers together this time, as he led me into that narrow hallway—where the line to the ladies' room was epic.

"Whoa," I said. "Wow, I forgot to pack my sleeping bag and trail mix."

Milo glanced at me. *Do you really have to…?* My *yes* must've been obvious, because he immediately added, *I don't mind. We can wait.*

You don't have to wait with me, I told him, even as the woman standing right in front of us smiled to reveal drug-blackened teeth.

"Want a third?" she asked, shouting over music that was loud even back here.

"A third of what?" I started to ask, but Milo cut me off with a very definite sounding, "Nope. Not into that."

"Wanna buy some—"

"Not into that, either," he said, even as he started, hesitantly and tactfully, to try to explain to me, *She, um, thinks we're in line to, uh, go into the bathroom together. The two of us. To, you know. Get jiggy. And she was offering to, um—*

Ew! I got it, and I was immediately embarrassed—more for not knowing what she'd meant. *I mean, not you and me* ew, *but* ew *at the thought of... And oh my God, you must think I'm so stupid.* Although he *had* just used the Mom-tastic phrase "get jiggy," but that was probably just to make me laugh.

I think you're sweet, Milo told me. *And funny. And definitely not stupid. But I also think I'm not leaving you alone on this line or anywhere else in this club.*

I nodded, grateful for his presence. *Thanks.*

Who was that girl in your vision? She was in your dream too. Milo immediately cut himself off. *Sorry. I really didn't mean to ask that. It's not my business. But this you're-in-my-head thing makes it hard to... I mean, I was wondering it, and even though I wouldn't have said it out loud if we were, you know, talking, it just kind of escaped because I was thinking it—*

It's okay, I reassured him, unable to keep from laughing. Usually taciturn Milo was practically babbling. *Really. It's not a secret.*

It kind of is, he countered. *I don't really know how I know this, but I do know that you haven't even told Calvin about her. Her name's Nicole, right?*

He was watching me with those eyes, his dimples nowhere in sight.

But then he smiled and touched his face with the hand that wasn't holding mine. *I think they make me look kind of goofy.*

I laughed. *Goofy. Right. Because random drug-abusing women in clubs always want to have anonymous bathroom sex with the goofiest-looking guys in the room.*

Milo laughed too, but then his smile faded. *It's okay if you don't want to tell me. I don't mean to overstep any bounds.*

You're not. And I kinda do. Want to tell you. Her name was Nicole—it still is, I quickly added. *She's not dead. Thank God.*

That's good, I felt him think as he tucked his hair behind his ear. The muscles in his forearm rippled as he moved and I tried not to stare. *I was afraid…*

She was my best friend, back when I lived in Connecticut. She was really smart but she was also really popular—which is harder to deal with than most people think. She started to get into drinking and drugs and… it got so that all she really wanted to do was party. She made some pretty big messes, and I was always there to clean them up.

And wow, I'm making it sound so crappy, but it wasn't. Not always. When she wasn't drinking, we had a lot of fun. She made me laugh. Anyway, it was a house party. A lot like the one at Garrett's. A lot of stupid high school kids doing things we wouldn't have been able to do if Mike's parents had been home that night. Mike Rizzulo. He was Nicole's boyfriend. That month. He was a total douche. I realized that even though my words were being sent to Milo through my thoughts, the voice I was using to communicate with him was wavering with emotion. *Sorry.*

It's okay, Milo said gently.

He was…gigantically stupid. But he was only part of the stupidity of that night. See, I should have been the designated driver, only my mother wouldn't let me get my license. It's beyond stupid. She thought she was— somehow—protecting me, but if I'd been in possession of Nicky's keys… I exhaled hard. *Anyway, the night was a disaster right from the start. Nicole and Mike had only been dating for about six weeks. It wasn't a long time, but for Nicky, that was pretty much an eternity. She really liked him.*

Milo nodded. The song playing out in the club switched to one that he liked, but I could feel his attention still completely on me.

Long, sad story short, she got pregnant. But when she told him—when Nicky told Mike—his response was to throw a party and not invite her.

Oh, no, I felt Milo thinking.

Oh, yeah. We found out about it—how could we not? And when we arrived, Mike was already making out with Jennifer Mills.

It had been brutal, and Nicky had been devastated. *We didn't even have the opportunity to slink away,* I continued, *because as soon as Mike saw her, he took the whole thing public. He told Nicky, right in front of everyone at the party, that the baby couldn't be his. That she was a big slut, that she'd slept with a million people—how about asking the rest of the football team if they were the father, blah, blah, blah.* I laughed out loud, humorlessly. *Thing was, Nicky had a reputation, but it wasn't real. What she did with Mike was a really big deal for her. He was the first.*

I could feel Milo's profound sadness.

But nobody believed her. And Nicky freaked. She went running out of there, and I followed her. And I got into her car with her—I guess I figured that since I'd driven with her before when she'd been drinking... I felt Milo wince, and I added, *And yes, I know that wasn't smart. But on this night, of all nights, I knew she was sober so I got in, and I wish that I'd said,* Let me drive, *or God, even,* Let me call my mom. *I wish I'd known Dana back then, or...you.*

I knew my eyes were filling with tears, and I willed them dry, staring ferociously at my hands, held tightly now in both of Milo's as the entire line shuffled slightly closer to the single-seater ladies' room.

Nicky was shouting at me, telling me to get out of the car. But I wouldn't. I was afraid of what she might do. All I kept thinking was that I should've kept her from going over to Mike's house. I should have stopped her. I should have known this would happen.

Milo interrupted me then. *It wasn't your fault.*

Stop being so freaking nice! I shot back at him, then immediately wished that my tone hadn't been so harsh. *I'm sorry. I just wish I'd done something different. I wonder if she would have driven that fast if I hadn't been in the car. But, finally she just took off, out of there.*

And I kept telling her to slow down, I continued, *but I think she was trying to scare me. She was driving and crying and swearing, and I know you and Dana don't think that I'm prescient, but Milo, I'm telling you that I knew. I knew—in those last few minutes—exactly when and where it was going to happen, but there was nothing I could do or say to stop her. I remember shouting at her, asking her if she really wanted to kill me too, and she...*

She'd called me a stupid bitch and said it was my fault for not getting out of the car when I had the chance.

Milo placed his other hand on the side of my face, and I leaned into it, feeling his solid warmth and strength, and wishing with all of my heart that I could turn one of my powers into an ability to rewrite the past. Surely there was a Greater-Than somewhere who had the talent and skill to demand a do-over—and actually get one.

She didn't mean it, I told Milo, even though I knew he could feel my doubt. Maybe my friendship—maybe *I*—had meant so little to Nicole that taking me with her as she killed herself didn't make her so much as pause.

We were going too fast as we approached a curve in the road. I'd felt the tires slip, heard the screeching of burning rubber as we slid across the asphalt.

Nicky had looked at me as she wildly spun the steering wheel, trying to keep the car in control. The expression on her face was one of pure horror, her mouth open in a silent scream as the car skidded sideways off the road. I shut my eyes, remembering the way the car started to roll—it was dizzying and terrifying, and it happened so fast that I don't remember hearing anything. Not the shrieking of bending and tearing metal, and not even that one final glass-shattering crash as we slammed into the trunk of a very solid tree.

The only sound I remember was a high-pitched buzz that faded as the world went black.

Then, just as quickly, the blackness lightened into a white fuzziness… kind of like a TV when the cable goes out, and the high-pitched buzz came back, louder and louder, until it became an actual noise, and I realized it was a voice, screaming—and that voice was coming from me.

I wasn't in pain—at least not that I could tell. And Nicky was next to me, in the driver's seat, her head slumped against the steering wheel. She had blood on her face, on her head, on her hands. There was so much blood—it was on me too. And I saw that a branch from the tree that we'd hit had come in through the broken window, and it stabbed into Nicky's side like a long, jagged knife.

I somehow pulled it out of her—at the time I didn't know how I'd managed to find the strength, but now I knew I'd used my power. Except it was the wrong thing to do, because after the branch was out, there was even more blood. God, Nicky was even breathing blood—it frothed from her mouth and her nose—only she wasn't really breathing. She was making more like a liquid gasp, the way I imagined it would sound if someone tried to inhale underwater. Her eyes were wide and white in her blood-streaked face. And she was staring at me like I should do something.

But there was nothing I could do. Nothing! I tried to find my phone, to call 9-1-1, but I couldn't find my bag. I searched for it, frantically, as I listened to her making those terrible, terrible sounds. *Where was my phone, where was my phone, wherewasitwherewasitwhere—*

You're okay. You're right here. You're with me. Milo interrupted the awfulness of the memory.

I gasped, and as my mind returned to the present, I opened my eyes. I was with Milo, and we were finally next in line for the bathroom. The drug addict who'd wanted to be our third gave us one last, longing look as she went in and closed the door behind her.

I saw all of it, Sky, Milo whispered in my head. *I'm so sorry.*

I couldn't do a thing. She couldn't breathe, and I couldn't even find my phone…

But Milo didn't let me continue. He overwhelmed me with a mantra, coursing through my consciousness with the strong rhythmic beat of the music around us.

Still thoughts. Still thoughts. Still thoughts.

And I breathed in his warmth through his hand on my face, as the serenity of his thoughts worked to calm my own.

"Thank you," I whispered.

"You're welcome," he answered, his mouth close to my ear. The noise of his voice was almost jarring after communicating purely through our minds.

"I can understand why you're dreaming about her," Milo said.

"Yeah, well." I shrugged, as if trying to act nonchalant or detached now would do any good. He knew exactly how I felt.

"What…happened after that?"

My mouth was dry. Maybe after I used the bathroom, I'd treat myself to a soda. "Well, paramedics showed up—someone saw the accident and called for help. Which was a miracle. If they'd gotten to us even a few minutes later, Nicky probably would have died. She had a punctured lung. It was bad."

Milo nodded.

"But it wasn't fatal," I continued. My voice was absurdly matter-of-fact, as if it was easier to talk about this in a tone that I might use to recite a grocery list. "We both went to the hospital. She stayed in the

ICU for weeks. I was discharged that night." I smiled bitterly. "Not a scratch on me. Of course."

That makes sense, considering who you are.

Don't you mean what *I am*, I shot back at him.

I think of you as a who *not a* what, Milo told me calmly. *How come Nicole never got a chance to apologize to you?*

I didn't bother putting it into a nicely told story. I just let him see the whole ugly, sorry mess. My mother having a near heart attack as she came to the hospital to find me. Nicky's parents, equally upset. The pressure they'd laid on me, as Nicky lay unconscious, to reveal the identity of the father of her child. The furtive and awful conversation I'd had with Mike in the hallway outside chemistry class, where I'd realized that he actually hoped Nic wouldn't survive. The sudden news from my mother that we were moving—immediately—out of state. My trip to the hospital to visit Nicky, still in a coma, only to discover that she'd finally woken up—and that her parents had already shipped her off to some private facility in Europe.

The official story was that she'd spend the next year "studying abroad." But everyone knew she was simply being hidden away for the course of her pregnancy.

She hadn't called, she hadn't texted, she hadn't emailed. She hadn't even sent me an old-fashioned letter.

I suspected that she was never coming back.

I didn't blame her.

"That must have been really hard for you," Milo said quietly as he let go of me, cutting our telepathic connection.

I looked up at him in surprise, but then realized it was finally my turn in the bathroom. Except it was more than that.

"Where the hell have you been?" Dana. Down at the end of the hall. Loud enough to be heard over the music.

No wonder Milo had let go of me, fast.

"I'll be right out," I told them both and escaped into the privacy of the incredibly disgusting bathroom, locking the flimsy door behind me.

Still, I knew that, even if I'd left it unlocked, I'd be perfectly safe. Because Milo—steady, strong, supportive, and sweet—would be waiting out there for me, ready to protect me.

From everything but my own stupidly treacherous heart.

———

"Girl, you held me hostage for damn near forever!" Calvin tried to sound annoyed, but I knew that a huge part of him had seriously enjoyed the last hour in Pretense. As he sat back down in his wheelchair in the front seat of his car, Dana's posture became visibly relaxed.

"I had to," she said simply. "Or else you would have interrupted what I was trying to do."

I tried not to slam the car door as I got into the backseat. "So now what?"

"You were talking to some pretty shady dudes," Calvin chastised Dana. "I was just trying to look out for you."

"I can hold my own," Dana said. "Believe me."

"And as long as I'm complaining," Calvin said, as he started his car with a roar. "The *Macarena*? I mean, seriously.

Dana laughed. "You were awesome."

I repeated myself. Louder this time. "Now. What?"

"Hey," Milo said soothingly, reaching for my hand, but I snatched it away. I didn't want to be soothed. I'd just spent an hour of my life getting us no closer to finding Sasha.

And yeah, *that* was why I was pissed. It had nothing to do with being forced to spend quality time with other people's boyfriends.

"Now we go to Taj Mahal," Dana announced.

I closed my eyes and flopped my head against the high seat-back. "Seriously? We're going to do that again?"

"And again, and again," Dana said. "Until your mommy says it's time for you to go home. Tonight, anyway. If we come up cold, we'll do your thing. But not 'til tomorrow." She looked at Cal. "Take a left out of the parking lot, Scoot."

I sighed and kept my eyes closed—even though I could feel Milo watching me. And sure enough, he did the one-finger-against-my-elbow thing and our connection clicked on.

Happy birthday to you, he sang in a not-unpleasant voice. *Happy birthday, to you. Happy birthday, dear Skylar...*

I opened my eyes and looked at him and fist-pumped—"Whoo-hoo!"—and we both started to laugh.

Dana turned in her seat to give us her WTF glare, and Milo took his hand away, digging in his pocket for another piece of gum.

CHAPTER TWENTY-SEVEN

"Car needs food," Cal announced matter-of-factly, breaking the too-tense silence as he drove us away from Pretense. Despite our ongoing failed attempts at finding any clues, Calvin was clearly still glowing from his vertical experience inside the club.

I couldn't blame him. But I also couldn't keep myself from feeling extremely *WTF-ish* about this entire sniffing-out-the-sewage-smell-in-the-haystack approach. We'd spent the whole night wasting time. I mean, I appreciated Dana's abilities and completely believed that she could use her mind-control powers to get vital information from nearly anyone—Percocet users notwithstanding.

But it seemed more and more as if my mysterious sewage smell was not as common as we'd first believed—or that it was, possibly, unconnected entirely to Sasha's disappearance. Maybe the traces of evil that I'd smelled out on the street and in the police station had merely been from fleeting evil-thought flatulence and not the result of someone completely, soullessly malevolent, like that old lady I'd envisioned exiting Sasha's bedroom window.

Regardless, I found myself feeling more and more frustrated as I thought about it, and I tried to remember all the times I'd smelled that smell. Surely there was some kind of pattern or commonality that I was missing. Kinda like what Dana had said about her sniff-out-the-Destiny-dealers approach. Find dealers who smelled like sewage, and then try to figure out what they all had in common, except... Maybe we were going about this back-assward.

Calvin found a sign for a gas station and pulled into the lot.

"I got this," Dana said, and as she got out of the car to pump the gas, I found myself thinking about that list she'd made on the napkin at the Pizza Extravaganza and I sat up.

"I need a piece of paper and a pen," I announced, and both Calvin and Milo looked at me in surprise.

Milo started patting his pockets as Cal reached into the cup-holder in the front and held up his phone. "You can use the note app on my phone," he offered. "Since you're obviously dying to start writing your novel."

"Shut up," I said, except I didn't really want him to shut up as I eagerly took his phone and clicked it on. I typed with my thumbs: "Times Sky Smelled Sewage" and then "1. Sasha's room, night she went missing." I backed up and made that a three instead, inserting "while babysitting for Sasha, Sunday night" as number one and "in nightmare before Sasha went missing" as two.

Milo leaned forward to see what I was typing, reading aloud so that Calvin could follow.

"Four was during a freaky daydream I had about the old-lady-thing climbing into my own window," I remembered, as I typed it in. "Five was outside my house on the Saturday after we first met Dana at the Sav'A'Buck"—had that really been less than a week ago?—"right before Garrett came over to help look for *Tasha*…"

"Six was when you barfed on the sidewalk," Cal reminded me, "when Garrett stopped to offer you a ride."

Six was really in a dream I'd had about Sasha, but as I was making this list, I discovered that I wasn't interested in the dreams and visions as much as I was in real-life instances of smell sensitivity.

"Thanks," I said. "Seven, the police station, when I found out Detective Hughes had died, and eight, right before the police swooped in and arrested Sasha's dad." I looked up at Milo and Calvin. "I think that's it. Now we have to figure out what all these things have in common, in addition to the smell. And FYI, I'm deleting all of the dreams and visions." I backspaced over two and four, which left me with six different instances.

"Police and police, for the last two," Cal suggested, but I was already shaking my head.

"That's not it," I said. "I know it."

"Why don't you go down the list," Milo suggested, "one at a time, and show me what you remember, starting right before you smelled the sewage. Maybe something will stand out." He held out his hand, and I realized what he wanted me to do. He wanted me to share those memories with him telepathically, like we'd done in the club.

Cal knew something weird was up between Milo and me, and he narrowed his eyes a little and said, "Or just talk through it, if that's easier."

But I shook my head, and lord, I hoped it wasn't only because the boyfriend-stealing monster inside me wanted to hold Milo's hand, and that it wasn't just a convenient excuse to say, "No, I think it'll be more complete, more detailed if we do it this way."

I purged all kissing thoughts from my mind and just did it. Grabbed hold of his hand.

And there was Milo, warm and familiar, inside of my head.

Start with the most recent memory. I don't know whose thought that was—it was possible we were both thinking the same thing. But I began with my recollection of the moments right before I smelled the sewage and spotted Edmund in the bushes near Calvin's house.

I was still upset from being scared that something terrible had happened to Cal. I was walking swiftly, and Kim's gym shorts were thinking about giving me a wedgie...

I hate when that happens, Milo thought.

The sun caught the bedazzled collar of a sweet-faced little dachshund, who led his elderly owner on an equally decorated leash.

I rounded the corner, and *boom.*

Milo pulled me sharply back from the memory of the smell, and I opened my eyes to find him looking at me.

I closed my eyes and ran the damn thing over again in my mind, more slowly, and this time I heard the jingle of the little dog's name tag and license. And I saw that his owner was limping a little—favoring his right leg. The stop sign on the corner reflected the sun, blinding me and making me glance down, and I saw that the dog had left a fresh deposit on the ground next to the pole. The old man had failed to scoop the poop.

I rounded the corner, and this time I stopped the memory before the smell.

Dog, collar, poop...

"Cat food," I said aloud, and pulled Milo with me into the memory of my excursion into the police station. I played my encounter with Sergeant Olga Moran on fast-forward—*Ba-dah, ba-dah, ba-dah, ba-dah, ba-dah, bahm!* She opened the can of cat food, and *boom*.

I yanked us away from the memory of the smell and dragged Milo into my recollection of Garrett stopping to offer me a ride. Cars pulled around him—including a white van. I froze the memory. Garrett's mouth was open, but it was the van behind him that I mentally pointed to. It had a cartoon image of a dog and the words *Doggy Doo Good* on its side.

I ran back to the memory from the police station, to Olga Moran and that cat food can—and sure enough, it was the Doggy Doo Good brand.

Whoa, Milo said.

Yeah. I was onto something here. I flashed into my memory of the morning I'd gone for a run with Garrett, when the doorbell had mysteriously rung. Had my powers done that? That wasn't important right now. I kept going. When I'd opened the door, no one had been there, but there *had* been a woman walking three little well-pampered dogs, right across the street. On leashes purchased, perhaps, from the big-chain pet store?

That left the first two times—both in Sasha's bedroom. Before and after her abduction.

Sasha smelled it too? Milo asked, and I nodded.

Maybe the person who'd taken her—creepy old-lady-thing or other—had been lurking outside the night I'd babysat. And maybe she'd had her pet...snake with her that she'd bought from Doggy Doo Good...?

Or maybe the smell is her, Milo suggested.

And I finished the thought for him: *And she spends so much time at the Doggy Doo Good that everything in the store is polluted with her stank.*

We both opened our eyes at once—as Dana got back into the car. "Let's move it, Scoot. On to the Taj."

"No!" Milo and I spoke in unison. "To the Doggy Doo Good."

CHAPTER TWENTY-EIGHT

"What the fridge is a *Doggy Doo Good*?" Dana asked, still annoyed.

We'd found the closest twenty-four-hour superstore on Cal's phone map.

It hadn't taken us long to drive there, and we now sat in the nearly empty parking lot, gazing at the warehouse-sized building.

"You haven't seen the TV commercials?" Cal asked her. "They're pretty freaking relentless." He started to sing. "Doggy Doo Good—"

"It's basically an upscale pet-store chain," I told Dana.

She snorted. "For people who'll only feed their puppies distilled water and designer chow. And you think…" She let her voice trail off. Her skepticism that we'd find anything here was written all over her face.

It was true. The idea that the woman who'd kidnapped Sasha—a woman who was pure evil—held down a second job at the Doggy Doo Good was pretty ridiculous.

Dana shook her head as she studied the door to the massive storefront.

"We need to go in," Milo said.

"I agree." To my surprise, Dana nodded. "Let's take a stroll."

The four of us approached the enormous warehouse of a store. It had wide glass doors that slid open to reveal a cavernous room filled with rows upon rows of doggy toys, dry food, canned food, collars and leashes, crates, and plush pet beds.

As we got close enough, we triggered the sensors. The doors swooshed open, and an overhead video screen clicked on to reveal a cartoon dog. "Rel-row," the dog greeted us cheerfully. "Rel-come to Doggy Doo Good!"

"Really?" Dana said.

"Let's just walk around," I started to say. But before I could get the words out, a blast of that god-awful stench hit me. The world turned white, and I was enveloped by an overwhelming surge of vertigo that sent me tumbling to the tile floor.

Screaming...all the screaming...too much...all those little girls with their terrified faces, arms and legs squished into cages like dogs in a pound...like animals, really, and screaming and screaming... A truck! They were in a truck, huddling together, shaking, screaming...pieces of rope hanging from the sides of the interior...or were those dog chains? Collars? Dog collars and leashes and huge bags of dried dog food, stacked in neat rows. And the deafening screaming... They wanted their mommies... Oh God, they were gonna die, they were gonna die theyweregonnadie, theyweregonna—

Still thoughts. Still thoughts. Still thoughts...

When I opened my eyes, Milo was kneeling over me, his big arms wrapped tightly around me.

I was too terrified to feel embarrassed.

Still thoughts. Still thoughts. Still thoughts…

My breathing steadied, and my heart rate slowed, and I realized that I wasn't puking my guts out all over the pet-store floor, even though I was still highly aware of the sewage stench.

And I knew, the way that I now know things, that as long as I kept my connection to Milo, I *wouldn't* throw up, no matter how overpowering the smell became.

And I realized too that my vision of those terrified little girls wasn't gone. It had slowed way down, as though Milo's presence inside of my head, with his calming mantra and solid warmth, was somehow permitting me to focus on individual images, one by one.

As much as I wanted to erase any and all of those terrible pictures from my brain, never mind avoid seeing any *additional* horrors, I bit the bullet and closed my eyes, willing the images to become more complete.

"Don't move me," I heard myself say to Milo—or maybe I hadn't said it out loud. Maybe I'd simply sent the message to him through my thoughts. Either way, he didn't budge.

And there it was. Someone—a man. A big man. In a room this time. A large room. Hot. Smelly, and not just with fish-fear, but with the stench of unwashed bodies. All those little girls were now in rows, chained to cots. The man was carrying a… What was in his hand?

I concentrated, but someone was talking—someone in the Doggy Doo Good store. It was one of the clerks. She was asking if I was okay.

What she didn't realize was that the sound of her voice was making it difficult for me to stay focused on the vision.

"Shut up!" I growled without opening my eyes, adding a *please*, because, damn, I sounded like the girl from *The Exorcist*.

The room became quiet.

And…a different man and a woman? Naked. Ew. They were kissing in a hot tub, but they looked kind of bored and… Was it…on TV?

No. A computer?

A computer!

Then back to the big man—fully clothed, a red shirt and filthy jeans—in the huge room, but he wasn't on TV. He was real. *And he was holding a…*

What was it? Was it a baseball *bat?*

The computer again… The lady's acting skills were overwhelmed by her apathy. Why was I seeing this? But as soon as I wondered, I realized that the computer screen had a clock.

8:04 p.m.

And then the vision shifted and I saw big eyes squeezed shut, little hands clinging to a teddy bear with its nose chewed…

Sasha.

Sasha. Alive.

"Sasha's alive!" I shouted. And I *knew* I'd said *that* out loud, because as I opened my eyes, a group of complete strangers all gasped in unison.

Dana and Calvin were there too, hovering close to me. Milo still held me, his eyes sad and solemn as he rubbed his hands up and down my arms.

I shuddered. "I saw…I saw so much."

Dana looked up at the small crowd of store clerks and warehouse workers. "All right," she said impatiently. "Show's over. Go back to your chew toys."

"Come on," Milo said quietly, guiding me as I shakily stood.

"You heard the girl. Stop standing around. There's nothing to see here." Calvin's voice was defensive as my friends help me walk out of the Doggy Doo Good.

When we were finally outside, Dana stepped in front of Milo, ripping him away from me as she grabbed my shoulders. "What happened in there?" she demanded.

"I saw Sasha." I nodded, driving my point home. "I saw her. Alive. She was asleep but she was alive. I have no. Doubts. About it."

Dana had already begun to shake her head. "No," she said. "Sky, we've been over this again and again. Sasha is—"

"Alive! I saw her! She was holding her teddy bear, and there was…a computer screen. Someone was in the room with Sasha. A gigantic man." I wrinkled my nose in distaste. "He was watching Skinemax. What kind of man watches that in a room filled with little girls?"

Calvin lifted an eyebrow.

"But I could see the little clock on the lower right-hand side of the laptop monitor," I continued.

Milo watched me. I knew he'd seen at least part of what I had, and I looked to him for confirmation.

"It read 8:04 p.m.," he offered.

"Right!" I exclaimed "See? Dana, do you see? It was happening in real time!"

"No, it wasn't." Dana grabbed Milo by the wrist, inspecting his watch. "It's nine oh eight."

It was a full hour later than I'd thought or felt or… It didn't make sense. I was so certain…

Dana continued. "The time was random. You're psychic, Sky, not prescient. It was a vision from whenever. Last week. Has to be."

That had been a real-time vision, I *knew* it. "No. I'm not wrong about this."

Dana silently held out Milo's wrist so I could look at his watch myself.

"Well," I said. "Maybe…the clock on the computer was wrong, or…" I looked at Milo, searching his face, hoping he'd have the answers, but his expression was one of helplessness. "Please," I exclaimed. "Tell Dana what you saw—what we saw. You know Sasha's alive, right?"

Calvin played with his phone as he sat next to us, clearly absorbing the heated argument despite his attention elsewhere.

"I can't… I'm not sure what that was, Sky," Milo finally managed.

Great. Even the guy who could read my thoughts didn't believe me.

"So I googled Doggy Doo Good," Cal offered, "and it says here that the main warehouse for the chain is in—"

"Alabama," I stated without hesitation.

"Dang," Calvin said. "I thought my 7G was faster than your piece-of-crap phone."

"I didn't look it up," I told him. "I didn't have to. I knew it. Like I know that Sasha's alive. She's somewhere north of here—I can feel it—and Alabama, well, it's north of here, right?"

Milo and Dana exchanged a long look.

"Right?" I demanded again.

Milo cleared his throat. "Those leaves that Sky saw in her dream? They were something called shagbark hickory. They definitely grow in Alabama."

"Fine," Dana said finally. "You think Sasha's in Alabama? Let's go to Alabama. I guess I don't have anything better to do."

I swallowed hard. "Really?"

But Dana was already marching toward Cal's car. "Come on, Princess!" she called. "Let's do it. Let's go! Alabama ho!"

I checked Calvin's face to see how he felt about the whole thing. He just shrugged. "I'll just call and tell my 'rents I'm crashing on your couch. It's your mom who'll flip out."

It was the truth. If I didn't make it home by my twelve-thirty curfew, there was a distinct possibility that Mom would notify the FBI, along with the Coast Guard and the Navy. And there was no way we could make it to Alabama and back by twelve thirty.

Still, being grounded for the next three decades was a seriously small price to pay if it meant finding Sasha and bringing her safely home.

"Cool," I said, not quite believing what I was agreeing to. "Let's do it."

The four of us climbed back into Calvin's car. Milo kept an eye on me as I buckled my seat belt—presumably to make sure I wasn't about to projectile vomit, faint, or burst into tears.

"Where are we going?" Cal asked.

"Alabama," Dana replied, stating the obvious.

"Gee, thanks. I kinda meant *where* in Alabama."

"I'll know when I feel it," I stated. "Just drive. I'll get us there."

———————

I'd never liked long car rides, and tonight was no exception.

Calvin tapped the steering wheel, releasing nervous energy in the form of a vague drumbeat.

I looked at the clock on the dashboard. We'd been driving for hours. My curfew had come and gone.

I was so grounded when I got home.

"Everyone awake?" Cal asked loudly.

"Are *you*?" Dana's look was challenging.

"I'm fine," Calvin scoffed, although I could tell he was getting tired.

"Pull over," Dana replied. "I'll drive for a bit."

Calvin began to shake his head, but Dana took the liberty of making him nod instead, even as his head tipped to the side. "I'd absolutely love it if Dana would drive my car right now."

As Calvin took the next exit, he added sullenly, "Your mind-control is mucho creepy."

"I do what I can."

He pulled into the parking lot of a boarded-up Corn Dog Palace. And as Dana and Cal worked to switch seats—Dana using her telekinesis to plop Calvin ungracefully into the passenger side—I took a moment to observe the very non-Southern-Florida trees around us and to pretend that Milo wasn't observing me.

"Alabama," I said out loud.

Milo nodded. "Alabama," he repeated.

Dana huffed and puffed in the wheelchair driver's seat, adjusting herself as she quickly became familiar with Calvin's special buttons. "It's kind of like driving a motorcycle," she said out loud.

"You sure you're gonna be a'ight?" Cal asked uncertainly. "I mean, it's not rocket science, but it takes practice."

"Which is what I'm doing right now," Dana said impatiently. "We're good," she added, pressing the button for accelerate. She got us quickly back onto the highway as if she'd been driving a car with hand controls for her entire life.

"Alrighty then," Cal said, leaning his head back against the seat.

"Alabama, here we come." What Dana was lacking in enthusiasm, she made up for with attitude.

"The end of this journey is taking us back to the beginning," Milo whispered quietly.

"What does that mean?" I asked.

"It means we're coming full circle here," Dana offered. She shook her head. "Frickin' Alabama," she repeated, and shook her head.

"Let's play the Would You Rather game!" Calvin announced cheerfully.

"Oh, no," I said.

"What's the Would You Rather game?" Milo asked.

"It's just basically Truth or Dare without the actual dare," I said. "But Cal has this unbelievable ability to come up with questions that suck."

"*You* suck," Calvin said gleefully.

"Who's going first?" Dana asked.

"I am," Cal said.

Dana glanced at him. "Are you asking the questions or are you answering them?"

"Asking," Cal replied. He crossed his arms. "All right! Dana. Would you rather…"

"Cal, seriously," I warned, grinning a little despite myself. "Cut her a break with the nasty scenarios."

"Fine," Cal said, pretending to sulk. "I'll have mercy on you. Um… okay, then I'll go off topic entirely and ask you a serious question I've been wondering for a while. Why is this so important to you?"

Dana frowned as she drove. "What do you mean?"

Calvin got more specific. "Why are you here? Why are you in this car right now, looking for a little dead girl you've never met?"

I rolled my eyes at the word "dead," aware that Milo was watching me. It bummed me out that he didn't believe me. I mean, I'd expected it from Dana and Calvin.

Cal continued. "I know you're such a Good Samaritan and all, but there's gotta be a reason you're putting so much time and energy into this."

Now Milo watched Dana.

She cleared her throat. "Maybe it's just what I'm supposed to do," she said.

"That's weak," Calvin argued. "Come on."

Milo leaned forward in the seat, chewing on his gum. "Dana?"

"Fuck you, Milo."

I frowned and impulsively grabbed Milo's arm. *Why do you let her speak to you like that?*

Milo's words cascaded through my mind as he laughed a little. *She doesn't mean it as… She's just… She has a funny way of saying I love you.*

I let go of Milo's arm. Dana loved Milo.

I hadn't had extensive experience in the relationship department, but last time I checked, *eff you* and *I love you* were two different sentiments.

Still, Dana was unique.

"Fine," Dana grumbled. "You wanna know why I'm here? Her name was Lacey Zannino. She was a gorgeous little girl with a big heart and a beautiful mind. She was funny and sweet and talented. And she was also my sister."

I lurched forward in my seat, not sure I'd heard Dana correctly. "Your…"

"Sister." Dana nodded, as my heart sank. "Lacey was my little sister. And those pieces of shit took her away in the middle of the night. They stole her body and her innocence, and then they stole her life." She swiped at her nose furiously. I knew Dana would rather die than cry in front of us. "And then, to make matters worse, they framed my dad. Who never would have hurt either one of us. He would have done anything for Lacey. Or for me. But now he's rotting on death row. And Lacey's rotting in an unmarked grave."

"Dana, I'm so—" I started.

"Don't," she warned, holding up a hand.

"So they never recovered her body?" Calvin asked.

"No," Dana said flatly. "They recovered nothing. The cops didn't care."

I knew what *that* was like.

"So then why do you think she's definitely…" Cal's voice trailed off.

"Do not. Say it. She's dead." Dana's voice actually quivered, her pain still so raw and horribly real.

I wanted to hug her, and I also knew that a hug wouldn't do a bit of good.

Finally, Milo spoke up. "It's important to both of us to find the people who are responsible for killing Lacey and...Sasha." He turned to look directly at me. "Whatever we find, Sky, it's going to help make it harder for these people to kidnap the next girl."

Cal's nod was determined. "Girl, I am so eff'n serious," he said, slapping a hand onto Dana's shoulder, "I got your back."

I looked at Milo. He took my hand.

I had no idea about... I nodded toward Dana.

I know. I wanted to respect her privacy. I wanted to wait for her to say something.

That day she was gone, I remembered. *Was she...?*

Visiting her father in prison, Milo told me. *She's allowed to see him every two weeks. Wherever she is, she makes sure that she gets there— although sometimes they make it hard by moving him around. He's currently in a maximum-security lockup in Georgia.*

"Oh God," I said aloud.

"Hey," Dana said sharply, peering into the rearview mirror at Milo and me. Quickly, I let go of Milo's hand. "Let's not have any back-seat *poor Dana* powwows. Let's just pretend that nothing's changed, because it hasn't. Lacey's still dead. She's dead. Got it? No more mind-talking or consoling or Kumbaya-ing. Conversation's over."

"Okay," I said quietly. Milo looked visibly uncomfortable, so I stared out the window, feeling worse than ever.

"It's going to be okay," he whispered to me.

And, sighing, I pretended with all of my might that I actually believed him.

CHAPTER TWENTY-NINE

I must have been dreaming.

It wasn't the jewel-hued clouds swishing lazily across the horizon that gave it away, and it wasn't the splash of yellow from the wildflowers as I all but floated through the field.

My unconscious had somehow accepted this as a normal scenario.

It was the fact that Milo and I were walking *hand in hand* through that aforementioned field—and the fact that for the first time in weeks I actually felt happy.

So, yeah. I *must* have been dreaming.

But my dream self didn't seem to feel as though waking up was high on my list of priorities. In fact, I found myself pausing for a moment in the center of the field, watching as billows of magnificent clouds provided a glorious backdrop to Milo's handsome face. And I found myself smiling.

He smiled back and pulled me close to him. I could have sworn I heard violins swoon.

Or maybe I'd tricked myself into believing there was music. Either way, my stomach was hovering in my throat, like I'd just soared down the highest hill of a roller coaster.

And then, his lips brushed mine, and all I could smell...or feel... or...something...was vanilla and sunshine. And love. Unabashed and unapologetic *love*.

This was no crush. This was the real deal, the Big One, the bona fide mondo emotion.

But before I had a chance to laugh out loud at the lovely sensation of his impossibly soft lips against mine, I felt my heart skip another beat, and I looked around me. The field was gone. And Milo and I were horizontal.

Horizontal...in a bed.

And love was still coursing through the air like it had its own individual pulse, but something else was casting a spell that lingered as it blew through the lit candles and brushed against the red rose petals sprinkled across the bedsheets.

It was desire.

I wanted Milo *bad*.

And then Sir Mix-A-Lot was blaring through Cal's car speakers.

Wait. Car speakers?

I awoke with a start, gasping as I sat up in the backseat of Cal's Audi.

"Ho boy!" I yelled.

From the other side of the car, Milo jumped in his seat, clearly just waking up too. He looked over at me, his mouth slightly parted, as if he were about to say something important.

Calvin waved to both of us from the front seat. "'Sup, guys? Done with your nightmares?"

435

I tucked my hair nervously behind my ears, willing my heart to slow down.

Dana had pulled off the highway and was parking at a rest stop.

"Nightmares?" Milo asked warily, shifting slightly in his seat.

"Yeah," Dana replied, grinning in the rearview mirror. "It's been almost an hour. You two have been moaning and groaning the whole time. I wanted to wake you up, but Cal thought it was funny."

I looked at Milo. Milo looked at me.

He'd been moaning and groaning. I'd been moaning and groaning.

I'd dream-molested him.

"Oh my God," I said, and swung the door open before Dana had a chance to completely stop the car.

"Wait!" she called, slamming on the brakes. But I didn't stop. I booked it toward the ladies' room, where I could be absolutely mortified by myself for at least a few minutes.

Maybe I'd just move into this rest-stop restroom for the rest of my life.

Yes. It was a good plan. I had running water and a selection of soft drinks and Cheez Doodles from the vending machine. It was an attractive alternative to actually coming out and facing Milo again, knowing that only a few moments ago I'd planted unbelievably erotic scenarios in his unconscious—against his will, to boot.

Unfortunately, however, I still had to find Sasha. So my genius plan of becoming the official reclusive hermit of the Chipley, Florida rest area wouldn't exactly work. I'd eventually need to bite the bullet and endure the walk of shame.

Of sorts. Because it was, after all, a dream. Dream shame, however, felt much like real shame.

Sighing, I went to the sink and splashed a good-sized amount of icy water onto my face.

I didn't want Milo, I didn't want Milo, I didn't...

I was screwed. I *so* wanted Milo to be my boyfriend.

Miserably, I tried to dry my face using one of those air blowers and finally gave up. I trudged out of the bathroom still slightly damp.

Cal's empty car was parked out front. I spotted Dana in line inside the convenience store. Calvin was probably still in the bathroom. And Milo was—

"Skylar!"

There he was. Of course. Waiting for me. His shirt was rumpled from sleep, and he'd already developed the slightest shadow of stubble on his jawline. On anyone else, it would've looked disheveled or messy. On Milo, it was...

Sexy.

I swallowed hard.

"Hey." He was clearly embarrassed, his cheeks tinged with red as he forced himself to meet my gaze. That only served to make him more attractive. "I just wanted to say that I'm sorry..."

I put a hand up. "Wait. Did you honestly just *apologize*?"

Milo frowned and bit his lip, a look that only exaggerated his deeply set dimples. "I...well, I feel kinda terrible, you know, about the whole dream."

"Milo! Seriously? What is wrong with you?" I put my hands up to my face. I wanted to look like I was exasperated, but the movement was mainly to cover the blush that had begun to spread across my cheeks. Unlike Milo, when I blushed I looked like a tomato. "I can't believe you're apologizing for something *I* did. *I'm* the one violating you in *my* dreams. You're the victim."

Milo laughed out loud at that. He raised an eyebrow. "Victim?" He shook his head as he said the word.

"Yeah! I mean, those are my dreams, and they're completely inappropriate and…pathetic…and…"

"It wasn't pathetic," Milo interjected. "And as for inappropriate, I was doing everything you were, so…you're not any more inappropriate than me."

"But you…"

"I'm pretty sure that dream was at least *partly* a product of my imagination. And, to be honest, Skylar? Even if it was all you, I really don't mind."

My jaw dropped. I didn't have time to respond, because Dana and Calvin were back outside and approaching us.

Milo bit his lip again, inadvertently showing off those infamous dimples. I wished he would stop doing that. It wasn't making me feel any better.

Dana's arms were filled with plastic bags of random goodies. She plopped a few of the bags onto Calvin's lap before looking up and glaring first at me and then at Milo.

"All right. What the hell's up?"

Milo smiled a little bit. Which pissed me off.

"Seriously," Dana continued. "You don't need a Skylar-nose to detect the tension right now. What just happened? Spill." She looked at us sternly.

I thought, for just a moment, about any number of white lies I could tell. But then I looked over at Milo, who was *still* smiling, and I opened my mouth.

"Okay. Okay, you wanna know what's up?" I exclaimed wildly. I pointed a finger at Milo. "*That's* what's up. *He's* what's up. And he won't stop smiling! Like this is funny or something. But it's not funny! I'm just a…a…dream molester. And *he* won't even let me feel bad about it because he keeps apologizing for something that *I* did wrong!"

I gazed at Milo, my voice quavering. "And that's why you're so goddamn freaking *wonderful*! Because you *do* stuff like that! And I'm just the dream molester *liar* who said she doesn't want a boyfriend, but I *do* want a boyfriend, and lying about it is the first terrible step on the slippery slope of full-on, unrepentant Greater-Than-power-induced sociopathic boyfriend-stealing behavior! And I will not do that! I will not become that!

"But I already did. I already am a monster, because I already lied *twice*!" I continued. "I lied about Tom Diaz, and the truth is that he wasn't *half* as cool as you are. And I'm sorry if I'm blowing your cover, but maybe you *aren't* so cool if you think it's okay to dream-cheat on Dana, but the thing is, I don't even think you're like that. You're just way too *nice*, so stop being nice for a second and be unforgivably lame so that I can at least have a fighting chance to loathe you. Because that's all I really want, Milo, just a chance to think you suck, but you won't let me *do* that!

"God! Just be annoying or gross or *something* besides absolutely amazing and wonderful and perfect and everything I've ever dreamed of—" I laughed out loud, and it sounded insane to my ears. "No pun intended—because otherwise I think I'm going to absolutely lose my shit if I haven't done so already. Which, I think I've done already, right? I mean, this is me losing my shit. Shit. Lost. Gone."

I took a deep breath and looked around me at three extremely stunned faces. Milo was still smiling. In fact, he was damn near grinning his ass off.

"Someone say something," I begged.

There was an extremely awkward and prolonged silence.

"Who's Tom Diaz?" Dana finally asked.

Milo took a step forward. "Skylar," he said quietly, even as I buried my face in my hands again. "I really don't blame you for those dreams. In fact, I'm certain I was orchestrating at least a part of them. That room we were in a little while ago—with the candles and the..." He tactfully left out the rest.

I nodded miserably.

Cal giggled.

"That was my apartment back in Santa Fe. You couldn't have possibly known what it looked like. That was *me*. Not you."

I looked up. "But you and Dana are..." And something in Milo's eyes made me stop. I glanced at Dana. "Dana said..." I stopped again and replayed that conversation we'd had at the Pizza Extravaganza in my head as I realized that Dana had never actually said the word *boyfriend*. She'd told me to back off, and that she and Milo had been together for years, but… "So okay, you didn't say it, but you certainly *implied* that Milo was your boyfriend."

Milo's smile disappeared as he turned to look at Dana as well. "Did you tell Skylar that?"

"No." She paused. "Well, kind of. I knew what she thought, and I didn't correct her misconceptions. Was it really my fault if she misunderstood?" It was Dana's turn to smile, just a little bit.

Milo was as furious as I'd ever seen him. "Dana! What the hell?"

"It was a test!" Dana replied defensively. She turned to me. "Congratulations, Bubble Gum, you passed. You are an honorable, loyal, and true friend." She turned to Milo. "As far as your potential girlfriends go, I confess to being really picky, but…she'll do."

Milo shook his head. "I don't believe you did that. You knew how I felt!"

"You're welcome," Dana said.

"Wait!" I interjected as Calvin continued to giggle uncontrollably. "So…you and Milo *aren't…*?"

"Milo's not my boyfriend, Sunshine. Never has been."

I looked at Milo, and he nodded. "Dana's like a sister to me."

"Oh," I said. "Wow."

"*Wow* just about says it all." Dana took the opportunity to grab Cal's shoulder. "Come on, Scoot. Let's bring these bags of junk-food goodness back to the car." The two of them moved briskly away.

I turned to look again at Milo.

"Skylar," he said, smiling again. "You should know that I think you're amazing and wonderful and perfect as well."

That roller-coaster feeling was back with a vengeance. "Really?" I managed, even though I could hardly breathe, never mind eke out a word.

"Really," he said. "And you gotta stop believing the crap you read on the Internet. Greater-Thans just don't become sociopathic monsters. And even if there was the tiniest chance that you *could*? There's no way *you'd* ever cross over to the dark side. It just wouldn't happen."

I wanted to believe him.

He must've seen my doubt, because he got serious. "I promise," he said, "if I ever see you start to lean in that direction, I'll warn you, and we'll have plenty of time to figure out how to stop it from happening."

It was that *we'll* that convinced me, and I managed to nod and even smile.

Then, like something out of the most amazing and romantic movie in the world—French, I would bet it would be French, with subtitles—he reached for my hand. And then, gazing into my eyes, he kissed the top of it. And *then*, he turned it over and kissed my palm.

Instantly, that same rush of vanilla and sunshine poured through every inch of me.

There. Do you believe me?

I looked at Milo as he let go of my hand, and then I smiled.

"Yeah," I said, reaching for his hand again. I didn't want him to stop touching me.

He intertwined our fingers, and we gazed into each other's eyes for a moment. I couldn't help it. I started to laugh.

I trust you. And I did.

I trust you too. His smile faded again. *You really do believe that Sasha is still alive, don't you?*

My gaze didn't waver. "Yes," I said out loud.

"Well, let's go find her, then," he said.

And, hand in hand, we walked back to the car.

Part of me wanted to fall back to sleep again, just so that I could experience at least one delicious Milo dream without any angst or guilt.

But when Dana steered us back onto the highway, sleep was the last thing on my mind.

"We're officially in a different time zone," Calvin announced.

Dana nodded gravely. "It's a long-ass drive to Alabama."

"I wish we knew which part of Alabama we were heading toward. Are we there yet?" Cal asked, his voice tinged with intentional whininess.

I closed my eyes, focusing on the ever-present mental tug. "We're getting warmer," I mumbled.

When I opened my eyes again, I looked over at Milo, who was gazing at me.

"Hi," I said.

"Hi," he said back.

We smiled at each other.

From the front seat, Dana made a barfing noise.

"Time zone!" Milo blurted abruptly.

All three of us jumped at his declaration. "What?" I asked.

"Time zone! Sky, don't you get it? We're an hour behind now."

Dana frowned into the rearview mirror. "And the significance of this is…"

Milo leaned forward. "Skylar's vision inside of that room, with the big ugly man and the computer… We all assumed the vision wasn't in real time because the clock was wrong, but it was an hour behind."

"It was an hour behind," I repeated, "because the clock and the computer and room—and Sasha—were in a different time zone."

"It was just after nine, our time," Milo continued.

"Which is just after *eight*, Central time," I concluded.

"Oh, snap," Cal said.

Dana shook her head, pessimistic as ever. "You're reaching," she said. But something about the look in her eyes as she glanced in the mirror made me think she wasn't entirely sure we were wrong.

Milo grabbed my hand. Immediately, a surge of energy worked its way through my bloodstream. *Let's work on what you saw.*

I locked eyes with him. *Back in the pet store?*

Yeah. I know you can remember it. Shoot it back to me. Let's review the images.

I winced, unsure if I was comfortable forcing such ugly visions onto somebody I admittedly really, really liked.

I can take it, he added. *I saw it the first time around. And I really, really like you too.*

Without hesitation, I blasted back through the scene. The walls materialized first, dark red and chipped. Then, like a camera panning out to reveal more of the set, I watched the room expand and grow.

Rows upon rows of dirty cots came into view, each one housing a tiny sleeping girl.

How many are there? And, try as he might, Milo couldn't mask the edgy tautness of anger that slipped through his tone as he tried to help me with the recall.

Five, ten, twelve...that's down one row...Two rows makes...shit. Twenty-four girls.

Twenty-four. Two dozen girls had been stolen from their homes and locked in some terrible, hot, smelly place, with a guard who—for some reason—scared the crap out of me.

Milo used his free hand to dig into his pocket for a piece of gum. I couldn't blame him, but the movement distracted me and the images started to fade.

But he felt me waver, and he took his hand out of his pocket and grabbed on to my arm instead.

Show me more.

I concentrated, and then the computer screen was back again, complete with a looping image of that movie.

Sorry, I said as I felt Milo raise a mental eyebrow.

Classy.

I wanted to laugh, but the idea of somebody watching sleazy movies as they guarded kidnapped little girls made me feel more sick than anything else. I wondered for a moment if Skinemax guy was the same sleazeball who had purchased the dog collars Dana had talked about.

I suddenly remembered a flash of an image: the big guard with the red shirt, his round face mottled with anger, spittle in the corner of his mouth as he brandished a baseball bat that was coated with…blood?

I recoiled from the picture, feeling my heart accelerate and my breathing grow ragged.

Still thoughts, still thoughts…

Milo had, of course, followed my entire thought process. He squeezed my hand. *Let's stay away from him for a minute and dissect the room. Look at the room, Sky. Where are those girls? What does it look like to you?*

I tried to hone in on details of the interior. I could see the peeling red paint, and the dirty floors…so dirty that they looked as though there wasn't any actual floor there—just hard-packed earth.

And hay. That was hay on the ground.

"It's a barn," I blurted.

I opened my eyes. Dana glared at us from behind the wheel. Calvin, who had begun to nod off, jumped in his seat.

"Yeah," Milo answered out loud. "I think you're right. I think we're looking at an old barn."

"Man, y'all have the weirdest conversations," Calvin said drowsily.

"Go back to sleep," I replied. Milo glanced at me and then leaned forward. "Cal, before you crash, may I borrow your phone?"

Cal handed it back to him, and Milo turned it on and flipped through Cal's various apps before he found what he was looking for.

It was a drawing app in which he could use his finger as a pen. He looked up at me and smiled. "I think we should try to draw a map."

I nodded. "Good idea," I agreed.

Dana tilted her head up and peered into the rearview mirror to see what we were doing. "Mind explaining what you saw?"

"It was the same thing as before. There was a big room—a barn— with two rows of cots. Twenty-four beds total. All filled."

Milo started to draw. To my surprise, he was an excellent artist. A clear picture of the interior of the barn, as I'd seen it, began to materialize on the screen.

"Where was the computer?"

I looked at Milo's picture. "There," I said, pointing to the front right-hand corner. "And there was someone else sitting over on the other side. The big guard with the bloody...the baseball bat."

Dana's eyes were focused on the road, but I could see her wince at my words.

"So two guards?" Milo said. I knew he was attempting to redirect my thoughts from the awful to the practical.

"Yeah," I said. "Two that I saw. I don't know how accurate my visions are," I added.

"So at least two guards," Dana offered. I was pretty sure I heard her whisper *I'm gonna kill 'em* under her breath.

"And where is the entrance?" Milo persisted.

I wasn't sure. I'd been so focused on the girls and the nasty guards that I hadn't had a chance to see exactly where the doors to the room were located.

"I think there's an entrance here," I said, pointing to the very front of the barn. "And I...I don't know. I'm pretty sure there's a back door somewhere too."

"It's okay. You're doing great," Milo whispered. He took my hand and squeezed it.

Thank you, I whispered back silently. And then I focused on the girls in the beds, all those cots in rows, metal frames planted deep into the dirt floor, chains keeping the girls locked to those frames.

I felt a fleeting thought race through Milo's mind. I almost didn't sense it; he was moving that fast.

What are you thinking? I asked.

He pointed out the window, where eerily familiar trees lined the sides of a highway that we'd both seen before. We'd finally reached the location of my dreams. Sasha had been here—I felt it stronger than ever. She'd tried to escape. She'd gotten away—but then they'd caught her. Hit her. Beaten her.

But not killed her.

I looked into Milo's eyes. *I've been thinking about that too—about all those girls in the barn. About all of the blood that was found in the back of Edmund's truck...*

I looked at him, eyes wide.

Sasha couldn't have possibly survived if she had lost all that blood at once, Milo continued. *But...*

I watched while he scratched his head with his free hand.

What if they were taking her blood in small amounts—enough to make the drug, but never enough at one time to actually kill her?

"Like milking a cow," I said, shuddering.

"*What?*" Dana and a now-awake Calvin both said.

Milo explained his theory to them.

Calvin sighed disgustedly. "Man, that is so effed up."

Dana nodded. "You're probably right," she said grimly. "But even so, taking blood from little girls, over and over and over again? It'll eventually kill 'em."

Milo interlaced his fingers with mine as I watched him. And I knew he agreed with Dana. Eventually it would.

He was thinking about Lacey, who'd been taken all those years ago. And I knew that Dana was thinking about her sister too.

"Maybe they give special treatment to the important ones," I offered. "Wow, that sounds terrible. What I meant to say was that maybe the people who make Destiny know which girls have a special, higher level of power, and they make a point to keep the goose with the golden egg alive. So to speak."

"I don't think they're that smart," Dana said.

"They're smart enough to steal dozens of girls and to frame innocent people with murder," I countered.

"I meant farsighted," Dana conceded. "And yes, they're plenty smart, except when it comes to long-term thinking, which ultimately makes them stupid."

"Still," I said, "Lacey was really powerful, right? Maybe she's still…"

"She's not," Dana snapped.

I cleared my throat. I knew I was risking Dana's ire. Still, I couldn't bring myself to give up hope. "Or maybe she escaped."

"Then where is she?" Dana's voice was harsh and bitter. "If Lacey escaped, then why didn't she come looking for me?" I watched her grip the steering wheel like she was wringing a neck. "It's been years, Sky. *Years.*"

I glanced at Milo, who told me, *It does seem unlikely.*

"When you've lost someone," Dana blasted me, "literally *lost* someone—for *years*—check back in with me. Until then, keep your Pollyanna shit to yourself."

I sniffed quietly and gazed out the window.

But then I jumped. "Hey! Exit. Now. Here."

CHAPTER THIRTY

The barn loomed large and quiet in the moonlight.

The magnetic pull had gotten so bad that it was all I could do not to leap out of Cal's car and start running straight to the building—straight to Sasha. She was down there; I could feel her.

"It's bigger than I thought it would be," Dana said quietly.

There were also two buildings instead of one.

We were parked on a tiny country road overlooking the small valley where the barn was tucked near a creek. We were waiting, our hearts in our throats—or at least mine was—for Milo to return to the car.

He'd gone out to do something Dana called a "sneak and peek." Basically that meant he was going to take a stroll in the dark near those two buildings—not one but two—where there were at least two guards, one very large and in possession of a baseball bat that he'd used before as a very deadly weapon.

Dana had used her two-rats-lurking-in-the-corner G-T skills to tell us that there were twenty-six people in the main structure—the barn—and six in the smaller Quonset hut that sat nearby.

Her theory—and Milo's—was that the smaller building was a lab where they cooked the enzymes and other elements from the blood that they stole from those two dozen girls chained to their beds. Cooked it into the drug known as Destiny.

What we were looking at was a "Destiny farm." And the fact that the men who ran it kept those little girls alive—whether for a day or a week or a month—was a surprise to Dana.

Who had to be thinking about Lacey.

"You okay?" I whispered to her.

She looked at me and her eyes were silver in the moonlight. "I want to kill them."

"Ditto," Calvin said. "But really, what we need to do now, as responsible citizens, is to call the police."

Dana laughed humorlessly. "Not happening, Scoot."

"Why not? I mean, worst-case scenario it's a false alarm and they don't find anything. But if you're right, y'all with your crazy visions and your psychic infrared, heat-seeker abilities or however the hell it is you know exactly how many people are in there...? If there *are* dangerous people in that barn, the police are going to have a few things we don't. Like, I don't know, *guns*, for instance?"

"For all we know, the local cops are dirty and taking a weekly percentage from these assholes," Dana countered. "You willing to take that chance? That when they show up, they hand us over to the bad guys, who kill us and bury us in the back forty?"

"You're just a ray of sunshine," Cal grumbled.

"I'm a realist," Dana corrected him.

"I still think this is too dangerous for us to pull off alone. We need help."

"We *have* help." Dana pointed to me, and then to herself.

There was a tap on the glass. I let out a yelp and then, realizing it was Milo, leaned across the backseat to unlock the door.

"God, you scared me," I exclaimed breathily.

"Sorry," he said as he climbed back in.

"How's it looking?" Dana asked.

Milo's face was grim. "It's bad," he said.

"Bad how?" I asked, not sure if I wanted to hear the answer.

"Well, it looks exactly like your vision," Milo told me. "Twenty-four girls and two guards are in the main barn. I was able to peek in through some air vents, over on the side, under the eaves."

"Did you see Sasha?" I asked eagerly.

Milo bit his lip. "I'm sorry. I didn't get close enough, and even if I had..." Even though he took my hands, he kept talking so that Calvin and Dana would hear what he had to say. "They've shaved the girls' heads. I don't know if it's a problem with lice or if they do it to intimidate or depersonalize them, but...they all look kinda the same. And they're all chained to their beds."

Nausea lingered in my throat.

"I'm gonna kill those scumbags. I'm gonna make them suffer." Dana's face darkened as she said what I was thinking.

"You're going to take a deep breath," Milo replied even as he sent me a *Still thoughts*. "You're going to be calm—because we need to stay logical and figure out how to best execute this rescue mission."

"So if we can't call the cops," Calvin said. "Isn't there someone, somewhere that we *can* call?"

Dana looked at him. "Like Batman?"

"Well, I don't know," Calvin said, before admitting, "yeah."

"I'm Batman," Dana told him flatly, which shut him up.

Milo spoke. "There are really only two organizations that I would trust to help out in a situation like this one. One's up in Boston—it's called the Obermeyer Institute."

"They're fast," Dana agreed. "They would get here as quickly as superhumanly possible. But they're just too far away. Calling them for help has us sitting on our asses, watching and waiting for about twelve hours. And I'm not willing to do that. If we wait, some of those girls'll die."

"Where's the other?" Calvin asked.

"It's out in California," Milo said. "Geographically, I think it's slightly closer, but it's not run the same way as OI, and it'll take them longer to go wheels up and to reach us."

Cal sighed.

"If this is too much for you, Scooter," Dana said, "let me know now."

Cal frowned, channeling all his nervous energy and turning it into determination. "Hell no." He looked at Dana. "Remember? I got your back."

Dana nodded. "Good," she said. She didn't smile, but I could tell that made her happy.

"Did you get a look at the second building?" I asked Milo, even as I peered down the hillside toward that prefab structure with the rounded metal roof. From this vantage point, we could see both buildings, the field and path between them, and the gravel parking lot that was on the far side of the barn. There were about a half-dozen cars parked there, along with what looked like a medium-sized truck.

"It's definitely a lab," Milo reported. "It's climate controlled. There's a huge AC unit outside. And there's a generator that was running when I went past. I'm pretty sure the building holds some kind of living quarters or barracks for the guards and lab techs too."

"Anything else?" Dana asked.

"There are six cars in the lot and—get this," Milo said. "The truck down there? It belongs to Doggy Doo Good. The company logo is all over it."

"Doggy Doo Good!" I exclaimed.

"Yeah. So, Sky, for what it's worth, you haven't been leading us on a wild-goose chase. I think the pet store's trucks are being used to covertly ship promising little girls all across the country to farms like these, where they bleed 'em dry."

I thought about the vision I'd had of little kids bouncing around in the back of a truck filled with leashes and dog food.

Dana let out a stream of curses, then growled, "I have a plan to get those girls out of there, but I flipping hate it."

Milo smiled briefly. "Does it involve me hot-wiring that Doggy Doo Good truck?"

"It does," she said. "We'll have to get some paint to cover up the logo. I mean, after we get those girls out of here." She punctuated her sentence with another f-bomb.

Cal cleared his throat. "I'm sorry, but I think I missed the part that happens between us sitting up here on this hillside and us painting that truck. And I think what you left out might be the most important part, because it involves freeing twenty-four helpless little girls from eight guards and lab techs who will probably object to our walking in, saying howdy, and unchaining them."

Dana sighed heavily, clearly frustrated. "What I *want* to do is rip their throats out, one by one. There's not a single person who works here, torturing and killing those girls for profit, who doesn't *completely* deserve to die a terrible, horrible, painful death."

"But what you're going to do instead is...?" Milo started for her, even as he squeezed my hand.

"I'm going to mind-control them," Dana said, in the same tone that she might've used to announce that she'd stepped into dog crap. She sighed again. "I'm going to get them out of here, because ripping their throats out might put those little girls into danger. Instead, all eight of them are going to be filled with an overwhelming desire to rush home. I'm going to make them believe that it's okay, that the girls'll be fine left alone here, chained to their beds."

"That's brilliant," I breathed. "Then we just walk in—"

"And get the girls out of there," Milo finished for me. "Dana can use her telekinetic skills to break all the chains."

"Then all we have to do is load the girls into the truck."

"And buy paint to hide the logo," Dana repeated. She sighed again. "Okay, let's fricking do this."

Cal stopped her with a hand on her arm. "Hey. As long as you're using what Sky so delicately calls your Jedi mind-screw, why don't you fill them with a burning desire to take a sample of Destiny and then add an equally insatiable urge for them to go straight to the police, to confess their criminal behavior? It's not the same as ripping out their throats, I know, and maybe the local police are crooked, but…maybe they're not. At least this way there's a chance they'll spend the rest of their lives in jail."

"Ha!" Dana smiled. "Scooter, I really like the way you think."

Milo's laughter was warm in the darkness. "And, as long as you're at it, Dane, let's make it even easier. Tell whoever has the keys to the Doggy Doo Good truck to leave them right in the ignition."

Dana nodded. "I'm likin' this plan better all the time." She took a deep breath and a cleansing exhale. "All right. Here's the deal in detail. Sky, you stay here in the car with Cal and keep an asshole count. Let's make sure they really all go before we walk into that barn. Milo, I want you around the back of the building, eyes on the back door."

"Just one thing before you go," Cal said.

Dana raised an eyebrow. "What's that, Scoot?"

"Can you, er, switch seats with me?" Cal wanted his wheelchair back, but he wouldn't be able to get into it without Dana's help.

Dana looked at him for a moment, her eyes squinting with suspicion. "You promise you won't pull some stunt and leave the car before I give the all clear?"

"I thought we were giving the all clear, since we're keeping count of the assholes," Cal countered.

Dana stared at him for a few more moments. "Fine," she said, making sure the inside light was switched off before opening the door and getting out of the car. And then, with not a lot of grace, she used her telekinetic powers to transfer Cal back into his chair—and into the driver's seat.

"Thank you." He smiled sweetly up at her.

"Whatever," Dana grumbled. She stood outside the car, waiting for Milo to get his butt in gear.

Milo looked at me.

"Please be careful," I whispered.

He smiled. "I will. And please keep the car locked while you and Calvin are out here. Okay?"

"Okay." I nodded. We'd parked off the road behind a thicket of brush. Even if someone drove up the hill instead of down into town, they wouldn't see us. Unless, of course, they were looking.

But why would they be looking?

Milo took another moment to gaze at me before wrapping his arms around me. *See you soon.*

I'll see you soon.

Calvin and I watched them disappear down the dark hillside.

"Come sit up here," he finally said.

I climbed up and over, into the front passenger seat, and sighed.

"I hope this works," Cal whispered.

"I hope so too."

We waited in silence.

"Look!" Cal exclaimed after a few moments. "Do you see that?"

Sure enough, several bright lights had clicked on, illuminating both the barn and a section of the metal building next to it. Then a group of men, dressed in everything from a white lab coat and medical scrubs, to jeans and a do-rag, to really dorky-looking plaid pajamas, headed purposefully around the side of the barn, toward the parking lot. Two men joined them, coming out of the barn.

"They're leaving!" I whispered excitedly. "Dana's mind-control is working!"

"This is effin' awesome!" Cal said as one of the men opened the door to the Doggy Doo Good truck and put something inside. The keys? I hoped so. "She's effin' awesome!"

"She is," I agreed. Without Dana, we wouldn't have had a fighting chance to pull this off.

One by one, the cars all pulled away, some of the men carpooling and leaving together. The headlights traveled up the driveway and then turned into taillights as the cars took a right, away from us, down the hill.

"Wait a minute, whose car is that?" Calvin asked. He pointed to the dark shape of a very large vehicle still parked a few slots down from the Doggy Doo Good truck.

Eight men had come out on the drive. Had one of them left his car behind?

But no, then I saw him—one last, lone man, standing outside the barn, almost absentmindedly swinging something—a stick or a rake or a cane—next to his leg.

He was an oak tree of a man dressed in a red button-down shirt and grimy, stained blue jeans. He stood staring after the last of those taillights, looking confused and annoyed, just swinging that stick, just swinging it, swinging…

"Oh my God," I whispered.

"What?" Cal asked. "What's wrong?"

Baseball bat. It wasn't a rake or a cane or a stick; it was a baseball bat.

It was the man from my visions.

And he wasn't walking toward his car.

Something had gone wrong. Dana's mind-control didn't seem to work on him.

"Uh-oh." Calvin was thinking what I was. "I wonder if he's taking some kind of painkiller."

"Like Garrett," I said.

"Now what?" Calvin asked, even as he started his car.

I shook my head. I didn't know. Where was Dana? But I spotted her, a tiny punctuation of a person compared to the monstrous guard with his lethal weapon.

She was flitting through the trees that lined the field next to the barn, careful to stay out of the beam of light that shone onto the gravel path. I held my breath, praying that the giant man wouldn't spot her, praying that she'd made note of the bat in his hands, even though he was now holding it tucked in close to his body, slightly behind his back.

Dana hid behind a clump of trees, and as we watched, the big guard seemed to know exactly where she was. He moved toward her slowly, carefully.

"He knows exactly where she is," Calvin breathed. "But she doesn't know he's coming."

"She's Dana," I told him, but I wasn't sure if I quite believed it myself. "She knows he's coming."

The guard moved closer. And closer.

"She doesn't know," Calvin said. "Oh, shit, she doesn't know!"

And he turned on the engine, put his car in gear, and hit the gas. We drove right down the hillside, through the field, bumping and bouncing our way directly toward the barn.

The big guard looked away from Dana and over at us, so that worked.

But Dana looked away from him as well, clearly freaked out and distracted by the sight of us barreling down the hill toward her.

Calvin's car bounced onto the driveway, skidding slightly on the gravel before coming to a stop.

And Dana took off running, making a beeline toward us, as she tried to put herself between us and the guard. Her sparkly dress twinkled as she sprinted, comet-like, toward the car.

She was fast, but the big guard was, surprisingly, faster.

"Dana, look out!" Calvin opened the driver's side door of the car and started to release the wheelchair ramp.

As if he hadn't distracted Dana enough.

"Get back into that car!" she shouted, and I grabbed at his arm, trying to hold him back.

And then it happened. She turned toward the big man, and she used her telekinetic power to spin him around, but she *hadn't* seen the bat he was carrying, and it extended his reach just far enough to clip her, hard, in the side of the head, with a horrible *crack*, which sent her down to the ground.

And she didn't get back up.

The guard with the bat had been flung by Dana's power, nearly over to the barn door, and he *did* get up, refreshing his grip on that bat handle.

And Dana *didn't* get back up.

I'd already let go of Calvin, and he'd gotten out of the car in a record-breaking amount of time. I followed him as he revved the engine to his wheelchair, dirt flying through the air as he whirled toward Dana, who was lying crumpled in the gravel.

Baseball Bat Man was moving toward her, weapon in hand, and I knew that I couldn't let him get anywhere near either Calvin or Dana.

And God, Dana was still lying there, so still.

I tried to move her. She'd had a theory that my telekinetic powers worked best in life-or-death situations, but I couldn't do it. She didn't move. And she didn't move. I gritted my teeth and she *still* didn't move.

So I finally did. I sprinted—full-force *sprinted*—away from both Dana and the nasty guard.

"Hey! Over here!" I belted out.

The guard looked up at me. He held the bat next to his ear, as if getting ready to hit a home run. I spotted a trickle of blood on the wooden surface. More dots of splattered blood…*Dana's* splattered blood…decorated his face.

"Come and get me, douche bag!" I shouted.

The guard charged.

And I ran.

And, yes, he was fast. But I *knew* I was faster.

Out of the corner of my eye, I watched Calvin scoop Dana up off the ground and onto his lap. Her body was limp, like a rag doll.

"Milo, where are you?" I shouted, even as I continued to sprint around the corner of the barn into the thick of an unkempt field of wild grass that lay between the two buildings. "Dana needs your help!"

In truth, Dana was probably dead.

"I'm gonna git ya!" the man growled. Even from so far away, I could still smell the overpowering sewage stench of his pure evil. It invaded my nostrils and clogged my throat, sending my head spinning and my stomach churning.

I could outrun this guy—but I couldn't do it if I was busy puking my guts out.

Still thoughts, still thoughts—it didn't work quite as well without Milo there to anchor me, but it helped enough to keep me up and moving.

Looking around wildly, I wished for one panicky moment that the field could provide me with at least one portapotty to explode onto my pursuer.

But no such luck.

All I had to work with was a stone wall that ran back behind the lab.

It wasn't much, but it was something.

But before I had the chance to focus my attention on the potential weaponry of dozens of boulders being flung through the air, I heard an echoing click behind me.

"Freeze, girl, or I blow your brains out!"

I stopped in my tracks. Hands raised in the air, I turned around slowly, my stomach filling with dread as I realized that the guard didn't just own a bat.

He also had a gun.

And it was pointed at my face.

The guard kept his mouth closed as he chuckled quietly, a low, thunderous sound that sent my skin crawling.

"I don't know who you are, or where you came from," the big guard said, "but judging from the things you can do, I'm guessing we could use some girls like you and your friend. The gimp's gotta go, though. Or maybe we'll just use him to make you cooperate."

I spat at him as I channeled Dana and told him to do the anatomically impossible.

"Or I could just bleed you dry now," he said, raising his weapon even higher. "That's probably the smartest thing to do. Keeping girls like you alive can cause trouble, and I don't want to get into trouble."

I was going to die.

I was going to…

"But let's do this inside," the guard said, gesturing with his weapon toward the barn, "so I can bleed you out proper."

I couldn't go in there with him. I knew, with a bone-chilling certainty, that if I went inside that barn with this horrible man, I would never come out again.

"Move!" he shouted at me. "I will shoot you. I *will* shoot you!"

It was then, without warning, that Milo stepped out from around the back corner of the barn, shouting, "Hey!"

He'd startled the big man, who fired his gun.

"Milo!" I shouted. I launched myself toward him as he did the same to me, and we hit the ground, arms and legs flailing as we each checked to make sure the other hadn't been shot.

Are you hit? he asked me.

I'm not hit. Are you hit?

I'm not hit. Oh my God, Sky. Are you sure?

I'm sure. Am I sure? Wait. I am. Are you?

I'm sure!

Oh, thank God! I clung to Milo, and he held me tightly too.

"Get up!" the guard's voice bellowed. "*MOVE!*"

Milo and I both scrambled to our feet as I asked him, *Is Dana all right?*

I don't know. I was hoping this guy would try to bring you through the back door. I was going to jump him, but then I was afraid he was just going to shoot you. I didn't know what else to do.

Our fingers interlaced, we clung to each other. Milo's vanilla scent calmed me down just the tiniest bit, helping me deal with the smell of the sewage. I leaned close to him and breathed deeply.

"Inside! Let's go!" The guard wanted us to walk in front of him around the side of the barn, toward the front door.

Back where we'd left Dana and Calvin. I looked at Milo and he looked at me. Neither of us moved.

If we go in the barn now, we die, I told him.

Milo squeezed my hand. *I'm gonna go for that gun. It's the only way.*

No, it's not. I'm gonna try to explode that stone wall, I continued silently. *Don't look, but it's on our left-hand side.*

Okay. I know what you're talking about.

You've gotta get ready to duck. I don't know how accurate I can be. My mind was whirling as I was trying to figure out what I'd done wrong. How had I moved Garrett, but not Dana?

Milo nodded almost imperceptibly.

Thoughts of everything I'd moved with my sporadic telekinesis skills raced through my head. The clogged toilet. The water bursting out of the fire hydrant. The sprinklers in the park.

I concentrated. And I concentrated, letting my heart pound and my pulse race as I tried to channel everything I was feeling.

And…

Nothing. Happened.

Why not why not why not? I was terrified, not angry—maybe that was the problem.

"Move or I will shoot your boyfriend!" the guard shouted at me.

Over my dead body! I tried to bolster my courage, but it was drowned out by *ohmygodohmygod.*

I'm gonna go for him, Milo sent to me over my inner noise.

"Don't you dare," I shouted at them both, adding, "Oh my God, I'm gonna throw up!" I doubled over, and then even dropped down to my hands and knees, hoping to buy some time. "Just give me a few seconds. Please, sir. I don't want to have to clean it up once we're inside."

That did it. The guard didn't want to clean up after me either, so he waited as Milo reached down to touch my shoulder as if comforting me, but instead to tell me, *I'm going for his gun.*

The boy had a one-track mind.

You have to make a run for it, I told Milo. *He's a lousy shot. If we go in two different directions, he won't know what to do.*

I am not. Leaving. You.

And *that* pissed me off. I glared at Milo, even as I leaned over, pretending to dry-heave. *You have to.*

No.

Yes!

No, Sky. Unlike some people, Milo didn't get louder when he was upset. He got quieter and more intense.

Please, I started, but before I could continue my protest, the lab exploded in a burst of orange and white, sending shards of metal and wood and billowing balls of flame and smoke up into the sky.

I felt Milo's surprise. *Did you...?*

But it wasn't me.

The guard stumbled, pushed down to the ground by the force of the blast, and I dodged a piece of flying wood as Milo let go of me and charged him, knocking the gun out of the man's hand.

They rolled together across the ground as I scrambled back to my feet.

Where was his gun? I hadn't seen which way it went. I tried to figure out the physics of where it might have gone, scrambling and feeling around in the high grass.

Flames licked the sky as the fire enveloped the now two-dimensional building. We were all close enough to feel the heat on our faces.

My heart was pounding, and I was nearly shaking with fear and anger. I tried to focus on the anger—where *was* that fucking gun?—and aim it again at the stone wall—when I realized that my telekinesis, at least the large-scale TK that was useful in a fight like this, was focused on moving water.

When I'd saved Garrett, I hadn't thought; I'd just done it. The human body was sixty percent water, and my innate skills had simply done the required task.

When I'd just tried to move Dana, I'd tried to move Dana. I'd also been laden not just with fear, but with doubt.

Right now, the nighttime ground was wet with dew, the grass slick beneath my feet, and I pictured the water coating the rocks in that field-stone wall, seeping into the granite. I could do this. I could *do* this. And with a roar, that stone wall exploded straight up into the air.

Holy crap, I was back, but I needed to do something that wouldn't kill Milo too. I tried to focus on hitting the guard, on pushing that sorry sack of H_2O away from my boyfriend.

I inhaled a big, smoke-filled breath of air, bearing down as my body filled with heat—both from the fire around me and the rage bubbling from within.

Unfortunately, the guard's grip was so strong that he pulled Milo with him, and they slid together, back through the tall grass.

"Milo!" I shouted. "Get away from him!"

But, despite Milo's strength, he was no match for the giant guard, and he couldn't get away, and he couldn't get away, and he couldn't get away...

And I was hanging on to my power, holding it back, trying to control it while I waited for the moment—just a heartbeat, a split second—when Milo scrambled free, so I could blast this son of a bitch straight to hell.

And then it happened. The guard hit Milo, the force of the blow pushed him back, and it was now or never.

I exhaled and let it rip, angry at my own fear, but certain it would work...

Whoosh!

With a rush of inexplicable energy, I released my power, sending the guard all the way across the field to the very edge of the burning building.

Dazed, Milo sat up. He was battered and bleeding—I could see an open cut above his eyebrow.

Meanwhile, the guard quickly scrambled to his feet, ready to go another round, even after I'd unleashed my fury.

For a panicky moment, the thought crossed my mind that this man might have powers too.

He was ridiculously strong.

But there was no way he shared my abilities. Otherwise, he wouldn't have had to use weapons like bats or guns—like the pistol he was pulling out of his waistband right at that moment. It was smaller than the first one, but that didn't mean it was any less deadly.

"Milo!" I yelled. "Run!"

"Hey! You!" A voice called out from around the corner. I whirled around, and there was Dana—very much alive, very much self-healed, thank God, and very pissed. Calvin hovered close behind her. "You really think you can mess with me and my friends?" she shouted.

The guard froze. He looked as though he was being scolded by a ghost.

After all, he'd beaten her senseless with a bat just a few moments ago.

"News flash, motherfucker. I. Pwn. You."

And, without any further warning, Dana lifted her hands up and blasted the guard with such an amped-up dose of kick-ass that the man dropped his second gun and sailed up, up, up, way into the sky, his cries disappearing as quickly as his body. It was like watching a human-sized balloon fade into the clouds. Wherever he landed, there was no way he'd survive the fall.

"Whoa," Cal and I both said, our mouths hanging open.

I closed mine and rushed to Milo's side. "You're bleeding!" I told him, crouching next to him in the grass.

"I'm okay," Milo reassured me, even though the cut above his eye was redefining the word *profuse*.

"Um, yeah," Dana said, slightly irritated. "I'm okay too...?"

I pulled Milo to his feet and moved him over to Dana, who had already gotten yanked down onto Calvin's lap. We both wrapped our arms around the two of them as I worked to not burst into tears right then and there.

"Thank God," I said. "I thought you were dead."

"Yeah, yeah," Dana replied impatiently, her body awkward and rigid as she endured the group hug. "I did too. I don't think I've ever healed that fast. It was almost as if..."

She was looking at Calvin, but when she saw my questioning look, she shook her head. "That's just a fairy tale, like Sleeping Beauty. Come on, Bubble Gum. We've got work to do."

I was curious—what fairy tale? But I didn't press her, because she was right. This wasn't over yet.

With the guards finally gone, we were able to stroll into the barn, no problem.

Once inside, though, reality hit me like a ton of bricks.

The place reeked of waste, urine, and sweat—and it wasn't the result of manifest emotions that only I could detect. These girls were literally eating where they shat.

Calvin gasped and stuck his face into the crook of his elbow. Dana grumbled something about a-holes under her breath. Milo clenched his jaw.

And I smiled. Because Sasha was there. I could feel her.

"Third bed, first row," I hissed to Dana.

Some of the little girls stayed asleep. Others shifted around, their chains clinking as they moved, frightened at the sight of us.

I rushed over to the bed, and there she was.

Sasha!

She looked so tiny lying there. Her head was shaved, but it was Sasha, without a doubt!

I felt Dana's presence behind me. She put her hand on my shoulder. "Let me." She blinked hard, and Sasha's chains broke open.

And I took her into my arms. "It's okay. You're safe now," I told her.

Her eyes opened, two pools of dark brown. "Sky," she whispered. "I knew you'd find me." But then she looked over at Dana, and she smiled, reaching up to cup Dana's face with her tiny hand.

"Lacey?" she asked. "You look like Lacey."

The change that came over Dana was startling. Her eyes filled with tears, and as she gazed back at Sasha, I knew she was holding her breath. "Do you know her?" Dana asked. "Have you seen her? Lacey?"

But in a flash, Sasha went from smiling to terrified, and she opened her mouth and started to scream.

"Sleep," Dana commanded, mind-controlling Sasha, so that the little girl's eyelids fluttered closed, and she dipped down again into unconsciousness.

Dana stood still, but only for a moment. Then, she turned, racing down the aisles of cots. Chains exploded as she used her telekinetic power to break the girls free.

"Lacey!" she called out. "Lacey Zannino! Lacey! Are you here?"

Little girls began to sit up in their beds, rubbing grubby hands across their drowsy, tear-streaked faces. I sat down on Sasha's cot, wrapping my arms around the sleeping little girl.

"Hey," Milo whispered from behind me. He put his own arms around my shoulders, even as I scooped Sasha onto my lap. "We have to get moving. These girls need to get into the truck fast, before any of the guards come back. We don't know their schedule. There might be another shift due to arrive."

I nodded, watching as Dana turned the room upside down searching frantically for her lost sister.

Quickly, Milo and I worked on carrying the girls out to the truck. So many of them were terrified, and once one started screaming, they all joined in. So Dana used her powers to make them all, like Sasha, fall back into a deep, peaceful sleep.

We all worked silently, steadily, quickly.

Calvin volunteered to stay beside the vehicle, keeping watch while Milo and I transported the former prisoners. I made sure to place Sasha in Calvin's arms before I headed back into the barn.

As I stepped back inside, I spotted Dana, a grim expression on her face as she lifted two little sleeping girls in her arms and carried them both toward the Doggy Doo Good truck.

"Did you find…?"

Dana shook her head as she handed the girls to Milo, who set them gently into the back of the vehicle. "Lacey's not here," she said.

"I'm so sorry…" I started.

But Dana raised a dismissive hand in the air, her face contorted. I realized that she had begun to cry.

"Dana, wait!" I called after her as she rushed back into the barn, unwilling to take even a few seconds of time to compose herself.

"Let her be," Cal said quietly, grabbing my hand before I had a chance to follow her.

Milo put his arm around me.

This sucks, I told him. *I get my happy ending—*

I know. Milo's voice calmed me. *We need to get the rest of the girls, though, and get out of here.*

I nodded, and started back toward the barn with Milo, my arm wrapped around his waist.

When we were on our way back out to the truck, it happened.

Just like that, the sewage smell was back. I stumbled, and Dana— grimly dry eyed again—grabbed the little girl I was carrying out of my arms, giving me a disapproving look.

I stood there, frozen, unable to move.

And then…I looked up to see her.

With gnarled, gray limbs and hollow holes for eyes, she stood against the backdrop of a swirling darkening sky, clouds churning, storm brewing. Her mouth curled up into a grotesque grin as ribbons of flowing, tattered cloth billowed ghost-like around her legs.

If I hadn't known any better, I would have pegged her for the devil in the flesh.

She was clutching a little girl, holding her tightly against her chest.

Calvin, Dana, and Milo were discussing logistics—Dana would ride in the back of the truck with the girls while Milo drove. I would sit in the backseat of Calvin's car with Sasha.

None of them seemed to see her, none of them noticed her, and I realized in that instant that I was having another vision.

A truly horrible one, in smell-o-vision.

Milo noticed that something wasn't right, and he came over to me. "Sky? You okay?"

He touched my arm, and his head snapped back, and I knew that he saw it too—everything I was seeing and hearing in my vision.

The woman pointed directly at me, and said, "*Skyyyylaaarrrrr!*" Her voice was echoing and omnipresent, rattling branches and blowing through the air like a strong wind carrying the stench of evil. "*I seeeeeeee you.*"

And then, like a subliminal message hidden within the frames of a film, the woman disappeared completely, leaving behind that foul odor that echoed in my head and a residual sense of impending doom.

Milo grabbed for me, pulling me tightly against him as we both gasped for air. "What was that?" he asked.

Let's just get out of here, I sent him. *Fast.*

As if on cue, Dana emerged from the barn. "Okay, that's everyone. Enough messing around, you two. We're getting the hell out of here."

Still a little dazed, I climbed into Calvin's car as Milo sent me one last worried look before he slid behind the wheel of the truck.

And, just as we pulled out of the driveway and onto the road, Cal and I glanced back to see the barn explode into a million brilliant pieces, lighting up the night sky.

No doubt about it—Dana was making damn sure that that facility was never used as a Destiny farm again.

CHAPTER THIRTY-ONE

"You missed a spot."

Dana pointed to the side of the Doggy Doo Good truck. She held a large roller dipped in black paint.

Milo saw the section and, with his brush, rolled over the last of the logo.

We'd parked on the side of a deserted country road. Inside of the truck, the twenty-three girls still slept soundly. On either side of us stretched seemingly endless fields. As the sun began to rise, the green expanse sparkled, dewy, in the foggy light.

"There," Dana said, satisfied as she stepped back to look at our work.

The truck was unrecognizable. Anyone looking for a missing Doggy Doo Good truck wouldn't look at it twice.

The four of us stood in front of the vehicle in silence.

"I guess that's it," Dana said, setting down her paint roller and wiping her hands off on her legs.

I studied her. Nobody had said a word about Lacey since we'd started this little art project. I was dying to talk to her, but knew it was the wrong time.

Still, it was impossible for me to *not* feel hopeful. Sasha had said Lacey's name. That had to mean something, right? After all, Dana hadn't believed that Sasha was still alive. And now we were bringing her safely home.

"What now?" Cal asked.

"Now Milo and I head west. While you guys were buying the paint, I got in touch with the team out in California. They're heading our way to pick up the girls." Dana placed her hand over her eyes to shield the ever-brightening sun as she spoke to Cal. "We can trust that these people will find their families, and keep them all safe in the meantime."

"So where are you meeting them?" Cal asked.

Milo stole a glance at Dana. "We don't know that yet."

Dana nodded. "It's an as-of-yet undetermined location, somewhere between here and there."

Cal made a face. "So basically you just don't want to tell us where you're going. Top secret, right?"

Dana shook her head adamantly. "No, Scoot. I'd tell you if I knew. Seriously. I'm not keeping secrets from you."

While Milo and Dana headed west, Calvin and I were taking Sasha back to Coconut Key. Dana had been adamant that, once we got into the car, we didn't stop until we got home.

"I figured out what you're going to tell your moms, and even the police, when they ask how you found Sasha," Dana said. "Sky, you're going to say you got a call on your cell phone from Sasha yesterday, asking for help. She'd escaped from the kidnappers, and she was so afraid, she made you promise not to ask anyone but Cal for help. Sasha's a smart girl, so she used Cal's emergency pin number to make a call from a pay phone. That why her call showed up on your phone as being from Calvin." Dana wiped one hand on the other, to indicate that the story was neat and tidy. "Finally, when you did end up finding Sasha, she was extremely disoriented—she couldn't even remember being kidnapped, or escaping, or even calling you for help."

Cal nodded solemnly. "Girl, that's masterful. You're brilliant."

"I get by." Dana smiled at him, and for a half of a second, she almost looked her age—and like a girl who'd just been called smart by a boy that she might've had a crush on.

I shook my head, thinking about earlier that morning, when Dana had all but returned from the dead—her forehead completely healed even after she'd gotten clobbered with a baseball bat.

I'd asked Milo about that fairy tale she'd muttered about, and he'd told me there was a myth among Greater-Thans that our power could be enhanced exponentially by true love. Kind of like Sleeping Beauty being wakened from a traumatic head injury, from just one kiss from her Prince Charming. Only in this version, PC rode around in a wheelchair, and SB was a kickass warrior woman.

Thing is, if Calvin really was Dana's true love, neither one of them seemed to have mentioned it to the other.

No doubt they'd figure it out in their own good time.

Meanwhile, Dana had turned away from Calvin and was staring into space, and I knew she was thinking about her sister Lacey and wondering. What had Sasha seen? What did Sasha know? We'd tried waking Sasha up again, but she didn't remember ever meeting anyone named Lacey. And then her fear had overwhelmed her, so Dana'd sent her back to sleep.

Dana now clapped her hands once. "All right! Cool! So we're good? Everybody knows what they're doing?"

"Yeah," Cal and I both said. Milo nodded.

"Awesome." Dana looked at Cal. "Oh. By the way. I'm putting Sky's training in your hands 'til I get back. So make sure she does her homework. And get the girl to eat. She's like a frigging bird and she needs those calories to keep up her strength."

"Will do," Cal replied, throwing an affectionate arm around my waist.

Milo glanced at me and Dana caught the look. "All right," she said impatiently. "Go say your mushy good-byes and whatever. Scoot and I'll be waiting over here."

I thanked Dana, and then Milo and I walked into the field a little bit, away from the former Doggy Doo Good truck. Through the grass I spotted splashes of yellow wildflowers. It was beautiful.

Milo took my hand, and little electrical shivers worked their way up my arm.

"I'm having…"

"…déjà vu," Milo finished for me.

And I laughed. "Yeah," I said. "You too?"

"Yeah. I'm pretty sure I dreamed this. Funny, isn't it?"

I turned and looked up at him. His eyes locked onto mine, and I felt the world tilt.

SUZANNE & MELANIE BROCKMANN

And, instead of answering his question, I bit my lip and grabbed the back of his neck, pulling him down toward me.

And he did exactly what I wanted him to.

He kissed me, his warm lips finding mine as I melted into his embrace, our two worlds melding into a moment that was as perfect as the new day dawning.

And, when we finally ended that incredible kiss, he held me close and whispered into my ear, "I'll only be gone a few weeks."

"Promise?" I whispered back.

I could hear Milo's smile as he spoke. "Promise. I'm not going to pull a Tom Diaz."

I laughed and then pulled away just a little bit so that I could look up into his eyes again.

We're coming back to get some more answers, Milo told me. *Sasha knows something. She has to.*

I nodded.

Of course I'd come back anyway, he added. I could tell that little comment was delivered to me accidentally.

Because Milo blushed.

Thank you, I said.

"Let's go," Milo said, grabbing my hand as we walked back to the truck. "The sooner I leave, the sooner I get to come back and see you again."

And, in that moment, just like in that dream we'd shared, I was really, truly happy.

At a little after noon, Calvin pulled up to my house.

There was a strange car in the driveway—an older model sedan that screamed Mr. Jenkins's name.

We went in through the garage, and my mom must've heard the door sliding up, because when I opened the entrance from the garage to the kitchen, she was standing there, waiting for me. And sure enough, Mr. Jenkins was standing directly behind her.

The look on her face—a mixture of relief, anger, fear, and hope—was one I'll remember all of my life. It was then that I knew—that *she* knew. About me. Who I was. *What* I was. And somehow, I knew that Mr. Jenkins knew too.

I tried for humor. "Would you believe it was a really, *really* long movie?"

It didn't get a laugh. I hadn't really expected it to.

"Skylar Reid," my mother started in a voice that shook with emotion, but then I stepped aside, and she saw Calvin, with little Sasha Rodriguez on his lap.

And I know I complain a lot about my mom. But when it comes to taking care of little girls who've been kidnapped and nearly killed?

She kinda rocks.

We never discussed it—my being a Greater-Than, and Momzilla probably having known it from the start. Maybe she was one too. But she didn't say anything, and I certainly didn't ask, not wanting to get into even more trouble. It was possible that she didn't realize that I was onto her and Jenkins. (Please God, don't let Mr. Jenkins be my father…)

Instead, we continued on as before.

I was grounded.

But Mom only sentenced me to a week, which really wasn't a terrible punishment considering the fact that I'd aged her at least twenty years when I'd disappeared that night.

And, really, Sasha had been brought home safe, which pretty much trumped my briefly limited social life in terms of importance. Plus, there were ways around Mom's rules.

Meanwhile, Carmen had a chance to finally hold her little girl in her arms again. And Edmund was released from jail. Both dad and daughter remembered nothing about what happened—but maybe that was a good thing, at least for now.

Still, it haunted me—that moment when Sasha looked into Dana's eyes and said *Lacey?* And if it was bugging *me*, it sure as hell was keeping Dana up at night too.

I liked the fact that Dana had been offered an injection of hope, though. Not because I knew for certain that Lacey was alive like I'd *known* Sasha was. I had no idea where the bad guys had taken Dana's sister, or if she was even still breathing. But I liked being optimistic. And, after Friday night, it kind of felt as if anything were possible.

As for the other little girls? They arrived safely in California. Just yesterday, I'd received a cryptic text message from a private phone number. It said: All safe. Still thoughts. Great dream btw. C u soon.

And, come to think of it, I *had* dreamt about Milo the night before.

Glancing at the text—for the trillionth time in two days—I smiled. I *would* see him soon.

It was early evening—a beautiful fall day in Florida. The breeze cascaded through my window. I put my phone in my pocket and headed toward my bed. Placing pillows and a few of my bulkier stuffed animals underneath the comforter, I worked to fluff the pile into the shape of a tall but skinny human. Then, I snagged the post-it note I'd written, pulling it off of my computer desk.

The note read: *Mom…goin' to bed early. Night. —Sky*

Maybe she knew, or maybe I'd just imagined that look in her eyes. Either way, we'd both keep playing this game. I stuck the note onto the outside of my bedroom door before shutting it silently.

Then, with ninja silence that would have made Dana proud, I snuck down the stairs, out the front door, and I ran around the corner to where Calvin was sitting, waiting for me in his car.

"Ready for some training?" he asked as I climbed into the passenger seat.

I nodded. The image of that horrible old lady crawled through my mind. I could still see the way she'd held on to that last little girl as she'd disappeared into the darkness.

"Cold?" Cal asked.

I realized I had shivered.

"Nah," I said, crossing my legs and leaning back in the seat. "Just ready."

"You're gonna be a warrior," Calvin replied. "It's pretty kick-ass."

I laughed a little bit. "Who's to say I'm not already?"

Calvin took a left turn and headed toward the beach. "I stand corrected," he said. "Seriously, Sky. You're gonna save lives."

Hell yeah I was. I *was* a warrior. And I wouldn't stop being one until I knew that girls like Sasha and Lacey were out of harm's way. But I needed Calvin by my side. "We are," I corrected him.

He smiled, and we drove for a moment in silence.

"All right," he finally said. "Question of the day. Would you rather have all the water you can drink, but have to drink it out of the dish of a dog with canine herpes, or be given only a teaspoon of very clean water to drink over the course of an entire day?"

I rolled my eyes. "Cal, you're ridiculous."

"You love me *so* much." Calvin grinned at me.

I shrugged and grinned back. Because I so did.

DON'T MISS WHAT HAPPENS NEXT

DANGEROUS DESTINY
A NIGHT SKY NOVELLA

AVAILABLE FALL 2014

WILD SKY
A NIGHT SKY NOVEL

AVAILABLE FALL 2015

ACKNOWLEDGMENTS

We would like to thank our agent, Steve Axelrod, and the entire team at Sourcebooks—our editor, the amazing Aubrey Poole, as well as Derry and Kate and Jessica and Todd and Danielle! And a big hug to Leah Hultenschmidt too!

Thank you to Jason Gaffney and his Mr. Right, Matt Gorlick; to Fred and Lee Brockmann; to Aidan; to Vern Varela and Buster; and to Dexter, Little Joe, and Boston-the-Cat. And a big shout-out to the Melanie Mania gang!

But most of all we thank Ed Gaffney (aka Dad), for his relentless calm in the storm. You are our hero, and without you, we'd be lost.

About the Authors

Suzanne Brockmann and her daughter, Melanie Brockmann, have been creative partners, on and off, for many years. Their first project was an impromptu musical duet, when then-six-month-old Melanie surprised and delighted Suz by matching her pitch and singing back to her. (Babies aren't supposed to be able to do that.) Since then, Mel has gone on to play clarinet and saxophone, to sing in a wedding band, and to run seven-minute miles. She has become one of Sarasota, Florida's most sought-after personal trainers. Suz has driven an ice-cream truck and directed an a cappella singing group, and can jog a twelve-minute mile when pushed. She is the multi-award-winning, *New York Times* bestselling author of more than fifty books. *Night Sky* is Melanie's first novel and the mother-daughter team's first literary collaboration. Each strongly suspects that the other is a Greater-Than.